TAKING THE HEAT

Eugenia Zukerman

SIMON & SCHUSTER
New York   London   Toronto   Sydney   Tokyo   Singapore

SIMON & SCHUSTER
Simon & Schuster Building
Rockefeller Center
1230 Avenue of the Americas
New York, New York 10020

SIMON & SCHUSTER and colophon are registered trademarks
of Simon & Schuster

Designed by Levavi & Levavi
Manufactured in the United States of America

1 3 5 7 9 10 8 6 4 2

Library of Congress Cataloging in Publication Data
Zukerman, Eugenia.
Taking the heat / Eugenia Zukerman.
p.   cm.
I. Title.
PS3576.U24T35   1991
813'.54—dc20   90-46847
CIP

ISBN 0-671-70874-0

For my daughters,
Arianna and Natalia

ACKNOWLEDGMENTS

I would like to thank my agent, Lynn Nesbit, for her enthusiasm; my editor, Marie Arana-Ward, for her tireless help and attention; my friends Julie and Michael Rubenstein, for their constant encouragement; and my husband, David Seltzer, for telling me to take the high road and showing me the way.

1

As in the womb the unborn
with the primordial light on its brow
has the rimless view
from star to star—
So ending flows to beginning
like the cry of a swan.

NELLY SACHS

❦ 1 ❦

ON THE FIRST DAY OF SPRING, THEO BRADSHAW'S MOTHER fell down the stairs and died.

"I should have insisted on that nurse," Theo said as we lay together on the king-sized bed in his apartment on the Upper East Side of Manhattan.

"She didn't want a nurse," I assured him. "You did the right thing." I kissed his neck, inhaling his musky smell, then nuzzled against his shoulder, his skin warm against my cheek.

It was almost a year since I had taken a wrong turn off the Taconic Parkway, gotten lost, run out of gas, and ended up knocking on the front door of a house to ask if I could use the phone.

"Come in," a voice behind the door commanded, and I hesitantly pushed the front door open, stepped into an airless vestibule, and saw someone seated on a chair in a corner of a darkened living room.

"Come here," the figure insisted. I stepped closer and saw that the speaker was old and frail, with a puff of white hair, her legs wrapped in a blue blanket. I thought of the flower fairy, the one my mother showed me how to find when I was a girl: carefully pull the petals off a pansy and inside you'll find something that looks just like a tiny little old lady with her feet in a blue bucket.

"Do you need some help?" I asked.

She was silent.

"Are you all right?"

"I got old," was the answer. "I just got old."

"I'm sorry," I told her, then wanted to kick myself for saying it.

"And I don't need a nurse!"

"I'm sure you don't," I agreed.

She squinted up at me, then seemed alarmed. "You're not from the agency?"

"I'm Nora Watterman. My car ran out of gas in front of your house, and I wondered if I could use your phone . . . ?"

She smiled, and offered me a cracker from a dusty silver bowl. "My son threatened to send me a nurse, against my wishes. What do you think of that?"

I took a cracker, politely popped it into my mouth, and crunched. It tasted like mildew and memories. "I think your son must love you," I told her.

"Love is one thing. Pity is another."

"So is concern."

She nodded slowly, thoughtfully at me. "My name is Charlotte Bradshaw. You can call me Lotty. And if you'll make some tea for me, you can stay for a cup."

"She was so strong," Theo sighed, twining his memories into mine. "Full of character. Passionate to the very end."

"Like her son."

"I'm not ending," Theo whispered, wrapping one long leg around both of mine. "I'm just beginning."

And with the abandon of the bereft, Theo rolled with me across the bed, and I half closed my eyes, free-falling through late-afternoon shadows into a purple light that grew luminescent as I floated and hovered and drifted. . . .

I was looking for the tea in her badly neglected kitchen that day, nearly a year before her death, when the doorbell rang.

"Nora . . . ?" Lotty called to me. I wiped my hands on a towel and headed for the front door. She stopped me en route. "If that's the nurse, get rid of her." She shot me a conspiratorial wink and shooed me toward the door. I opened it, and standing before me was no one dismissable. With burnished gold hair and a strapping physique in a pinstriped suit with a crimson tie, this visitor stepped into the vestibule with complete authority.

"How is she?" he whispered to me.

I hesitated, the smells of wool and leather and aftershave mingling in my head with his concerned words. "She's all right, I think."

"You *think?*" He eyed me with alarm and I suddenly wished I were wearing something presentable instead of a ratty sweater and an old denim skirt.

"I just got here," I stammered. "I just met her."

He exhaled an impatient puff of air. The scent of exotic spices wafted my way. "Are you qualified?" he demanded to know.

"Theo?" Lotty called out, having heard his voice.

"Mother?" Theo called back, striding right past me, brushing my sleeve. I followed him into the living room where he was bending to kiss his mother. He did it on both cheeks. "Are you all right?" he asked pointedly, turning to glance back at me. I stood there, embarrassed, my arms awkwardly folded.

"I am indeed," she declared.

"Good. It's the top agency in the area. I knew they'd send the best nurse they had."

"Nurse?" Lotty asked. Then she burst out laughing. I could feel myself blush as Theo looked at me questioningly and his mother announced, "Meet my guest, Nora Watterman."

"Ah," Theo said, nodding to himself. "My mistake." He looked at me differently now, warmly, appreciatively, so it seemed. Then he smiled at me, a smile that was a little off center, just slightly, just the perfect touch of imperfection. "Forgive me."

11

"Apologize to *me*," his mother chided, her voice heating up. "You will not interfere with my life. I can still take care of myself. I would rather fall down the stairs and die than ask a stranger for help."

Theo's arms flew into the air and came down in muted defeat against the rough wool of his jacket.

"I'm sorry," he sighed. "I just don't know what to do."

"Call the agency, cancel the nurse, have a cup of tea and then help Nora Watterman fix her car," his mother instructed. "*That's* what needs doing."

"I was just passing by," I explained. "And I ran out of gas and . . ."

"Ah," Theo said again, and I smelled a mix of ginger and mint on his breath, or was it anise, chervil, tamarind, bergamot? It was a sweet yet indeterminate aroma, evoking blossoms, dream gardens, languorous afternoons. . . . "And so you knocked on the door and my mother invited you in and asked you to make tea," Theo concluded, then turned to Lotty. "You asked a *stranger* for help?"

At this, his mother sat straight up. "I merely asked a new friend for a favor. There's a difference."

Theo looked at me for a long moment. "Yes, there is a difference," he conceded softly. And instantly, there was.

In Theo's bedroom, it grew dangerously late. "I want you to come to the funeral," he whispered. He pushed a lock of golden hair out of his eyes and there was great sadness in his face. He seemed suddenly fragile, his noble features crumpling. "I need you to be there for me."

I folded him into my arms as if he were a boy and I the mother he had just lost. I stroked his forehead while he wept, my tears mingling with his.

I was ten years old when my own mother died. I could still see her lying in the shiny coffin so comfortably padded with ivory satin. I held tight to my father's hand and stared at her closed oval eyes with their long black lashes that would never again brush like wings against my cheek for a goodnight butterfly kiss. I studied the nose that she would never again let me squeeze while she made a silly goose honk. I surveyed the reddened lips that would never again utter, "Katchki Dredel," or other nonsense pet names. And a fury raced like wildfire through me. Before my father could stop me, I seized my mother by her stiff and unbending shoulders, and shook her, screaming, "Mama, stop it! Stop it!"

My mother died when she was young. Lotty had lived a rich, full life. But death, like life, is not concerned with fairness, and grief knows no distinctions.

"Just come, sit in the back of the church," Theo insisted when I finally got up and rushed to dress to make the five-fifteen train back to Corbin's Cove. He wound a sheet like a toga around his body, looking once again powerful and worldly, yet weary and ineffably pained.

"You know I can't," I protested through the woollen neck of the jersey I was pulling on. "Nobody in your family knows me, and someone will wonder about me." And there were other, more pertinent, reasons. As my head emerged from the tunnel of material, I caught a glimpse of myself in the mirror—black curls flying like snakes around a face that would, I thought, turn anyone to stone.

"My beauty," Theo said, blind to the guilty eyes that stared into his. "You're so pale."

"I'm so late."

He stared at me, the determined glint back in his eyes. "Please come. Please be there."

If I had not been so unnerved by his mother's death, or so filled with the sudden self-loathing of the adulteress, or so panicked about getting home late, I might have had the courage to say no. Instead, I threw my arms around his neck for a last kiss and whispered, "I'll be there," before grabbing my canvas bag and racing, frantic, out the door.

2

I LUGGED MY CANVAS BAG WITH ME EVERYWHERE.

"My flute's in it," I was always explaining. "I can't leave it." But, in a manner of speaking, I already had, years back, when I met Bernie that steamy summer up in Vermont when I was playing a Vivaldi concerto and he was in the audience. I had worn something gossamer and he came up to me after the concert and said, peering down with his hawk-sharp features into my uplifted face, "You look like a nymph but you play like a goddess." And I, Nora Lind, who swore music was my entire life, gave up the dream of taking the music world by storm. I gave it up, at age nineteen, just like that, for another dream, a calmer dream: to be Mrs. Bernard T. Watterman.

"I hate a woman with saggy lips," Bernie would tease, to induce me to practice. Eight years older and centuries wiser than I, he spoke of mutual respect, mutual fulfillment. He would support my every effort. "Babylove, break the sound barrier," he would say, to wish me luck as I'd step onstage. But, at home, cuddled in his warm and sturdy embrace, my goals quickly modulated into a quieter key. I would never stop playing the flute. I would just find a way to make music fit into my life, instead of the other way around.

Corbin's Cove is a small town some fifty miles north of Manhattan. Upstream from Scarsdale and Dobbs Ferry, it is decidedly more downscale—a mix of modest commuters, blue-collar workers, and a growing group of artists and craftspeople. With its saltbox homes and wooden cottages it looks more like a village on Cape Cod than a suburb of the Big City. Shortly after our marriage, when I surprised us both with my instant pregnancy, Bernie and I drove up the Hudson and found a nine-room house in Corbin's Cove. Although it needed lots of work, it came with a barn, apple trees, and a pond, and compared to the three dark rooms on West Eighty-eighth Street where we were holed up, it was a palace. The public schools were good, we were told, and it would only take Bernie an hour on the train to get to the city to the CBS television studios and less than that to drive to La Guardia so he could conveniently fly off to produce his pieces for "Vista," the weekly news program to which he had just been promoted.

Linden Hill. We jokingly named our place after the scrawny little linden out back, to make it sound like an estate, and after all the hours Bernie spent hammering and sanding and painting and all the trouble I took hanging wallpaper and making curtains, it ended up looking grander than we could ever have imagined. It was comfortable and cozy, and I felt safe when Bernie was away. Nicky dug in the dirt, explored the pond, picked the apples, or roamed with his dog Harold—a.k.a. Prince Hal, or just Hal. We watched with pride. Both city kids, we had given our boy the kind of childhood neither of us had. A little brother or sister would have been a welcome addition, but it just never happened, and neither of us felt the need to explore the medical reasons. Bernie had his work, I had my music . . . when I could fit it in. I thought to have a card made up: Nora Lind of Linden Hill, Flutist. But I was Nora Watterman, Mrs. B. T., and I had no real desire to advertise. I was content as wife, mother, and part-time music maker. I played in local chamber music groups, taught at home, and practiced when possible. More important, I had a family, a close one, a strong one. Ours, I was constantly told by friends, was an enviable life. Over the years, the tree that was little more than a twig when we arrived had sprouted into a magnificent arbor, its leaves and blossoms signaling spring each year with a golden flourish. Linden Hill. It was more than an estate. It was a home. A haven.

3

"THERE ARE NO WRONG TURNS," STEPHANIE COMMENTED when I told her I had taken one, and what had happened. "Freud said that."

"There are no jokes," I corrected. "*That's* what Freud said."

"Oh no?" Stephanie challenged, somber, then with a smile sneaking across her glossed cheeks, she asked, "Did you hear the one about the Polish violist . . . ?"

"No, thank you." I stopped her, stood up and gazed out the window at Fifth Avenue and the runners circling the reservoir in Central Park. "I've had enough of musicians and their endless stupid jokes."

"I'm glad you came to town. It's so refreshing to be insulted before breakfast."

I ignored the rebuke and nibbled on the skin around one fingernail before confiding nervously, "I'm scared."

"What else is new?" Stephanie assessed me with a frown. "You're thirty-fucking-seven and frightened of your own shadow. Look at you."

True, in a long flowered skirt, baggy sweater, and scuffed boots I suppose I did not exactly exude confidence, and, true, I should have at least tried to tame my Medusa hair before getting on the train in Corbin's Cove.

"You look like you've been electrocuted." Stephanie frowned.

"I have been."

"Oh, please. *Mensch* up, will you?"

"It's wrong. I know it is."

"Look, you've been married seventeen years and . . ."

"Eighteen."

"Eighteen years and you've been faithful all that time."

"Until now."

"So are you a criminal? Are the police after you? Do you hear sirens?"

My eyes filled up. "I hear my heart breaking," I whispered, and my oldest and dearest friend, with whom I had shared my secrets, my sorrows, my ups and downs since we had met at the age of fifteen that fateful summer at Deerwood Music Camp, heard it and watched it, too, as my face began to fold inward like a fan. Stephanie swept across the room in her lavender caftan, her blond hair cascading over her shoulders, the shoulders that one critic called "consummately creamy," as he reached to describe the physical attributes of America's foremost woman violinist, the international superstar and media sensation (not to mention single and unwed parent) Stephanie Saunders. She took me in her arms and held me tight and I could feel my hot tears burning through her lavender silk, but still she didn't pull away until I did, sheepish and red-eyed.

"I feel like a jerk," I hiccoughed.

"You are a jerk," Stephanie said, dabbing at the salty stain.

"And I ruined your pretty party dress." I pointed.

"You'll buy me another one."

"The hell I will."

We exchanged a look and I managed a smile, Stephanie a laugh, her head thrown back, looking as bewitching and magical as she had the day I met her at camp, down at the swimming hole, as she emerged through the swamp wearing a bikini, holding a bullfrog by the legs, yelling, "I kissed him! I'm waiting!"

"Mommy, come!" a little voice commanded, bringing me back to the present, and a miniature Stephanie skipped into the room, flaxen hair in pigtails, eyes sparkling with mischief. Stephanie scooped her daughter, Jill, into her arms and kissed her, then handed her over to me for a hug.

"Nowa," the child said and gave me a kiss, the touch of her satin skin and the apple smell of her breath reminding me, in a rush, of my own young motherhood—the velvet of Nicky's hair as I held him in the rocker and sang to him, a Polish lullaby my mother had sung

17

to me, so very long ago, *"Ai, lu lu, kolebka z marmuru. . . ."*

"Do you love him?" Stephanie asked.

"Love?"

"You know, the feeling that's supposed to accompany all this commotion?"

I brushed my lips against her daughter's downy forehead, and began to waltz slowly around the room with her in my arms. "When I'm with Theo," I sighed, "it's like I'm dancing with Apollo!" Our waltz got faster and faster, making my partner giggle as I twirled and sang my lover's praises. "He's dashing, and refined and caring. And he makes me feel alive, and valued, and cherished, and desired, and dizzy!" Off balance, I stopped and kissed Jill.

"More!" she demanded, while her mother evaluated the evidence.

"I'd say you're in love."

"I'd say I'm in trouble." My mood darkened as equilibrium returned.

"If it's tearing you apart," Stephanie said, reaching for her child, "then end it."

I fluffed the hem of Jill's lacy dress as I handed her back to her mother, and thought of Theo's gentle hands reaching under my skirt and the way he touched the inside of my upper thighs and told me I was his great love, the love of his life, his only one.

"I can't," I blurted, trying to hide the turmoil I knew was traced across my forehead, trying to steady my fingers as they caught in the curls I was attempting to calm, trying to pretend my eyes were not flaming like pilot lights against the whiteness of my cheeks.

Stephanie studied me knowingly. "Then you better have breakfast," she said, and led me toward the smell of fresh-baked muffins and coffee being prepared by Pearl in the kitchen.

4

FRIDAY THE THIRTIETH OF SEPTEMBER. EMBER DAY, MY EN-
glish datebook (the special brown leather one Bernie had
brought me from London) told me. Fire Day would be more
like it, I thought, wondering how I had let a little spark
rage into a blaze that was now out of control. "4 P.M. Dr.
Rotman," I saw scribbled on the roster for the day. But
there was also a small star penciled in the lower-right-hand
corner—my secret code, meaning: Meet Theo at The
Apartment for lunch. How could I have forgotten to cancel
Dr. R's lesson? I would never be back from the city in time.

You are no good at this, I told myself, all the prevaricat-
ing, pretending to be where you will not be. You've canceled
Rotman three times this month. Call Theo. Cancel *him*.

"Hello, Dr. Rotman?" I heard myself say into the phone.
"I'm terribly sorry to do this again, but an emergency has
come up and . . ." What kind of an emergency? he wanted
to know. "A medical emergency," I improvised. "I have to
see a specialist in the city, and I'm afraid I won't be back
until . . ." I was not to worry about the cancellation, he
assured me, his voice appropriately therapeutic. He was a
psychiatrist whose Friday hours from four to six were kept
sacrosanctly free for flute instruction, even though the tone
he produced rivaled a steampipe's and his sense of rhythm
was skewed. He responded to my very gentle suggestions
by stamping his foot and muttering "Idiot!" to himself.
Progress did not concern Dr. Rotman, he had informed me.
Process did. Friday from four to six were the hours he most
looked forward to all week.

"Nora," Dr. R. told me. "Whatever this emergency is,
I know you have the tools to handle it."

"Thank you, Doctor," I said, and promised without fail
that the following Friday we would have an extra-long lesson, and, yes, I would play with him the Kuhlau duet,
Opus 81 number 2, which he had prepared. I could not

wait to work on it with him, I lied. But it was a good lie. It was important to differentiate: good lie, bad lie. Trouble was, the line between was beginning to blur. Good and bad untruths were piling up like kindling, feeding the fires of my infidelity.

It might have been Ember Day in England, a day for fasting and penitence, but I was neither English nor Catholic, and far from penitent as I put on my new black bikini underpants with the little satin bow in the front and dressed for a lunch that would not require utensils.

5

BERNIE WAS ASLEEP ON THE BLUE COUCH. IT WAS MANY months after Theo and I had begun our secret meetings. Bernie knew nothing. He certainly seemed to sense nothing. Life just went on as it always had for B. T. Watterman, with his wife and son safely ensconced in a quaint house on the banks of the Hudson.

"Producers are the unsung heroes of TV news programs," his boss, Gus Morrison, always said. And maybe Bernie *was* heroic. He told his stories of dodging bullets, braving tornadoes, being there when the going got rough. But what about at home? Where was the hero then? Asleep on the blue couch. He was tired. He worked hard, he deserved to come home and crash, didn't he?

Now he slept fitfully. Prince Hal lay on the floor beside the couch, exhausted from the run Bernie had forced him to endure up hills and down, and, from the looks of the carpet, across that boggy field out back. Harold's halcyon days had been spent with Nicky, from whom he'd been inseparable, until Nicky's puberty robbed the dog of his playmate. Now Nicky had better things to do, and Hal, an aging golden retriever, had to make do with an occasional pat on the head from me and the odd romp with the master of the house. Standing at the doorway of the den, I gazed at Man and his Best Friend with annoyance. It was not just that I had vacuumed and spruced up the place that very morning and now there were mud and wet leaves all over. It was not that at all.

I sighed, and Hal cocked one ear but didn't open his eyes. Bernie did not budge. His bald monk's crown was still gleaming with damp from the run.

"Hair is left over from monkey time," I had consoled him when it began to fall out years back. "I'll love you even more when you've evolved." And when a pate that was round and unblemished eventually emerged I thought it complemented his strong, prominent features, making him look powerful and undeniably sexy.

Here was my husband, his stocky, sweat-suited body spread out with abandon, and his wet Nikes adorning the arm of the couch. It was a sight that would have warmed my heart . . . before Theo. And still should, I reminded myself. Bernie was still the father of my son, and he was still my husband, with the hearty laugh, generous smile, and bear-hugging warmth everyone adored.

"Bernie's a giver," Gus told me at the annual "Vista" Christmas party. "The guy just doesn't stop."

Gustav Morrison just doesn't know, I thought, but smiled dutifully. He might have given at the office, but when Bernie got home, it was to sleep, to have his laundry done, his food cooked, and his wife and son on call. Now that Theo was in my life, I realized I had been handmaiden to the king for lo those many years, a servant to Bernie's needs, unaware of my own. Now that mine were finally being met, and royally, I felt entitled to my secret realm, protective of it. While, deep inside, a stew of conflicts bubbled away, I tended it carefully, adding a dash of remorse, a jot of self-justification—whatever would keep it from boiling over. There would be no mess in *my* kitchen.

Bernie opened his eyes and, seeing me standing there, smiled contentedly.

"Come here," he said, and held out his hand.

I felt my cheeks turn red.

"Look at you," Bernie teased, pointing at my face. "Come here and I'll give you a real reason to blush."

Guilt beat against my ribs like a prisoner demanding release. But I was not about to set it free.

"What's the matter with you?" Bernie asked.

"Nothing," I said, startled. Then, recovered, I bestowed my most winsome smile upon him, and walked like a wife toward his outstretched arms.

❦ 6 ❦

NICKY WAS GALLANT WITH ME. AT ONLY SEVENTEEN, HE WAS my protector, my chevalier.

But that was before I began coming home late from rehearsals that did not exist, from restaurants that were never visited. Now Nicky's every glance jolted my conscience, for even if he suspected nothing, my fear was that he knew all.

"So was it good?" Nicky asked me as I walked into the kitchen one evening, frazzled. He was dipping a cold chicken leg into a jar of my homemade salad dressing. The evening news droned on behind him on the small TV I reluctantly agreed to allow in the kitchen. Nicky munched on the bone. Oil stains dotted his black pullover. He wiped his chin with the back of one hand and looked at me, disdainfully, I thought.

"I was going to make spaghetti just for the two of us," I offered, placing my canvas bag on a cluttered counter. Nicky belched loudly. I glowered at him.

"Sorry," he apologized, then announced, "I'm outta here." He stood up, tossed the chewed bone toward the garbage pail.

"Two points!" he called as the basket was made. He turned to grin at me. I was not charmed. "You didn't answer my question. Was it good?"

"My rehearsal?" I asked, hoping my cheeks were not still flushed with postcoital content, hoping that Nicky's smile was just his normal wise-ass grin and not the smirk of discovery. "It was okay," I said, as casually as I could. "How was school?"

"Hell High, Ma? How good could it be?" Nicky zipped up his varsity jacket, and shook a lock of sandy-colored hair out of his face. Tall and muscular, with arctic-blue eyes and angular features that I knew would be called *chiseled* as he grew into them, Nicky had an aloof, impervious air about him, a style he copied from the bright young studs of current movies. His father called it arrogance; I said it was just a phase. However, it did appear that Nickolas Watterman, a high school junior with a very average transcript, was not about to burn up the world. Add to his undistinguished record an intense relationship with a feckless high school dropout of nineteen who had worked for the last three years as a scooper down at the local Baskin-Robbins, and it looked to us as if our boy was well on the way to nowhere.

Nicky put out his hand. "Keys?" he asked with a little boy voice and a very adult wink.

"You know I'm not giving you the car on weekday nights."

"Why not?" As if he didn't know.

I sighed. Maybe if I treated him like a grown-up, he would act like one, so I said, "I really was looking forward to having dinner with you. You like my spaghetti."

"I *love* your spaghetti," Nicky gushed. "And I love you. You're hot, Ma."

"Oh?"

"All my pals think so, too. Makes me proud."

"Thanks," I said, oddly flattered.

"And I'm glad you're not like all the other mothers, either, into money and status and stuff."

"Who says I'm not?"

Nicky winked at me. "I know you. You've really got it together. That's what I told Kelly, and I told her you play the flute and you know what she said?"

"What?" I could not wait to hear the gem from Kelly the scooper.

"She wanted to know if you played the panpipes, like Zamfir, or a gold one like Jimmy the Greek?"

We both laughed. "Is that the cutest?" Nicky wanted to know.

"It's certainly the dumbest," I said, instantly regretting it as Nicky's mood crashed.

"You think the whole fucking world knows the name Jimmy Galway? You think the whole fucking world cares?" he bellowed.

"Sorry," I said, hands up. Nicky was staring at me. Could he know about me and Theo? Impossible. I was being paranoid. I had simply insulted his girlfriend. I would make amends.

"It was very snobby and elitist of me. I really am sorry," I said. But he just kept staring. "How can I make you believe me?"

Nicky grinned. "The keys, please, Louise," he said. I wanted him to forgive me, but at what price? I was not about to be bribed.

"What about your homework?"

"It's done. And it's brilliant."

I looked doubtingly at him. I put my hands on

my hips, and Nicky copy-catted me, which he knew I loathed. I took my hands off my hips, and sighed, which Nicky knew would not be wise to copy. Instead he placed his palms together and rested his forehead against the fingertips, in a pose that I knew he hoped would look penitent. He was adorable. I had to give in. I caught him watching me out of a corner of his eye as I reached inside my canvas bag, grabbed the car keys, and lobbed them toward him.

"A little low and inside," he announced as he caught them, "but a hit is a hit. Thanks."

I flashed him an annoyed look just to seem parental, but he blew me a kiss and breezed out the door, letting it slam behind him.

I winced at the thud, then perched myself in front of the television set. I reached for a chicken leg from the plate Nicky had left out.

"A strong storm is moving in from the Midwest," the weatherman droned from the TV screen. I dipped the chicken into the bowl of salad dressing—just because it was there—and was surprised the taste wasn't half bad. The forecast finished with concerns about local flooding and a warning of possible electrical activity in the area.

A pang of loneliness washed through me. I thought of the summer storms in the cabin in Maine we rented one wet July, when the lights would go out and we'd make a fire in the fireplace, toast marshmallows, the four of us— me and my two men and our faithful dog, and it seemed that nothing, not the howling of the wind, nor the pounding of the rain, nor the deep and endless darkness could possibly ever harm us.

"SOMETHING'S GOING ON IN YOUR LIFE THAT MUST BE AWFULLY
good," Martin Kramer said, pointing his bow at me as he
leaned back in his chair and let his cello rest against one thigh.
We had just rehearsed the "Shepherd's Lament" of the Trio
in G Minor for flute, cello and piano by Carl Maria von Weber,
and even *I* had to acknowledge that the little flute cadenza
at the end of that movement had been played with a supple-
ness, a grace, and an ease that were remarkable. Most remarkable was that *I* had played it. I had only been practicing
the flute an hour or two daily—not enough, I knew, but all
I could manage, given the exigencies of my newly complicated
life. But, strangely, it seemed my playing had grown stronger.

"You sound great," Jenny Bowers said, agreeing with Martin, taking a bite of her candy bar and a swig of cold coffee.

"Really?" I said, sounding doubtful, but knowing there
had been a change. Every time I picked up the flute and
took a breath to play, I felt a warmth flowing through my
veins and knew I could do things on the instrument that
had seemed impossible . . . before Theo. Now I could
shape phrases like a seasoned sculptor, I could shade my
tone with delicate colors, and there was a depth to my sound
that I no longer needed to dive for—it was just there. My
fingers delighted me with a new reliability. Where once
there were flaws, now there was flight.

"I'm inspired," I admitted.

"Who is it?" Martin wanted to know.

"It's you," I teased. Martin patted his curls into place
and beamed angelically.

"Whatever it is, keep doing just what you're doing,"
Jenny suggested as she got up to stretch, her ample midriff
spilling out from under a tight red sweater.

"Unless it's immoral," Martin cautioned. But before the
curve of my smile could flatten, he added, "In which case,
do more of it."

We laughed and then Jenny sat down and we launched into the final allegro, with me playing the tricky runs and treacherous turns like a tightrope walker who knew no fear. I stopped at the scherzando section to ask Martin if he could play a little softer: "The flute has the melody, and . . ."

He raised one eyebrow, peeved, I thought. "No kidding," he said, "so I have to cover you up or everyone will hear how much better than me you sound."

"Are you a professional or are you a putz?" Jenny put in cheerfully.

"A professional putz?" Martin mused, then instantly turned serious and waved his bow at us for attention. "Letter E, ladies," he whispered. "And I'll play soft." Then looking to me he said, "Take it away, Nora baby!"

And I did, thinking that the next concert of the Tri-State Chamber Music Players would please the crowd at the First Unitarian Church of Washington, Connecticut. It would certainly please one member of the audience in particular who I knew would be sitting there, in the back, feigning impartiality as he listened to the flutist with whose lips and tongue and dazzling articulations he was deeply familiar.

❦ 8 ❦

"YOU PLAYED MAGNIFICENTLY, MRS. WATTERMAN," THEO whispered to me after that concert when he managed to mill around to my side at the crowded reception held in the church's vicarage.

"Thank you, Mr. . . . ?" I replied, pretending not to

know him, pretending I was not thrilled that my lover had been present to hear me. Bernie was conveniently in Cleveland and Nicky was at home studying for a test. I was a free woman—for the night. Theo took my hand and squeezed it, then moved off and allowed others to come up and offer compliments. Discretion was the order of the evening: we would demonstrate no association, let alone affection. But out of the corner of my eye, I kept seeing him proudly watch me, hands tucked into the pockets of his gray suit, a maroon cashmere scarf wrapped around his neck, looking dashing and urbane and leonine, with that mane of hair, those invincible eyes. He certainly was king of his own jungle—at age forty, chief executive officer and owner of the brokerage firm Bradshaw International. Amicably divorced, he even dined, on occasion, with Melissa (his ex) and Porter, her new husband. His two children were away at boarding school. Melissa kept the twenty-room house in Scarsdale, while Theo was content with his three-room pad in New York.

"I was living in *exile*," he told me, soon after we had met. "It's so exciting to be right here in the heart of it."

He rhapsodized about the city's museums, the theater, and especially the concerts. Having once aspired to a career as a pianist, he owned a Bechstein and harbored a bittersweet regret. He had to be coaxed to play through a Bach sonata with me.

"This could be the end of a beautiful relationship," he said, resisting.

I tempted him with a kiss and a challenge: "There's one way to find out. . . ."

He stumbled his way through the undulating triplet accompaniment of the sarabande from the Bach Sonata in E Flat, as I floated the melody delicately above him. But he stumbled with sensitivity.

"So it's over between us . . . ?" he nervously asked before the last note faded.

I sat down on the piano bench beside him. "Don't be ridiculous. You're good," I exaggerated. "We could make beautiful music together."

"We could," he teased, kissing my neck. "And you really think I'm good?"

"I do. I think you could have been a first-rate soloist if you had wanted to."

"No," he disagreed, while unbuttoning my blouse. "I was efficient but earthbound. Not like you. You've got wings."

If I did, I was sure Theo had given them to me. I was certainly soaring that night as I slyly caught his eye, then looked away, pretending indifference, feeling exultation. I was in love with a handsome, successful, utterly elegant gentleman who, for some reason, returned my affection. What was it he saw in me? I was certainly not a polished gem, a trophy. Nor was I footloose and fancy-free. I knew nothing about the world of business and finance, nor did it interest me. Was it that my flute filled the void of his abandoned dreams? Or was it that the imposed secrecy of our connection made the music sound so sweet to him?

"You're frowning," Theo whispered, startling me. "But I want you anyhow." Then he touched my arm and headed for the cheese and crackers, and I couldn't help smiling. I worried someone might have noticed. But no knowing glances turned my way. No one seemed to have the slightest suspicion, not Martin or Jenny or any of the others. So, when a decorous amount of time passed, I said my goodbyes and regrets that I had to be leaving so soon, and got into my car alone as if eager to drive home. Then, with my pulse racing, I saw Theo's BMW waiting for me up ahead, as planned, and I understood what Stephanie meant when she once said, "A wonderful concert followed by a daring night with a debonair lover—there is nothing like it."

Nothing, I thought, as I drove too fast down winding roads, following the red lights of Theo's car to the country inn where he had taken a room for the night.

"I have to go home," I said at one in the morning. "I told Nicky . . ."

"Call him. Say the party's still going on," Theo urged,

then pushed his body against mine to show me that it was.

"Darling . . ." I objected, but I felt his flesh enter mine again and I heard myself groan with a pleasure that could not be controlled, and I stayed and stayed until it was two in the morning and I was beside myself with panic and guilt.

"Call Nicky," Theo directed, trying to calm me. "Tell him you had a flat tire, and everything's fine, you'll be home soon."

I called and was surprised by the wifely voice that answered, until I realized it was my own voice, Nora Watterman's, Mrs. B. T.'s, on the answering machine. I was trying to sound natural as I left the message about the flat tire, when a worried voice picked up the phone, and said, "Ma, I'm here. Where are you? I'll come get you."

I mumbled that the tire was almost fixed and I was on my way.

"God, I got scared," Nicky admitted, then laughed. "Now I know what you must feel like when I tell you I'll be home by midnight and I'm not."

"Yup," I agreed, and swallowed hard. My son, my darling son, worried to death about me, while I'm out betraying his father. A pretty picture.

"How was the concert?"

"It was all right," I managed to tell him, wondering how I had raised this angelic, caring child when I was so callously capable of deceit. "Go to sleep, honey. I'm sorry I had you worried."

"Hey, no problem," Nicky said, "Drive safe. Love ya."

"Don't torture yourself," Theo insisted, as a flood of self-recrimination poured out of me.

"I just feel rotten. Evil. Awful."

"Nora, I love you. And you love me."

"And that makes it okay?" I looked at him, blanket pulled up under his chin, relaxed, smug, I thought, as I struggled to dress. "Well, it's not okay. Not for me it's not. Not anymore." I stuffed my arms into my coat sleeves.

30

"Then leave him," Theo commanded. He was suddenly on his feet, naked, arms around me, brushing away my tears as he kissed me and whispered that everything would be all right, that he wanted to marry me and that we would be happy together, he knew it. He would take care of me, he would take care of Nicky, he would take care of everything. "You're right. It's not okay anymore," he agreed. "It's time to tell him."

Tell Bernie? An icy spike of fear jabbed me at that thought. "I can't," I blurted. "I just can't."

Theo held me by the shoulders at arm's length, studying my face. "You know you can't keep living a lie forever."

"I'm not living a lie!" I twisted myself out of his grasp and turned angrily away.

He said nothing, but I could hear the disappointed flap of a shirt as he shook it out. His belt clinked as he pulled his trousers up. He zipped them closed. "I know this is not easy for you," he said, tugging at the back of my coat, coaxing me into his arms again. "It's not easy for me, either."

He looked tired and grim. But he held me and assured me he understood, he would not push me, he only loved me, he only wanted me to be happy, he would wait, he would be patient.

But could I? I *was* living a lie and didn't something need to be done about that? But what was it I wanted to do, and why didn't I know? I agonized as I sped home toward my son, toward my compromised home, toward my no longer comfortable bed. But when I crawled into it, after creeping into Nicky's room and planting a light kiss on his forehead, I was amazed how easy it was simply to close my eyes, out the world, and sleep.

❦ 9 ❧

"STROGANOFF?" GUS ASKED, AS HE STOOD BESIDE HIS AS-
signed chair at our dining-room table, regarding the large
dish I had just placed on our prettiest lace tablecloth.

"I hope you don't mind," I said, knowing that the cho-
lesterol conscious would be on red alert.

"Mind? I love it!" he said, pulling a chair out for Pamela
Wright, a new editor on "Vista." It was one of those dinners
I gave several times a year for Bernie's pals at work, the
guest list varying, with the exception of Gus, his boss, who
was always present.

"He *is* on a polyunsaturated diet," Midge Morrison announced about her husband, shooting him a cautionary
look. "But I'm not going to say a word."

"Bet your ass you're not!" Gus told her, buttering a piece
of bread and biting into it.

"They're putting all sorts of hormones in cattle feed,"
Pamela kindly contributed, while self-consciously pushing
some bleached-blond hair out of her eyes. "But personally,
I don't think about it." Then she laughed, a haughty little
inhalation of a laugh. She was tall and languid and of that
indeterminate age around thirty when a single woman, no
matter how independent, has pangs of desire for partner-
ship. Bernie poured her a glass of Bordeaux. I was spooning
out egg noodles when I caught a look between the two of
them that went right through my eyeballs into my gullet.
With a rush of recognition I saw that Bernie wanted her,
if he hadn't already had her. The bastard! I was furious.
Outraged. The nerve of them, putting on this farce right
in front of me! Hold it, I told myself, *you* are the one having
an affair. But at least I hadn't stooped to sticking Theo right
under Bernie's nose! I couldn't help surveilling the two of
them all evening. Bernie spilled a drop of wine on his shirt
and Pam was instantly dabbing at it with some Perrier.

"Aren't you supposed to use white wine?"

"For what?" Pam wanted to know, regarding Mel Brackman, her putative date, with the contempt his question inspired in her. Further evidence, I decided. She's being mean to Mel because it's Bernie she's after.

"Something about the opposite color wine getting out stains?" Mel theorized.

"It works," Midge concurred, "I got some Burgundy on a beige silk blouse, and a dab of Chablis took care of it. Must be in the enzymes." Then she crunched with difficulty on the green beans I had deliberately undercooked.

"Thanks," Bernie said to Pam, patting her hand a little too gratefully after she had made the entire front of his shirt wet.

Shop talk consumed the rest of the meal—cutbacks at the network during the cheese and salad, rumors and guessing who-with-whom during the meringues and strawberries, and a barrage of bitter complaint about accommodating the national attention span during the coffee.

"That interview with the kid who kept poison spiders? I had to cut a great soundbite about black widows because it was fifteen seconds over the limit," Pam told Bernie, spinning her little web.

"Three minutes. That's it for your average Joe," Bernie said to all of us, as if it were news. "Is that pathetic?"

"That's how long it takes your average Joe to fuck, too!" Gus chortled. "Now *that's* pathetic!"

Midge pretended to be horrified by the kind of language she had been enduring from her husband for the past thirty-six years.

"If they fuck at all anymore," Mel offered, "with all these diseases around." He got a roll of the eyes for his effort from Pamela whose hand I thought I saw going under the tablecloth in the direction of my husband's thigh. Hands off! I thought to tell her, but who was I to take offense?

Who was I, indeed? Not the happiest of hostesses for this dinner party, that was certain. By the time midnight rolled around, Gus and Midge were fighting about who would drive home, Pamela and Bernie were tucked in a corner talking, and I was stuck discussing the difficulty of finding fresh buffalo mozzarella with Mel who, it turned out, was not just a producer but also, as he informed me, "profoundly into food."

"What's your problem?" Bernie wanted to know, as he entered the kitchen after the others had left, to find me angrily doing dishes. He cut himself another hunk of Brie and stuffed it in his mouth, a rivulet of runny cheese pouring out of one corner.

"Nothing," I said, averting my eyes.

"Nothing?" Bernie was not convinced. "You didn't seem to have a great time tonight."

"Didn't I?"

"No. You didn't."

I handed him a dish towel. He groaned and grabbed it. "Producers don't do dishes?" I asked, not nicely.

"Don't get sarcastic."

"Sorry."

"And don't apologize. I hate that!"

"Oh, you do? Well, I'm just trying to keep this civilized, that's all."

"Civilized!?" He growled, then stopped. We looked at each other, both bleary, bloated, distressed.

"You want to talk?" Bernie asked.

"What's there to talk about?"

Bernie whacked at a chair with his towel. "You make me so fucking frustrated sometimes, you know that?" His voice was cold, bitter.

"Well, I'm sorry . . . I'm not sorry. I'm tired. I cooked all day. And I just feel like the domestic."

Bernie was frowning, his forehead knotted up. Hal whined for attention and Bernie scratched him behind one ear. "I thought you loved to make these dinners, Nora."

"I thought so, too."

"So now you don't?"

"Not when no one notices."

"They noticed!"

"It's not *they* I care about." I was about to cry or to explode or both. Instead I just glared at my husband.

"What the hell do you want from me?" he asked.

"I don't know," I blurted. "But it's something I'm not getting, that's for sure."

Bernie laughed, infuriating me. Now he spoke slowly, as if to a foreigner, "What is it, Nora, that you are not getting?"

He was so arrogant, in his tight jeans and cowboy boots, his white shirt with a cravat he probably had put on to make Pam think him artistic. To me he looked like a thug, an emotional mugger coming at me down a dark and dismal alley. I would not run.

"I'll tell you what I'm not getting," I started, my voice quivering. "I'm not getting friendship. I'm not getting support or caring or understanding or one single thank-you from you or . . ."

The phone rang just in time, silencing me. Bernie picked up the receiver.

"Yeah?" he said, then listened, then grumbled, "Nicky's out. Call back tomorrow, okay?"

"See what I mean?" I couldn't stop carping after he hung up.

"What now?!"

"Call back tomorrow, *please?* Can't you *ever* say please?"

The muscles in Bernie's jaws tightened as he said, through clenched teeth, "Why should I?"

"Because manners are the tact of the soul." An elegant retort, I thought, for someone who quit school at nineteen to marry B. T. Watterman with his master's degree.

"Who says?" Bernie was amused, crippling my confidence. "Come on. Who're we quoting here?"

"Someone."

"You don't know. You don't know *anything*, Nora, do you know that?" He was yelling.

"Oh, and you do?" I yelled back.

"I happen to be informed. Well-informed!"

"That's your job."

"It's everyone's job." He tilted his head, looking at me like a teacher working on a trick question.

I laughed. I couldn't help it. It was all so funny and stupid and sad.

"Nora?" Bernie asked softly, as he, too, seemed to realize how ridiculous we both were. "What's this all about?"

It's about a marriage in peril, I thought to say, a life about to crumble. But I offered a simple, "I don't know," instead.

Bernie gave me a friendly smile, pulling at his cravat, loosening a few buttons of his shirt. "I'm sorry, babe," he said.

"Me, too."

"It's late and I'm tired." He circled his arms around me. "I'm also an asshole."

"So am I." I kissed his cheek, then leaned against his solid chest, closing my eyes, feeling safe, out of the war zone, back home.

He swept me up and carried me, apron and all, out of the kitchen, flicking off the lights with one elbow on the way, and preventing my feigned objections with a kiss that caught me off guard and kept me very quiet. When we got upstairs to the bed and he slid me onto the covers and lay down beside me and continued kissing, I wanted to say, No, I'm tired, don't. But then an image of him with Pamela slipped into my head, and I found myself suddenly embracing my husband with an urgency that surprised and inspired us both.

❧ 10 ❧

IT WAS WINTER. THE LINDEN LEAVES WERE LONG GONE AND snow fell, muting the landscape. I had not seen Theo in several weeks. I had not wanted to. I had claimed that the elements, as well as the demands of music and domesticity, were keeping me away. But Theo correctly sensed my withdrawal and gallantly agreed to meet me halfway. I demurred, but, finally, after a long and lonely weekend during which Bernie slept and ate and hardly spoke, I said Yes. Please.

"Mr. and Mrs. Jack Frost?" I laughed when Theo told me how he had signed us in at the Happy Wayfarer's Motel in Hartsdale. I threw my coat on the orange polyester bedspread in room 103 and asked, "What did the lady at the desk say?"

"Not a word. She took the cash and handed me the key and said 'Have a pleasant stay, Mr. Frost.' " His voice was deep, his eyes were undressing me. We were in a tacky motel room, with a TV nailed to a crumbling bureau, and a radiator beating jungle drums but emitting no warmth. Yet just seeing Theo unbutton his shirt cuffs caused a lava flow of heat inside me. As I helped him with the buttons on the front of his shirt and reached in to fondle the fur on his chest, he pressed me to him whispering, "I think it will be a very pleasant stay, don't you?"

Yes, I murmured, yes, as his hands slid ever so pleasantly under my skirt and we fell together onto the bed on top of the coats and clothes, and neither of us noticed the chill as we tumbled across the wool and leather and licked at each other like hungry wolves, then disappeared into a deeper lair of desire.

Emerging, finally, we huddled limply together under the grimy sheets. Theo pointed at the painting that hung over our heads—conestoga wagons in a circle, cowboys blowing up red men as they attacked from the bluffs above. "How about that in our living room, right over the La-Z-Boy Recliner?"

I laughed, but Theo turned serious and said, "I want a home with you Nora. It's time." I longed, suddenly, for my own living room, not this seedy box on a highway, halfway between home and nowhere, and I wondered why I was there anyway, lying next to a man I hardly knew who was entreating me now to change my whole world.

"I mean it, Nora. Leave him," he said, adamant.

"You promised not to push," I reminded him.

Yes, he had promised, but this half-life of lies and limits was taking its toll. His patience was fraying, he wanted the whole cloth. I, on the other hand, was swaddled in ambivalence, struggling, but immobile.

"You're ready. I know it," he prodded me. "And you know it."

I had no reply. "Nora," Theo said, propping himself up on his elbows. "Do you love me?"

"You know I do."

He raised one doubting eyebrow. "Or am I just the crowbar you're using to pry your own way out of prison?"

I objected. "My marriage is not exactly a prison."

"Not exactly."

"Not even remotely!"

"Then why are you here with me?"

My eyes filled with tears of frustration. "I don't know."

Theo held me and stroked my hair and said, "Either we face up to this thing like grown-ups, or all it can ever be is an affair. Affairs are for cowards. Those who can't make a move and take the consequences."

"Easy for you to say," I grumbled. "You're divorced."

"Because Melissa made her move. Declared herself. I respect her for it."

"Well, great for her!" I huffed and turned away.

"I love you," he whispered, tracing a heart with one finger on my back. "But I want more. I deserve more. So do you."

A terrible sadness pressed down on me, a crushing

weight. "I do love you," I said, trembling. "But I have a whole *life* with Bernie. I belong with him."

He kissed my forehead. "You were a baby when you married him. As a woman, you're just beginning to blossom."

Did one divorce in order to flower? What about vows, sacred promises? Should I break mine for the sake of my own growth? But then I remembered that I had already broken the vows, that the transgressions were made willingly and now consequences were growing like weeds, fast and furious, choking me.

"I'd rather wilt and die than hurt my family," I told Theo.

"You've hurt them already," he said, and even though I knew it was true, I dressed in stony silence and answered his, "Meet me at the apartment on Friday?" with a curt, "I'll call you."

When we slipped stealthily into our separate cars outside room 103 to go our separate ways, I turned to blow a kiss to Theo but his head was leaning resolutely against his steering wheel and he was deep in thought. I shifted into reverse and backed slowly, quietly away.

❀ 11 ❀

A FEW MORNINGS LATER, I WENT TO VISIT LOTTY BRADSHAW and found her huddled in the kitchen in front of a hot stove, wrapped in blankets, the furnace being "on the fritz," as she put it, the rest of the house uninhabitable.

"When did it stop working?" I wanted to know.

"Yesterday afternoon."

"And you sat here overnight?"

Lotty nodded. Turned up to broil, the gas stove was warming the kitchen, but it was an ancient contraption, with blackened burners and a rusty door and it looked as if it could blow up any minute. "Lotty," I asked, horrified, "why didn't you call the police, or the fire department for help?"

"Now why would I do a damn-fool thing like that?" She was wearing a salmon-pink chenille robe with a moth-eaten scarf around her neck. Stalagmites of white hair stuck out from her scalp. She glared at me with clouded, rheumy eyes, but her mind was clear. "I'm not incompetent, you know. I called the Five-Star Furnace Company and demanded repair service."

"And what did they say?"

"They said they've had lots of emergencies. I'd have to wait my turn." She wiped her dripping nose on a napkin, then swore, "Hell will freeze over before those boys get here!" She gave an exasperated huff, and reached out for the silver brick I held in my hands—walnut-date bread wrapped in foil. She thanked me and placed it on the table in front of her.

"Why didn't you call Theo?"

Lotty raised her eyebrows. "I didn't want to bother him."

"Why not?"

"He's got worries of his own," she said.

"Is he sick?" I asked, the sudden notion filling me with dread. Maybe he had been hiding a heart condition, a weak lung, a . . .

"Healthy as a horse." Then she glanced slyly at me. "Are you two perfectly happy together?"

"Perfectly," I assured her.

She knew about us. She was delighted, and, true to form, took all the credit: "If I hadn't asked Nora to tea, you never would have met," she had boasted to her son. But when we made plans to visit her together, Theo insisted I pretend to be divorced. His mother was old-fashioned, he said, and would never approve. We did go to see her, once, as a carefree couple, but it was a charade that troubled me. I decided it would be better to make future visits to Lotty by myself. It felt somehow *seemlier*. Besides, I enjoyed her more when I had her to myself. There was something so cozy about just the two of us, talking, laughing together. Her house was only half an hour from mine, so every few weeks I could fake an errand in Dobbs Ferry and stop by, bringing home-baked breads or flowers to the woman whose wit and wisdom I admired, whose determination to stay alone and alive touched me, whose affection warmed me. She was the mother I imagined mine might have miraculously become. And she was a link between me and her son, tightening our connection with her stories, her albums of faded photos.

"Theo at two," she would say, pointing to a picture of a tow-headed boy in shorts holding a pail and shovel in one hand. "He was a holy terror. Bashed his sister Bernice over the head with that shovel."

"Why?" I would want to know.

"She deserved it. She was three years older and knocked over a castle he'd spent hours building. But she required ten stitches over one eye."

"How awful."

"Not for her. Poor Theo felt so badly, he locked himself in his room and wouldn't eat or drink until we broke the door down and threatened to force-feed him."

And so at these visits I was able to gather details of Theo's life, bright bouquets of insight into the man who had made me feel so newly awake, so truly valued, so very alive. But he was also the man who was now making demands I could not possibly meet.

I took Lotty's two icy hands in mine and rubbed them, then held them up to my cheeks to warm them. Lotty Bradshaw's body might be cold, but I could tell her mother's intuition was burning on all cylinders.

"Is something bothering you?" she asked.

41

"Will you let me call the heating company again for you?" I offered. But she was not ready to change the subject.

"I have a feeling things are not clear between you and Theo."

I flushed. "Why would you say that?"

Lotty looked at me, leaned toward me. "Why haven't you moved in together?"

"We don't want to rush things."

"You're not kids. You should know what you want."

"It's not that easy, Lotty."

"Of course it is." She studied my face. "Unless there is some difficulty I don't know about."

I was not about to reply. She sighed and looked at me for a long moment, then said, "Go ahead. Call those damned furnace fellows. I'd appreciate a little heat around here."

"Remember me?" the service man asked me, when he arrived, on the double, after I had phoned the company to tell them their client was aged and weak and that their inattention constituted criminal neglect.

"Well done," Lotty complimented me after the call. "But you might have left out the part about my decrepitude." Then she had winked and I knew my indiscretion would be overlooked . . . that once.

The service man removed his hat, glanced at me, and said, "I fixed your boiler a couple years back."

"You did?" I asked, worried about being remembered.

"Over by Corbin's Cove," he persisted. Then, scratching his head, he unfortunately retrieved the name. "Mrs. Watterman?"

Lotty's head spun around. She looked at me, studying my discomfort, my shifty eyes, as I said, "That's correct," to the man.

"You've got that friendly dog and a jogger husband, right?"

I froze. I thought to say, We're divorced. But I simply nodded.

Lotty pointed the serviceman toward the cellar door and

when he had descended into the frigid depths she held one shaky finger up toward me. "You're still married, aren't you?"

"Yes," I admitted, my cheeks hot with humiliation.

"Then why the song and dance about being divorced?"

"I never wanted to lie to you. . . ." I began in self-defense, but she waved her hand for silence, having something more important to tell me.

"As a sin, I'd say adultery is way overrated." She unwrapped the silver package that sat before her on the table. "But I will tell you what's wrong with it." She broke off a corner of the bread. "It weakens the floorboards of your life." Then she popped the crumbs into her mouth, tasted, nodded approval, and told me not to worry, it would be all right, everything turned out all right in the end.

But she was wrong. Things turned out badly all the time. Terrible traumas were visited for no reason even on the innocent. I had known this all my life. My mother had taught it to me.

Her name was Elena Miklavska. They came to get her when she was eleven. She only had enough time to put on her tattered brown coat and take the doll her mother had made for her before they grabbed her and threw her onto the truck that was transporting children to the camps. Her parents and her older brother, Nickolas, had already been taken away. She would never see them again. The truck took them to a special train, and they were packed into the cars like livestock. My mother hugged her doll as she huddled in a corner. Through a hole in the floor of the car she could view the tracks and, since they were going slowly, she saw an occasional wildflower. "Pretty flower," she showed her doll. "We are going to a place where there are flowers everywhere."

Six months later the war was over and my mother was sent, doll-less, with other orphans to the United States where she went to live with an aunt in Brooklyn. She learned English, sparkled in school, and married my father,

Ezra, a second-generation American Jew whose parents had come from Poland before the war. They changed their name from Galindski to Lind and their fate from certain death to impoverished survival. Their son Ezra fared better. He went to Brooklyn Technical High School and became a tile layer for a small contracting firm. A quiet man with a good heart, he was no match for the fiery Elena, whose moods jumped like fleas, irritating him endlessly. They fought and fumed. Their marriage was a battlefield. I wondered why they stayed together. But when my mother died of polio when I was ten, my father nearly expired from grief. He wept and wept, recalling her grace, her warmth, her goodness. Their differences never existed. He, too, spotted only the flowers.

But I, their only child, saw only shadows and darkness and I felt an anger that knew no end. My beautiful mother was dead of polio at a time when vaccines had nearly wiped the disease off the face of the earth. What monstrous memory could have caused Mrs. Elena Lind to refuse vaccination?

"I will not stand on line and be given a shot for some little disease. Polio is just a cold," she had declared. "And God knows what those doctors are really pumping into people."

Ezra went on laying tiles while I grew up in our little apartment in a brownstone on West Twenty-third Street. We shared our breakfasts and dinners at the Formica table in the well-tiled kitchen. I cooked simple things Elena had taught me, and Ezra did the dishes. He was silent but generous, and gave me everything I wanted—music lessons, a silver flute, summers at music camps. But, when I turned fifteen, he gave me something I did *not* want—a stepmother named Sonia who wore push-up bras and stiletto heels and smoked Romanian cigarettes, blowing putrid rings from her painted cherry lips as she played canasta with my father in our newly redecorated gaudy living room, Ezra laughing, eyes glimmering. His joy was my only consolation for the punishment of Sonia's presence. A widow, she had one son who died when he was three. I was certain she had killed him, strangled him in his bed, but the official description was liver disease. As for Sonia, emphysema was to be her painful fate. She and Ezra moved to a retirement village in Arizona where she lived out her last suffocating days, smoking to the very end. Ezra stayed on in Arizona, laying tiles for other retirees, sending an occasional card to Corbin's Cove: "I am fine. You are well, I hope. My best regards to your husband and son. Your loving father, Ezra Lind."

Sitting silently with Lotty Bradshaw in her kitchen, I missed my mother with a pain that was as sharp as it had been the day I lost her.

"Come on, now," Lotty finally said to me gently. "There are worse woes than the marital variety."

I picked my head up as Lotty handed me a slice of bread, and, pointing to the kettle, she suggested that a cup of tea with honey and a dash of Jack Daniel's would wash the crumbs down very nicely.

✤ 12 ✤

"PERSONALLY," STEPHANIE ANNOUNCED, DRAPING A MAUVE organdy strapless gown over one arm, "I think you deserve Theo. Compared to Bernie the Bull, he sounds like a prize stallion."

"What do you know about it?" I snarled, hating to hear Bernie insulted. Heaped on the injuries I had inflicted on my husband, it was cruel. But Stephanie was not the inflictor, and her stunned response to my nasty outburst shamed me. "Stephanie, I didn't mean to . . ."

"Hey," she said, stopping my abject attempt, "our friendship is beyond apology, isn't it?"

I stood mute, but Stephanie went on, cheerily humming to herself as she continued packing for yet another tour.

I meant to ask her where she was going this time, but my mind only fixed on one thought. I had not stopped seeing Theo. The floorboards of my life were in danger of collapse, but I persisted, shoring up my marriage with more lies, my liaison with empty promises.

"I'll burn in hell," I announced.

Stephanie looked up. "Jews don't believe in hell."

"What if they did?"

"I don't think having an affair merits eternal flames, do you?"

She knew what I was talking about without even asking. She always did.

"What is your big problem with this?" she asked.

"I'm married."

Stephanie threw her hands in the air. "So what is marriage about?"

"Mutual trust."

Stephanie flicked her golden tresses from one shoulder to another and arched her eyebrows at me. "Yeah. But what else is it about?"

"Is this a test?"

"I'm just trying to make you feel better."

"You're doing a lousy job," I complained, getting up from her bed, being careful not to topple the piles of evening gowns that surrounded me.

She pointed at me to take my seat. "Listen to me."

I obediently plopped back down, causing a silk slip to waft to the floor.

"Let's say you're a little weak in the mutual-trust department right now." Stephanie plucked the slip off the floor and, with the flair of a magician, folded it into a tiny square and stuffed it into an ivory satin carrying case made for the frequent, yet very feminine, traveler. "But marriage is also about mutual independence," she continued lecturing. "It's about being supportive of the other's work, needs, dreams. Now it seems to me you've always been there to bolster Bernie. But vice-versa?"

I shrugged. Still flushed from a tryst uptown, I had stopped by Stephanie's since the next train home was not for another hour. Now I wished I had opted for a hard wooden bench in Grand Central. It would have been more comfortable than this conversation.

"How can you stand it, all the travel, all the trouble?" I suddenly wanted to know, changing the subject for the sake of comfort and showing that I was capable of thinking of something else.

"I *can't* stand it," Stephanie confided. "I just do it for the flowers."

"You don't even take them with you, all those roses you get after concerts."

"I know. I leave long-stemmers in bathtubs in hotels around the world. It's wicked."

"It's wonderful," I sighed. "How many concerts this time?"

"Five. In six days, three cities."

"Grueling."

"That's why I don't look a day over eighty-five."

"You look gorgeous." It was true, even in the elephant-gray sweat suit she was wearing. Stephanie Saunders was statuesque and sculpted to grow finer as she grew older. She no longer had the peachy luminescence of the ingenue, but the womanly glow that had replaced it was even more luscious.

"What about Jill?" I wondered.

"What about her?" was her decidedly defensive reply.

"How's she doing?"

"Fine. When I'm here." Her mood suddenly clouded. "She's—what did the nursery school teacher tell me with that *tone* of hers? Oh, yes. 'Jill is a little anxious when Mommy's away.' "

47

"Did you tell teacher that Mommy has to go away because she is an artist and because she needs to make money?" I asked, trying out the tone myself.

Stephanie looked up at the ceiling, then back down at me. Then she sighed deeply and asked, "You think she'll forgive me?"

"The teacher?"

"No, you moron. Jill."

"Forgive you for what?"

"Abandoning her. I *am* her only parent. I leave her all the time."

"You take her with you when you can, when it's good for her, when it's good for both of you." Then I had an idea I should have kept to myself. "You *could* let her stay with her father once in a while."

She frowned and said fiercely, "The sperm donor? That bastard! Are you kidding?"

"He *did* want to marry you, don't forget," I reminded her, which only fueled her fires.

"*Before* I got pregnant, don't forget," She flung a strand of pearls into the suitcase and hissed, "Talk about abandonment."

"But he came around after her birth and wanted to marry. . . ."

"Please." Stephanie stopped me. "End of subject."

"What about forgiveness?" I urgently needed to know. "What about mercy?"

Stephanie ignored the question and held up an emerald number with a rhinestone-studded bodice. "Too froufrou?"

"Who'd you get it from? Imelda Marcos?"

"Touché!" Stephanie admitted. She tossed the gown into the reject pile, and continued packing. I played with the silk tassles on a long paisley scarf, braiding them, unbraiding them as my thoughts took up the inevitable strand.

"How do you suppose it will all end?" I couldn't help asking.

"Do you want it to end?" Stephanie probed, knowing exactly what I was talking about again.

"I haven't a clue," I confessed.

"I say you're *entitled* to Theo. You think only husbands have the right to screw around?"

A tidal wave of jealousy hit me. "Do you know something about Bernie you're not telling me?" It was that damned Pamela, I knew it. . . .

"Christ!" she groaned. "Of course not. All I'm saying is sometimes a little something on the side can make you happier at home. You want my advice?"

"No way."

"You're getting it anyhow," Stephanie insisted, then stopped folding silks to wag a finger at me. "Don't write any love letters. And even if there are pictures of you and him naked in unnatural poses, deny it to the end. Am I making myself clear?"

I felt the blood drain from my head. "I'd die if Bernie found out," I whispered.

"Then, honey," Stephanie counseled, "there's your first clue."

⚜ 13 ⚜

"DEAR THEO,

This is the letter I never wanted to write. . . ."

Then why are you writing it? I asked myself. I crumpled up the paper and took another piece. I was in the kitchen, sitting at the oak table that Bernie had sanded and I had finished many years before, the one we had found together at a local antique fair. Bernie had haggled the price down from twenty-five to seventeen dollars.

"The damn thing's falling apart!" he had objected, pointing out its many defects, while I looked away, mortified. But he prevailed, and we carted off our prize, tied it to the top of our battered station wagon, and with our puppy yapping and our sweet baby cooing, we drove off down a country road, the very picture of the perfect young family.

Now I was seated at that venerable table, tearfully penning a farewell to a man who had never set foot in our house but whose existence threatened to cause it to crumble.

"Darling Theo," I tried. "I love you and cherish every moment I have spent with you. But I have come to realize that there is no way I can ever leave my family. And so, even though it pains me more than I can say, we must stop meeting. It is no longer fair or right or reasonable to continue. . . ."

Hal looked up as yet another balled-up piece of paper flew over his head on its way to the wastebasket. I couldn't get it right. I would never get it right, and besides, it was cowardly to send words. I would have to confront Theo, face to face. But that would only end with his pleadings, my protestations, and the inevitable embrace. . . .

I groaned, and the dog's sympathetic whimper made me smile. I got up, yawned, and noticed a hanging plant that looked parched. Standing on a stepstool, watering can in hand, I poked at the soil, sprinkled a generous amount of water, and saw a spiderweb stretched across one corner of the window. After I wiped it away, the fingerprints on the refrigerator door caught my eye, and before I knew it, I was cleaning the kitchen, furiously berating myself for letting it get so out of hand. How could I have left those grease stains on the stove for so long? Why hadn't I waxed the wood floor before the finish came off? Why hadn't I . . . My eyes wandered to the balls of paper in the waste basket and I remembered Stephanie's warning. I emptied the basket into the kitchen sink, took a match, and lit each crumpled piece of paper individually. I watched the edges curl up, turn black, fall away. Smelling something charred, Hal began to bark and rub himself against the backs of my legs.

"It's not a barbecue," I told him, booting him gently away. I watched the last blackened, soggy bits slide down into the disposal, then turned it on, the smells of orange peel, onion, and burnt paper reaching my nostrils in one final affront. Tears rolled down my cheeks, partly from the aroma, mostly from frustration and confusion and a pain that started in my gut and got stronger as it coursed into the cavity in my chest.

14

"SPIN THE SOUND," I COAXED. "NICE, NICE, KEEP IT SPINning, support the sound . . . yes! Beautiful!"

Dr. Rotman finished the first phrase of "The Dance of the Blessed Spirits," by Gluck, to the accompaniment of my encouragements, and then raised his flute in the air, exuberant as a baton twirler after his team made a touchdown.

"Wonderful!" I exclaimed, truly pleased with my least talented but most tenacious student.

He was catching his breath, beaming at me through his wire-rimmed glasses, contentedly pulling on his beard, when I said, "Now let me hear you do it again. This time try playing it with the same intensity, but softer, pianissimo."

Rotman's face fell. "It was too loud?"

"It was really lovely," I assured him. "But I just think the opening statement should be gentle, more introspective. Orpheus has just reached the underground. He's pleading with the keepers of the gates of hell to release Eurydice, the love of his life. Would he dare be so . . . shrill?"

Dr. Rotman, seething with insult, stretched himself up to his full five feet two inches and screeched, "I was *shrill?*"

"Not shrill, just a bit, um . . . piercing."

"Idiot!" Rotman screamed, and stamped his foot, grinding his teeth and gyrating like Rumpelstiltskin on the rampage.

"I didn't mean to upset you," I said, touching his arm, which made him jump even more. "Doctor," I persisted, "I'm only suggesting a very subtle dynamic shading."

"I play like a pig," he replied sulkily.

"You certainly do not."

"A swine. Oink-oink!" And suddenly, Dr. Milton Rotman, the distinguished psychiatrist, was darting around my living room uttering odd, piggy grunts.

"No one is above improvement," I tried to reason.

"You are!" he said accusingly. "There is nothing you play that doesn't sound simply first-class."

"That's not true."

"Is."

"Isn't." I sighed. "I have plenty of things to feel guilty about."

Dr. Rotman wheeled around. His professional antennae went up. "Now why would you use that word, Nora?"

"What word?"

"*Guilty.*"

"I didn't say *guilty.*"

"Did. You said, and I'm quoting, 'I have plenty of things to feel *guilty* about.' "

"I did not. I said I have plenty of things to *improve* on."

His superior expression galled me. "Nora, I am a *listener.*

I get *paid* to listen. And you may have *thought* you said one thing, but your *subconscious* spoke another for you."

So what if it had? A twinge of annoyance made me snap at him, "Are you going to play the flute, or are you going to play Dr. Freud?"

"Defensive!" he gloated, pointing a finger at me. "What is it you are feeling guilty about?"

The urge to murder you, I wanted to say, but blurted a very terse, "Nothing."

"Nothing?" He played with the adjustment of the head joint of his flute and looked at me. "How's your *medical* problem, Nora? We've missed four lessons because of it. . . ."

The front doorbell rang. I sighed. Saved by Stuart Milliken, my six o'clock Friday night student. So what if he was thirteen and sullen? It was better than a fiendish forty-year-old shrink. "I think our lesson time is up, Doctor."

I excused myself, put my flute on the closed lid of the piano, and went to open the door. I left Stuie in the front hall to peel off his scarves and boots and sweaters while I returned to dispatch Rotman.

"I'm running late," I told the doctor, hoping he'd get the hint.

"You're very tense, Nora."

"It's my nature," I said, impatiently straightening a pile of music on the piano.

Dr. Rotman took out his cleaning rod and wrapped a fresh white handkerchief around it, poked it into the end of his flute, slowly swabbing it out. "You spoke very emotionally about Orpheus. Does his plight interest you?"

"Not particularly." I picked up my flute and fingered a scale, noisily clicking the keys.

"Then perhaps Eurydice? Imprisoned. Helpless. Is that how you feel?"

"I *feel* that my next student is here. . . ."

But Rotman was on a roll: "You know you can stop feeling helpless. You can stop feeling like a victim. That is, if you want to."

"Did I *say* I feel like a *victim!?*" I huffed.

"Denial?" Dr. Rotman mused, peering at me over his glasses. Then he snapped his flute case shut and chirped, "See you next Friday," just as Stuie Milliken slouched across the carpet toward me, defiantly announcing, "I didn't practice. So don't expect miracles."

❧ 15 ❧

SUN WAS GLINTING ON THE SNOWBANKS, AND THE SMALL cluster of shops in Tudor-style buildings at the center of Corbin's Cove was humming like a hive as I pulled up to the curb to do some errands. In the window of Earth Arts I saw a pottery class earnestly throwing clay onto their whirling wheels. Leon Dubrovner, the young and fiery instructor, moved among his acolytes, flailing his arms. I walked right past Baskin-Robbins without turning my head. I had no desire to see Kelly, Nicky's Empress of Ice Cream.

I was passing Molly's Frocks when I saw Doris Walker, in a bright red coat, coming at me like an unexpected stoplight. Doris was undoubtedly on her way to Lovin' Lathers to get a haircut or a facial or a full body massage. Married to Tommy Walker, and the mother of Stan—a classmate of Nicky's—she was also the lover of Brad Positano, a wealthy builder who was the husband of the very put-upon and long-suffering Paula, who was the mother of Sylvia, who was, so Nicky told me, now dating Stan (the Schnoz)

Walker. There were some pretty close families in Corbin's Cove, and the ancient art of gossip was practiced with the special vengeance of the small town.

"Did you hear about Lou Simone?" Doris asked me.

"Who's Lou Simone?"

She batted her disbelieving lashes. "Captain of the hockey team at Corbin High?"

"What happened to him?" I knew a question would quicken the encounter.

"His mother has cancer." She leaned closer. "Cervical."

"How terrible."

"And his father is back on the sauce."

"I see."

She tilted her head, closed her eyes to look pained, then smiled and asked, "How's Nicky and how's that Bernie of yours?"

"They're fine, just fine. And how's . . ."

She had her arms crossed and her head tilted to the other side as she whispered, "Must get real lonely with him out of town so much. When the cat's away . . . ?"

I just squinted at her and smiled as if amused. She patted her hair and bubbled, "Well, bye, then. I've got a ten A.M. and Jean-Claude will kill me if I'm late!"

Gourmet Goodies was packed. I waited on line for a pound of Colombian Heart-o'-the-Jungle Beans for Bernie's coffee, and back outside in the dazzling light I bumped into Selma Divan and Trish Vanderthorp who asked me to join them for espresso at Toujours, the patisserie around the corner.

"Love to," I told them, "but I'm off to Grunder and Vlicks."

"Getting screws?" Selma giggled.

"Many," I bantered back and as I walked away toward the hardware store I heard a murmur behind me. Were they whispering about me? Had they been gossiping with Doris Walker? So what, I told myself. They couldn't possibly know. Besides, there was nothing to know. Not anymore. Not since the harrowing evening Theo and I had spent at The Hound and Hare in Millbrook.

"Don't do this," he had whispered.

"I have to," I told him, tears dripping into my wineglass. I wanted to end things in a setting where words would be final and caresses impossible. The restaurant was formal and far away and so stuffy that I would say what needed saying and be done with it.

"You're making a mistake. You will regret it, and then what?"

His words troubled me, but I was firm. "I'm doing the right thing," I said.

"Right for whom?"

"For me."

Theo shook his head. He looked at me for a long moment, then took my hand and kissed my wrist. He turned my hand over and held my palm against his cheek, closing his eyes. "I love you, Nora," he said. His eyes fluttered open. "I always will."

I had not counted on his elegant acceptance. A part of me hoped he would beg me to reconsider. A large part. But Theo Bradshaw was not a man to beg.

We stood outside together in the slush of the parking lot. A misted moon peeked from behind pewter clouds.

"I'll be there if you ever need me," he said, his white silk scarf blowing in the wind. "Or want me."

Want him? For a fleeting moment I imagined being naked with him in the back seat of his car. But I was in total control of myself, serene with my decision.

I cried all the way back to Corbin's Cove. But as Linden Hill appeared out of the fog, I felt a great cloud lift, and I was home, safe at last.

The next evening Bernie came home from a trip, and if he wondered why Nicky was out and the table was set as though for a banquet and the candles were lit and I was wearing a low-cut knit dress, he kept his questions simple. I flung my arms around his neck when he walked through the door.

"Whoa," he said. "What's going on here?"

"Nothing," I teased, then snaked my arms tighter around his neck, kissing him with a deep repentance he took for desire.

"You'd think I'd been gone for months," he joked, pinching my bottom as I went to the kitchen to pour two glasses of wine. I was the one who had been gone for months, but did it matter? I was back. We were together. I was his own true wife. Again.

⚘ 16 ⚘

MARCH CAME IN LIKE A LION. THAT MEANT IT WOULD BE A mild spring. I marched through the month in a storm of emotions, buffeted by strong urges to call Theo, calmed by my capacity to maintain silence. I was recommitted to my marriage, and although Bernie seemed to be more absent than ever, even when he was home, I held to my resolves and hoped the reward would be future happiness: April showers would bring May flowers and then, in the summer, we planned a vacation, just us three Wattermans out in the wonders of the West. It would be the summer before Nicky's senior year, the last summer we could attempt such a trip, since the following summer he would consider himself a College Man, and would no doubt not want to suffer such fools as his parents.

July would be a month worth waiting for. I imagined a wonderful closeness amid the adobes and ancient ruins of the American Natives, me and my men, trudging the well-worn trails of the national parks, forging a fresh family path of our own.

But then, on the first day of spring, Lotty Bradshaw fell down the stairs and died, and I rushed to her son's side, to share his grief, and, despite all resolutions to the contrary, to share his bed.

This is understandable, it is natural, I told myself as Theo undressed me and I did not, could not, protest. It would not happen again. Never. But there, embracing, flesh against flesh—it seemed to keep Lotty with us, for the moment. And wasn't it the moment that mattered, with everything so fragile and evanescent?

The night before Lotty Bradshaw's funeral, at which I had pledged my presence, Bernie called from Butte, Montana.

"Hi, my baby," he said, and I could tell from the relief in his voice that his work was done and he was on the way home.

"Hi!" I responded, hoping my strained enthusiasm could be hidden with monosyllables.

"What's wrong?" Bernie asked.

"Nothing. Why?"

"Your 'hi' was low."

"I'm reading," I lied. Lies, again! When would I be done with them, once and for all?

"What're you reading, mousie?"

Mousie. Why did he use such idiotic epithets? Baby. Mousie. Then there was the worst: cutes. Theo's endearments had elegance and style: beauté; beloved. But the comparison was unfair, I told myself, and marriages were not to be measured by nicknames.

"The King Must Die," I answered, spotting it on the kitchen counter among the cluster of books Nicky had obviously failed to return to the library.

"Sounds sad."

"It is."

Silence. "How'd the shoot go?" I asked, to fill in.

Bernie sighed. "Copper mine closing, town depressed, people desperate but dignified. And they stick me with Duane Kirkbridge, the dumbest correspondent in the pool. Get this. We're interviewing a guy—thirty years in the pit and now he's out of work—we're getting a great soundbite, the old boy's quoting from the Bible, something like 'What good getteth a man from his labors.' He's got tears in his eyes, I signal the cameraman to go in tight on him, and Kirkbridge cuts him off with some jerkoff comment like, 'That's very moving.' "

"You'll edit it out."

"And lose the whole sequence?" Bernie was practically shouting.

"I'm sure you'll find a way to save it." Here goes, I thought—his bombast, my bromide. Will he ask how I am, what I'm thinking, what I'm feeling? No. And it's just as well, since how could I say, I'm sad because the mother of my lover just died? So I drummed my fingers on the metal edge of the counter and let him puff away, interjecting an occasional "you're right," or an "of course you will."

There was a momentary pause, which Bernie broke with, "I never read it."

And now for the non sequiturs, I thought. Time to play, What's Bernie Talking About Now? It annoyed me. But it kept me sharp.

"Me neither. I read her other one about Pompeii, so I thought I should read this one."

More silence, then Bernie said, "You seem sad."

"It's just the book." Lie of omission. Did it count?

"Are you almost at the end?"

"Almost."

"Maybe the king won't die after all."

I laughed. "Bernie," I said, with real warmth. I missed him suddenly, and felt real remorse at having sullied myself again. Grief was no excuse.

"I'm coming home," he said.

Not before I pay my respects to Lotty! "When?" I asked, and held my breath, eyes shut, waiting for the answer.

"I'll get to O'Hare by midnight. Hilton. Then the sunrise special to the Apple so I can be home for breakfast. What do you think?"

"Great!" I said, out of breath, and then added, out of habit, "I'll start slingin' the hash."

"That's my girl."

Bernie's girl was going to cry. I bit my lip and heard Bernie say, "Sleep tight, Tinker Bell."

Tinker Bell! I hung up and groaned. But I did not weep. I sighed with womanly resignation instead, and reached for the phone to tell Theo I would not be able to attend the ceremony, to tell him that what happened the day before at his apartment would not happen, could not happen again, ever. I dialed his number and let it ring and ring. His answering machine did not pick up. Undoubtedly, in his condition, he forgot to turn it on. I pictured him at the funeral parlor, looking at the painted waxen corpse they would tell him was his mother.

"She looks well," I imagined them telling him. "She looks just like she's sleeping."

I put the receiver back in its cradle, then went outside and looked up at a diamantine sky. Concentrating on the brightest star, I wished Lotty Bradshaw eternal peace and a place of honor among the spirits of the flower fairies, and I promised her that I would visit her grave, bringing garlands of pretty pansies to place beside her silent stone.

❧ 17 ❧

"YOU KNEW I WAS COMING, SO WHY DID YOU PUT THE CHAIN on?" an aggravated Bernie asked me as I opened the back door for him the next morning.

"Sorry," I said. "I mean, I locked it when Nicky left for school. Habit." I took the garment bag he handed me and asked, "How was the trip?"

"Air-traffic delay, car wouldn't start, traffic on the Deegan." He dropped his suitcase onto the kitchen floor where it landed with a dull thud, and looked at me. He was tired, annoyed, but in his leather bomber jacket with the black scarf I had gotten him for his birthday tossed jauntily around his neck, he was, I thought, looking a little dangerous, and a lot attractive.

"You're very handsome," I said, dangerously.

Bernie clasped me to his leathery chest, and kissed me. "And you are very nuts," he replied, then buried his nose in my neck and said, "but you smell good."

"Must be the cranberry muffins," I said, pulling away. "Just made them. Want one?"

"I want something else," he said softly, squeezing my buttocks, lifting me toward him.

Despite visions of the funeral I knew had just taken place, our fifteen minutes on a kitchen chair—me straddling, naked, his cold jacket still unzipped, the metal teeth pressing against me—was somehow quite satisfying, life-confirming, marriage-strengthening. Here it was, my reward of, if not happiness, at least a hint thereof, and not in the future but at the very moment, there, as I bent to gather my hastily discarded clothing. Bernie gave my bottom a playful swat. He demanded one more kiss, then let me run upstairs to wash.

The phone rang just as I was about to set foot in the shower. Bernie will answer, I thought. But as the ringing

61

persisted, I realized that he was probably stuffing a muffin in his mouth, or slugging down some orange juice, so I called out a bouncy, "Got it!" and dashed to answer.

"Theo!" I whispered, horrified.

"I had to call. You said you'd be at the church, and when you weren't . . ." His plangent voice broke off and my head was pounding with the thought that Bernie might have picked up at the last moment and could be listening.

"Nora," he urged. "I must see you."

"Please!" I begged back. "I can't. Not now. Not ever." And I hung up, then rushed into the bathroom, locked the door, and leaned back against it, as if to keep the demons of destruction out. Then I got into the shower and soaped up, lathering myself into a frenzy of self-confidence. By the time I had rinsed off, dried, wrapped myself in a terry-cloth robe and pulled my hair back into a slick ponytail, I was thoroughly reassured, ready for anything.

I stepped out of the bathroom to see Bernie, standing at the window, arms folded in front of his chest, staring out at the budding linden tree, its branches shimmering with the faint yellow of its new leaves. A sparrow landed on a limb, tilted its head, and seemed to look first at Bernie, then at me.

"Must be spring!" I said, sounding light, feeling faint. Bernie's face was ashen when he turned it toward mine. His lips were pressed into a tight, thin line. But he said nothing.

Then nothing is wrong, I concluded, and walked to my closet, reached inside for the red plaid dress that I knew was his favorite.

"Makes you look like a country girl," Bernie had said. "Real fresh. Innocent."

And you are innocent, I told myself, if you say you are, if you act innocent, you will be innocent. . . . I buttoned up my dress, silently chanting that litany, knowing his eyes were on me.

"Who was that?" he asked calmly, simply.

"Who was what?" I answered. My legs were trembling. My head began to spin as he looked at me, accusingly.

"Nora," my husband said, his voice burdened. "I picked up the phone."

"And?" I asked ingenuously, holding onto the door frame of the closet for support.

Bernie's eyes drilled into me. Deny it to the end. Stephanie's advice. Follow it. I walked toward him, ready to reassure.

"You've been seeing someone?" he half asked, half accused.

I stopped in front of him, but the simple "No" that could assuage his fears, save the day, would not come.

"Have you?!" he demanded to know. "Answer me!" His eyes were wild. He was looming before me like a bad dream, dark, ominous. I wanted the nightmare to be over, I wanted the Bernie I had just clung to on a kitchen chair, my loving husband, not this lurking beast.

"Yes," I said.

Bernie stared at me for a long moment, a moment that seemed to last forever. He was breathing heavily, quickly.

"Do you love him?" Bernie asked.

"I love you," I answered instantly, honestly. I sank down to the floor on my knees in front of the tribunal that was my husband. I did not fear a verdict. I felt only an over-whelming sense of release, as if I had been wandering through a tangled maze and the truth would somehow lead me into the clear light.

Bernie placed one hand on my head, as if in benediction. Or was it to crush my skull? His fingers dug into my scalp, he began to squeeze.

"Nora," he asked, still breathing hard. "Why?"

"I don't know," I answered, having no explanation, but worried that his grip would tighten if I made no attempt. "It just happened."

"Affairs don't just *happen*," Bernie said, pulling his hand away as if stung. He began to pace around the room, tense as a tiger.

Affair. The word sounded suddenly so evil, so sordid. "It wasn't an affair," I claimed. Bernie made a sharp hissing sound as he whirled around toward me.

"Having sex with someone to whom you are not married,

when you are married, is called having an *affair*," he instructed. Then he roared, "At least by normal people, people who don't just fucking let things happen to them! What'd he do? Tie you up, rape you?"

I had no reply. Bernie slumped down onto the edge of the bed and stared straight ahead. Then he buried his face in his hands and his whole body shook. I pulled myself off the floor and sat down beside him. I put my hand on his shoulder. He did not move away.

"Who is it?" he asked calmly, emerging from behind the wall of his hands. His face was wet.

"No one you know."

"That's nice," he said, as if it were. He wiped his cheeks with the backs of both hands, and turned to look at me. "Why did you tell me?" he groaned. "Why?"

"You asked," I said softly.

"That doesn't mean I needed to know!" he yelled. "I didn't need to know!" He squeezed his eyes shut, then opened them and slammed his fists into a pillow, sending it into the air. It landed on the bedside table, knocking over a glass that did not break as it hit the carpet, but rolled slowly under the bed. Bernie stood up and, towering over me, demanded, "How long have you been seeing this person I don't know?"

I looked away. "I'm not seeing him anymore," I said.

"Then how long *were* you seeing him?"

"What's the difference?" I sighed.

"What's the difference?" he asked, his sarcasm searing. "Come on, babe. Was it a night, a couple of days. What?"

I heard him pick something up from the bureau, hitting it against his palm. My brush. Just a few weeks, I thought to say, brush it off with just a few weeks.

"How long?" he asked, again.

"Since last spring." I couldn't help it. The words just came out.

I looked around to see Bernie nodding his head, taking this in. "Last *spring*," he mused, then he slammed the brush back onto the bureau. "*Last* spring? We're not talking about an affair. We're talking about a whole fucking *relationship* here! For Christ sake, Nora!"

"I never meant to hurt you," I said.

He picked up a photo in a heart-shaped silver frame of me holding a small Nicky. He was quivering with an effort to control himself. He tapped the glass, then put the picture down. "I'm afraid that's not good enough," he said, through his teeth.

"I'm sorry," I added.

"And neither is that. Sorry just isn't good enough."

He looked at me, a long and sorrowful look. Then he turned, carefully as a convalescent, and slowly walked out of the room. I heard his footsteps beating heavily on the stairs, and when the back door slammed, I neither winced nor wept. I lay down on my side, curled myself up into a small ball, closed my eyes and breathed slowly and carefully in and out, in and out. I let bubbles and iridescent fish swim into my head, remembering the time we went to Virgin Gorda and Bernie showed me how to use the snorkle, and I put my masked face into the water for the first time and an entire universe of light and color exploded before my dazzled eyes. I lay there on the bed, breathing in and out, and finally fell into a deep and dreamless sleep.

18

"He'll be back," Bernie's mother told me. "They always come back."

She would know. Gilda Watterman had survived The Rover, Mo Watterman, who had been a traveling salesman, supplying dry goods and novelty items to drugstores up and down the eastern seaboard. He would tell Gilda he was going on the road for a week and not return for two. His excuse was always the same: he was too tired to travel at night.

"I should fall asleep at the wheel?" was his chronic defense. "You want me to come home in a coffin, I'll come home in a coffin!"

But Gilda knew it was not exhaustion that kept her husband from making it home on time. It was a string of sweethearts, from Miami to Bangor.

"But none of them could hold a candle to me," she confided. This was proved by the fact that Mo eventually always trudged back to Brooklyn, burst through the front door, waving a wad of orders at his "old lady," carrying a stuffed toy for his daughter, Linda ("Princess Lindy"), under one arm and a model airplane kit for "my boy, Bern" in his briefcase.

"He was a provider, what can I tell you?" Gilda rationalized. "Does a good man have to be perfect?"

It had been three days since Bernie left. He had not communicated with me, or, as far as I could tell, with Nicky, and he was a father who always called his kid.

"I thought he was supposed to come home Tuesday," Nicky said, somewhat concerned.

"The shoot got complicated," I told him.

"How come he didn't call?"

"He did. You were at school. . . ."

"He always calls at night. No matter how late. No matter what."

"They're shooting at night. All night."

Nicky looked at me, tugging at the tab on his jacket zipper. "Something goin' down here?" he asked.

"Don't be silly," I answered easily, and handed him a double fudge brownie I had just baked—sweets to soothe the suspicious.

"Next time he calls," Nicky said, "tell him to get his ass on home, okay?"

I did not take exception to the turn of phrase. I merely

nodded and cut another sugary brown square to pass to the outstretched hand before me.

When Nicky was at school, I cried constantly, hopelessly, pathetically, telling myself to stop, telling myself, Enough. Only fools weep. *Mensch* up. Pull yourself together. I tried diversionary tactics, like practicing. I would bring the flute up to my lips, inhale, and something between a howl and a scream, coming from the very center of my body, would find its way through the instrument, startling me and causing Hal to fold his ears back against his head and cower under the piano. I thought to write an amusing article for *The Flutist's Quarterly* called "Fifteen Ways to Correct Your Sound While Sobbing." But the thought only made me cry harder.

As for my swollen, red eyes, I told Nicky it was allergies.

"You look like a frog," he announced.

"That cute, huh?"

"It's a good thing Dad got delayed. I mean, men have left women for less."

I just stared at him like an amphibian.

"Hey," he said, giving me a nudge. "Joke?"

But I was not tickled. Not by Nicky and certainly not by the situation.

Bernie had not shown up at work. This I discovered by calling the office ten times a day, disguising my voice, asking for Bernard T. Watterman.

"I think he's on location," one secretary told me.

"Bernie's not available," said another.

When I finally got up the nerve to use my own voice and call Gus, he told me, "He called in sick."

"Did he tell you we're having sort of a . . . *crisis* at home?" I dared ask.

"Sort of . . ." Gus admitted.

"He hasn't called. I'm getting worried."

"I'm sure he's okay."

"Do you know where he is?"

Silence. "Nora," he finally said. "Patience is a virtue."

"Fuck virtue," I said, hoping to shock Gus into disclosure with his own kind of locution. "I need my husband."

"Maybe you should have thought of that a year ago," he said, his tone nauseatingly self-righteous.

I bristled. So Bernie told him. I could just imagine Gus's response. "Leave the slut," he had undoubtedly counseled.

I worked up the guts to ask, "Did you give him any advice?"

"Who, me? Hey, I'm not the kind of guy to pass judgment or interfere or anything."

Sure, I wanted to say, but stated simply, "I appreciate that, Gus."

"Yeah. Well, don't worry. And if I hear from him, should I tell him you're looking for him?"

"Yes!" I urged. And added the most plaintive "Please!" Gustav Morrison had probably ever heard.

"Put your mind to rest," Bernie's mother told me during our phone conversation. "Whoever she is, he'll get tired of her."

"It's not another woman," I insisted.

"Are you sure?"

It's another man would not have gone over well with Gilda. So I sighed and said, "I'm absolutely certain."

"Only fools are certain," Gilda cautioned. "And the wife is always the last to know. I'm telling you, like father, like son."

I had no response.

"You call me, then," she insisted. "The minute you hear from that *shtunk*. And you *will* hear from him."

"Of course."

"And don't be too harsh on him. It doesn't help. Believe me."

"I won't."

"He loves you, Nora. And he loves his boy. So don't get crazy, okay?"

"Okay."

But I did get crazy, frantic, quietly hysterical. How could I not, now that I had lost everything? At the moment of my confession I felt a riptide of love for the man I had betrayed. What could have possessed me to want someone else, when I had Bernie, who was earthy and real and warm? I loved my husband more than I ever had, more than on that first day in Vermont, more than on our wedding day, more than on our son's day of birth. If he would just come back, I would make it up to him, I would find a way, I would do anything, anything, anything. . . .

It was late Friday afternoon. Nicky was upstairs, his stereo blasting. I could hear him laughing, talking on the phone. Prince Hal was curled up like a burlap sack at my feet as I stood at the sink, polishing a pair of brass candlesticks. They had been my mother's, given to her by the aunt she went to live with when she first arrived in the States. An avowed atheist, my mother still could not stop herself from lighting candles on Friday nights.

"It doesn't mean a thing," she would respond to my questions about the Hebrew words she would chant. She would turn out the lights, and light two white candles, then close her eyes, and make circles with her hands right above the flames. She looked so beautiful, her head lowered, the candles throwing a radiant glow onto her face, and the melody she sang was so sad, so mysterious, so very evocative.

"Why can't you tell me what the words mean?" I persisted each time the ceremony was completed. My mother would not answer, and Ezra, in his white shirt and tie was always preoccupied carrying in the big bowl of soup his wife had cooked.

One Friday Elena sighed more deeply than usual at my question. "It means, the Jews suffer and die, but a good meal goes a long way," she reluctantly disclosed. And for the longest time, I believed her.

. . .

"Why are you doing this?" Nicky wanted to know, later, as we stood together in the dining room and I placed my mother's gleaming bronze candlesticks on the table before us.

"It's Shabbos."

"Since when are we religious?"

I took a match out of its little box and said, "This isn't about religion."

Nicky scratched his head. "You into devil worship or something?"

I gave him a look. "Just indulge me," I requested. "And don't laugh. Or you're dead. Okay?"

Nicky put on his most serious expression. "Go," he said.

I lit the candles, then traced circles in the air, shut my eyes, and without even trying to remember what came next, I found myself singing the words I had last heard years before. When I finished chanting, I opened my eyes, and saw my son studying me.

"Mom," he finally said. "That was nice. I sort of wish you had done it before. You know, like when I was a kid."

I was surprised, and felt an instant twinge. "Do you think I deprived you of your heritage?"

"Hell no. I mean, I was the one who said no way, when you wanted me to have a bar mitzvah."

"Maybe we should have insisted. . . ."

"I'm glad you didn't."

I did not believe him. We sat down and I ladled out a bowl of soup for my son.

"What does it mean, the thing you just sang?" he asked.

"It's a prayer," I answered, knowing this from my father, who had translated it for me properly, after my mother had died. "It asks for our home to be consecrated by these candles, for them to shine on us with the light of love and truth."

Nicky nodded thoughtfully. "And how come you circle your hands over the candles like that?"

"I don't know," I answered, realizing I had never questioned that gesture.

"So how come you did it?"

I shrugged. "My mother did it."

"That's pretty stupid," Nicky commented. "To do something just because your mother did it, not even knowing what it means."

"There are things you just understand without asking," I said, in self-defense. "Obviously you circle your hands over the candles to welcome the Sabbath into your home."

"Obviously," Nicky agreed, then winked. He knew that I had made it up. I winked back. There were things my son understood without asking. I wondered, with discomfort, if his father's absence was one of those things.

But Nicky just blew on a spoonful of soup, then asked, "Did your mother keep kosher and everything?"

"Hardly."

"Is that a yes or a no?"

"No. She didn't even believe in God."

"But she *did* light the candles. How come?"

"Your grandmother had her quirks."

"You're always putting her down," he commented, between slurps of soup.

"I am?" I wondered if it were true.

"Yeah. You talk about her like she was some kind of lunatic."

"I don't mean to," I said, troubled by his observation. "She was a very secretive woman, a damaged woman—the war and all—but I did love her, I guess I . . ." A lump in my throat stopped me.

"Could I have a piece of bread?" Nicky asked, noting my distress, while pointing at the basket. "Are you okay?"

"Sure," I said, touched by his concern. My chevalier. My son. I broke off a piece of bread for him. It was still warm.

Nicky sniffed appreciatively at the freshly baked rye scent. "Dad loves this bread."

I said nothing. Nicky looked at me. "How come you didn't wait till tomorrow to make it?"

"What's happening tomorrow?"

Nicky stuffed a huge wad of rye bread into his mouth. I was about to reprimand him when he mumbled, mouth full, "Dad comes home."

"Dad? Tomorrow?" I dug my fingernails into the palms of my hands in an attempt to keep calm.

Nicky looked at me quizzically. "How come you don't know?" he asked, washing the bread down with another slurp of soup.

"How come you do?"

"He called."

"Dad?"

"Well, *yeah*." He frowned with confusion, then went on. "While you were cooking."

"He didn't ask to speak to me?"

"He just said, 'Tell her I love her.' "

I gasped with surprise.

"He always says that," Nicky added. "What's the big deal?"

"Nothing," I agreed.

"Then why are you crying?"

I rubbed at my cheeks with my uncurling fists and laughed, realizing I was.

My son pointed a finger at me. "I think you're being secretive. Like Grandma Elena. You're hiding something."

"I am," I said, jumping up from my seat. "The fried chicken. Your favorite!"

And as I darted off into the kitchen, I heard Nicky say to his dog, for my benefit, "Hal, were your parents weird, too?"

19

WE WERE DOWN AT THE POND. BERNIE HELD MY HAND, AND with his free one he was skipping rocks for my amusement. The water was murky, but stirring with spring mysteries— tiny bubbles bursting suddenly on the surface, pollywogs wriggling, insects hatching, testing their dewy wings.

"Did you see that?" Bernie yelled, pointing at the ripples in the middle of the pond.

"What?"

"Seven bounces with one stone. Seven! And my lady love doesn't even notice." Bernie pulled me to him, pretending anger, but the look in his eyes was all affection.

"I've never been so happy," I sighed. He kissed me, tenderly, with a new gentleness. Birds chirped. A bee buzzed overhead. At that moment I thought that Linden Hill was the loveliest spot on earth, and that I was the luckiest woman alive.

"I think we should dredge it this year," Bernie said.

"The pond?"

"No," he said, as if to a moron. "The bathtub."

"You don't have to be sarcastic," I said sweetly.

"Don't get on my case, Nora," Bernie said, his voice oddly menacing. He stood before me, a pained expression on his face. Then he turned away.

"Hey," I said, wanting him back. "What's wrong?"

He shrugged, kicked at a rock, and said, "Come on. Let's go check out the barn." He grabbed my hand, and began to run up the hill, me keeping pace, both of us suddenly laughing like teenagers.

We were hauling old cartons out of the barn, piling them up for removal.

"Wait a sec," Bernie said, pulling a pack of baseball trading cards out of one box. "Maybe Nicky still wants these."

"Doubt it."

"Phil Rizzuto . . . Micky the M—" He looked up at me. "These could be worth something."

"Be ruthless. That's what you said when we started this cleanup detail, sir," I reminded him, with a sharp salute.

Bernie smiled weakly, then thoughtfully shuffled the cards. "Do you have a picture of him?"

"Of who?"

"It's of *whom*," he corrected, with no small annoyance. "And you know very well of whom I mean."

I folded my arms and took a deep breath. "No, I do not have a picture of Theo."

"Is he a hunk?"

"No."

Bernie was unconvinced. "A pretty boy?"

"No."

"So what is he? A *GQ* kind of a guy with a dimple in his chin and Armani suits, or the more rustic Lands' End type? Smokes a pipe and wears red plaid shirts?"

"What's the difference?"

Bernie shrugged nonchalantly. "Call me curious. I just wonder, was it his dashing good looks, or his youth—he is, you've said, five years my junior. Correct?"

I nodded coldly.

"With a full head of hair?"

"Yes. Fair hair. Luxuriant," I said meanly, then quickly added, "but I prefer yours."

"I don't have any. Or haven't you noticed?"

I blushed with remorse and fury as Bernie continued his caustic questioning. "Well, then, was it his money, or, better yet, his fancy hydraulics that swept you away . . . ?"

Bernie cupped a hand behind one ear, comically awaiting a reply.

"I'm not on the witness stand," I grumbled.

"Oh, but you are," he insisted.

I glared at him. "Why do you keep doing this?"

"Doing what?"

I hissed annoyance.

"Oh, so I'm not allowed to ask about the perfect Mr. Bradshaw?"

"He's not perfect. Neither am I. Neither are you. And I don't see the point," I said softly.

But Bernie did. "You betray me for a year with this guy," he reminded me. "I leave you for a minute. I swallow my pride and come back. But I'm not allowed to ask questions?"

Yes, Bernie had returned, for which I was grateful, truly grateful, and willing to pay the necessary penance. But he was unpredictable as a puma, one minute purring, the next lunging, and the price of penance seemed way beyond my reach.

"What do you want to know?" I asked, braving a beastly response.

Bernie was silent, the muscles in his cheeks undulating. "Nothing!" he finally said. "I don't want to know a fucking thing about the asshole."

"Good," I said, feeling the color rise in my cheeks. "Because I don't think it would be very constructive. You won't ask me about Theo. And I won't ask you any questions either."

"About what?" he goaded.

"About anything or anyone you don't want me to know about."

"Don't do this, Nora," he warned.

"Don't do what?" I asked, as if I did not know. I had vowed to do anything and everything to make it up to Bernie. And I was trying my best. But it suddenly occurred to me that Bernie might not be without some blame himself. I had seen the way he looked at Pamela. And husbands do screw around. Hadn't Stephanie said that?

Bernie threw the baseball cards back into a box. "Are you accusing me of having an affair?" he demanded to know.

"Would I have a reason to?" I retorted, unable to stop pushing.

"No!" he yelled and spun around. He marched into the barn and then came storming back toward me. He stood still in front of me and said, softly, "You haven't asked where I went when I left home."

"No, I haven't."

"Does that mean you don't care?"

"I care. Of course I care," I answered, trembling now. "But don't tell me."

"You'd rather imagine where I was, than know for sure?"

If confrontation was the name of the game, I could play it as well as he. "You were with what's-her-name. Pamela," I said, hoping I was wrong, knowing as I said it that it was true.

"Yes, I was," Bernie admitted. "I thought, if Nora can do it, so can I, but you know something?" He looked up at me, his eyes tearful. "For a few nights, it was very nice. But I had to end it. I just couldn't bear hurting you like that. I didn't have it in me." He sighed before asking, "How did you do it?"

"Please," I said, touching his arm. "Stop."

He shook my hand off. "I'm really curious," he insisted. "You betrayed me. Day to day. You took a year of happiness away from me. And you were so good at it!" He sniffed. "So good."

His words chilled me. He was right. I was evil. Hateful. Mea culpa, mea culpa. I deserved his punishment. Yet if he, too, had strayed, why was he without regret? Why was he so relentlessly righteous?

"If you think I'm so awful, then why did you come back?" I asked, tossing my head, defiant.

He wiped his eyes. "I'll tell you why," he said, standing up, pointing at the house. "There is a family here. And I think of my son, bringing his son here to see his grandfather." He grabbed my hand. I did not pull away. "I see grandchildren here, Nora."

"So do I," I said, the thought choking me with emotion.

Bernie wrapped his arms around me, and held me very tight. "I want to get over this," he whispered, "I want to find a way to get over this thing!"

"I love you," I assured him.

"I love you, too."

We stood there, for a long time, outside the barn, like two drowning swimmers, clinging to each other, until Bernie broke away and said, "Let's paint it."

"Paint what?"

"The barn." He cocked his head and gazed at the dull gray shingles. "Red. What does red do for you?"

"Everything!" I answered, wishing it could.

❧ 20 ❧

I SHOULD NEVER HAVE LIT THOSE CANDLES. WHO NEEDS THE light of love and truth, when the former blinks on and off and the latter glares relentlessly as a bare bulb? Under the blinding light of truth, I continued to withstand the interrogations of my husband with as much dignity as an avowed offender could muster:

"Did you ever spend the night with him?" I was asked.

"Define 'the night.' "

"Did you ever wake up in the morning with him?"

"We had sex. You know we had sex. So what's the difference when and where and for how long?"

"The *difference*," Bernie would explain in that slow, patronizing tone of his, "is that a wife is someone who wakes up in her husband's bed."

"Even when her husband is away?"

"*Especially* when her husband is away!" Bernie would bellow, then pace around the room, and come back at me with yet another question: "Did you ever sleep with him and then come home and sleep with me?"

I sighed, impatient, but answered no.

"Why not?"

"I wouldn't do that," I told him. "I just couldn't. I never did."

"Good!" he gloated. "I never poked around in his slime. That's one thing to celebrate."

"I don't think there's *anything* to celebrate," I said, sadly. "About me. About you. Or about *us*."

"How right you are," he would furiously agree. "And whose fault is that?"

Before I could respond, he had turned on his heel and marched back out to the barn where he picked up bucket and brush and slathered red paint like knife wounds onto the gray shingles.

But then there was the light of love, which spluttered and dimmed, yet when it sparked, seemed to illuminate the landscape like fireworks on a blackened sky.

One warm and muggy weekend, the pond was dredged. Jim Carley and his partner, Snaky Johnson, came out to the house with their huge truck and, manning an intricate array of hoses and pumps and a generator whirring like a cyclone, they sucked all the silt and muck out of the water.

"What about all the little embryos and larvae down there?" I yelled to Bernie, who stood right beside me. "Aren't we killing a lot of tiny creatures?"

"Don't you understand about balance?" he yelled back, sounding like Mr. Feturgiotis, my ninth-grade biology teacher, who gave me a C for spelling phylum with an F. "We're cleaning up the ecosystem!"

"I see!" I screamed back, my head pounding with the rumble of the generator.

"Gotta give 'er a good week or two before everything really settles down," Snaky informed us when he finished. "It's like after a good fight with the missus." He winked at Bernie. "Takes a minute till the clouds clear. Then . . .

how sweet it is!" He guffawed, and Jim Carley swatted at him with the sweaty T-shirt he had just taken off. Bernie glanced at me meaningfully, and as the dredging duo rumbled off, he snuck one hand under my sweater, and nibbled at my ear, whispering, "How sweet is it?"

I held my hand out in answer, and led him behind the barn where, lying on a bed of cool moss under miniature white clouds of apple blossoms, I showed him.

❦ 21 ❧

BERNIE WAS READING THE NEWSPAPER AFTER DINNER.

"Didn't you read it at work?" I asked. It was his daily routine, first task to read the paper. "Can't *do* unless I know what's doing," he always said.

"If I did, why would I be reading it now?" Bernie peered impatiently at me over his glasses which were perched halfway down his nose. Then he went back to the metropolitan section and left me to wonder whether he really had ended it with Pamela, and whether she, instead of the paper, had been his morning priority. Mine was now to finish cleaning up the kitchen, a task in which he once used to take part and pleasure.

"Where's Nicky?" he asked, when he had finished the business news.

"In his room."

"Wrong," Bernie informed me. "He went out right after dinner."

"He did?" I had not seen him leave, nor had he asked permission. "He's not supposed to, on a school night."

"So why didn't you stop him?" Bernie asked, his manner decidedly critical.

I did not appreciate his tone. "Why didn't *you?*" I asked back.

"You're the one who made that rule, Nora."

"You agreed to it," I reminded him. I folded up the wet dish towel I had been using and took a seat across the kitchen table from my husband.

"How's he doing?" Bernie demanded to know.

"You mean, in school?"

"Of course I mean in school."

"We'll find out when he gets his report card in June. He says he's been doing better."

Bernie gave me a doubting look, then pulled a piece of paper out of his pocket, waved it at me. "Not if his S.A.T. scores are any indication," he informed me, and handed the paper to me.

I studied the numbers and knew they were well below the average.

"He won't get in anywhere!" Bernie announced.

"There are colleges that will take him," I mumbled, feeling the impact of my child's failings, wanting to protect him. "State schools . . ."

Bernie took his glasses off and began to twirl them by one earpiece. "Where the hell have you been, Nora?"

"Me?"

"Yeah. You. Why didn't you know your son needed remedial help for this goddam test? Why didn't you pay attention when attention needed paying?"

Taken aback, I had no answer.

"Well, we know, don't we," Bernie responded for me. "You were busy boffing the beautiful Mr. Bradshaw." He stood up and walked around behind my chair, leaned down and hissed into my ear, "Instead of going to the PTA meetings and college counseling sessions, like other concerned parents. Instead of getting your son a tutor, you were tooting something else." He stood up and spoke as if to an audience: "Not her flute, folks. God knows we haven't heard her practice in months. She was playing another instrument, wasn't she?" He turned back to me, his cheeks rippling, waiting for my response.

I stood up and carefully slid my chair back under the table. "There are things I will take the blame for," I told him, my voice controlled. "But this is not one of them."

"Oh?" he taunted. "Really?"

"Really," I said. "And for your information, Nickolas has two parents, and I would have thought the one with the master's degree would have made it his business to pay attention to the college process."

"I'm bringing home the bacon! I'm traveling! I'm in fucking Duluth and you expect me to attend college conferences?"

But I had turned and walked out of the kitchen.

"Come back here, goddam it!" my husband called after me.

I was halfway up the stairs and not about to reply.

"Did you hear me? Nora!"

The next thing I heard was the pounding of Bernie's feet as he ran up the stairs and grabbed me by the elbow, spun me around, nearly making me fall. "How dare you not answer me?" His face was the color of aging steak as he screamed, "Out! I want you to get out of this house!"

"Bernie . . . ?" I tried to reason. "Nicky's S.A.T. scores are not . . ."

He growled at me, shoved me into the bedroom and flung open the door to my closet, pulling everything out—dresses, scarves, purses, shoes, boxes. Everything.

"Stop it!" I yelled at him. "Will you stop it?!"

But he kept heaving items into the center of the room, and when he was finished, he shoved me onto the pile, and said, between his teeth, "Get out! I want you out of my house in fifteen minutes!"

Then he reeled out of the room, bumping into a chair, kicking it and slamming the door behind him.

I held my breath for a very long moment, then let out a sob and buried my face in a cotton dress, a new floral one, purchased to please him.

Where would I go? What would become of me? I could not bear to be forced to leave my son. But did I have a choice? Yes, Bernie had wandered, but only for a moment. I was the true culprit, the adulteress, the demon mother. Bernie would tell Nicky now, and he would hate me forever, never speak to me again. I saw myself, canvas bag in tow, hitchhiking on a highway, homeless, penniless—destitute. I curled up and cried and cried.

The doorknob turned very slowly. I sat up, realizing my fifteen minutes had expired and I was about to be evicted. But when the door creaked open the raging beast I expected to see bursting through the door was now just a man, head lowered. He walked heavily toward me and sat down near the pile of clothing on the floor beside me.

"Nora," he said, picking up a pink sweater. "I want it to go away. But it just won't."

I wiped my nose on a floral sleeve and said nothing.

"Sometimes," he said, stroking the sweater, "I'm sitting in my car, and this picture slides into my head, you with this other guy, this *Theo* . . . and I get crazy. I pound the dashboard, I . . . ." He raised a fist, then opened his hand and showed me an empty palm. "It's so unfair," he went on bitterly, tossing the sweater onto the bed. "You told me about it and it was over for you. Finished. Done. But, don't you see, that same moment, for me, that was when *my* torment *began?*"

How could I answer, when what was done was done and "Sorry" was not good enough? I had sinned, I had transgressed, I had admitted my guilt. But had I willfully planned to hurt my husband? My adultery was unpremeditated, not intended to harm others, a folly in the first degree, not worth, in my opinion, a lifetime of punishment. Surely there was a statute of limitations. I understood his rage, his disappointment, his deep and devastating pain, but didn't anger diminish with time? Yes, I told myself. He will get over this in time. I will wait it out. Patience can be a virtue after all.

"Say something," Bernie urged me, tentatively touching my hand. "Please?"

I gazed slowly around the room at all the familiar objects in their places, the mirror over the bureau we bought when we married, the jewelry box with the diamond pin Bernie had presented to me when Nicky was born, the painting of a baroque woodland scene we had picked up in a flea market. I looked at Bernie, my partner in it all, and felt that to be without him would be to halve myself, to break apart. To die.

"Nora?" Bernie said. "Please?"

I looked at him, then at the gutted closet. "Now that it's empty," I said, pointing at it. "Could we paint it?"

A smile crept slow as an inchworm onto his pale and sorry face. "Yes," he whispered. "Of course we could."

❦ 22 ❦

ONE MORNING WOKE UP, STARTLED BY A LOUD, SCRAPING noise, like metal dragging on cement. I listened for it, but the house was silent. I checked the clock. Nine. Nicky and Bernie must both have tiptoed out without waking me. I ached all over. I felt my face and was surprised it was wet. Then I touched my pillow, and it was damp, and I realized I had been crying in my sleep. But why and for whom?

No dream image surfaced in my sleepy mind. Bernie was right, painfully and precisely accurate. The moment I revealed Theo, he had disappeared. It was not even that I had forgotten him. It was as if Theo Bradshaw had never existed. I could not recall the color of his eyes, the shape of his head, the lilt of his voice, the voice that for an entire year had lured me sirenlike into forbidden and dangerous waters.

"Am I just the crowbar you're using . . . ?" Theo's words haunted me. Yes, I had used him. I was not only an adulteress. I was a callous, calculating one. Had I cared about my lover, really cared, deeply, sincerely? If so, then how was I capable of shutting him out, stopping up the feelings, forgetting him so entirely, so completely that I did not even dream of him?

Sitting in the kitchen in my bathrobe, Prince Hal at my feet, I was sipping coffee, watching "I Dream of Jeannie."

"Master," the ponytailed bimbo dressed like a belly dancer beseeched, "please don't be angry with me. I only wanted to talk to her."

"But how can you? She's dead!" her bug-eyed lord protested.

"I'll just conjure her up from the Other Side," Jeannie explained, and when her master hit his forehead in disbelief and looked out at the audience of one, who was me, I remembered my dream:

The cemetery seemed vast and arid, like another planet. The people in black, the box in which my mother was trapped, the huge marble slabs surrounding us were all intergalactic objects, not of this earth, and therefore could not touch me. I did not cry, not when the mysterious Hebrew words were intoned, not when my father tried to jump into the grave and had to be restrained, not even when I was asked to drop a handful of dirt onto the top of the coffin. I just did it, dry-eyed, no questions asked, no tears shed. And when we left my mother there, covered with cool, wet earth, we drove out of the cemetery through an open wrought-iron gate. I turned back and saw the gates being closed slowly, and I heard them clang together, a cruel, scraping sound that echoed louder and louder, and I saw that I had become the gatekeeper. It was *me* standing there, a fierce and hateful creature who was clanging those gates shut with force and finality, a hideous grin on my face.

"Then you do forgive me, master?" Jeannie was whining, when I stopped daydreaming my dream.

"Of course," he simpered. "But it's off season in this house for séances, is that understood?"

"Oh yes, master!" the dream mistress sighed and, hugging her lord and keeper, winked right at me over his shoulder.

❦ 23 ❧

HE LUMBERED UP THE STAIRS. TONGUE HANGING OUT, PRINCE Hal was having trouble getting to the top. I put the pile of clean towels I was carrying into the linen closet, then squatted down beside the dog.

"What is it, old boy?" I asked him, and the whimper of his reply and the pleading in his fading brown eyes made me reach for the phone.

"Sorry to bother you," I said. "But I think there's something wrong with Hal."

"What?" my husband wanted to know. He was in the editing room and obviously did not appreciate the interruption.

"He could hardly make it up the stairs, and . . ."

"Have you been feeding him leftovers?" he asked accusingly.

"No. Of course not. And I don't think it's his stomach."

"What he eats affects his entire body," he said in a slow, testy voice. "I've got to get this piece finished, Nora. So why don't you do the obvious thing? Call the vet and take the dog in?"

"Okay," I said, and hung up, feeling stupid and contrite and quite annoyed. Hadn't Bernie spent the last fifteen years with the dog, too? And what was so important about the piece he was editing, except, maybe . . . the editor? Was Bernie still involved with Pamela? The thought angered and saddened me. But I had something more important to take care of and would not allow myself to waste time on trifles.

"Good. That's a good dog," Dr. Calibrian told Hal, as he turned him on his back and began feeling his belly. Hal whined and looked up at me and I stroked him under the chin and told him he was the best dog in the whole world and he was going to be okay.

"Mrs. Watterman, when did you first notice this mass?" the doctor asked. He pointed to a swelling just below the rib cage.

"I . . . we . . . he seemed fine until today. . . ."

"It's a tumor. Unmistakable," the doctor said, palpating it again, making Hal groan. "And it didn't develop overnight."

He looked at me reproachfully. How could I not have noticed it? And did I somehow cause it?

"Is it . . . benign?" I asked, sickened.

"We'll do a blood workup on him," he said, gently turning the dog onto his side. "And then we'll know what needs to be done."

Hal mewled and licked at my hand and I bent down and kissed him on the top of his head, between the ears, and inhaled his woolly scent before helping the doctor hold him down to draw the blood that would determine his fate.

Driving back home with Hal lying limp on the seat beside me, I remembered him, many summers before, chasing Nicky down a wooden dock on a lake in Maine and diving in after him. They surfaced together, two golden boys, both howling with pleasure. Sunlight sparkled on the water, as they chased each other from water to dock, back and forth, over and over, jumping and splashing the long afternoon away.

24

BERNIE WAS UP ON A LADDER PUTTING THE FINISHING touches on the shingles on the western side of the barn. He had called me to come inspect his work.

"It's fabulous," I told him.

"Yeah?" He squinted into the low afternoon sun to look down at me. "See anything I missed?"

I surveyed the shingles and noticed one small gray patch in a corner. I was about to point it out, but decided, Why dampen the spirit of renewal and renovation when I could easily touch it up myself one day while he was at work?

"It's perfect!" I congratulated him.

He puffed out his chest, mugging proudly, then handed the brush down to me. I stood on tiptoe, but could not quite reach, so I jumped up to grab it, startling Bernie, he later claimed, making him lose his balance and fall backward, bucket and all.

"You're lucky you didn't land on your head," Nicky told him later, as the three of us waited in the hospital emergency room for the results of the X rays.

"Ow," was Bernie's only comment. He was lying on a gurney in a hospital gown, two limbs swelling, right arm, left leg. He tried to move his injured arm, and winced.

"Don't force it," I suggested, and he glowered at me.

"Don't fucking tell me what to do," he hissed.

"Hey," Nicky protested, on my behalf. "What'd Mom do?"

"Ask *her*," Bernie said, then groaned as he tried to move his left leg.

Nicky looked at me. "What'd you do?"

"I'm up on the ladder," Bernie quickly told his son. "I'm trying to hand down the brush to her and she jumps up at me like a crazy cat."

"You jumped at him?" Nicky asked me.

"I couldn't reach the brush," I whispered, guilt grabbing at my voice.

"Like a crazy cat," Bernie repeated. Then he pressed his lips together and grimaced.

"I'm sorry you're in pain," I told him.

"Sure," he said, sulky as a child.

"She said she was sorry!" Nicky said, coming to my defense.

"She's sorry. She's sorry for lots of things, isn't she?" Bernie said, staring at me with no visible affection whatsoever.

"Like what? Mom, what are you sorry about?" Nicky was looking from his father to me, wanting one of us to answer, when a young man in a white coat strutted into the room, holding up a stack of X rays, announcing cheerily, "Nothing broken, just a couple of sprains and a torn ligament in the knee. You'll need a cast on the leg to immobilize it, a sling for the arm, a little bed rest and a lot of love. . . ." Then he saw three morose faces staring at him, two vertical, one horizontal.

"Who's the patient?" he teased.

Bernie was hardly amused. "Who's the doctor?"

"So you fell off a ladder," the doctor persisted. Then he turned to me. "Or did *you* push him?"

I did not even attempt a smile.

"Get me a doctor," Bernie demanded sternly.

"I'm Dr. Kimmelman," the young man seriously introduced himself. Then, pointing to the swelling limbs, he said, "And I'll put you in plaster faster than you can say 'Kimmelman eats Mozartkugel.' "

Bernie's eyes were scrunched shut. He was shivering with pain. "Just do it," he moaned as Kimmelman motioned for me to get out of the way so that the husband whose heart and limbs I had mangled could be wheeled past.

✣ 25 ✣

BERNIE WAS LYING ON THE BLUE COUCH, LEG PROPPED UP, arm anchored across his chest, eyes wide open, staring at the ceiling. Prince Hal was on the floor, a white bandage wrapped around his midsection. They both heard me enter the room, and turned disinterested eyes in my direction.

"Peach tart," I told Bernie, placing the tray I was carrying on the coffee table before him. "And some tea. And your pills." I pointed to a pretty brass thimble filled with prescribed painkillers. "And your morning paper." I handed him the rolled-up *New York Times* I had tucked under my arm, and Hal cringed, worried that he was about to be punished.

"You're a good boy," I cooed, squatting down to reassure him. Hal was licking my hand, eyes closed. Despite the vet's advice that the humane thing would be to put him to sleep, Bernie had opted to remove the dog's malignant tumor and to hope for the best. Now, post-op, and filled with medications, Hal was befuddled and uncomfortable but bearing up like a prince, which was more than I could say for his silent master.

"Anything I can get you?" I asked amiably. Bernie looked up from the TV page, expressionless, then reached for the clicker and turned on a talk show. "Husbands without Prostates," was the subject. Bernie flipped to an old film, *Waterloo Bridge*, and sighed, settling in for a few more moody, melancholy hours.

"Well, then," I said, to no one in particular, backed out of the room, and wandered toward the kitchen to prepare the ointments and bandages for the dog's morning dressing change, and the barley soup for Bernie's lunch.

As I was chopping onions, eyes watering, there was a knock on the back door. My mother-in-law floated into the kitchen like a dirigible, balancing a large pot on the shelf of her ample stomach.

"Stop crying, I'm here," she said, pointing at my face. A diamond ring circled her fleshy finger like a tourniquet.

She slid the pot onto the kitchen table, and folded me into her doughy arms, then pushed me away, slapped at my cheeks and said, "Eat, Nora. Look at you, scrawny as a chicken. You want to keep your man?" She pulled off the cover of the pot and tilted it to show me. "This will put a little meat on your bones."

"A brisket. Thank you. It's so nice of you to . . ."

She waved at me to skip the niceties, as she sank into a kitchen chair. "Will he walk again?' she whispered.

"Of course. It's just a torn ligament and a sprain. The cast is to keep it immobile. He'll be good as new in no time."

"Too bad. After what he put you through? He deserves a permanent limp, at least. Got any Diet Coke? I'm dying."

We sat together at the kitchen table, sipping two Diet Cokes, and I felt worse and worse as Bernie's mother continued to berate her son. "It serves him right, for what he did. And if he thinks there is not a God up there . . ." She stopped to point and to look at the ceiling. "You never heard of dusting, Norala?"

I looked up and saw another spider's web stretched like a hammock from one corner of the room to the overhead light. "I've been so busy, what with Bernie and the dog and . . ."

She waved me silent again, patting my hand. "A spider has a right to a house, too, so stop feeling so bad. How's the baby?"

"Nicky?"

"Who else?"

"Nicky is seventeen."

"You think I can't count?"

"No. I mean, yes, of course you can count. Nicky's fine. He's just swell."

"Top of his class?"

"Not exactly."

"My daughter, Linda? You remember her?"

"Of course. My sister-in-law."

She leaned toward me confidentially across the table, squashing her breasts against the hard wood. "A phone call to Lindy the sister-in-law once in a while, this is too much for you?"

Lindy the Loser and her boring brood. If Bernie couldn't be bothered to contact her, why was I responsible? I took a deep breath and dutifully pledged, "I'll call her."

Gilda nodded, eyes closed in acceptance of my promise.

"Good. She's a lovely girl. And that little Rolanda of hers? A *beauty*. No. A *great* beauty. She has all the boys in Woodmere panting at the door. And Joshua? A genius. What can I say?"

Gilda poured herself another glass of Diet Coke and looked me over. "You're pinched like a prune, Nora. This man, my son, is aging you. Put something sweet on the table. You'll eat. You'll fill out."

I obliged with a plateful of my best chocolate chip cookies and a chest filled with the worst remorse.

"Bernie's not the only one to blame here," I began as Gilda munched a cookie. "In fact . . . Gilda. What I am going to tell you may shock you. . . ."

"The brunette from Dubuque?" she asked, stunning my confession into silence.

"What brunette?"

Gilda looked at me, eyes wide. She hesitated, but then continued. "Lindy's best friend, Karen, the corporate lawyer—she should have married Marvin Rabinowitz if you want my opinion—anyhow, she was in Dubuque a year or so ago, and saw them, Bernie and this brunette, at a bar in the Hilton. . . ."

A year or so ago? If Pamela was a blonde and a recent conquest, then who was the brunette? Obviously a different woman. Another woman. I tried to keep my voice from quavering. "Saw them? Doing what?"

"You know."

"I don't."

She fidgeted, arranging herself in the chair, brushing brown crumbs off her purple blouse. "It was probably nothing. Just a one-night stand. Men who travel have their needs, you know. . . ."

I was quiet, taking this in, imagining Bernie at a bar with some brown-haired broad, smooching the night away. And how many nights, and how many broads? And how stupid could I have been to assume that Pamela was an isolated incident, a reaction to *my* reprehensible behavior? *Me?!* Bernie fooled around on the road. Probably often, if not all the time. In eighteen years I had met *one* man outside of my marriage to whom I responded with care and affection. Yet I seemed to be the sole offender. Was this just and right and as it should be?

"What's with you?" Gilda was asking, looking at me, concerned.

"It isn't fair."

"If life was fair," Gilda declared, posing like a portly pinup, "we'd all be at the Fountain Blue doing the cha-cha-cha." Then she slapped my arm. "Cheer up, Nora. You look like Bette Davis on a bad day." She pushed the table away from her chair (although her intention was vice versa) and rose, slow as an iceberg. "Now tell me where my boy, Bern, is," she requested, out of breath. "I'll give him a kiss and be on my way. A mother-in-law lasts longer in short doses, you think I don't know this?"

❧ 26 ❧

"DO I LOOK LIKE TOM CRUISE?"

"Who's Tom Cruise?" I asked my dapper son as he turned around slowly in his tuxedo.

"Tom Cruise? The movie star? You've never even heard of him?"

I nodded no.

Nicky stared in disbelief. "What planet are you from?"

"Mars. And from up here, Tom Cruise can't compete." I kissed him on the cheek. "Kelly's a lucky girl."

Nicky's smile flattened. "Mom . . . ?"

I could see him struggling. "What? You can tell me. Anything."

But whatever was on Nicky's mind did not find its way into words before his father, now without cast, limped into the living room, held onto the back of a chair, regarded his only child and said, "You look like a million bucks. The ladies'll love you. Go kill 'em, kid."

"Kelly is the only woman I care about," the romantic lad announced.

"A one-woman man, hunh, like your Dad?"

Nicky's knowing, keen blue eyes blinked. "Just like my Dad."

"But you'll fall in love a few thousand times before you find that final one woman," Bernie said.

"I've found her. Kelly's my one and only."

Bernie slung a paternal arm around him. "I'm glad you like her so much, son."

"I love her."

"You're a junior in high school."

"So?"

"So you've got a lot of living to do."

"That doesn't mean I can't feel love yet."

Bernie squeezed Nicky's shoulder, then stepped back to study his boy. "I believe you're capable of deep and true feelings. I believe you're in love. I believe in you, Nicky."

A megawatt smile lit up Nickolas Watterman's face. He hugged his father hard, almost knocking him over.

"Bust my other leg and I'll bust you!" Bernie hugged his son. Nicky looked up at me and beckoned me to join them, saying boyishly, in his now deep voice, "Mommy?"

And I reached my arms around my son, circling his father into the embrace, squeezing Nicky between his two parents, making our family sandwich, The Watterman.

"Easy on the mayo," Nicky whispered, as he always had when we squeezed too hard. I pulled away, almost tousling his hair, but stopping myself in time. He was a man now, and moussed to perfection and on his way to his junior prom.

Bernie winked at him. "I envy you."

"Well, you can't come," Nicky teased.

"Have a wonderful evening," I told him.

"And be home by"—Bernie waited for the exasperated click of the tongue, which came on cue, and then surprised the clicker with the word—"dawn."

"I think I can handle that." Nicky smoothed his jacket, adjusted his carnation, and tipped an imaginary top hat at us as he waltzed gracefully out the front door.

27

BY MID-JUNE THINGS WERE MENDING. BERNIE WAS BACK AT work, walking easily, treating me kindly. I had put Pamela and the brunette in the past. Bernie seemed to have Theo in perspective, too. Prince Hal was hanging in. Nicky was out of school, having squeaked by with passing grades. He got a summer job at Earth Arts, where he helped Leon Dubrovner keep his wheels well greased and his floors clean, and where he discovered, one night after hours, that he liked the feel of clay in his hands. Leon showed him how to throw it, shape it, and sometimes let him sit in on classes.

Bernie's response to his son's new interest was less than enthusiastic. "They did that in the sixties," he grumped and, stepping on the accelerator, passed a truck in a no-passing zone. "What if he ends up moving to Vermont, making pots and baking bread?"

"There could be worse things," I replied, wanting to say, Slow down, it's raining and the road is slick.

"Not in my book."

"Nicky has an artistic flair. Leon Dubrovner said . . ."

"Leon Dubrovner is a fool."

"End of discussion."

Bernie speeded up. "You do that all the time, cut things off, shut down the shop." He shot an angry glance in my direction. "Then you tell me we don't talk enough. You can't have it both ways, you know. Or haven't you learned that yet?"

"I've learned that it is possible to talk, really talk, only when the person you're talking to can be open and interested in any point of view other than his own. Watch it!"

Bernie swerved, just missing a Wagoneer as it skidded out of lane. Rain was pummeling the car. Visibility was practically zero. Bernie wiped at the fogged windshield, and reluctantly slowed down.

"Maybe we should pull over?" I dared suggest.

Bernie inched over to the shoulder of the road, and stopped the car. We sat staring into the rain, window wipers ticking lonely seconds away, rain beating its relentless tattoo.

"You're right about me," Bernie admitted, without looking at me. "I hold on to opinions like a terrier and won't let go. I'm that way with grudges, too."

So much for perspective. I leaned wearily back against the headrest. Bernie checked his watch, and sighed.

"Are we going to be late?" I asked.

"Maybe we should forget it."

"You were looking forward to it."

"Was I?"

"You asked me to get the tickets."

"You hate musicals."

"But you don't. I'd like to see you enjoy yourself."

Bernie turned toward me, leaning one arm on the steering wheel. "You are a very good and giving woman."

"Thank you," I said, feeling a tingle of warmth in my veins.

Bernie took my hand and looked affectionately into my eyes. "But I can't stand it when I feel happy with you."

I gasped for breath, as if socked in the stomach, and pulled my hand out of his. "Why?"

"Because I know I'm only pretending."

"Pretending what?"

"That it doesn't hurt. It still hurts, Nora." Shadows flickered across his face. He was half in darkness, or was it half in light? And where was I? Pushed away. Far away.

"I never meant to hurt you," I repeated for the millionth time. Mea culpa. Mea culpa. But then Gilda's revelation slipped like a splinter into my thoughts, making me flinch. Was I just going to let it sit there and fester? I closed my eyes and squeezed the words out: "No more than you meant to hurt me."

Bernie's forehead wrinkled. "How have I hurt you?"

I hesitated. Maybe I should leave well enough alone. But things were not well enough. "You told Nicky you're a one-woman man, Bernie."

"Well, I am," he blustered, sitting up, his body tensing. "I'm not seeing Pamela, if that's what you're implying."

"I'm not implying anything," I stated. "I know there were nights on the road, before Pamela, when you did not sleep alone." I said it simply, without rancor, yet I could feel a prickle of electricity emanating from Bernie.

"There's a big difference between an occasional one-night fling, and a love affair that lasts an entire year."

I should have known not to test his unyielding stance, but I had already begun. "There's no difference," I claimed. A heavy clap of thunder sounded in the distance.

"You were *intimate* with that man. I didn't even *know* these women."

"How sad," I said, and moved away from him, up against the door. I leaned my cheek against the cool glass of the window. "And how dangerous. And how many of *these women* did you spend the night with?"

"None of your goddam business. You don't have a clue, do you? You don't have a shred of moral decency in your body, Nora." He was leaning toward me. I pressed my cheek hard against the glass.

"And you do?" I was not afraid.

"Yes, I do. I know what's right and what's wrong, which is more than I can say for you!"

"Bernie," I said, placing two firm hands against his chest, pushing him away. "I forgive you. To forgive is right."

Bernie slid back over to the driver's seat and tapped his fingers on the wheel. "Who told you?" he asked. "About those . . . women?"

I shrugged, and wiped at the condensation on the window. The rain was drumming harder, and cars were pulling off the road, lining up in front and behind us, headlights on, wipers swishing, forced by a summer storm into a few seconds of immobility. "I wonder how many couples in these cars are happy." I pointed to the queue. "I wonder how many are miserable, how many are fighting, how many . . ."

"There were only a few, Nora," Bernie interrupted. "I swear it. And only because they were there and only because I was lonely. And every time it was awful and I felt bad and I thought of you and wanted you, only you. . . ."

"It's okay," I whispered.

Bernie looked at me for a long moment. "It's letting up." We listened to the slow ping of drops and saw cars gliding back onto the wet black ribbon of road.

"Think we can get there for the second act?" I asked.

"Doubt it."

"Sorry we missed it."

"I'm not."

"No?"

"I feel very close to you right now," he said, touching my arm, forcing a smile. "And it feels very good. Everything's out in the open. We can start fresh. . . ."

His voice had a hollow ring to it. Things may have been out in the open, but the landscape seemed barren, in need of much toil and tending. Could any effort make it flower again?

"We can start fresh," I echoed, my head pounding, my empty stomach complaining. "But first let's get a couple of burgers and a large order of fries."

Bernie winked at me. "That's my girl," he said, squeezed my knee, and started the motor.

◈ 28 ◈

I BEGAN PRACTICING AGAIN, WITH A PASSION. OR WAS IT WITH a vengeance? I clung to my flute as a shipwrecked swimmer to a piece of driftwood. It was my lifeline, my saving grace, my way of staying afloat. I spent hours at it, inspired by something I could not name. And I practiced in the barn. Now that it was cleared out and newly painted, it was, I discovered one sultry morning, the perfect place to pipe a tune, to turn a phrase, to spin a sound. I had wandered out there barefoot, looking for a trowel to dig up the soil around some roses. Sunlight was pouring through the windows; there was a sweet woody smell and a cheerfulness to the place. I heard birds singing, crickets clicking. I took a deep breath and sighed and missed something terribly, missed it physically, and I knew instantly what it was: the cool silver feel of a flute in my hands, placed just under my lower lip, catching that stream of air, turning a sigh into sound.

And so the barn became my studio, my sanctum sanctorum, *sans* telephone, *sans* interruption—my refuge. I practiced scales, études, orchestral excerpts, anything and everything, hour after hour. And then I would improvise, make melodies up as I went along, just for myself, just for the sheer pleasure of it.

"We'll build cabinets out there, turn it into a proper music room for you, won't we, Dad?" Nicky offered one hot June night as we sat around the kitchen table.

"I like it just the way it is," I said.

"You have a concert coming up?" Bernie wondered.

"No. I kept July free, for our trip. . . ."

"Then why are you practicing so much?"

"I just like to."

"Art for art's sake, haven't you ever heard of that, Dad?" Nicky challenged.

Bernie shook his head. "You two with your flutes and your pots . . ."

"What's wrong with flutes and pots?" Nicky said, bristling.

"Your father's just joking."

"The hell he is."

"Cool out," Bernie said.

"*You* cool out."

"Stop it. Both of you," I put in.

My two men glowered at each other.

"Do I have to go with you?"

"Go where?" Bernie asked his son.

"That trip out West. You two go alone. Have a second honeymoon. How about it?"

"Your mother bought the tickets. Apex fare. No refunds. And we've made hotel reservations."

"I'll pay you back."

"Nicky!" I said, surprised and hurt.

"I have a life, Mom," he said. "I can't come. I'm sorry."

"Damn right you're sorry," his father warned. "And you *are* coming with us, life or no life. We've been looking forward to this family trip for months. And no son of mine is going to spoil it. Is that clear?"

Nicky's hands curled into stubborn balls. "You can't force me."

"No? Who pays your bills? Who feeds and clothes you, wise guy?"

"I'll move out. I'll make it on my own, I'll . . ."

I headed him off at the pass: "You'll see Indian ceramics out there, Anasazi artifacts, Navajo pottery. . . ."

His face relaxed. He uncurled his fists. "Leon has a book on it."

"Borrow it," Bernie ordered, pushed his chair back, and stood up.

"I will!" Nicky threatened.

"Good! And we'll have a good time!"

Bernie turned on his heel and stormed out of the room, Nicky shouting after him, "We'll have a good time? Hell, we'll have a great time! We'll have a fucking fabulous time, won't we! One hell of a happy family time . . . !"

My hand on his arm quieted him. He looked at me, angry tears in his eyes.

"Maybe we will," I whispered. "Maybe we fucking will."

Nicky smiled sadly, hung his head, then buried it for a brief moment in my shoulder before bolting out of the room and up the stairs.

❦ 29 ❦

STEPHANIE STOPPED TO SEE ME ON HER WAY UP TO TANGLE-wood. We met at Baskin-Robbins to treat Jill to some ice cream and to talk.

"Letting such a thing happen! You ought to be arrested!" an outraged woman said to Stephanie as she passed our table on her way out of the shop.

"It's chocolate, not shit!" Stephanie informed her. I wiped at Jill's face and hair with a napkin, trying to blot up some chocolate fudge ripple. Her white organdy dress was dotted with dark smudges. She giggled like a minx and said, "Messy me."

"Yes, you're a messy monkey," I told her, gritting my teeth in that silly way adults will when overwhelmed by an utterly adorable child.

A hand holding a pile of napkins slid in front of my face. I took the offering and looked up to see Kelly the Scooper smiling at me with her wan, empty face. Strands of pale, limp hair hung over her shoulders like sauerkraut.

"Thank you."

"Want some water, too?"

"It's okay," Stephanie told her. "I've got other dresses for her out in the car. . . ." She pointed through the plate glass window to the white stretch limousine that was poised to whisk her up to the Berkshires for a weekend of performances with the Boston Symphony.

I introduced them. "Stephanie Saunders, this is Kelly, Nicky's . . . girlfriend."

"Pleased to make your acquaintance. Are you the famous fiddler?" Kelly asked.

"I do play the violin." Stephanie preened. Applause pleased her. Recognition delighted her. She was unashamed of her lust to be known. "Do I *need* the fame?" she was quoted as saying in an interview in *Vanity Fair*. "Does a fish need tartar sauce?"

"I've heard your record."

"Which one?"

Kelly looked heavenward for help. Then she took a shot at it. "Shogun?"

"Shogun?"

"It's sort of gypsy music by a French guy."

"*Tzigane*, by Maurice Ravel?" Stephanie guessed.

"Yeah. That's it." Kelly grinned, showing the overbite Nicky found so adorable. "Could I get your autograph?"

"Well, of course," the superstar answered and, reaching into her designer handbag, produced a packet of five-by-seven black-and-white glossy photos of herself, signed one with a flourish—To Kelly with Love—and presented it to her newest fan.

"Gee, thanks!" Kelly said, then turned to Jill and held out her hand. "How's about you come with me and I'll take you back to the kitchen and wash that goop off your puss?"

Jill eagerly took the proffered hand, jumped off her seat and without so much as a wave to her mother, skipped alongside my son's Insignificant Other.

"What a sweet girl," Stephanie whispered.

I looked at her, shocked. "Sweet? She's stupid and slothful and . . ."

Stephanie flicked her compact open, twirled a pink lipstick at me. "You're jealous."

"Jealous! Of that twit?"

Stephanie smeared lipstick the color of bubble gum onto her lips and looked at me. "That twit has a sparkle in her eyes. And a shape on her. And she's sleeping with your son. Of course you're jealous."

"Who says they sleep together?" The thought had occurred to me, but I had always managed to dismiss it.

Stephanie raised her eyebrows. "Earth to Nora . . ."

I refused to acknowledge the carnal truth. "You just like her because she asked for your autograph."

"Maybe."

I sighed. "Nicky's got so much more than she does. I wish his sights were higher."

"His hormones are raging. Give him a break." She blotted her lips. On her, even the most ludicrous color worked.

"God, I hope they're not . . ." I mused.

"Not what? Fucking? Of course they are. Nora, wake up and smell the cappuccino, for Chrissake."

How could she look so relaxed, glamorous, and controlled as she said such things? In a gauzy white cotton outfit, her hair tucked into a turban, she was irritatingly lovely as she casually called my attention to my son's loss of innocence.

"I refuse to believe you," I told her.

"Avoidance is not just a tendency with you. It's a way

of life," she announced, then careened like a hit-and-run driver into another attack with, "You look terrible, Nora. Brush your hair. Wear some clothing."

I picked up an edge of my long skirt and angrily waved it at her. "What do you call this?"

"You've had that *shmatte* for fifteen years."

"So? It still fits."

"Unfortunately." Stephanie took another sip of her vanilla malted, musing as she studied me. "You miss him, don't you?"

I knew she meant Theo. But try as I might, I could not summon up an image of the man. He was tall, thin, with fair hair, of aristocratic bearing and gracious demeanor. But what did he look like, really, and who was he, and what was all that heavy breathing about anyhow, and where had it gone?

"I know it's hard." Stephanie patted my hand, taking my silence for suffering. "How's Bernie treating you?"

"Like a goddess," I lied.

Stephanie dropped her compact and lipstick back into her bag and gave me a look. "Translation: doormat. Right?"

I shrugged, and stirred the melting mound of peppermint ice cream that sat in front of me. "Look, I deserve it."

"The hell you do. You've paid up. You've worn the hair shirt. What the hell does he want?"

"He wants to forgive me. But he can't."

"Then leave the bastard."

"He's my husband. I hurt him. So he's hurting back."

Stephanie slapped an impatient hand on the table, putting her malted in jeopardy, catching it just before it tipped. "If it was a simple reprisal, I'd say okay. You'll recover. You'll rebuild. But constant bombardment?" She leaned across the table and whispered dramatically, "Are you going to let him make you into his own little Lebanon?"

Stephanie smiled at me, pleased with her own little analogy, awaiting a reply. But I had none. She pointed a dainty finger at me. "Take some vitamins. And call me, when you've had it up to here." She made a stagy sweep with one hand across her forehead just as Jill, face clean, dress freshened up, skipped toward us, holding Kelly's hand.

"Mommy! Mommy! I want Kelly to come!"

"I can't, sweet pea. I've gotta work," Kelly explained, stooping down, circling an arm around her waist. "But maybe you'll stop in again, someday, okay?"

"No! Come! Now!"

"Jill!" her mother warned her, making her pout, stamp her feet, and rev up for a proper tantrum.

But Kelly, seeing the storm clouds gather, nodded toward the waiting limo. "I bet I can run out to that car faster than you can!"

"No you can't!" Jill defied her.

"Bet I can." And the two of them raced out of the shop, Kelly lagging behind. They reached the car, breathless, giggling like little girls, Jill turning to squeal at us, "Me first! Me, me, me!"

❧ 30 ❧

OUR TRIP WAS A WEEK AWAY. IT WAS HOT OUT WEST, so *The New York Times* weather page reported, and a pair of shorts would probably be more comfortable than blue jeans. I tried some on in Molly's Frocks in Corbin Center and was observing myself in a khaki pair when a familiar voice slid like an earwig into my head.

"Nice legs. But I'm sure all your men tell you that!" In the three-way mirror I saw Doris Walker laughing, head tilted to one side.

"Bernie and Nicky and I are going out West together," I felt compelled to explain.

"Doing the redneck circuit, I suppose? Yellowstone, Grand Canyon, and such?"

Doris Walker annoyed me intensely. "No," I coolly told her. "Mesa Verde, Canyon de Chelly, Chaco, et cetera."

"Upscale, aren't we?" Doris twirled a hand, then whispered, "Last couple I knew who did the canyons got divorced."

"I'm sorry to hear that."

"And I'm sorry to hear that you and Bernie are having your differences, too."

Flames leapt up my cheeks. I turned away from the fiery image in the mirror to face Doris. "Bernie and I are just fine."

"Well, good. I was worried, after what I heard." She looked at the price tag dangling from the waistband of the shorts. "Thirty-two for these? Try Banana Republic. You'll find the same thing for . . ."

"What have you heard?" I could have bitten my tongue off for asking, but there it was, said and done.

Doris looked over my shoulder, then pulled me toward a rack of swimsuits. "My friend Brad . . . ?"

Lover, I might have corrected, but just nodded, not wanting to impede the path to disclosure.

"He's in the city sometimes and he always goes to this bar on Tenth Avenue, Mulrooney's. And he sees them there." Doris looked suddenly contrite. "I feel bad for telling you, but I think you should know about Bernie and the blonde."

I summoned up an entire junior high school acting career to fake the laugh I hoped would sound wildly amused. "I'm sure it's an editor he knows. They work together. They're just friends."

"Do friends stick their tongues in each other's mouths?"

I began to cough. "Recently?" I asked. "Brad saw this recently?"

Doris fingered a plastic hanger. "Last week?"

I could hardly breathe. Bikinis and maillots blurred before my eyes as I felt faint with fury and humiliation.

Doris tilted her head and touched my arm. "I'm sorry to be the bearer of bad news. But I, for one, think it's high time for women to let each other know when their men are cheating on them, don't you?"

I swallowed hard. "What about when it's the other way around, Doris?"

"Honey," she confided, "men don't know what they don't want to know. I could stick a picture of me and Brad doing it right under Tommy's nose and he'd just say, 'What's for supper?' " She laughed. "Well, I'm running behind. Nice to talk with you, Nora, and I'd buy those shorts if I were you. I'd buy two pairs!"

❧ 31 ❧

B FLAT, THE SECOND B FLAT ABOVE MIDDLE C—MY FAVORITE note. Debussy's evocative piece for flute alone, "Syrinx," starts on that B flat, snakes around it, and keeps coming back to it, tracing a melody that is sad yet filled with a melancholy solace, a solace that restores, revives. And I certainly needed reviving, now that I knew Pamela was back in the picture. Or was she? Doris Walker could have made it up. In any case, I could not, would not, let idle gossip affect me.

So I practiced, starting my day in the barn on B flat,

edging into it softly at first, finding the center of the sound, then holding it, sustaining it until it felt just full enough, and only then would I begin to diminuendo, softer and softer, until B flat vanished in a wisp of air.

It was my last morning in the barn before our trip. I had planned on a few early hours before taking Hal to the kennels, and doing the last-minute packing and organizing. Bernie was asleep in the house. Nicky, reluctant but resolved about accompanying us the next day, was already at Earth Arts, having a last lesson with Leon. The dog was asleep in the sun at the side of the house.

I held a B flat, for a long, long moment. Then I resolved down to A, a clear open note, a solid note, and easy to sustain. Then A to A flat. I was winding down chromatically toward middle C, but somewhere around low G, I heard it—a high-pitched sound that pierced my long note like a balloon, making me stop playing, stand still and listen. I nearly threw my flute down onto an old picnic table and as I raced out of the barn toward that horrible sound, I prayed for it not to be what I knew it must be: an animal in pain.

He lay on the side of the road in a heap, blood oozing out of his mouth. The driver of the car, a young girl, was shaking and crying, "I didn't even see him. He ran out in front of me from nowhere!"

Bernie, in pajama bottoms, was on his knees, patting Hal's lifeless head. "How could you not see him?!"

"It wasn't your fault," I told the girl.

"What can I do? How can I make it all right?" She sobbed and rubbed at her eyes.

Bernie looked up at me, accusation in his eyes. "You let him out of the house?"

I sank to my knees next to my husband and put my cheek against Hal's still-warm body. "He followed me out toward the barn. Then he got tired after a few steps and lay down in the sun. I never thought he'd . . ."

"He's an animal. Animals are unpredictable, a wounded one especially! What the hell is wrong with you, Nora?"

I blocked Bernie out, and kept stroking Hal's fur, trying to imagine his last few minutes: lying in the sun, listening to a silver flute. Revived by a high B flat, he must have gotten up and loped happily around the house, smelling the air, feeling strong, even young again. Was it the scent of a squirrel or perhaps a rabbit that sent him running out so recklessly into the road? Or was it just the sound of a silver flute that animated his ancient bones?

"He died so horribly," Bernie said. "And it could have been avoided." His eyes charged me with the lengthening list of my crimes, and there was no alibi, no excuse, nothing that I could ever say or do to bring Hal back.

We buried him near the pond between two birch trees. Nicky and Bernie dug the grave, while I prepared the prince for that dark and final resting place, wrapping him in the old brown blanket he loved to lie on at the foot of Nicky's bed. I also filled his food dish with flowers and tied ribbons onto his worn leather collar. Then we gently lowered his wrapped body and the artifacts into the earth, and each of us attempted a few words.

"Bye, old boy. Be good," was all Bernie could manage before his voice caught, and he rubbed at his eyes, smudging dirt across his cheeks.

It was my turn and I tossed rose petals on top of his body and said, "Thank you for being ours. We loved you, Hal, we . . ." Unable to finish, I turned to Nicky who, dry-eyed, took Hal's well-chewed rubber ball out of his pocket and let it roll down into the grave.

"Let's hope you'll need this where you're going," he said. Then he took a handful of dirt and sprinkled it over his dog.

A boy and his dog. Both are gone, I thought, as Nicky handed me a shovel, and I looked up at the chiseled features of an earnest young man.

❧ 32 ❧

We drove in silence, cutting a swath through Colorado from Denver southwest toward Mesa Verde. The road wound up and down mountain passes, in and out of ghost towns, through tourist meccas, and on and on. Windows down, the wind whipping a hot breeze around our faces, we were like three strangers, trapped together by a quirk of fate. We stopped, we started, we ate mediocre meals, we snapped pictures at lookout points. We crossed the Continental Divide, a family divided. Bernie was simmering with resentments. Nicky was reluctantly and silently there for the ride. And I felt like a hostage dragged along on the very trip I had planned, the trip that was meant to mend all rifts, heal all hurts, bring us together again, the three of us, the Watterman family.

We had spent a night in Aspen, as per our itinerary, where we heard Stephanie play an inspired Sibelius concerto with the Aspen Festival Orchestra in a tent in the open meadow below Red Mountain. The setting was breathtaking, the atmosphere electric, and Stephanie swept the audience away. But after a standing ovation in which Bernie energetically participated, he pleaded exhaustion and a headache and refused to go backstage.

"Just come with me, tell her you liked it," I urged.

"You want me to wait on line with all those asswipes to say something insipid and feel like a jerk?"

"Fine. I'll go with Nicky."

"Do I have to?" our son groused.

So I went backstage alone.

"Nora!" called an old Juilliard crony who was teaching bassoon at the Festival, as we waited for our moment with the soloist. "You haven't changed a bit. Still playing?"

"Sure," I said, smiled and wondered what life might have

been like had I kept at it, *really* kept at it. Would I have been a Stephanie Saunders, standing there at the head of a receiving line, shaking hands after each concert like a bride, or would I have failed hopelessly, given music up entirely, sold real estate, worked in an office, become a dental hygienist, a hair stylist, a . . .

My reveries were interrupted when my turn came to say something touching, or clever, or both, to Miss Saunders.

"You've done it again!" I gushed.

"I tried!" Big hug. "I knew you were here. It helped." She lied. I knew her mind had been partially on the music but mostly on the conductor, who was the music director of the Festival. Bartolomeo Siepi, at twenty-nine, was the new wonder boy from Milan. He had shocks of shiny black hair and big bedroom eyes and seemed to be Stephanie's summer enthusiasm.

After I finished my obligatory backstage business, Bernie declined to come with me to the party in Stephanie's honor. Nicky preferred to hang out and catch the action in the pedestrian mall in the old Victorian town rather than accompany me to clink a glass of champagne against Stephanie's in a crowded salon at the historic Hotel Jerome.

"Where're your men?" Stephanie asked me at the party. It was jammed with people in designer jeans, weighted down with tons of turquoise Indian jewelry and fringed chamois jackets.

"Bernie's back at the hotel—headache. Must be the altitude. And Nicky's on the prowl. You know how it is."

"Steph!" someone shrieked, and tried to pull her away from my side, but she delayed them with a kiss, then propelled me into a corner, and asked urgently, "What do you think of him?" Her eyes wandered to Bartolomeo who, in fashionably wrinkled wheat-colored linens, was gazing back at her from across the room.

"Uh-oh, Steph," I cautioned. "You're not thinking of canceling everything and hanging out here with Mr. Smoothie, are you?"

"No way." She wore a tight violet pantsuit and her blond hair was flying as she gesticulated extravagantly. "Would I cancel Tchaikovsky in Ravinia with Levine, or Mozart G with Rudiakowski in Salzburg?"

"Yes."

She glared at me.

"And who the hell is Rudiakowski?" I asked.

"Marek Rudiakowski and the Cracow Chamber Players?"

"Is this another one of your Polish jokes?"

Stephanie looked at me as if at a heathen. "Rudiakowski is a genius. And Cracow happens to be one of the great cultural spots on the globe."

"So is Sioux Falls."

"Your ignorance is appalling," she lamented, and looked for her beau, who was surrounded by young lovelies. Stephanie swished her blond hair and whispered, "What do you think of him? Isn't he wonderful?"

Wonderful? He was obviously a playboy. A roué. A heartbreaker. And hardly worthy of Stephanie Saunders. "He seems a little young," I said.

"Barto is the most mature man I've ever known."

Mature? I was her best friend. It was my responsibility to warn her, wasn't it? I could not let her make a fool out of herself over this cad. "But, Steph, how long will this last?" I began. "A weekend . . . if that long? Look at him. He's a *conductor*, for Christ sake. He can't help himself. He's putting the moves on everything in skirts."

I nodded in the direction of Barto, who was coralling some brunette into a corner. Stephanie's shoulders slumped. The glimmer went out of her eyes.

"Miss Saunders, may I just ask you . . ." a high-pitched voice entered our airspace like a mosquito.

"Of course!" she instantly purred, and turned to me with a frown. "Thanks for wrecking my party."

"I'm sorry."

"Don't be sorry. Just don't be so fucking frank all the time. You'll find it's not always necessary. Or nice."

Stephanie glided off into the open arms of the admiring throng, leaving me to stand alone in a crowded room.

I walked back to the motel through the bustling old town, where guitarists twanged melodies to the moon and lovers strolled idly arm in arm. I thought of Theo for the first time in months. I wondered where he was, and with whom, and whether he thought of me, too, from time to time, and whether he had been right when he said I would regret leaving him. But it was not regret I felt. It was determination. Although I worried that Bernie might be back at the motel at that very moment, whispering sweet nothings into the phone to a distant but devoted Pamela, and although we had neither made love nor been loving to each other in many days, still, we had traveled so far down the road of life together, that to part ways after all we had been through was just unthinkable, for either of us, wasn't it?

Back at the Roaring Fork Motel, I spent a sleepless night, tossing and turning beside Bernie, who slumbered through my contortions without so much as a twitch.

The next morning I called Stephanie at her condominium in the Mountain Queen to apologize.

"I'm practicing," she said, and hung up. I sat holding the phone, staring out the window at lush snow-capped mountains. Stephanie Saunders, my closest friend, had just cut me off coldly, angrily. Hung up on me! Stephanie!

"Who was that?" Bernie wanted to know.

I dropped the phone back onto its hook, then pushed my nose into the air. "The Mountain Queen."

"Who's he?"

Although I laughed long and hard, it was a lonely laugh, and at my own expense. I stood up, snapped a suitcase shut, calling out with false bravado, "Let's blow this two-bit town."

And as we drove away, past the music tent, past the opulent rustic mountain palaces and the fluttering aspen leaves, I bit my lip and thought of one more adjective I could now add to the lengthening list modifying my tarnished name: friendless.

"Could you turn the radio on?"

"There's no reception," Bernie said.

"Not in Gunnison there wasn't, but that was hours ago," Nicky reminded him.

I reached toward the radio to turn the knob, but Bernie's hand stopped mine.

"Let her turn it on!"

"Don't tell me what to do," Bernie growled at the back-seat driver.

"Your father prefers to drive without music."

"Ma, why are you always translating for him?"

"Don't call *her* ma, and don't call me *him!*"

"Yes, sir, Father sir!" Nicky barked.

"And don't be smart with me, or . . ."

"Or what?"

"Please!" I begged them.

"Can I drive?" Nicky asked.

"Shut up!" was the answer.

An unhappy silence prevailed again, while the three of us spun away from the vortex of the storm, each into our own quiet corner of concern. I tried not to think but to concentrate on the distant rims of mountains, the forests, the streams and just let it all streak past, hoping that with the passage of time and place, we three Wattermans would reach our destination delighted to be together.

"What are you thinking about?" Bernie's voice startled me.

"Nothing."

Bernie glanced at me cuttingly. "Don't say I never try to make conversation."

"*I'm* thinking how nice it would be to hear some music."

"Well, no one asked *you*," Bernie told Nicky. "And you should have brought your Walkman."

"I gave it to Kelly."

"That was nice of you," I mindlessly said.

Bernie guffawed.

"What's funny?" Nicky wanted to know.

"Nothing."

"Your father just . . ."

"Ma, stop translating! What's funny about Kelly?"

"I'm not laughing at Kelly. I'm laughing at your mother."

114

"Why?" Nicky demanded.

"Just because."

"Do you have a problem with Kelly?" Nicky asked.

"Not me," Bernie said, smiling.

"Ma?"

"Your mother can't stand that girl," Bernie jumped in.

"That's not true!"

"Why deny it?" Bernie asked me. "Here we are together, the three of us. It's an opportunity to tell the truth. Tell it like it is."

"You say one more thing about Kelly and I'm getting out of this car. Okay?"

I craned my neck to see my son's indignant face.

Bernie shot a look into the rearview mirror and seemed oblivious to the turmoil he was creating.

"What the hell are you trying to do?" I asked. Bernie just snickered and kept going, and as he turned left at the junction of 550, heading into the setting sun toward Telluride, he flipped the radio on, twiddling with the dials until a station came in loud and clear with the country western twangs of "Lyin' Eyes. . . ."

"How's that?" Bernie twisted his head to ask his son.

"It sucks."

"Well, hey, boy, I like it. It kinda rings a bell, now don't it mother?" he hopelessly mimicked the accent and narrowed his eyes in my direction. The air turned thick and acrid with tension.

"There is something awful happening in this car," Nicky announced. "And I want out."

"Suit yourself," Bernie said and, pulling off onto the shoulder, screeched to a stop. Dust swirled around the car. A hawk circled in the air above us. But Nicky did not move, and none of us said a word for what seemed a very long time until, finally, Nicky leaned forward and hooked his chin over the rim of the front seat. Bernie wordlessly leaned his head against one side of Nicky's face, and I leaned mine against the other.

"I *do* like Kelly," I said. "She was sweet with Jill the other day. She's a nice person."

"She's more than nice," Nicky said.

"I'm sure she is, son," Bernie said. "And I'm sorry I teased you."

"Do you miss her a lot?" I asked.

"Yes."

"It's hard to leave your girl," Bernie mused.

"Especially now," Nicky sighed.

"Why's that?" I asked.

Nicky's silence made us both turn to look at him. He was rolling words around like marbles in his mouth.

"Spit it out, son," Bernie suggested.

Nicky looked up at him, then smiled his flashiest, cutest smile and said, "Nothing."

Bernie playfully grabbed Nicky's head, tousled his hair, and said, "Then get your ass up here and drive this tub. We want to hit Telluride before it's dark, don't we?"

⚜ 33 ⚜

IT WAS SIX IN THE MORNING. I WAS WALKING THROUGH Telluride, a town composed of a few colorful streets filled with Victorian houses left over from the boom days of silver mining. Telluride was surrounded on three sides by steep rocky walls that rose up around it, kept it cozy and closed in, like a mountain slipper. Bernie was asleep at the Billy-the-Kid Motel. I had not slept at all, and when, at dawn, I wandered out into the pale streets of town, I was not surprised to find my son wandering, too.

"Rough night?" I asked him.

"Not for me."

How could he know his parents had retired to their conjugal bed only to turn back to back, not touching, each edging toward respective precipices?

"You look terrible," Nicky noted.

"I am terrible," I sighed.

"I don't think so."

"Well, you're my guy."

He took my arm, and we strolled together.

"Things with you and Dad, are they okay?" he asked.

"Well, of course."

Nicky squeezed my arm. "Don't bullshit me, Ma. It's like you two are just going through the motions."

"Maybe we are. Maybe that's what marriage is about. Maybe that's what *life's* about."

Nicky gave me a look. "I wish I thought you were kidding me."

I sighed. "We're having a bad patch. We'll get through it."

"Well, don't stay together just 'cause of me."

"Thanks for your permission. But your father and I are still an item with or without you."

"Yeah?"

"Yeah," I said, trying to believe it.

"Okay. Cool," he said, pretending it was.

The town was stirring. A runner in shorts, sneakers, and a ten-gallon hat dashed past us, making us giggle. Then a whiff of something sweet hit us both at the same time.

"Mm!" Nicky pointed at the bakery. We gazed longingly into the window at fresh muffins and cookies and doughnuts, each sprinkled with a light dusting of confectioner's sugar.

When I was pregnant with Nicky, the world smelled to me like sugar doughnuts. Everywhere I went—the grocery store, the butcher, the cleaner, the dentist—the scent of powdered sweet dough seemed to be in the air.

"Don't you smell it?" I'd ask Bernie. He'd wrinkle up his nose, sniff and twirl an index finger at his temple, then point it at me.

"Pregnant women are supposed to crave pickles and ice cream. But my wife? To her, the world smells like sugar doughnuts," Bernie delighted telling all our friends during Nicky's gestation.

"Maybe it's an omen," someone suggested.

"Something to do with a circle? The kid'll be an egghead?"

"Better name it something that starts with an O."

Olivia. Oscar. Obadiah. Onyx. I actually considered a few O-names, just in case the constant odor really did mean something. Was it a portent? A symbol? A sign? And when my son was born, so pink and squalling and healthy, I decided the doughnut smell had meant something after all. I would name the boy Nickolas, after my mother's brother, who had been exterminated in Poland. Five years older than Elena and idolized by her, Nickolas had dreamed of going into their father's business. He had pictured the sign above their shop: Miklavska and Son—Pastries Extraordinaire.

"A penny for your thoughts," Nicky said.

"Due to inflation, that'll cost you ten dollars."

"Forget I asked."

I squeezed his arm. "I was thinking about *you,* if you must know."

He nodded. "Do you ever regret it?"

"What?"

"Having me. I mean, you were so young."

"I was twenty."

"But don't you wish you waited or anything?"

I looked at the strapping young man at my side, with his eager eyes and sweet smile and said, "Not for a second."

"Excellent response. Now you can buy me a dozen of those to prove it." He pointed to the Belgian waffles piling up on a plate inside the store, and steered me toward the opening door.

❧ 34 ❧

MESA VERDE. MIDAFTERNOON. WE WERE WAITING IN LINE
with whining kids and cranky parents and cameras clicking
and voices competing, for our turn to take the trail up to
the Cliff Dwellings. Having driven at dawn from Telluride
to Cortez, Colorado, only fourteen miles from the national
park, we had checked into the Mountain Flower Motel, and
were now enduring the long, dusty wait with varying degrees of impatience. Nicky, in cut-off jeans and a T-shirt
fanned himself with a just purchased cap that said "Cute
Ute" on the visor. I was boiling hot, even in my khaki shorts
(one of the two pair I had purchased at Doris Walker's
provocation) and a sleeveless cotton top. Bernie, in a Ha-
waiian shirt left over from our last vacation two years before
and a pair of running shorts, seemed the least comfortable
in the crowd.

"I hate waiting in these frigging lines," he grumbled. "It's
worse than Disneyland." He adjusted the rim of the sailor's
hat he was given when he produced a piece on the '84
America's Cup for CBS. Coupled with the palm trees on
his shirt, the chapeau added a salty touch.

"You don't go to the national parks in July," a nearby
woman in tight madras shorts and a sombrero told us. "Unless you're crazy like us. Right, Marvin?"

She whacked a small man in a safari hat on the back. He
wheezed and snorted at her, "Stuff it, Mildred."

"Remind me never to let you plan a holiday again," Bernie whispered to me.

"Remind me never to go on one with you again." I tightened the bandana I had wrapped like a gypsy's around my
head.

"No problem." Bernie wiped at his sweaty neck with a
shredding tissue and turned to Nicky. "Having fun?"

Nicky was observing the park ranger, a pretty young
woman with long, sun-tanned legs and a confident swagger,

sporting an official green hat. She headed toward our over-heated group.

"At last," Nicky sighed. "A natural wonder."

"We may never know why the Anasazi moved to the cliffs," Natural Wonder told her group of forty motley tourists as we clambered single file up the scorched path behind her, heading for the Cliff Palace, the largest ruin in Mesa Verde. "They had no written language. And so we know nothing of their thoughts and feelings. But we do know it took them seventy years . . . please, sir, do not allow your child to dangle her doll over the edge. It's a long way down. . . ."

The canyon floor spread out seven hundred feet below us with jagged brush and spiky brambles. Bernie, walking right ahead of me, suddenly stumbled. I reflexively grabbed his shirt, but he had already caught onto the rope barrier at the edge of the path and was safe, if shaken. The people behind us gasped and stopped short.

"Sorry," I apologized to them as Bernie grimaced and shook himself free from my grasp. "Damn knee," he groaned, "The bad one . . ."

"Are we all right back there?" Natural Wonder called, hearing a commotion behind her.

"We're fine!" Bernie called up to the guide and stoically limped onward. Five rough wooden ladders, each at least ten feet long, led up to the entrance of the Cliff Palace. Bernie climbed them like a martyr.

When we forty followers had made it up the ladders into a vast natural alcove wedged into sheer rock high above the canyon floor, we gathered around for more information from Natural Wonder. I tried to ask Bernie how his knee was, but he shushed me, and nodded toward our guide.

"Imagine the men in their loincloths, women wearing only a small apron," she waxed poetically. The crowd tittered. Bernie laughed a little too loud. I saw that he was sweating profusely, and no doubt suffering. Nicky, who had been walking up ahead and had not seen Bernie's near fall, paid rapt attention as the descriptions continued: "This area here, the courtyard, so to speak, was a very busy place, with children, dogs, and turkeys—yes, imagine that, wild turkeys, and not the kind you drink—running around. Some boys might have been over here, mixing mortar or plaster to cover walls that needed repair. Men were coming and going with game from their hunts, crops from the fields above, and firewood from the canyons down below. . . ."

I moved away from the group and caught shards of monologue as I wandered through the remains of the ancient dwellings on my own. "Coils of clay . . . tools of stone . . . carrying jugs of water, one at a time . . . called a *kiva*, this pit was the religious center for the clan . . . and this small hole was called a *sipapu*—a symbol of the Great Sipapu, through which it was believed mankind had entered the world. . . ."

Wooden flutes and hollow drums sounded in my imaginings as the apricot light of late afternoon flickered on the stones. I noticed Nicky edging away from the others, losing himself, as I was doing, in the shadows and echoes of the centuries.

In that dry air, climbing up and down the perilous stone wall they called home, men and women clung to life for a millennium, braving the brutal winters and the incendiary heat of summers. But then, when the rains stopped and starvation threatened, and nothing that could be said or done in the kivas seemed to help, the Anasazi moved on, leaving the homeland of their ancestors, deserting the canyons and the tablelands forever. Who was it who decided it was time to give up? Did some chief give the signal, or did they just straggle off, one hungry family after another? And who was the last to go? Was it man, woman, or a small child? Maybe a dog, staying to chomp on a bone, left over from one last hopeful meal. . . .

"Nora?" Bernie's voice cut short my reverie as he limped to my side. "Astonishing, isn't it?"

"Yes," I agreed, pleased that my spouse was as moved as I.

Bernie actually smiled at me. Then I felt something cool and pleasant slide against my palm and I realized it was his hand, my husband's, taking mine in his as we stood together for a brief affectionate moment on the brink between past and future, gazing out over the vast panorama of canyons and flat mountain tops where once the ancient tribes farmed and flourished.

"Remember the time I did a piece on the mailman of the Grand Canyon, that guy who delivers letters to the Yavapai Indians who still live down there?"

I remembered, and completed the often-told story, as a wife will. "And you rode a horse for seven hours down into the Canyon and you got so stiff they had to carry you out?"

Bernie smiled at me again and pointed to a bulging knee that had turned purplish gray.

"Oh God," I said.

"It's the Yavapai problem all over again. You'll need a helicopter to get me out of here."

"You'll lean on me and Nicky. . . ." I looked around for our son, and saw him in a corner of the cave, squatting down next to Natural Wonder, studying something. "Nicky!" I called.

He stood up and strode toward us, eyes bright with excitement. "There's bits of pottery over there. They traded, jars and mugs and stuff. It was like their most important product, and . . ." He saw his father's brow, braided in pain. "Who died?"

"My bad knee," Bernie pointed at it. "Only worse."

"You push him again?" the Cute Ute asked me.

I gave him a dirty look. "He twisted it all by himself on the path up. He's having trouble walking."

"I can carry you," Nicky instantly offered his father.

"Doubt it."

"Want to bet?"

. . .

One arm draped across his son's shoulder, Bernie hopped on his good leg as Nicky bore the brunt of his weight. I walked behind them.

"A little ice and you'll be fine," Natural Wonder said when we had made it back down the path to the Group Gathering Point. "Have a nice night." She winked at us, then posed with her arm around Mildred (in the sombrero) while Marvin (in the safari hat) took their picture for posterity.

Back at the Mountain Flower in Cortez that night, Nicky was asleep in the room next to ours, while Bernie, in pain, his leg packed in ice, propped up on pillows, watched the "Tonight" show. He drank beer, crunched Doritos, and seemed in a strangely good mood for a man in such discomfort.

"So much for Canyon de Chelly and the rest of it," he said.

"Maybe the swelling will go down."

A doubting look confirmed the necessity for a change of plans.

"Well, we'll do stuff that doesn't require hiking. How about Durango? We could take the old train that goes up to . . ."

Bernie beckoned me toward the bed. I sat down carefully beside him. "You and Nicky will have to go on alone. I don't want to spoil your trip."

"What are you saying?"

"I'm saying you can drop me off at the airstrip in Gallup. I'll get myself back to Corbin's Cove, and you two will do the canyons. . . ."

Leaning against the headboard of a king-sized bed, Bernie was proclaiming himself a free, if injured, man.

I burned with suspicion. "It's Pamela. That's why you want to go home, right?"

Bernie puffed ostensible annoyance. "I've told you, I'm not seeing her."

"So you've said. But unfortunately you two have been seen together."

"Oh, really? Where?" Bernie folded his arms across his belly and looked at me, as if amused.

"A bar on Tenth Avenue."

He raised his eyebrows at me. "Mulrooney's? It's the CBS hangout. Everyone goes there."

"Everyone doesn't embrace there."

Bernie laughed, wheezy intakes of air. "Hey, I'm an affectionate guy, a hands-on kind of fella. . . ." He stopped laughing. "Who told you this garbage?"

"A friend."

"Excuse me, but no *friend* would concoct a romance out of innocent comaraderie."

I nodded silently, acceptingly. Doris Walker was certainly no friend. And even if her report rang regrettably true, who was I to expect loyalty from my husband? If he was still seeing Pamela, it was not only my fault, it was my punishment, and perhaps the proper one. I stood up and walked slowly, sadly toward the window. The moon was full, shedding a ghostly light on Sleeping Ute Mountain, which rose like a giant statue in the distance.

I pointed to the mountain silhouetted against the sky. "It's supposed to look like the body of a warrior wounded in a fight against the Spirit of Evil."

"How would you know?"

I turned back to meet his eyes. "Says so in the motel brochure."

"And does it say who won?"

"No," I courageously informed him. "But I'd guess the warrior lost, since the spirit is still hanging around here. . . ."

Bernie gazed at me with disdain. "At least he fought it, instead of giving into it. . . ."

Hands on my hips, I tilted my head daringly. "Were you always so self-righteous, or did it develop slowly, like an ulcer?"

"Nora," he sighed heavily. "Do you or don't you want our marriage to work?"

I took my hands off my hips, untilted my head and said straightly, "I do. Of course I do."

"Then stop trying to push it off the edge, okay?"

Just before dawn, sleepless and restless, I tiptoed into the bathroom and pulled on a skirt, sweater, and a pair of sneakers. As I slipped past my sleeping husband to exit the stuffy motel room, the oddest urge propelled me to grab my canvas bag, sling it over my shoulder, and carry it with me.

Outside, behind the motel, the air was cool and clear and a fading blue light dusted the cactus and sagebrush. I followed a footpath that led across some flatlands toward the Sleeping Ute Mountain. Long grasses drenched with dew brushed against my ankles, cooling me with their moist strokes. A marmot dashed across the path, squeaking an alarm as he disappeared down a hole. Something rattled near me, and I worried whether snakes could be a danger. But danger or not, I kept going farther away, toward the mountain.

The flute, it has been said, was a magical incantatory tool for primitive man, a way to summon up spirits, a way to send dreams spiraling. And so, when I reached the feet of the Sleeping Warrior, I slipped my flute out of my canvas bag, out of its case, pieced it together, and began to play. What spirit was I attempting to summon as I sent silvery sounds into the damp morning air? Was I calling up Evil in order to enter battle where the warrior left off? Or was I simply wishing that a small dream could come true, that all hurts would heal, knees and hearts, and that the threat of Pamela would vanish and that Bernie and I, truly and completely reconciled, would live out our days together happily? I piped a languid tune in a minor key, and, as if by magic, the sky turned aquamarine, the color of cool Caribbean waters. But then the sun slipped above the horizon like a fiery dragon's head, roaring with heat. Rattling sounds seemed to rise all around me. No snake slithered by, but filled with strange premonitions and a sudden cold sweat, I hastily packed up my flute and ran back to the motel.

Returned from my mountain pilgrimage, I took a long tepid shower, worrying that I might wake Bernie. But with his knee bolstered by pillows, and his brain dulled by pain-killers, he was still out cold at eleven. Even Nicky's loud knocking on the door didn't wake him.

"Shh." I nodded toward his sleeping father, then pushed him back out the door and stepped outside of the air-conditioned motel room to talk, closing the door behind us.

"How's his knee?" Nicky whispered as we stood outside, sweating in the sudden heat.

"I don't know yet."

Nicky sighed and shifted his weight from one foot to the other. In shorts, sneakers and his Cute Ute cap, squinting in the bright light, he looked like an eager camper, ready for activity.

"Are you bored to death?"

"Never. I've watched fifty-three episodes of 'Leave It to Beaver,' and it's not even noon."

"Did you have breakfast?"

"Only twice. Great coffee shop." He pointed across the parking lot toward the motel lobby where a glass wall afforded a view of people sitting in orange booths, chewing and gesticulating. "At seven I had pancakes and blueberry waffles. At eight, I came back for a couple of vein-blockers, over easy. . . ."

"With hash browns."

"Of course." He looked at me sweetly, wanting something. "So if you're going to let the old man sleep all day, could I have the car?"

"To go where?"

"Anywhere." He took off his cap and fanned himself. "Just to tool around, take a look. How'd you guys like lox and bagels for brunch? Maybe I'll find a deli."

"In Cortez?"

"You never know." A thought crossed his mind and he caught it. "There's also a museum of Indian artifacts we passed yesterday. I'd like to get a good look at those bowls and stuff."

"You're really interested, aren't you?"

Nicky moved into the shade and leaned back against the door to our room. "Mom, I really want to do this. I really want to make things with my hands." He held them both up. "I think I could be an artist. Leon thinks so. I mean, I know you guys think it's for airheads, but . . ."

"I take it very seriously, Nicky. I take *you* seriously."

My son, my handsome, serious son whispered, "I'm thinking of applying to some art schools, in the fall, you know, for college . . . ?"

Maternal pride and relief surged. "Nicky, great!" My boy had found a passion, after all. He would pursue it, he would be fulfilled and happy. "So where will you apply? Let's see, there's Pratt, there's Carnegie, there's . . ."

He stopped me with a palm held up. "First I've got to get a portfolio together. I'm coming to this kind of late. . . ." Worried, he bit at the inside of his cheek and looked to me to say, Green light. Go.

"Hey, you'll do it, you'll get it together. You can do this. Leon will help. I'll help."

He beamed at me, confident, handsome, then asked, "You think Dad will approve?"

"I think he will."

"And if he doesn't?"

Nicky looked to me to reassure him, just as he had since he was small, just as he had after his first step, his blue eyes wide with wonder and triumph. "You can count on it," I promised, knowing I needed a private session to present the idea to his father, who had other things in mind for his son—something secure, with a tangible future.

Nicky gave me a big, sweaty hug. "So can I have the keys, please, Louise?"

I hesitated.

"Just for a ride, Ma? Just in the name of bagel research?"

I put a finger to my lips and tiptoed back into the room, picked up the car keys from the bureau where they lay beside a black Bible, and without waking Bernie, backed out of the room again.

"Thanks," Nicky said as he took the keys and headed for the car.

"Come back soon."

He nodded and rolled down the window, calling, "I love you!"

"Love you, too!" And I waved goodbye to the future artist extraordinaire, to my chevalier, the light of my life, my son. "Be careful!" I added with a mother's sudden reflex, but he was already out of sight. Gone.

"Why the hell didn't you wake me?" Bernie grumped when I shook him gently and told him it was afternoon. The swelling in his knee had gone down, and when he attempted to stand he found that he could miraculously put weight on his leg. He took a few tentative steps.

"Hey, I can walk!" he crowed.

"Great." Had my incantation worked?

"It's a miracle!" He jokingly closed his eyes, crossed himself, tried a few more paces, then beamed at me, "All right! Today, we drive to the Canyon de Chelly. What do you say?"

"Really?"

"An Ace bandage and I'll be ready to hit the trails!" He stepped gingerly toward the bathroom.

"So we're not changing plans after all?"

Bernie turned to look innocently at me and shrugged. "Not unless you want me to go home."

Had my fluting finished off Pamela, too? I smiled. "Of course not."

Bernie blew me a kiss, and as he turned on the shower he yelled, "Is our Boy Scout ready?"

"I'll go see if he's back."

"Where'd he go?"

"Just out. I let him have the car for a while. He was getting kind of antsy."

"And you don't know where he went?"

"He's a big boy, Bernie."

"When did he leave?"

I looked at my watch. I hadn't realized it had been so long. "An hour or so," I lied, knowing it was more like two.

Bernie stepped back into the room, annoyed. "So he could be gone for the day, for all we know."

"I'm sure he'll be back soon."

"What the hell kind of parent are you, Nora, not to give him limits, not to . . ."

A knocking on the door stopped him. I flew to open it, shooting a smug look at Bernie, expecting Nicky. But it was not what I expected.

I knew, before the police officer spoke the words. I knew by his expression, his stance, by the way he asked, "Are you the mother of Nickolas Watterman?" But even after I identified myself, and even after he spoke the words, "There has been an accident," and even after he repeated himself twice, in case I had not heard or comprehended, and told me how sorry he was, how it had been instant and on impact and therefore without pain, still I could not react. It was like being deep under water, pressure unbearable, unable to surface, caught, trapped, until, realizing there had been some mistake, I was surging up, powered by a sudden desperate hope, gulping for air, screaming, "No! No! No!"

Bernie, at my side, caught me as I fell to the floor. I woke up on the bed, both Bernie and the officer leaning over me, Bernie ashen, the color of emptiness. And we were empty, void, drained of the blood of our blood, bone of our bone. Our son, our only child, had been crushed beneath the weight of a twelve-wheel rig that was carrying tractors and traveling too fast and could not stop for the red light at the junction of highways 160 and 166, where Nicky was turning left out of Manuel's Taco and Deli just three miles from the motel. A dozen squashed bagels in a bag in the backseat were extracted by the highway patrol, smeared with what had been one container of cream cheese and another containing Manuel's extra hot salsa. Nicky was on his way back to the motel with brunch for his parents— bagels with hot salsa, a southwest surprise, meant, no doubt, to make us smile.

Clutching at each other, Bernie and I were taken to the county morgue in Cortez. People in uniforms and white coats slid in and out of vision and it was Bernie who felt faint when they said, "We need you to identify the body," and I who helped him into a chair and brought him water. Then we both followed a white coat into the cold room where, laid out on metal, covered with a sheet, was, we were told, Nickolas Watterman, in whose pockets had been found a driver's license, a dog tag marked "Harold," a key for room 127 at the Mountain Flower, Cortez, a snapshot of a girl, one stick of Juicy Fruit gum, and twelve dollars and sixty-three cents.

"I think she should wait outside," the white coat said, indicating me.

Bernie looked at me. I nodded No, and so he took my hand and we approached the table together.

Nicky always slept like that, sheet pulled over his head. "Who do you think you are, King Tut?" I would tease him, and yank the sheet down, but then, in the morning, when I would peek in to see if he was up, he would be shrouded again, completely covered, fast asleep.

Swollen blue skin, eyes shut, a gash across the forehead, nose battered, the mouth and jaw so badly damaged. . . .

"Yes, this is my son," Bernie stated bravely. But, no, I could not agree with him. Nicky's eyes could wink, his mouth could smile. This was not my son, Nickolas Watterman. Nicky had just gone out to buy bagels. You can't die buying bagels. But then someone was screaming, loud piercing wails, the cry of someone in pain, a pain that cannot be endured and will never go away.

Bernie clapped one hand over my mouth and shook me. I stopped screaming and shuddered and looked away from that mutilated young face. I took his father's arm and we walked together out of the room, out of the morgue. We stumbled, weeping, out into the parking lot, into the scorching heat of day, where we both writhed around like two bodies being cremated. Officers rushed to calm us, to comfort us, to help us into a squad car, and with no siren, no flashing lights, no sign that anything at all had transpired, they drove us back to the Mountain Flower, and offered to stay with us, help us make arrangements.

"Thank you, but we'll be all right," Bernie said, knowing we could not, knowing that nothing would be all right for us ever again.

❧ 35 ❧

WE BURIED OUR SON QUIETLY AND QUICKLY, IN THE JEWISH tradition. Everyone in Corbin's Cove said we were both so brave, we were both holding up so well. Bernie arranged the funeral at a temple we had never attended, but the rabbi was kind and attentive and when he stopped by to ask us for anecdotes to use in his eulogy, I cried, and Bernie's mother, who had taken charge of the house, herded me upstairs, put me to bed. I lay there, in our now barren bed, staring out at the linden tree, smelling Gilda's cooking, waiting, waiting for it to be over.

Stephanie turned up, jet-lagged and rumpled, after being informed of the accident by one of our friends. She had canceled performances in Salzburg. She had come.

"I thought our friendship was finished," I said when she arrived.

"Nora," was all she could say, and she buried her head in my shoulder, muttering, "Why Nicky? Why?" Her tears burned into my neck, and crying, too, I held her.

"Thank you for coming," I told her as we wiped our eyes.

"Nora," was all Stephanie said, and I looked at her and wondered if she knew I was waiting, waiting for it to be over.

Many people came to the funeral, Nicky's friends, ours, the family, Bernie's sister and her children, cousins, aunts. My father flew in from Phoenix, looking frail and unshaven. He spoke few words, but his eyes said much, and when he took my hand and rubbed it against his cheeks so I could feel the stubble, as I had done with delight so long before, he burst into tears and had to drink two vodkas straight up to calm down. He slept on the blue couch in the den and offered to tile the kitchen floor for us.

There would be a scholarship in Nicky's name at Corbin High. He would be remembered. His friends came by to visit, to tell us what a great guy he was, a terrific friend, a real live wire. Leon Dubrovner gave me a small pot that Nicky had made just before we left on our trip, glazed in a crackled blue. It was a whimsical thing, delicate, its neck tilted just slightly as if to say, I'll hold one flower for you, just one.

"It's called a pinch pot," Leon explained. "You take a ball of clay and with your thumbs you push and shape it into a bowl, and it's one of the most difficult things to do, to get the walls just the right thickness, the body of it globed just right. And Nicky could do it so easily, and with such charm." Leon shook his head slowly. "He had such potential, such promise."

I took the little vessel and held it in my hands, and closing my eyes, I pictured Nicky's hands holding that very clay, shaping it. I imagined my hands on top of his, and I could almost feel the veins in his fingers. I cried and nearly dropped the pot.

Kelly sat on the sofa, red-eyed, looking like a lost rabbit. She asked if she could see Nicky's room and I realized she had never visited our house before, never been in Nicky's room, or in his bed. Was Nicky ashamed to bring her home? Or was it us of whom he was ashamed, his particular parents, whom he knew would be so unwelcoming to this girl?

"Second door to the left," I told Kelly, pointing the way, but when I heard sobs coming out of the room, I went in after her. Lying face down across his bed, she was inconsolable. I sat down beside her, and patted her back and told her that he had loved her, he had loved her very, very much.

"I don't understand," she sobbed.

I patted her back. "I know, I know."

Then she sat up, and looked at me angrily. "Why did you have to make him go on that stupid trip anyway!" And she marched out of the room, leaving me seated on my son's bed, staring at assorted pennants and posters and books and a collection of tapes neatly organized in cigar boxes on top of his bookcase. I picked up a water-filled plastic paperweight Bernie had brought back from Alaska with a polar bear inside, and when I shook it, snow fell. I watched it, waiting, waiting for things to settle.

Doris Walker sent flowers and came to the house with her son Stan (the Schnoz) and hugged me hard. Stan stood beside her, shifting his weight from one foot to the other while rubbing at the famous nose that was, I could not help thinking, just as Nicky had once described it to me, "a sausage with nostrils."

"I'm sorry about your son," Stan told me, averting his eyes, but it was I who felt sorry, sorry for noting his nose instead of his sympathy. It was I who felt sorry, sorry,

sorry, for everything. And sorry was not good enough, sorry did nothing. Sorry was of no use at all.

Trish and Selma and every vague acquaintance in the Cove visited us and raved at our strength, our courage in the face of such misfortune. We accepted these odd compliments with silent shrugs that people took as further evidence of resilience. "And you and Bernie are such a Together Couple," Trish observed. "You give each other such comfort."

The Together Couple barely spoke to each other. What could be said that could possibly give comfort? We hardly acknowledged each other. Bernie's eyes burned with such blame that to look at them was to face the fires of the sun. And so an occasional glance was all I could manage. Nor would we touch each other. To touch each other would be to remember everything, to feel everything, to release torrents of pain. And so we kept the floodgates bolted, and stood apart yet beside each other, accepting the condolences, the expressions of deep regret, the exclamations at our remarkable bravery. And I waited for it to be over.

Dr. Rotman offered to recommend a colleague for me to see so that I could work through the manifestations of grief with all its conflicting emotions.

"You seem to be in a state of denial," he told me.

"My son is dead."

"Good. That is to say, it's good that you know this, that you accept it."

Know it? I saw it, I saw my son's remains. It was I who gave him the keys and sent him to that destiny. I knew it all right. I accepted it all right. Now all I had to do was wait.

Stephanie asked me if she should call Theo.

"What for?" I asked, the idea absurd. But then I thought of him, golden, godlike Theo Bradshaw. He, too, had stopped existing. But if I could make him real, make him spring back to life, then maybe Nicky, too, could be some-how restored to me. And so it was I who made that phone call, jolted by a sudden memory of Theo's touch, and his words, "I will love you always, Nora, I will always be there for you. . . ."

"Who may I tell him has called?" his secretary asked.

"A friend. May I speak to him, please? It's important."

"I'm afraid he's out of town."

A pause while I tried not to sound desperate. "When will he be back?"

"In three weeks."

"Three weeks? Why so long?"

"Look, miss," she said snootily, "why don't you just leave your name, and . . ."

"Forget it." I hung up, and impatiently brushed at tears as they rolled down my cheeks. What did I want with Theo Bradshaw anyhow? Besides, how could he possibly help? And why would he be away for three weeks, except for a vacation, or maybe . . . a honeymoon? After all, nothing was forever. And he deserved to be happy with a woman who was, no doubt, worthier of him than I. I felt a mo-mentary pang at the thought, but only momentary, because really, it did not matter. Nothing mattered anymore.

Finally, the funeral and a procession in limousines and a burial. Stephanie dressed me in some black designer outfit that felt too big and too short, but she said I looked just fine, I looked lovely. Then she asked if she could do some-thing to my hair, just to make it look a little less, um, awful. We both smiled as she attempted a French braid, gave up and made do with a low ponytail roped into a black ribbon.

At the cemetery I stood beside my husband, Bernard T. Watterman, and we wept uncontrollably and those around us sobbed, and the casket was lowered and we all went home, and the waiting was almost over.

• • •

A few days later, the flowers had wilted and the phone stopped ringing. We were not going to sit for the seven days of ritual mourning. "Life is for the living," Gilda told me, as she packed her pots and prepared to go back to Brooklyn.

Stephanie reluctantly took off for Europe, leaving me a list of hotels and phone numbers and making me promise to call her, collect, if I needed anything, anything at all. Bernie decided to go into the city to work, telling me to order a sedan from the local limo company to take my father to the airport. For some reason, he did not think I should drive just yet. He looked worried when he left, asked if I was okay, and told me to call him if I needed anything.

My father cried when he said goodbye. He took my hand and rubbed it against his cheek before slipping into the shiny black car and disappearing down the country road where his grandson had ridden a bike and chased a ball and skipped and played with his dog. I stood in front of the house, listening to the sounds of a high summer morning, the cicadas thrumming, the heat rising. I went back into the house, the empty, silent house one last time. And when I was certain that there was nothing more to be done or to wait for, I went upstairs to the medicine cabinet and poured ten pills out of a bottle, checking the label to make certain it was the right one. I saw a face in the mirror as I tipped my head back to swallow, and if it was mine, I did not recognize it. I had lost my son. I had lost myself. And so, nonexistent, I walked out of the house and down to the pond, stopping for a moment at the mound, now covered with moss, under which the faithful, noble Prince Hal lay. Then, making certain no one was in sight—no neighbor, no salesman, no wandering child—I went to the edge of the pond and, without hesitating, I walked straight into the water with my shoes and clothing on.

I felt the cool liquid surround me. My feet sank into the soft bottom as I struggled to walk out far enough. Water bugs skimmed by. A dragonfly looked at me curiously and flew off. I leaned back and floated, squinting at the bright sun, waiting for sleep to close my eyes and let me sink, soundless, into the silt and weeds below, deep into the unremitting darkness I deserved.

<h1 align="center">❧ 36 ❧</h1>

AT JFK, THE COMPUTERS WERE DOWN. MY FATHER'S FLIGHT to Phoenix was delayed and overbooked, and when chaos ensued, Ezra Lind, who could not stand conflict of any kind, reclaimed his bag, waited in line for a cab, and took it back to Corbin's Cove. When he arrived at Linden Hill, the driver demanded seventy dollars' cash, and since Ezra did not have it, he entered the house, looking for me to loan him the money. Perhaps it was the kind of parental radar I sorely lacked that made him search for me outside. And had we not dredged the pond, he never would have seen me there, lying face up at the bottom, bubbles still coming out of my mouth.

Rashid El Hammadi, the driver of the taxi (medallion number 3405A) dived into the water, pulled me out and performed CPR for which he later became a recipient of the Good Samaritan Citation from the City of New York. I was rushed to the local hospital, had my stomach pumped, and woke up, nauseated, my father and my husband peering into my face.

"Hi," my father said, and waved as if I were too far away to touch.

137

Bernie took my hand in his. "Nora," he said sadly.

I blinked, trying to comprehend what had and what had not happened. Then I felt a burning in my eyes, and I turned my face toward the wall and cried.

Bernie took me home, and, to please him, I agreed to see a psychiatrist. Dr. Rotman recommended an analyst, not a rigid Freudian, he said, but rather, an all-purpose practitioner, "a real people person." Dr. Horace Young was a man of sixty-something, with white hair, runny eyes and a habit of tapping on his yellow legal pad as he waited for me to speak. And he had to wait, since I had no desire to say anything. Not to him. Not to Bernie. Not to anyone.

"What comes to mind?" Dr. Young would repeat and repeat. "Are you thinking about your son?" he would ask. "Are you grieving?"

"Nora, I'm in pain, too," Bernie told me, his forehead furrowed. "It hurts. It's constant. But it won't get better by itself. We have to make an effort. What good does it do to just sit here?"

I shrugged. It was 7:00 P.M. and I was in the same bathrobe I had worn for a week. I would take it off once daily in order to pull on a skirt and a shirt for my requisite noon visit to Dr. Young. Then, having said nothing to him, I would come back, undress, and either crawl under the covers in our bed again or wander into Nicky's room and look at his things. Sometimes I would lie on his bed and close my eyes and picture my son at different points in his life, trying to be chronological, trying to remember everything, and keep it in order . . . his first word (button), his first solid food (banana), his first step (in the kitchen), his first book (*Pat the Bunny*), his first jacket (navy blue with gold buttons, size toddler 2), his first loose tooth (left front incisor). I had lost track of the days since my incident in the pond. My father had stayed on, with the mistaken idea that I needed company. Now he sat beside me in the kitchen, silent, too, surveying the floor, calculating, no doubt, the number of tiles that would be necessary to cover it.

Bernie sighed. "I can't take this much longer, Nora," he said, and if he meant it as a threat I could not tell, nor did I care. He could leave for good. Or he could kick me out. What did it matter? What did anything matter?

"I think she should come stay with me in Phoenix for a while," Ezra surprisingly offered, speaking to Bernie as if I were not present. "I think that would be the best."

Bernie was silent for a moment, then he turned to me. "Nora," he asked carefully, "would you like that?"

Would I like it? There was nothing I liked or disliked anymore. I could not even muster the enthusiasm to make another attempt to end my life. I could hardly get out of bed in the morning. I was useless. But at least I could stop being a burden to Bernie. My father would take me to his home. I would figure things out from there.

"I'll go," I said.

"Are you sure you want to?" Bernie asked.

"Yes," I said, thinking of that retiree community in the parched desert where old people flocked to spend their last sunny days, and where perhaps, if I were lucky, I would wither up in the heat like a dry leaf and simply blow away.

"Shall I call the travel agent?" Bernie asked.

"Please." I stood up and pushed my chair back into its place at the kitchen table.

"When would you like to leave?"

"Now," I told my husband, and without looking at him, I went upstairs to pack.

I took a small suitcase out of my closet. In a slip I wrapped the little pot Nicky had made and cushioned it between two skirts and some socks. Two sweaters and a blouse seemed adequate, my brush, some underwear, one pair of shoes, the photo of Nicky and me in the heart-shaped frame.

"Need any help?" Bernie entered the room and leaned against the door frame.

"No," I said. "Thanks."

Bernie hooked his index finger like a question mark over his nose as he studied me. "There's a flight tomorrow at noon. I left the return open. Is that okay?"

"Fine. Thank you."

Bernie sighed. "So when do you think you'll be coming back?"

The house was so quiet, like a cliff dwelling deserted by the living, haunted by the echoes of a golden time, a time when there were laughter and footsteps and a dog's eager bark. Now there was nothing left, not even a kiva in which a prayer might be spoken. And so, resolved as a squaw, knowing that nothing could be said or done, knowing that it was all over and time to go, I looked at my brave husband for a long moment, memorizing his angular features, his round and unblemished skull, his sad but discerning eyes.

He came toward me, knowing, too, that I could not answer his question. And we leaned against each other heavily, sorrowfully, like two survivors, bracing against the unbearable weight of a long shared life that was now over.

"I'll call you, Nora. If you need anything . . ."

Need? There was nothing I needed.

He pointed at the small suitcase. "That's all you're taking?"

I nodded.

"What about this?" He picked up the canvas bag with my flute in it that lay on the dresser.

"What for?"

Bernie shrugged and said no more. But when we got into the car to go to the airport the next day, he handed that bag to the driver, hoping I would not see. Then he turned to find me looking at him, annoyed.

"Take it," he insisted. "Just take it."

❦ 37 ❧

ON THE PLANE TO PHOENIX, A BABY CRIED. SEATED ACROSS
the aisle from us, the mother cooed to it, cuddled it, her
voice rising and falling. The baby calmed, then copied its
mother, her aahs and oohs and ups and downs, maternal
music imprinting like birdsong. How linked we are, I
thought, mother and child, by the key and color of our
voices, the melody, melisma, cadence, and phrasings of our
intimate music. I could hear Nicky's voice lingering in my
ear. Even though it was now silent, it was a music that
would not fade—our music, his and mine, our voices, one
voice.

I had sung to Nicky. And I played my flute for him,
nursery tunes, gentle melodies. He would sit at my feet
and clap his hands, and when he was three, Bernie brought
him to a chamber-music concert in which I played. I saw
Nicky, seated in the front row of the audience, staring at
me in my evening dress as if he had never seen me before,
his eyes wide with surprise. And after the concert, he whispered in my ear, his little fingers dancing around my neck,
"I said bravo to you, Mommy."

I took the handkerchief my father produced from his
pocket, and dried my face.
"I'm sorry," I told him. "I can't stop thinking of Nicky."
He patted my hand. "Why should you stop?" Then he
stood up, stepped over my legs to get into the aisle. He
walked away, came back with a glass of water, and handed
it to me.
"I don't want any."
"You are going to the desert." My father forced it into
my hand as he settled back into his seat. "Drink." He
pointed a paternal finger at me, and just to feel like a daughter again, I dutifully drank.

❦ 38 ❦

"WHY, THIS MUST BE NORA," A WOMAN SHAPED LIKE A DUMP-ling exclaimed as she sashayed toward me, arms out-stretched. Her cheeks were apple red, and her head was crowned with a doughnut of white hair.

Seeing her, my father stood up straight and became a strapping fellow of seventy, not the same old man who had shuffled off the plane with me, barely able to carry the plastic bag filled with various tile samples he had collected from Rutland Ceramics in Corbin's Cove.

"Meet Claire," he said, beaming, as she embraced me and then turned to my father, asking if he had enjoyed his trip.

"We buried my grandson," he reminded her.

"Oh yes. So you did. Well, we'll have to meet at a happier moment, next time. But here we are. Shall we go?" She shook a set of keys at us and smiled.

My father took my arm. "We'll get the luggage and meet you right outside the baggage claim. How's that?"

"Koochila moochila!" Claire trilled, and toddled off.

We were outside waiting for Claire's green Toyota, which was nowhere in sight. "She's just a friend," he protested, when I teased him about his ladylove. "One of many." My father a ladies' man? I took another look at him. He *had* married the Romanian bombshell, Sonia, I reminded my-self. And he had moved to the desert with her. He had become a stranger to me. But now he had offered me a refuge, this stranger, my father. Wouldn't I intrude on his life? And why had I not considered his needs? How could I have been so selfish?

"Are you sure I won't be in your way?" I asked him.

"What do you mean?"

"I mean, I don't want to cramp your style, or anything, you know, with Claire . . . ?"

"Claire has her own home. I help her. She helps me. That's the way our little town works."

I sighed. "I won't be any help to you. I'll just be in the way. I shouldn't have come. I think I should go back. I . . ."

His eyes misted as he patted my arm and said, "I've been longing for a visit, a real visit, with you."

I leaned over and kissed his cheek. "I'll try not to let you down. I'm not good company right now."

"A daughter is the best company a man can have, no matter what." He turned away, embarrassed, saying, "Now where is that woman?"

Claire's green Toyota had yet to appear. It was so hot I could feel the sidewalk burning through my sandals. I looked at my watch. "It's been twenty minutes, Pops."

"Pops?" My father smiled. I had never called him that before. But it seemed to fit him, this stranger, my father. It sounded just jaunty enough, just right. He nodded, liking the name.

"Maybe something happened to her."

"Last time Claire took me to the grocery store, she waited in the car, forgot what she was waiting for, and drove off." He chuckled. "Left me standing on the curb, two big bundles in my arms."

"Alzheimer's?"

"Shhh!" he cautioned. "Don't say that word."

"Why not? It's nothing to be ashamed of. It's an illness."

"It's a curse," he corrected me. "Claire's just forgetful." He picked up his suitcase and nodded for me to come with him. "Let's go. We'll take a taxi."

The cab driver, a retiree himself, lurched down the highway, heading toward the "adult village" where children and pets were allowed only as visitors. Brief visitors. Sunrise Villas, ten miles north of Phoenix, was where my father had lived for the past twenty years, twenty years without the sounds of children's laughter or dogs barking. We had visited him there once, after Sonia died, when Nicky was little, but his house was stark and unadorned, and our son's boisterous enjoyment of a sprinkler in the backyard had so annoyed the neighbors that they called the police, who came to investigate, sirens blaring. Bernie was outraged, and we left in a cloud of recriminations, never to return.

"Bunch of fucking crazy senescent assholes!" Bernie growled as we drove away.

" 'Nescent assholes!" Nicky echoed from the backseat with all of Bernie's bravado plus some. " 'Nescent assholes!!"

My father was hurt by our refusal to come back to Sunrise Villas, and our offers to fly him to Corbin's Cove to visit were usually answered with: "I'm tired. I'm too old. I have too many floors to do." I could only remember three times that he visited us at Linden Hill—on our tenth wedding anniversary, for Nicky's thirteenth birthday, and, of course, for the funeral—and during his stays, my father was a laconic presence.

We turned right, under the terra-cotta archway marked "Sunrise Villas," rolling past well-watered lawns and colorful gardens. A few old-timers pedaled by on bicycles. At one stop sign we waited for a golf cart to turn, its two passengers waving at us.

"Hey, Ezra!" one man called. "See you tomorrow at the tournament!"

I looked at my father. "Golf, Pops? You play golf?"

"Hell yes." He rubbed his hands together. "You don't expect me to sit home and knit, do you?"

The taxi stopped on Hollyhock Lane in front of a house I did not recognize. A green Toyota was in the driveway. Delicate flowers lined a path of white pebbles leading up to a trellised front entrance where pink bougainvilleas hung.

"This is it?"

"I think so," my father teased. He was smiling. Why had I only remembered my father as sad and somber, when, in fact, he was a man who smiled?

The front door opened as Claire poked her head out and called, "What took you so long? I've been waiting forever!"

I followed my father around his house as he proudly showed me his fully tiled kitchen with its intricate pattern of yellow-and-white squares on the floor and its walls done in a blue-and-white fleur-de-lis pattern. Then there was his pride and joy—his bathroom, just off the master bedroom, covered top to bottom with rare English antique hand-painted country tiles that he had collected through correspondence with antique shops in London—here hounds in pursuit, there a deer leaping, here a shepherd playing a flute.

"Now follow me," he ordered, eyes sparkling. I hadn't seen his eyes sparkle since he played canasta with Sonia in the living room on West Twenty-third Street. But, then again, I had seen him so infrequently since then. Why hadn't I insisted that we visit him again after the sprinkler fiasco? How could I have denied him the joy of seeing his grandson grow? And now there was no way to make it up to him. None.

He set my bags down in a little room with a rocking chair, a rolltop desk, and a bed covered in white lace. There were crisp pansy-printed curtains on the windows, and a view of flourishing rosebushes in the backyard.

"This is your room," he said, and I burst into tears. I did not deserve such a lovely room. How could he offer me so much when I had given him so very little?

"There, there." A soothing voice said over his shoulder as Claire came in, silencing me with a warm embrace and a plan: "Wash your face and then we'll take you to the club for dinner."

"What club?" I looked at my father.

"The Sunrise Country Club—golf, tennis, swimming, and dinners with dancing and music."

"And it's Thursday, so the music is extra-special to-night." Claire closed her eyes and clasped her hands, humming to herself.

Dinner, music, dancing? The idea horrified me. "I can't."

"Wear one of those miniskirts," my father suggested, ignoring my resistance.

"I don't have a miniskirt. And I can't go with you." I realized I was sounding like a twelve-year-old. "I won't!"

"You will. And you'll wear something fetching. Give the old geezers a thrill."

"All three of them!" Claire laughed, and pulled my father away from the door, saying, "Now where should we take your little girl for dinner?"

❧ 39 ❧

THE CLUB'S DINING ROOM WAS LARGE AND ROUND, FILLED with circular tables surrounding a parquet dance floor. Couples were dancing. Odd couples. Pairs of old women glided together across the slick surface, gazing into space, smiling as if lost in memories of former partners, former loves. An occasional male moved among the female twosomes, cutting in, giving each girl a whirl, then moving on.

"Do you dance?" I whispered to my father.

"Do I have a choice?" he quipped, then pointed to a cream-colored grand piano, complete with candelabra, at which an elderly gentleman with a bouffant mane of white hair sat, crooning into a microphone, "Trust Me with Your Heart, Again, Arlene." Finishing that song, the pianist reached to his left to twirl the dials of a rhythm-and-sound machine and chose a bossanova beat to accompany his own rendition of "My Garden's in Need of a Peach Like You."

"Victor Victoriana," my father said. "He plays the club every Thursday night."

I nodded toward the dance floor. "Is Thursday night ladies' night or something?"

My father smiled, nodding No. "Most people come to the Villas as a couple. But the men die off. You ladies are the stronger sex."

"C'est la vie!" Claire sighed. "My dear Edward passed on just a few years ago."

"Twenty," my father whispered to me as Claire sighed and swayed to the music. "Turn-of-the-century tunes," she said. "How I wish I had lived then."

"Didn't you?" my father jested.

Claire poked him in the ribs, miraculously getting his joke. "Oh, Ezra, you card! I was born in eighteen-nineteen, and you know it."

"Nineteen-eighteen," he quietly amended as an ancient woman dressed in an antique garden-party outfit slowly approached us to say that our table was ready. We followed her, or tried to. We were constantly stopped along the way by outstretched hands—friends of my father's, wanting to meet me.

"This is Ezra's daughter, uh. . . ." Claire fumbled for my name.

"Nora," I helped, and shook hands with a table of six senior citizens, five female, one male.

"She just lost her husband," Claire confided to them.

"Son," I corrected, my throat closing, the room spinning as Victor announced in his mellifluous tenor voice, "And now, sung with great success in nineteen-oh-four by R. J. Jose, written and composed by Mr. Paul Dresser, here is, 'Your Mother Wants You Home, Boy, and She Wants You Mighty Bad.' "

. . .

147

"Lamb patties, meat loaf, or baby duck?" our waitress shouted. She was no spring chicken. She was wrinkled and stooped, and spittle collected on her lower lip as she awaited my choice. How could she possibly manage to hold up a tray?

"I'll take the lamb."

"The loaf?" she shouted, and then I saw the hearing aids, one in each ear, so I shouted back at her, "I said, the lamb!"

"No need to screech, dear," Claire said to me, then, turning to the waitress, she was about to state her preference, when the choices suddenly eluded her. She elbowed my father. "You order for me please, Ezra." She tapped on her head. "I'm all turned around up here tonight." Then she hummed along with Victor while gazing dreamily at the ladies on the dance floor.

Dad was doing a fox-trot, changing partners like a pro, tripping the light fantastic. Claire sat beside me, eating my chocolate pudding, having already devoured hers and my father's.

"When do you suppose they'll bring the dessert?" she asked, but I was too absorbed watching my father weave and spin to answer. Years fell away as he moved among the women. He was handsome, trim—a debonair dancer. And he seemed to be enjoying himself. Was it possible, I wondered, that this man who had buried two wives was now having the time of his life with these decaying creatures among whom he had chosen to spend his waning years? These figures floating across the dance floor seemed suddenly unreal. Were they specters, phantoms, fleeting astral images? Where was I anyhow? Watching the dead dance? I closed my eyes tight, opened them again. Skirts swirled before me. Shoes tapped and turned. The room began to spin round and round and there was a ringing in my ears as everything faded and I grabbed onto the tablecloth and slipped slowly off my chair.

"Nora?" My father was sitting next to me, holding my hand, smiling. "Are you feeling better?"

I looked around. I was lying on a chintz couch in some lounge area, my feet propped up on pillows. Aging female faces peered over my father's shoulder, and I heard a chorus of comments: "It could have been the lamb. . . . It was that long flight. . . . She's just upset. . . . Maybe she's pregnant. . . . She looks just like Snow White, doesn't she. . . ?"

The flock was then parted by a tall man with white hair who reached for my wrist, taking my pulse. I blinked and recognized him.

"Mr. Victoriana?"

"That's just for the stage," he said. "Victor Stillwell is my real name. But you can call me Doc." He concentrated on his watch for a moment. "Down to ninety. Now that's a lot better."

"You're a doctor?"

He pulled the lids on my eyes up, peered into them. "Retired long ago. But I still know a case of acute syncopus when I see it."

I stared at him. "What does that mean?"

"It means you fainted. But you seem to be fully recovered now." He turned to my father. "I'd take her home, Ezra, give her warm milk with honey, put her to bed."

"No! Tea with vodka! Brandy and milk! Hot chocolate! A tuna sandwich!" the chorus piped up.

But Doc ignored them, stood up and straightened his candy-striped tie. "I've got to get back. I promised Mrs. Pendleton a chorus of 'Till I Met You I Never Knew of Love Sweet Love.' "

"Sorry I ruined your evening."

"You didn't ruin it at all," my father insisted.

"We had a lovely time," Claire said as she drove too

fast down Hollyhock Lane. "Except of course, it was sad."

"What was?" Ezra asked.

"That young girl passing away. And right at our table." She slammed on the brakes and the car squealed to a halt. "Well, here you are. It was so good to meet you, Norma."

"Nora," my father told her, and kissed her on both cheeks.

"Good to meet you, too," I said.

We got out of the car. My father bent over to say, "Good night, Claire. See you tomorrow."

She poked her round face up at him. "Eight A.M. And don't you be late, or you'll miss your starting time. You plan to win that tournament, don't you?"

"I plan to try. I'll be ready at eight sharp."

"Koochila moochila!" she trilled, and sped away, burning rubber as she rounded the corner.

I followed my father into the kitchen and sat down opposite him at the table. He slumped in his chair, looking distressed. "She shouldn't be driving anymore," he said, playing with a straw basket filled with napkins.

"I know." I was relieved he brought it up. It worried me. Claire could easily cause an accident. My father could be killed. I could be the one to let such a thing happen. Again. "Talk to her," I urged. "Reason with her."

"I've tried." Ezra rubbed at his chin, feeling the midnight bristles. "She won't listen."

"Then learn to drive yourself."

"And be one more menace on the road?" He crossed his hands in front of his face as if fending off a demon. When he lived in New York, his assistant drove him to their jobs in his beat-up van. For personal travel, he used the bus and subway. He would respond to my urgings that we get a car with, "Why would any sane person want a car in New York City?" But I begged him to consider a secondhand rattletrap, anything, just so we could take a drive, just so we could get away. But Ezra Lind was not a restless man in need of movement or change. And so there was no car then and no car now, and my father was allowing his life to be endangered by this dotty old lady, Claire.

"Some days she's sharp as a tack, and others . . ." He bit his lower lip, then smiled. "She was very good to me when Sonia went. Very good."

I nodded. I had not even appeared at Sonia's funeral. I was expecting Nicky at the time, and I made some excuse about not being able to fly. The truth was, I resented Sonia and felt no loss at her departure from this world. But she was my father's wife, and he was deeply bereaved, and what kind of a daughter was I not to have rushed to his side, as he had so willingly done for me? What kind of a daughter was I allowing my father to be in mortal danger now?

"I'll rent a car and drive you wherever you need to go," I offered. "I'll *buy* a car." The thought stopped me cold. With what would I buy a car? Money. The subject filled me with an instant dread. I had none. I did not even have my own bank account. The tiny sums I had made teaching and playing were mere pennies compared to Bernie's substantial salary. Having caused our tragedy, I wanted no further claim to our joint account. Nor could I stay with my father and sap him of his savings. And why had I never addressed this issue? I was penniless. Homeless. Childless. I began to tremble like a stray dog. "Dad," I whispered, wanting to ask for advice, for solace, for help. But my father was off in his own thoughts, far from the concerns of finance and housing.

"You should have seen Claire fifty pounds ago." He closed his eyes, as if to summon up that svelte image. "She was a dancer. Modern. Danced with Martha Graham in the early days. . . ." He opened his eyes and looked at me. "She and I used to kick up our heels at the club. You should have seen us!"

I tried to sound interested. "I wish I had."

Lost in his memories, my father lapsed into silence. I could not trouble him with my woes. We sat quietly together, father and daughter, at the kitchen table, as we had so often in the past.

"Feels like old times on West Twenty-third Street," I said, pretending nostalgia.

He looked up and his eyes were heavy, his voice muted. "Old times on Twenty-third Street. Sad times." He placed one hand on top of mine. "I wish I could have done better for you."

"You did just fine, you gave me so much. . . ."

He silenced my praises by pressing down hard on my hand. "No, Nora. I gave you so little. Your mother's death killed something in me. I shouldn't have let it."

"What could you have done?"

"I don't know. I don't know. But something."

He shook his head, then pressed harder on my hand, and I remembered my mother's hands—long, tapered fingers, delicate wrists, and her right forearm so very permanently marked with small blue numbers, the color of midnight. I remember those hands gracefully braiding my hair as she spoke to me before breakfast, urging me to walk briskly to the bus stop, not to talk to strangers, to eat all of my sandwich and to promise not to hit Mickey Harrigan, no matter what the provocation, nor to call Mrs. Ingpen, my teacher, Mrs. Pigpen even behind her back because one day she might hear, and then what?

"Don't let Nicky's death kill something in you," my father insisted, taking his hand away, bringing me back from daydream to the darkness of that moment.

I looked up at him. "How can I stop it?"

"Be strong. Fight it."

"I've lost my child," I whispered. "My only child. What is there left to fight for?" I folded my arms on the table top and buried my head in them and sobbed. My father stood up, and I felt him take my head between his hands, just as he had when I was sick as a child, hunched over the toilet, heaving. My mother could not bear to see me suffer, she said. So it was always my father who would stand over me, holding my head as he held it now, letting me retch with sobs until finally they subsided and he slid back onto a chair beside me, mumbling, "There. It's over. You're better."

I shuddered with the aftershock of crying and attempted to focus my bleared vision. My father looked gaunt and

152

pained. My outburst had upset him. My presence was a burden. I should have known it would be. Why had I inflicted myself on him?

Ezra was studying my face, a wan smile flickering around his mouth. "You look a lot like your mother."

"Really?" I had kept very few photos of Elena Lind. I did not like seeing them. I had shoved them into some closet somewhere, and I could not even remember where I had put them.

"Same eyes, a little puffy now"—I dabbed at them with a napkin as he went on—"same high cheekbones, that noble forehead . . ."

Noble? What could possibly be noble about me? I wondered as my father's eyes moved to my rat's nest of hair and he commented, "But of course, in your mother's day, a woman kept herself well groomed."

I managed a smile. "Is that a suggestion, Pops?"

"No." He assessed my head as he would a floor. "But it wouldn't be a bad idea, now that you're single, to try to look your best."

Single. Was I? Bernie and I had not said a word about a formal separation. Our son was dead, and there was no reason for us to be together anymore, and I had left. But, yes, we had separated. Yes, I was single. Yet the thought of trying to look good seemed preposterous. For whom, and with what intent?

"I'm sorry," my father said, seeing my face fall again. "I keep hurting your feelings."

"No, you're right," I told him, then, just to make him feel better, just to please him since that was the very least I could do, I asked, "Know any good hairdressers around here?"

QUEENIE TWIRLED ME AROUND LIKE CLAY ON A POTTER'S wheel. She stopped the chair, chomped on her gum, then, looking over my shoulder at her own reflection next to mine in the mirror, asked, "You're sure about this?"

I gazed at the tangle of black curls tumbling down my shoulders. A woman's hair was supposed to be her crowning glory. But what glory could I possibly claim? I studied Queenie as she stood peering into the mirror beside me. Clad in a leopard-print jumpsuit, wearing magenta lipstick, yellow eyeshadow, her head wrapped in an orange turban, Queenie looked predatory, eager to tear hair out by the roots. "I'm sure," I told her, shutting my eyes as I felt her yank a comb like a claw across my head.

She cut and cut. And talked and talked: "So, after I left Alexandre of Dallas, I tried L.A. But, you want to know something?" She waited for one grunt from me, then went on. "That town does not love hair. It tortures it. Me? I love hair. I'm passionate about it." Click! Click! "I love to take a mess like you and transform. Oops. Hope I didn't hurt your feelings?" Grunt. Click. "It's my specialty, transformation, if you really want to know. That's why I'm at the Villas once a week." I felt a stream of hot air hit my earlobe as she whispered, "These old bags with the blue hair? They trust me. I'm young. Well, twenty-eight. Young enough. At least my hands don't shake like every other hairdresser around here. I come into town, scissors blazing, and I make these blue-haired stiffs look like girls. Girls! They love me. And the tips I get here? I could live on the tips!" Click. Click. "You're the first woman under sixty I've ever had in this place, you know that?" Grunt. Click. "And for sure you are going to look like something when I am through with you!" Click. Click. Click.

Eyes open, looking into a large lollipop of a mirror I held

up to my face as instructed, I saw the back of a head reflected in the wall mirror. The nape of the neck was exposed. I thought of the nape of Nicky's neck, and how I loved to plant a kiss there when he was little, where it indented just below the globe of the skull, and how like a thin stalk his neck was, holding up the large flower of his head, and what a miracle it was, that fragile neck on that strong little boy. . . .

"So, what do you think?" Queenie asked, pulling the lollipop out of my hands, turning me around to face myself in the wall mirror. I blinked. A woman with short black spikes poking out around her face looked back at me. Her complexion was yellowish. Her large blue eyes were open wide. She looked demented.

"It's fabulous!" Queenie insisted.

An old woman with wet hair stood beside us, impatient for her turn. "You'll get used to it," the wet lady told me, shooing me up and off the chair.

Dazed, I handed Queenie a twenty-dollar tip, and as I walked, wilting, toward the cashier, silver-blue heads turned to stare at me in disbelief.

Outside of Guillaume's Beauty Parlor, a Cadillac Seville pulled up to the curb and a man in Bermuda shorts and golf shoes got out. He looked around for someone, saw me, and did a double take.

"Did you win the tournament, Pops?" I asked the man, as if nothing had changed, as if I were recognizable.

"No," he said, blinking.

Touching the absurdly stiff bits of hair poking out around my face, I couldn't help smiling.

"You're not crying, " my father noted. "You're very brave."

"Isn't she, just?" the driver of the car agreed as she came up behind us. "I'd be hysterical if I were you . . . I mean . . ."

My father saved her with an introduction. "This is Eleanor."

"Pleased to meet you, Eleanor," I said. In a peach suit

and matching pumps, a scarf around her neck, her white hair swept back, her handsome face powdered, Eleanor was dressed for the occasion. Any occasion.

"Where's Claire?" I whispered as Eleanor returned to the driver's side of the car.

"Friday lunch is with Eleanor," my father whispered back, adding a preemptive, "We're just friends."

My father the ladies' man. He had never seemed to me to be the type. But there was Eleanor, at the wheel, eager, attentive.

I sat like a thistle between the two of them in the front seat. "Here's what we'll do," Eleanor said, leaning over the wheel to peer into my face. "We'll drop Ezra off, then we'll go to my house, wash out all that mousse, and see what's left."

"I like it as it is," I said.

"It's awful," my father blurted. "I'm sorry. It's my fault. I was told Queenie was the best hairdresser in town."

"By whom?" Eleanor wanted to know.

"Claire."

"Claire? Well, no wonder! She meant Jeannie, not Queenie! Jeannie at Guillaume's for goodness' sake! Everyone knows *Jeannie's* the best. Really, Ezra!"

"I think it looks okay," I piped up in my father's defense.

"It's terrible," the defended disagreed.

"If you come with me, I'm sure we can improve it," Eleanor offered.

"Go with her, please," my father pleaded. "You don't want to walk around looking like you've been butchered, do you?"

Yes, was the answer. Yes, I liked looking mutilated, shredded, spiked. I felt brutalized. Why not look it? But I could see that my father was hurting. I had caused enough pain. I would go with his lady friend and get fixed.

"It's very chic, very feminine, very Kikki in Paris," Eleanor decided. I sat at her dressing table in a red silk bathrobe—hers. Blow-drier and brush in hand, she nodded approval, then pointed at the arsenal of makeup massed on the table before me. "Red lipstick, a little eyeliner, some pencil on the brows, and you'll be ready for the Rue de Rivoli!"

I'm only doing this to please my father, I kept telling myself, as Eleanor attended to the good grooming my father said he admired. But I could not help seeing how different I looked. How, for lack of another word, good. A slim woman with short black curly hair brushed elegantly away from her face; full, sensuous lips and deep-set blue eyes with long black lashes gazed back at me from the mirror. There was a sadness around her reddened mouth, a mysterious quality in her expression. She looked fragile, tentative, yet her eyes burned like two intense flames.

"Try this on," Eleanor was insisting, holding up a beige suit made of raw silk.

"I really don't want to. . . ."

But Eleanor was unzipping the skirt. "Come on. Just for fun."

"Fun?" I asked. The word sounded foreign, odd. Yet when Eleanor zipped me into the short, snug skirt, helped me on with the tailored jacket, tossed a long rope of pearls around my neck, and threw me a pair of high-heeled shoes, I found myself prancing across the oriental rug in her boudoir, stepping high, tossing my head, feeling, for a brief moment, light as air.

Eleanor insisted I keep the suit, the pearls, and the shoes. "Please, do me this one favor," she pleaded. "My late husband owned ten department stores, and they still send me designer samples every season. There are only so many items my closets will hold." Then her maid, Consuela, came in with a crystal pitcher of iced tea with fresh mint, and we each had a tall glass of it while Eleanor regaled me with vignettes from her days as a young girl when she studied voice at the Paris Conservatory and led *la vie de bohème* until, of course, she met Todd.

"And then you stopped singing?"

"To marry Todd Randolph, heir to the Randolph Stores?

Who wouldn't?" She dabbed at her lips with a mono-
grammed cloth napkin and smiled at me. "Don't get me
wrong. I loved him. And I kept singing—in the shower!"
She laughed until regret crept like a sly cat into her eyes.
"That was in the dark ages, of course."

I sipped my tea rather than talk about it.

"If I had it to do all over again," Eleanor sighed, "I would
have been more daring. Like you."

I nearly laughed. "Me? Daring?"

"But you are," she insisted. "I can see it in your eyes."

"God, I wish that were true," I confessed. "I feel like
such a coward."

"Feeling and being," Eleanor mused as she twirled the
sprig of mint around in her tea, "that's the trouble with us
women. We confuse the two."

❦ 41 ❦

WIDOWS WALTZED, ONE AFTER ANOTHER, THROUGH MY FA-
ther's house. After the forgetful Claire, and the regretful
Eleanor, there was the dramatic Marlene, whose husband
had owned a costume shop in Denver. Her inheritance
allowed her to dress according to her ever-changing
moods—fiery flamenco skirts, dashing circus spangles, ad-
venturous safari outfits. Then came the merry Alice for her
weekly Saturday-night date with Dad. A redhead of sixty-
eight who had just lost her fourth husband, Alice drove a
hunter-green Porsche, perfect for two passengers.

"But you can scrunch up in the back," she said, urging me to come along. I pleaded a bad back.

"Since when?" my father wanted to know.

"I'm tired," I tried.

"You slept till noon."

"Headache."

"Take something and come with us."

I racked my brain, and remembered the one excuse that had always worked when I was a girl: "I have to practice."

My father smiled at me, then bragged to Alice, "She plays the flute like a dream. A dream!"

I lay on my bed for a long time after they left. I had no intention of taking out my flute. It hadn't even been my idea to bring it with me. If Bernie hadn't foisted it on me, it would still be sitting in Corbin's Cove. I had no desire to play the flute. None. I tried to sleep, but I had already put in twelve hours the night before. The house, empty and quiet, was oppressive. I gazed at Nicky's little blue pinch pot, which I had carefully placed on the bedside table. I had plucked one rosebud from my father's backyard to put in it. Petals were opening, dark red, like clotting blood. The photo of Nicky and me in the heart-shaped frame stood next to it. As I looked at it, a sudden sharp pain overwhelmed me. I moaned, rolled off the bed, knelt on the floor in front of the table, and cupped my hands around the blue clay pinch-pot vase. I began to sob, and letting go of the vase, I slid down onto the rug and cried and cried until, finally, I wore myself out. I lay very still. The rug was rough, scratching my cheek. I stared ahead and there, under the bed, directly in my line of vision, was my canvas bag, where I had shoved it the day I arrived. My flute was in it, the flute I once played like a dream. Nicky liked me to play the flute. "I said bravo to you, Mommy." I could still hear him telling me that. Bravo. A big word for a little boy. A word that must be earned. The thought made me sit up. I wiped my eyes, then reached under the bed for my bag, pulled out my flute case and put the silver pieces together. I stood up and brought the flute up to my lips. I would never hear my son say bravo to me again. But he

had said it once, and he had meant it. I took a deep breath.
I would try to honor that memory.

❦ 42 ❦

NOW THE DAYS PASSED MORE EASILY. I WOULD SLEEP LATE,
get up, have a leisurely breakfast with my father, or, if he
were out with one of his ladies, or off tiling a floor, or
playing golf, I would eat by myself. Then I would shower
and groom and dress. Eleanor's gifts kept piling up—a
blow-drier, makeup, perfume, suits, scarves, jewelry. I
tried to refuse her presents, but Eleanor would pout and
say, "Don't deny me this great pleasure."

"She really wants you to have these things," my father
would say.

"I have no daughters, and my son's wife is a tank. It's a
joy to find someone slender who can use these things."

"Maybe you could give them to the homeless," I suggested. My father frowned as Eleanor fretted, "My Lanvins
and Chanels? Nora, I thought you understood them."

What I understood was that my closet was filling up with
fancy hand-me-downs, and by wearing them I not only
pleased Eleanor but also gave my father the impression that
I was putting myself together again.

And perhaps it was no mere impression. Each morning,
after showering and slipping into an Eleanor Outfit, I would
place a fresh rose in Nicky's blue vase, then amble into the
living room carrying my flute. It was difficult to make a

decent sound after so many long weeks of silence. But, thinking of Nicky, picturing him in my head, I would begin, on B flat, with long tones, holding one note at a time, trying to shape the sound, to color it, to let it open up like a blossom. And my tone improved. Then I would move on to scales, arpeggios, études. What had once been mere drudgery was now sheer pleasure. Where once I had labored like a horse in harness, now I rolled, jumped, twirled, flipped, and flew like a bird. I had brought no music with me, and so I relied on memory, and was surprised at how much I had retained. I could retrieve whole sonatas, concerti, endless melodies, opera tunes, orchestral excerpts. And then I would improvise—a medieval chant, a gypsy czardas, an American folk tune, a turn-of-the-century song. I would embellish and embroider ornaments around the melodies, like a jazz player on a riff. And it was this new-found flair for filigree that gave me an idea for gainful employment.

"My Thursday nights have been so lonely up here," Victor Victoriana oozed into the microphone. "But tonight, I am delighted to announce that I shall share the spotlight with the very lovely, the very young and talented, the very heavenly—Miss Muffet!"

And, wearing a big smile, looking like a Watteau shepherdess in a creation supplied by Marlene, I entered the dining room of the Sunrise Country Club, flute in hand, and took my place in the curve of the cream-colored piano, keeping my distance from the heat of the blazing candelabra on the piano top. I arranged the sheet music Victor had photocopied for me and, listening to an A from the piano, I tuned up.

"Our first piece will be 'The Herd Girl's Dream,' " Victor announced, "by August Lavitsky." He poured out a cascade of broken arpeggios, and began singing the bucolic melody through which I twined a flowery flute obbligato. I was nervous at first, but candlelight flickered gently around me, faces smiled. I imagined myself at the turn of the century, in a salon in a Victorian house in the country, playing for friends, and the jitters disappeared.

"Treasures That Gold Cannot Buy," "Look for Me When the Lilacs Bloom," "Only a Bunch of Violets"—songs surged up at me from the pages, but I easily improvised embellishments over the vocal line—trills and flourishes and fancy cadenzas. The listeners lapped it up, danced as if enchanted, complained when we took a break, and begged us to play on past eleven.

At midnight, Victor closed the keyboard and kissed me on both cheeks. "You're the best thing that happened to me since Rosemary Clooney sang 'Pretty Kitty Doyle' with me in 1954 when she visited her aunt at the Villas." Then a shadow of worry crossed his face and he reached for my wrist. "You're not feeling faint, are you?"

"I'm fine, Doc. Fine." And I was. I had made music. I had given people pleasure. It felt good.

The manager of the club, Jack Winkler, waddled over with a crisp hundred-dollar bill. "You were a big hit, young lady. I'd like you back next Thursday, okay?" He handed me the money while shifting a toothpick from one side of his mouth to the other.

"It's up to Doc," I answered. I did not want to horn in on his territory.

Doc bowed toward me. "It would be my great honor." Then he turned to Mr. Winkler. "Only next week, you'll have to pay her two-fifty."

The manager spit out the toothpick. "That's a little steep, isn't it?"

"For a soloist from New York? My dear man, she commands thousands when she plays Carnegie Hall."

Winkler spluttered and wheezed and grudgingly conceded.

"I've never played at Carnegie Hall," I whispered to Doc as Winkler receded toward the cash register.

"Well, you know how to get there," Doc said, collecting his sheet music, blowing out the candles on the candelabra. "Now, about rehearsal. How's Monday at three?"

❀ 43 ❀

THURSDAY CAME AGAIN, AND THE NEXT THURSDAY, AND THE next, and Victor Victoriana and Miss Muffet packed the Sunrise Country Club. Jack Winkler was pleased and my father was bursting with pride. I wanted to donate my earnings to our household expenses, but my father would not hear of it. "You are my guest, you are my daughter, and you will keep the cash, is that clear?"

And so, stashed in my lingerie, my treasury increased while I practiced and rehearsed with Doc and played at the club. I began to yearn for more lasting melodies than "They Call Her April, but She's My Queen of the May." I missed Mozart and Beethoven and I even began to fantasize about playing chamber music again, maybe even being in an orchestra one day.

I worked hard and lost track of the time, and as weeks blurred into months, the sharp pain of my loss was softening around the edges. I thought about Nicky all the time. But I cried less. I slept less. I had some energy again. I began to cook for my father, to entertain his lady friends, and to clean his house. And it was while sorting out some boxes in his laundry room one day that I found a carton marked "Elena." I was about to open it, but something stopped me. What could be in it but old photos, letters, documents? Harmless things. Yet a cold sweat crept over my skin and I quickly shoved it back into the dusty recesses of a cupboard. Why would I want to see old images of my mother, fading relics of the woman who had left me, a small child, to face the cruel world without her? And yet, there I was, so many years after her death, standing in a stuffy laundry room, closing that cupboard door, whispering "Mommy," until I was no longer whispering it, I was calling out for her, just as I had when I was in the last throes of giving birth to Nicky. What had escaped my throat in the delivery room were not mere sounds or curses or vague cries for help. I remembered taking one last deep, desperate breath and, bearing down, I had screamed with all my might, "Mommy!!"

Bernie kept in contact. "Is there anything you need?" his distant voice would ask me during our brief phone calls.

"No."

"Your father tells me you're playing the flute again."

"I am."

"Well, that's great."

"Thanks. And how are you?"

"Good."

"That's good."

And there would be silence followed by terse goodbyes. Hanging up, I would wonder how it was that eighteen years and one son had come and gone so fast and that the man with whom I had spent all those years and raised that son was now just a detached voice on a telephone.

❧ 44 ❧

DUSTCLOTH IN HAND, I ANSWERED THE FRONT DOOR.

"Are you Nora Watterman?" asked a man holding a large basket of flowers.

"Yes."

"Then this is for you."

The bouquet was too big and beautiful and could not possibly be meant for me. But the receipt had my name on it, so I signed it and carried the basket into the kitchen.

"Happy Birthday," the card said. "Your real present will arrive on the twenty-ninth. Love, Stephanie."

My birthday. I had totally forgotten it. Was it already the nineteenth of December? And was I thirty-eight, or thirty-nine? Nine, I decided. Thirty-nine? How did that happen, and where was I on my last birthday and how could I be almost forty? I sat down hard on a kitchen chair and I remembered my previous birthday, which had been spent with some man named Theo in his bachelor pad in New York. Bernie, who had been out of town, had awakened me with a phone call and a painfully off-key rendition of "Happy Birthday" followed by a promise to bring me something upon his return, which he never had. Then Nicky made me breakfast—two overcooked eggs and some burnt toast—but he had brought it up to me on a tray, along with a present: a pair of white knit slippers that were eventually chewed to bits by Prince Hal.

"I love them!" I had told him last December 19.

"Really?" His face was shiny, his eyes bright with pleasure.

"Honest."

"You can wear them in bed. That's why I got them. 'Cause your feet are always cold, right?"

"Right."

And he had kissed me on the forehead and said he'd be late for school if he didn't hustle, then he clattered down the stairs and out the back door, my son, my lovely, sweet son. Then I, his brazen, deceiving mother took a train to meet a man named Theo Bradshaw. Had I loved him? I could not remember. And what had it been like, all that stealthy planning and dangerous embracing? No nerve endings twinged to remind me. I was dry as the desert, drained of all passion.

. . .

"You're upset?" my father asked, when he entered the kitchen and saw me, weeping into the flowers.

"I'm just so touched," I told him, and handed him Stephanie's card.

"Oh my God," he said, looking sheepish, "is it really your birthday?"

And at that, voices yelled "Surprise!" and bodies burst into the kitchen, carrying cake and champagne and presents.

"She's really very happy," my father insisted as I wept and wept and weathered the hugs and pinches with as much pluck as I could muster.

"Here's to many more," Eleanor toasted.

"More what?" Claire wanted to know, while Alice downed her third glass of bubbly, and Marlene, dressed in an aviator's costume for the occasion, cut the cake.

"I want you to eat all of this," Doc commanded as he gave me a huge piece. "No one loves a scrawny flutist."

My father gave me music he had sent for from New York—the Bach flute sonatas, Bärenreiter edition, and the complete Handel sonatas—and a wooden music stand he had inlaid with antique tiles.

"Happy birthday," my father said, shyly accepting my grateful hugs and kisses, and he handed me an envelope. "This came in the mail today." Opening it, I found three tickets marked "Cracow Chamber Players conducted by Marek Rudiakowski, with Stephanie Saunders, violin soloist, Phoenix Symphony Hall, 8:00 P.M., December 29."

So, to hear Miss Saunders play would be my "real present." What an egotist! What arrogance! How very like Stephanie. And how very wonderful. I could not wait to see her. Stephanie!

"What is it?" my father asked, seeing my flushed face.

"How would you like to go to Stephanie Saunders' concert with me in Phoenix on December 29?"

"I'd love it, but how will we get there?"

"I'll take you," said four female voices in unison. And

166

Claire, Eleanor, Alice, and Marlene glared jealously at each other.

"How many tickets did she send?" my father asked.

Four faces turned toward me. I cleared my throat. "Three," I said.

"Then let me go with you," Doc intervened. He winked at me and turned to the ladies. "Nora owes me, after all I've done for her, don't you think?"

❦ 45 ❦

THE HOLIDAYS CAME AND WENT. CHANUKAH AND CHRISTMAS merged at the Villas, and there were parties with paper snowflakes and dreidels and songs sung about wise men and menorahs and it all passed quickly and strangely. On Christmas day it was not only snowless, it was 103 degrees. There was a special Christmas buffet dinner at the club, and even with air-conditioning, the ice sculpture of Rudolph the Red-nosed Reindeer melted and crashed into the plum pudding. Doc and I performed holiday favorites for that dinner, Doc in a Santa outfit, I dressed as an angel, courtesy of Marlene, of course. After a particularly poignant rendition of "I Saw Mommy Kissing Santa Claus," Doc leaned over and whispered to me, "Thank God we get to hear some *real* music in a few days!"

Real music. My longing for it had turned to lust. I devoured the Bach sonatas my father had gotten for me, I

167

lingered over the Handel. I tried to play them with Doc, but he could not keep up. "I'm all heart and no technique, my dear," he apologized. "You need to find yourself a proper pianist."

But how? And where? I wanted to make music. *Real* music. But with whom and when?

"Victor Victoriana and Miss Muffet?" Stephanie chortled into the phone when she called a few days before her concert, to make sure I planned to attend. Then she modified her amusement with, "I think it's great that you're playing the flute again."

"It passes the time."

"It does more than that."

"Not when you're playing obbligati to tunes like 'Take Me with You to the Land of Love.' "

Stephanie laughed, then suggested, "So find some good people to play with. Start a group."

"Here? With these old-timers?"

"There have got to be young players in Phoenix. Ask the Symphony. Call the local union. Take some auditions."

"I couldn't."

"Why not?"

"I just . . . couldn't."

"Of course you can. Hey . . ."

A dangerous silence. I knew she was scheming.

"I'll talk to Rudiakowski. Bring your flute on the twenty-ninth. You'll play for him, after the concert."

"No way!"

"Why not? Just to get the hang of auditioning?"

"I'd rather hang myself."

"Nora, you're not feeling like doing the old Ophelia number in the pond again are you?"

Leave it to Stephanie to remind me. "No," I told her. "And I'll thank you not to make fun of me."

"I wasn't . . . I didn't. . . ."

"Forget it."

"Okay. Okay. I can't *wait* for you to meet Marek, anyhow." She said his name with definite warmth.

"What happened to Bartolomeo?"

"The Italian stallion had a wife and kids back in the stable."

"Sorry."

"You're sorry? You should have seen how sorry he was after I told him his career was history."

"Stephanie, that's outrageous."

"What's wrong with revenge?"

"Everything."

"Well, don't worry. I can't hurt his precious career. He's too talented. And drop-dead gorgeous. And charming. And a scumbucket. In other words, a superstar."

"Forget about him."

"I already have."

"And the Polish prince?"

"Marek?" She hesitated. "We're old friends. I was supposed to play with him in Salzburg. But I canceled to come to the States for Nicky's . . ."

"Funeral," I finished for her. "You can say the 'F' word." How could I be joking about it when visions of the cemetery were flashing through my head—the hearse, the coffin, the crying, the long black limousines . . . ?

There was surprised silence for a moment, until, trying to sound bouncy, Stephanie continued her story. "So I told Marek I'd squeeze the Phoenix date into my schedule to make up for it. So it worked out just great, didn't it?

"Ready!" I announced, on the twenty-ninth of December, striding into the living room in an Eleanor Outfit—a simple red suit with a short skirt, pearls, and high-heeled black patent-leather shoes, my hair artfully blow-dried, my makeup discreetly applied. Doc whistled, and my father, in his best blue suit, nodded his approval.

"Shall we go?" Doc suggested.

"I've already gone," my father answered in all seriousness. Then, just as he would if I were still his little girl, he turned to me to ask, "Nora, did you make a wee?"

❧ 46 ❧

STEPHANIE NEARLY DROPPED HER STRAD. "MY GOD," SHE whispered when she opened her dressing room door at the Phoenix Symphony Hall. "What happened to you?"

"I got a haircut."

"But it's wonderful! But you're stunning!" she blurted, staring at me, amazed. Then she put her violin down on a table and hugged me so hard that little circles from the sequins on her gown imprinted into my jacket.

Stephanie kissed my father, who shyly said, "Good luck tonight."

"Dr. Victor Stillwell," I said, introducing Doc, who shook Stephanie's hand and told her how he admired her artistry, how her Brahms concerto with Muti and the Philadelphia was the definitive performance as far as he was concerned, and that to hear her play the Mozart D major tonight would be like seeing the sun come up over the Alps.

"Thank you, Dr. Stillwell," Stephanie said flirtatiously. "And I hear you are a superb pianist."

"I was a superb doctor. As a pianist, I am passable. But I've been inspired of late by your friend's flute playing."

Stephanie smiled at me. "She's good, isn't she?"

"Good? She's superb. She's lyrical, expressive. She's a fine artist. Like you. But *you* . . ."

"*I,*" Stephanie interrupted his effusion. "I better warm up or you may wish you had stayed home tonight."

"Never!" Doc sighed, and I was utterly astonished to see that Stephanie was attracted to him.

"He's seventy-five!" I whispered to her when my father and Doc left the room to allow us "girls" a moment alone.

"So? He's still sexy."

"You're hopeless," I told her. Then I kissed her on both cheeks. "But you're the best."

"Me? Look at *you*, Nora." She shook her head. "I can't get over it. It's like someone touched you with a magic wand!" Then, fearing my sensitivity, she quickly added, "Not that you were chopped liver before. But now . . ."

"Gefilte fish?"

She laughed, and hugged me, and whispered, "Wish me luck."

"You don't need it."

"Say it anyhow."

"Okay. Good luck," I said, smiling at her, my friend, my oldest and dearest friend.

Marek Rudiakowski was small and burly with a trim beard. He rushed onto the stage like a man about to miss his train. Then he leapt aboard the podium, bowed deeply toward the packed audience, and, whirling around, arms in the air, he slashed a downbeat before the applause died away. A warm string sound filled the hall as the Cracow Chamber Players gave a precise yet robust performance of a concerto grosso by Arcangelo Corelli. The group, numbering about two dozen, played with energy and intensity, and I watched their faces with interest. *Character* was the word that came to mind. The men looked gentle, refined. The few women, with high cheekbones and wide, smooth faces, were undeniably attractive. Cracow. The name resonated in my head. Where was the city of Cracow anyhow? Somewhere in the land of Chopin and Paderewski, somewhere in the land of my mother's birth, in the land of my mother's sorrow. . . . I remembered her standing in the kitchen, listening to the radio, telling me, "Chopin wrote fifty-three mazurkas while he was in France living with a woman who dressed like a man. He wrote them because he was homesick for Poland, where the women wore skirts, such lovely skirts, beautiful embroidered skirts. . . ."

After the Corelli, an oboist and two horn players took their places, and Stephanie Saunders swept onstage, causing the audience to gasp at her dazzling gown and her shimmering hair and her gracious manner. Whispers died down as she tuned her violin, then nodded to Marek to begin, and as the introductory tutti heralded her entrance, a fierce concentration crossed her face and she launched into her opening notes with the kind of grit and guts that transformed a simple D major triad into a powerful statement. Her sound had a clarity and sheen to it, her phrasing an ethereal simplicity. I cried in the andante cantabile and smiled through the rondo and rose to my feet with everyone else in the hall to join the tumultuous ovation that followed the final notes.

"No one is allowed back here," an usher warned as my father, Doc, and I tried to go backstage at intermission.

"I am Miss Saunders' best friend," I announced importantly, and pushed past him anyhow.

We hurled superlatives at Stephanie, but, astonishingly, she was disgusted with herself. "Didn't you hear that scratch on my high C sharp in the middle of the slow movement? Christ, I sounded like a cat in heat, and my last entrance in the rondo? Pig City!"

She fumed and fretted about her performance, then, turning to Doc with a coy smile, she asked, "Did you really like it?"

I tried not to roll my eyes while Stephanie hungrily gobbled the good doctor's praises. A loud warning bell, beckoning the audience back into the hall, was a welcome sound.

"You two go ahead," Doc suggested, shooing my father

and me out of the dressing room, calling after us, "I'll come in a minute!"

"I'll bet he will," I whispered to my father, who looked shocked for a second, then shook an amused finger at me as we joined the returning throng.

⚜ 47 ⚜

WAITING FOR THE SECOND HALF OF THE CONCERT TO BEGIN, I listened to the cacaphony of the musicians warming up— the chaos before the clarity. Was the flutist of the Cracow Chamber Players nervous? An older man with white hair, he looked secure as he tried out his solos, his difficult runs and turns. I thought of the days when I had played first flute in the Juilliard Orchestra two decades earlier. I remembered the jitters before the first chord, then the urge that would charge through my veins at the very last moment, turning nerves into excitement, making me champ at the bit, eager for the challenge. Now, as Marek thrust his baton forward, it was almost as if I were on that stage for the downbeat of Beethoven's Fourth Symphony, as if *I* were playing that pianissimo high B flat, in tune with the B flats an octave below in the other winds. My ears prickled with attention to the strings as they moved in their portentous downward phrase against the sustained octaves. Floating over that string sound, drawn into the mysteries of Beethoven's introduction, like a leaf on a stream, I edged toward the tumbling waters of the allegro vivace. Marek's beat was clear and crisp, and I could have followed him easily. I would have spun out a silver banner of sound, not the tired rag of a tone being warbled by the white-haired player who was up there. *I could be playing this part*, I thought. *I could be playing it better.* But I knew it was one thing to think so from the safety of a seat in the audience. It would be another actually to prove it. It would require a job. And a job would require an audition, and an audition would require confidence and guts. . . .

Backstage, after the concert, Stephanie introduced me to the maestro. "This is Nora Watterman, my best friend. She's a fabulous flutist!"

"I can see," Marek said, looking me up and down. He took my hand and brought it toward, but not quite in contact with, his lips. "You will play for me one day?"

"I'd like to," I dared.

"I'm having problems with Laszlo, my flute," Marek confided. "Could you not hear?"

"I thought he sounded excellent."

"You are generous." Marek patted my cheek. "I like this. But Laszlo?" He shook his head. "He has a problem with health, but he will not take the curation, because he worries I will replace him for permanence. I assure him, I would not, but he worries and so it goes on. . . ." He shrugged and looked at me. "So you are a great flutist?"

I blushed and stammered, "I'm okay."

"She's wonderful!" Doc offered.

"And she's even Polish!" Stephanie joshed.

"Really?" Marek wiped his face with a towel, while assessing me. "From where?"

"Her mother was born in Warsaw," my father explained. "So were my parents."

"*Czy pan mówi po polsku?*" Marek asked.

A strange look crossed my father's face. "No, I don't speak Polish," he said coldly. "I prefer Yiddish."

Marek clapped my father on the back. *"Nu? Was machts du?"*

"You speak Yiddish?" Stephanie asked, surprised.

"But yes," Marek said, beaming. "I played with the Jewish children when I was a small boy in my village, before they went away."

My father began to cough and Stephanie asked, with forced gaiety, "So, where shall we go for dinner? I'm starving!"

❧ 48 ❧

THE WINE FLOWED, AND THREE OF THE FIVE OF US WERE getting giddy. My father sat silent, carefully cutting his Cajun chicken. Doc was driving, so he stuck to Shirley Temples—ginger ale with cherry juice. But Stephanie and Marek were toasting each other, getting tipsy, acting as stupid as musicians will after a concert, and I downed glass after glass myself, while Doc tried to add a touch of intelligent conversation.

"It's quite unusual for a chamber orchestra to do Beethoven symphonies, isn't it?" he asked.

"Beethoven doesn't mind!" Stephanie hooted.

"I mean, isn't it usually done with more strings?"

Stephanie slapped the table. "Four for every fiddle!" And Marek put an arm around her, squeezed her, kissing her sloppily on the cheek.

I shrugged at Doc and smiled at him as Stephanie popped a really important question: "What's the difference between a violist and an onion?"

The three of us were already giggling, while my father just stared, and Doc smiled indulgently and said, "I give up."

"Nobody cries when you chop up a violist!"

Marek laughed so hard he was choking and crying and when he finally came up for air, he pounded on the table, then asked, "What are you calling a violist in a Polish orchestra?"

Stephanie and I looked at each other, floored. Was there a musician's joke we had not heard?

"What *do* you call a violist in a Polish orchestra?" Stephanie, the straight man, asked.

Marek was giggling, about to say the punch line, then he scratched his head and pulled on his beard, annoyed with himself. "I can't find word." He drained his wineglass. "In Polish, it is *powtórzenie*."

"Redundant," my father translated, a small smile slipping wryly across his mouth.

With Stephanie dangling from one of his arms, and me from the other, Marek navigated a path from the restaurant toward Doc's waiting car, where he and my father sat waiting patiently for me. As Marek leaned in the window to say his elaborate and hearty goodbyes to the two men, I careened toward Stephanie and whispered, "Are you in love with him?"

"No way. We're occasional lovers. He's married."

"Stephanie!" I gasped.

"What's wrong with that?"

"The same thing that was wrong with it with what's-his-face, Bartolomeo."

"Totally different."

"Why?"

"Because Bartolomeo didn't *tell* me he was married!"

176

. . .

"It was my very big pleasure to meet you," Marek said, his face too close to mine, his breath sour.

"The pleasure was mine," I slurred. "It was a glorious concert! Magnificent!"

"But you are a passionate woman!" Marek exclaimed, grabbing me. "This is good. You must play the flute like an angel! A passionate angel!" He kissed me loudly on the mouth. "You will come and play for me?"

Luckily, my father had gotten out and was pulling me from the clutches of the ardent maestro.

"I'll call you!" Stephanie promised as I banged my head getting into the car.

"*Dzię*kuję!" Marek was yelling. "*Bardzo Dzię*kuję!"

I leaned my head out the window and remembered to say, "Good luck with the rest of the tour!" before we drove off. Then I slumped back into the car and deposited the contents of my stomach all over the backseat.

❦ 49 ❦

"DRINK THIS." I WOKE UP THE NEXT MORNING AND SAW MY father sitting on the bed beside me, holding a glass. "Doc brought it over. It's his own recipe for hangovers."

So that's what the anvil smashing inside my head and the dead rats in my stomach were all about. The past evening's events washed through me, and I grabbed for the glass. "Ugh!" I spluttered, drinking the foul potion. I fell back on my pillow and tried to focus on my father's face. He was smiling at me, looking amused.

"I'm glad you think it's funny."

He nodded. "I'm just pleased to see you taking part again."

"In what?"

He sighed. "Life."

I played with a button on his shirt. Button. Nicky's first word. "What was my first word?" I asked my father.

Surprised by the question, my father looked at me and shrugged, then rubbed his chin. "I should remember such a thing?"

"Right," I said, hurt. "It's the sort of thing only a mother would remember."

He patted my disappointed hand. A wave of nausea and sadness made me turn my head away. The bed jiggled as my father stood up suddenly and announced, "I must show you something. I'll be right back."

If he had something to show me, he certainly took his time getting it, which was a good thing, because when he returned, I had dozed off and now woke up feeling vaguely human.

"Come, look," he was saying, as he placed a carton on the floor and sat down beside it. I recognized the box marked "Elena," I had discovered some weeks before. I had not wanted to look inside then. I certainly did not want to now.

"Look. Look at this." My father was waving a photograph at me. "You are a carbon copy. Come look."

"I don't feel very well. . . ."

"This will make you feel better," he promised. "Come here!"

Woozy, but wanting to please him, I crawled out of bed and sat down beside him next to the carton. I reluctantly took the picture, glanced at it, and my mother seemed to gaze back at me like a mirror image. Her hair was lighter in color than mine, but it had the same curl and texture, and it was swept away from her face, revealing the same shaped eyes and nose as mine. Her full lips were opening, as if to laugh or to cry, I couldn't tell which.

"That was taken the year she died," my father said heavily. "She was only thirty-five. And look at this one." He handed me another photograph.

We were at the beach. Riis Park, near the city. I remembered the rancid smell of the subway we took to get there, the suffocating heat. In the photo, my mother was wearing a one-piece bathing suit and holding a small girl by the hand—me. I was looking up at her, as if in wonder, and she was gazing off, out to sea. She was slim, with a terrific pair of legs and a confident posture. Was that my mother? Or was the next photo the real Elena—wearing a hat, a short dark dress, standing in front of our brownstone on West Twenty-third Street, furtive eyes avoiding the viewer? Or was that she in this picture of both parents— Dad looking strong and silent, my mother, primly dressed, with a starched collar and a look of panic on her powdered face?

"She was a beauty, wasn't she," my father stated rather than asked. "She loved you so much."

My eyebrows arched. "Really?"

"Do you doubt it?"

I looked at him, hard. "Do you really want to know?"

"I'm asking."

"Okay. Yes, sometimes I doubt this great love of hers."

"She adored you," he insisted.

"Leave it, please."

But he was agitated, determined. "She did! Never did a mother love a child more!"

"Please. Stop!" But he would not, nor would the anger that was bubbling up inside me.

"She only loved you. She never raised a hand to you. She never did anything to hurt you!"

"She died!" I blurted.

"You think she died on purpose? Are you crazy?"

I glared at my father and tried to lower my voice. "Parents are supposed to act responsibly," I said in a controlled voice, "parents who love their children. When there is a killer disease that's preventible, a parent gets inoculated. So you tell me, if this woman loved me so much, why the hell didn't she get a polio vaccination?"

My father was breathing heavily. "I promised her never to speak of these things."

"What things?"

"Things that happened to her. Over there."

"Oh, please," I protested. "Not the old Holocaust number again."

My father was pointing accusingly at me. "Yes, it is the old Holocaust number, Nora! And it was not a minuet, let me tell you, young lady! And it left its mark. On your mother! On me! On you! And it is indelible. It is forever. Forever! Don't you understand?!"

The veins in his temples were pulsing. His face was livid. I was afraid he might have a stroke. "I'm sorry," I mumbled, groping for his hand. But he would not take mine. And sorry was not good enough.

My father sat for a long time, turned away, breathing with difficulty, his shoulders rising and falling.

"Are you okay?" I kept asking. "Pops?"

He finally looked at me, and spoke calmly, gently. "Look, Nora. You lost a son. It was a terrible accident. But your mother lost her entire family, and it was no accident and it was terrible. She never wanted you to know how terrible."

I reached up, and my father took my hand and put an arm around me and squeezed hard.

I stared at the box. A sudden grim curiosity took hold of me. "What else is in there?"

"Look for yourself," he said.

I hesitated. "Are there photos from Poland?"

"Not one."

"No family pictures?"

"Nothing. No one survived. No one."

"Then what's in there?"

"Are you afraid to look?"

"Of course not," I lied, and just to seem cavalier, I

reached into the box and pulled out a packet of papers tied in a red ribbon. "Love letters?" I asked, handing him the packet.

My father untied the papers, and perused them. "Reparations," he explained. "Your mother was going to file for them. But she never did."

"Why not?"

"She decided money would not repair anything."

I nodded. "And this?"

My father looked at the envelope I handed him. "It's a letter from Poland."

"What about?"

Opening the letter, my father scanned it, and folded it again, slipped it back into the envelope. "Your mother had some correspondence with this person, just before she died. She knew him in the camps. . . ."

"And?"

My father was shaking his head. "A *meshuggener*. Crazy! Can you imagine, he went back to live in Cracow after all that?"

I was staring at the Polish words on the envelope. *Ciesclaw*, must be the name. All those consonants. Then an address. *Szeroka, 7. Cracow.* Ciesclaw from Szeroka Street in Cracow. A real mouthful. "What does the *meshuggener* say?"

My father twirled one finger near his temple, babbling, "Hello, how are you, how is life in luxurious America, etc., etc."

"Seriously." I handed the letter back to him. "What does it say, *exactly?* Please."

My father impatiently flattened out the paper. " 'Dear Little Elenka . . . ' A nut case. She was already thirty-five."

"No comments. Just translate, okay?"

He rolled his eyes, then read to himself, mumbling, before continuing: " 'I am living in Cracow, working in a factory. I married Magda. You remember Magda, don't you? She was on the transport with me from Zamosc. She

181

is now living in Israel, because the life here was hard and I am not easy to live with. I wish her well. I have no bitterness toward her, or toward anyone, for that matter. I am grateful to be here, to be working, to have a nice apartment, even if the pipes leak. How is your life in America, with all the luxuries? I have not forgotten you, Little Elenka, your smile, your kindness, nor have I forgotten that but for you, I would not be here, writing this letter. I wish you well, and your family, and may God bless you. Your friend, Stanislaw Ciesclaw.' "

My father patted the letter and slid it back into its envelope.

" 'But for you I wouldn't be here'?" I looked at my father. "What did he mean?"

Dad shrugged. "I asked your mother. She said she did nothing to help him. She was eleven. He wasn't much older. What could a child possibly do?"

"But he said . . ."

"Look, the man is a *meshuggener*, what can I tell you?"

I nodded slowly, wondering about the crazed Stanislaw Ciesclaw, who had chosen to live in the land of his torment. And I wondered about my mother: her "smile"? Could she have been smiling in the camps? And what about her "kindness"? Had she been caring for others during her own duress, graceful under the worst of all possible pressures? What if she really did save this Mr. Ciesclaw? Was it possible?

"Nora?" My father was peering at me, concerned. "Are you all right?"

"Just thinking."

"About?"

"About Mom. About how I know so little about her, or her life. . . ."

"Here. Look at this. This tells you about her." He put a little wooden box into my hand and gestured for me to open it. Inside, tied with a tiny pink ribbon was a lock of curly black hair. A piece of yellowing paper was in the box with it. I recognized my mother's ornate European script. "Nora's first haircut," it said.

"She saved everything of yours." My father reached into the carton to find a packet of my first drawings, my first school reports, my medical records. "You see how she loved you?"

I saw. But it was painful to see and to remember. We were such a pair, she and I. "Like from a cookie cutter!" my mother would say when we would peer into a mirror together. "Now . . . the big cookie gobbles the little cookie!" Then she would nibble my neck, making me shriek with terrified delight. But it was not I who disappeared. It was she whose life was taken away slowly, inexorably, and she was gone before I had a chance to know who she really was.

Compelled by relics and memories and a deep, abiding sadness, I asked my father the forbidden question: "What *exactly* happened to her during the war?"

He closed the little wooden box containing the lock of my hair. "What happened to your mother during the war she left behind. Over there. Far away. Where it stays."

"Pops," I pushed, "it's time for me to know now. She's not here to tell me. You *must* tell me."

"I promised her. . . ." He rubbed at the stubble on his chin.

"Sometimes it's appropriate to break a promise."

"Not this one. And don't ask me to."

"I'm asking."

He sighed. "You know what happened to her."

"I know her parents and her brother were taken away, and she never saw them again, but do we have records of their deaths?"

"There are no records."

"Then how can we be sure they died?"

"We can be sure. Dead sure." My father's face hardened. "And that's enough for now, Nora."

Frustrated, I tossed a pile of papers back into the box. "That's *her* line. 'Noraleh, enough about the war. This is not a subject for a little girl. . . .' " I stared at my father. "I am hardly a little girl. And I say the subject needs to be addressed now."

"Why now?"

"Because now . . . I miss her. I want to know her." My chin began to tremble, but I swallowed hard and looked at my father. "Help me to know her. Please."

He studied my face. Then he picked up a photo of Elena, and gazed lovingly at it. "She had a doll named Kasha when she was very small. And she loved her bedroom, which was painted green. With lace curtains. And she would lie on her bed with Kasha and pretend the green was a forest and the curtains were clouds. . . ."

My father's eyes were pained. It was hurtful for him to talk about my mother and it was cruel of me to demand more information. But I could not stop. "*And?*"

He sighed before reluctantly attempting more. "*And* she had a happy family. A beautiful childhood. Then she was taken to Auschwitz, where her childhood ended, where she got very sick and nearly died. But she survived." He turned his palms up and shrugged. "And that's all you need to know."

Anger churned its sharp blades inside me. "How do *you* know what *I* need to know?" My voice was rising. "What if *I* need to know everything, every little detail, like when did my mother get sick and what exactly was wrong with her and how high was her fever and who took care of her and what did they give her to eat and where did she sleep? Who are *you* to tell me what *I* need to know?"

He took my hand. "I am your father. And I love you."

"I *know* that, damn it!" I yelled. "But if you won't tell me, where do you expect me to find the answers?!"

My father began slowly shuffling papers and photos. "I expect you to stop asking questions," he said, and gently placed the remaining relics of my mother's life back into the cardboard carton marked "Elena."

❦ 50 ❦

I WANDERED OUT INTO MY FATHER'S BACKYARD BAREFOOT, TO pick a rose for Nicky's vase. It was night, and the air was very still. A pale moon, delicate as an empty eggshell, dangled in the sky. High overhead a jet left its vaporous trail. Where was it going? Who was on it? And why were they traveling? Suddenly I was on that plane myself, watching the eggshell moon through a small, square window.

"Nora?" the woman next to me asked. I turned to find my mother sitting beside me, smiling.

"Where are we going, Mommy?" I asked, leaning my head on her shoulder, inhaling her sweet perfume.

"Far away," she said. "Over there."

"And how long will it take to get there?"

"Not long," she promised, and tucked a blanket around me. "Here's someone to help you sleep."

She handed me a doll with curly blond hair, dressed in a pink satin smock and little white shoes.

"Her name is Kasha," my mother said.

I held Kasha tight and looked up into my mother's face and she brushed her lashes against my cheek like butterfly wings and I felt something warm and wet on my nose.

"Are you crying, Mommy?" I whispered. She did not answer. "Are you sad?"

"No," she insisted, as her tears rolled down my face and I tasted the salt. "Not anymore."

I sat up, and blinked in the bright morning light. I looked at my watch. Could I have been asleep for sixteen hours? Horrified by my sloth, I hopped out of bed and headed for the shower.

I closed my eyes, tipped my head back, and let the nozzle spray over my face. My dream came back in a rush as the warm water poured like my mother's tears down my cheeks.

Why had she cried in that dream? She said she was no longer sad. Were those tears of joy because we were traveling somewhere together? She and I had never taken a trip, except to the beach.

"Can't we go somewhere?" I would nag.

"Why should we go when we have everything we need right here?"

"To see things."

"Such as?"

"Such as the alligators in Florida. And the mountains in Wyoming. And the stars in Hollywood."

"You are *my* little star," she would say, beckoning me to her for a hug. *Beckoning me to her.* I dropped the soap as that phrase rang in my head, and by the time I had finished showering, an idea had appeared like a wisp of a cloud on a clear sky. I dressed and the idea kept billowing, taking shape, gathering force.

I pulled the atlas off the living-room shelf and opened it to a map of Europe. There it was, over there, far away, nestled among the Germanies, pillowing Czechoslovakia, directly below Sweden—Poland, the land of my mother's birth and my father's ancestry, the land of my heritage. What was it like, this land over there, so far away? I turned to a larger map of Poland and found Warsaw in the North and Cracow in the Southwest, and, only a pin-dot away from Cracow—Oświęcim! My mother used to say that word like a curse—*Oświęcim!* The Germans called it Auschwitz. And they did not curse it. I stared at that word for a long time, repelled by it, drawn to it. I even had the strange urge to go to Oświęcim, to have a look for myself, to see that place of execration. What would I find? I did not know exactly. But if I went to Cracow, I could visit Mr. Ciesclaw and talk to him myself, find out about my mother, about everything that happened. Then, perhaps, finally, as my father wished, I could stop asking questions.

Yet how could I pay for such a trip? I had my Miss

Muffet money stashed away, but it would barely cover the cost of a plane ticket, let alone living expenses.

Thwarted, I shut the atlas, and slid it back onto the bookshelf. I would not go to Poland. I would not go anywhere. I had no money, no resources. I would stay in the Villas forever. I would cook for my father. I would play at the country club. I would wither up with all those widows and waltz the rest of my life away, unless I could find a place to go and a job to go with it. . . . My pulse raced as a thought jolted my body, and I lunged for the phone.

"Are you crazy?" Stephanie yelled into the receiver. "Are you your own Polish joke?"

I had called her early in the morning in Albuquerque, the next stop on her tour with Rudiakowski. I had interrupted her practicing. She was not delighted. "I need a job," I told her.

"Okay. But *there?*"

"Cracow is one of the great cultural spots. You said so yourself last summer."

"I was lying. Cracow is horrible. There are no vegetables. You'll get depressed."

"I am depressed. And dependent. And I can't keep draining my father forever. I need to get out of the Villas before I ossify."

"So why don't you audition for a job right here in the good old United States of America?"

"Because I'm too inexperienced. And I'm too old. There are all these whiz kids who can play rings around me. If I get a job abroad, I can come back here and then maybe I'll have a chance."

"Poland is not just *abroad*, Nora, and you know it. Why would you want to spend time in a country everyone is trying to get out of?"

"Things are changing there now. All those reforms, all that freedom . . ."

"All those anti-Semites. Remember Auschwitz?"

"It's right next to Cracow."

"Great," she sneered. "You can spend your weekends there."

"Maybe I will."

"Jesus, you are perverse!"

"I'm not perverse. I'm practical. Marek's flutist needs medical treatment, but he worries about being replaced. I'll offer myself as a *temporary* replacement."

"I hate to break it to you, but there's a second flute back in Cracow who's supposed to be young and pretty and very willing. . . ."

"So that's exactly why Laszlo won't take his medical leave. She's a threat. But me? I'm just an American, doing this to help out until he's better. Get it?"

"No, I don't get it. Unless . . . you don't have the hots for Marek, or something, do you?"

"Are you kidding? He's repulsive! I mean . . . I didn't mean to insult you, or . . ."

She was silent.

"Steph?"

"Forget it."

"I'm sorry."

"Yeah, you are. You're a sorry sap. You want to go to Cracow for some cockamamy reason you're not telling me. What is it, Nora. More self-punishment? Haven't you paid enough penance?"

"It's not about that," I said.

"Then what? Why the hell would you want to go there?"

I could not tell her about my dream, about my mother, about my compulsion to go. It was all too personal, too vague. How could I explain it? How could she understand it? "I'm just tired of sitting around feeling sorry for myself," I finally said. "I get the first positive, independent idea of my life, and I call my best friend for encouragement. Why can't you be there for me?"

I heard her pluck her violin strings. "I am," she grumbled. "I'm here. And you're right. Play for Marek. At the very least, you'll have one audition under your belt, right?"

"Right." I smiled and looked at my watch. "Do you think he'd be willing to hear me at five?"

"Today? You could get here this afternoon?"

"Why not?"

"But we're in the middle of New Mexico. You're in Arizona. Isn't Albuquerque far from Phoenix?"

"Nothing is far from Phoenix," I told her. "Not anymore."

❧ 51 ❧

ALICE SHIFTED INTO FIRST AND FLOORED IT. I FELT THE WIND whip around my face as the desert streaked by, all orange and rose and aquamarine in the dusty sun.

"Halfway there, and flyin' low!" Alice yelled. In her goggles and racing helmet, wearing bright orange coveralls with "Le Mans" scrawled over the breast pocket, she had risen to my request for a ride to Albuquerque with demonic glee. Hell-bent on breaking her own record of Phoenix to Albuquerque in five hours, twenty-three minutes, she was only too glad to have a reason for taking that trip.

"Five hours nineteen!" she crowed as we hit the city limits. "Now you go ace that audition, and I'll visit my favorite body shop." I thanked her profusely and crawled out of her Porsche in front of the Hotel Rancho Paradiso, knees knocking, bladder bursting. I heaved my canvas bag onto my shoulder, and headed for Miss Saunders' suite for a pee and an hour of practice before my big moment with Marek.

"*Leonora* Three?" he asked, and I tossed off the flute solo from Beethoven's overture with the necessary panache.

"Brava!" Marek applauded. "Do you have *Daphnis?*"

I swooped up Ravel's slinky scale to the haunting solo in *Daphnis and Chloë*, playing the long, aching line with sheen and luster.

"Superb!" Marek sighed. "Brahms Four?"

I knew he meant the sustained passage in the flute's lower register from the last movement of the symphony. I played it with a full-bodied sound, mellow yet strong.

"Such a tone," he sighed. "Sensuous. Voluptuous."

"Thank you."

Marek smiled up at me from his armchair, nodding. "You have not to thank. It is me and it is Laszlo who are thanking *you.*" He rose to his feet, holding on to both lapels of a jacket that strained to close around his expansive middle. He paced back and forth across the room, then stopped right in front of me, his eyes penetrating, his breath overwhelming. "Your idea is a genius, my dear. And now that I hear you, and you are perfect, I am completely convicted. I will have you!"

Trapped inside Marek's sudden bear hug, I tried to breathe and to focus on the future. I pictured a warm welcome from my fellow musicians, I heard strains of Mozart, I saw myself onstage in the country of my ancestry.

"Who would have thought these things would ever be possible—cooperations, friendships between our countries?" Marek pulled back, letting me breathe and nod my head in agreement. "Now, with the nice politics, everything can be arranged one-two-three! Visa is not a problem, but we cannot pay in hard currency. You can accept your salary in zlotys like the other musicians?"

"I don't expect special treatment."

"But you will have it! I will arrange for you a very nice apartment in Cracow belonging to a professor who is in

Vienna for some semesters. Will this be satisfying?" He headed for the telephone, glancing back at me for an answer.

"Sounds wonderful," I supplied.

"And I am close friend with the deputy minister of culture in Cracow, Mr. Lukasz Slezick. I am calling him right now. He will be very pleased for the publicity!"

"Publicity?"

"Of course." Marek dialed and tried out some copy as he waited for his call to go through: " 'Harmony in Our Time—American Flutist Comes to Make Substitution for Polish Colleague with Kidney Stones That Do Not Pass in Cracow.' What do you think?"

But before I could suggest some edits or question Laszlo's condition, Marek was yelling into the phone in Polish, and a mix of excitement and anxiety was sloshing through my own stomach, making me sit down, dizzy at the speed of events.

✌ 52 ✌

CRACOW CANNOT BE COLDER THAN THIS, I THOUGHT, AS I navigated my way down Fifth Avenue toward the Polish consulate, wind whipping around me mercilessly as I passed glittering store windows filled with spring fashions. I turned up the collar of the red wool coat Stephanie had loaned me, and barreled onward toward Madison Avenue.

"Take a mink," she had pleaded, as we picked through her coat closet.

"I'm allergic."

But she knew better. "To what? Looking good? Don't tell me you're one of those hypocrites who won't wear dead animals, but has no problem eating them?"

I shrugged. When Stephanie was on a roll, I knew enough not to get in her way. "How about something in sackcloth?" She yanked the red coat off its padded satin hanger. "Would this be humble enough?"

With its bright gold buttons, black braid trim, fitted waist, and long, flaired skirt, the red coat reminded me of one I had seen in Macy's, when, as a girl, I had gone shopping with my mother. I had loved it, and longed for it, but we could not afford it. I tried on Stephanie's and twirled around, making the skirt billow.

"Don't tell me Madame is pleased?" she sneered.

"Madame is delirious." I stopped twirling. "But do you think it's too bright? I don't want to call attention to myself or anything. . . ."

"Babe," Stephanie said, "with a face like yours you'll get looked at whether you like it or not. Or should I buy you one of those ugly wool hats to scare away all the men?"

"I'll buy my own accessories, thank you very much," I bragged. "I have saved my salary from the country club. Over two grand."

"You're rich!" Stephanie exclaimed. "You take two thousand bucks to Poland, and with the rate of exchange, you'll need a goddam wheelbarrow to carry all those zlotys home."

Home. The word sounded as displaced as I felt. Home. I had no home anymore. Linden Hill was just some house on a hill in some distant town. A man lived there named Bernard T. Watterman. Once he and I were married. We had one son. But he died.

"Could we meet for coffee before you go?" Bernie had asked when I called him from Stephanie's to request my passport.

"Coffee?"

"We have some things to discuss."

Separation, no doubt. Divorce. The division of our

192

worldly goods. "You can have everything," I told him. "Just send me the papers and I'll sign."

"Nora . ..." He cleared his throat and sighed. "I'd just like to see you."

It would be painful. It would remind me of Nicky. It was a bad idea. "I can't," I told him. "I'm busy."

"I see," he said, then hesitated before asking, "I suppose you're dating someone?"

Dating? Me? What a bizarre idea. But Bernie was silent, waiting for an answer, and I formulated one that seemed adequate, that sounded adult: "I'm not ready to socialize."

He cleared his throat again. "I think it's important to see people. For both of us."

"Suit yourself," I said. "I'll sign anything you want me to."

I could hear him fidgeting at the other end. "Do we want to do something so formal?"

"Can divorce be informal?"

"Divorce?" He sounded shocked.

"Isn't that what you want?"

"How about we just leave it until you get back? See how things go."

"Whatever."

" 'Whatever'? I hate that! It's such a cop-out!"

"Sorry," I muttered, although I was not sorry. Not anymore. I was leaving Bernie's bailiwick, going behind the recently parted iron curtain, where, despite the dawning of a new era, it would still be dark and dismal enough without his reproach.

"Did you see the article in the *Daily News*?" he asked.

"What about?

"You. Your trip. How it signals artistic exchange between U.S. and Poland, yatta, yatta . . . nice picture, too."

"Really? I wonder where they got it." As if I didn't know. Marek had requested all my publicity materials and was making good use of them already.

"It's your old photo, in the yellow dress."

"The one that makes me look like a duck?"

Bernie chuckled. "I haven't seen you in a long time, Tinker. . . ." His voice trailed off, then he came back with, "So, I bet you'll have a swell time."

"I'll be working."

"I'm sure you'll have time for fun."

"I don't think people have fun in Poland."

I could hear him breathing heavily. Then he said, "Take care of yourself, Nora."

Take care of myself? Had I ever? A mother and wife for as long as I could remember, I took care of my son and my husband, yet the idea of doing things for myself, by myself, was daunting. I had never traveled anywhere alone in my life. Yes, I made the reservations, planned the trips, but it was always Bernie who led the way through customs, exchanging money, hailing cabs, finding hotels, paying bills, beating paths, running interference. . . .

Take care of myself? "I will," I told him, as if I knew how. "And you, too," I added. "Take care."

Vice-consul Patinsky had a mole on his chin, with two dark hairs sticking straight out of it, like antennae. It was hot in his office, and dark, but I could make out oriental carpets on burnished parquet floors, wood-paneled walls, and on his vast oak desk, piles of paper, and a plate with a half-eaten chicken sandwich and a slice of pickle.

"Your photographs are of no justice," he said, as he attached them to my visa with a thunk of his stapler.

"Thank you," I said, watching his whiskers wiggle, wanting suddenly to laugh. It was comical. Me, getting a work permit from a man with antennae. Me, going to Europe. *Eastern* Europe.

"Do you speak Polish?"

I bit the inside of my cheek. "No," I admitted. "My parents spoke it like a secret code, you know, so I would not understand."

"Yes. Parents." The whiskers twitched. "It is a difficult language."

"All those consonants," I said, a laugh bursting through

the ropes of my restraint. Vice-consul Patinsky laughed, too, like a sea lion asking for fish, his whiskers vibrating.

"You will do well in my country, I can see," he predicted. "You have a sense of humor. In Poland, this is important, to laugh."

"I'll try to remember." I giggled foolishly as he handed me my passport and led me out into the waiting room where somber citizens were patiently waiting on the long line I had bypassed, thanks to a phone call from Maestro Rudi-akowski. Outraged eyes burned into mine as I breezed past, making my smile fade fast, and my steps quicken as I ran down the steps of the consulate into the ominous arctic wind that greeted me.

Disoriented, I walked east instead of west and found myself on Park Avenue, far from Stephanie's apartment, frozen, no buses or cabs in sight. This is how you will feel in Cracow, I told myself. Alone. Cold. Miserable.

I shuddered and kept walking. Two more days and I would be getting on a plane and going to that alien place, that bleak tundra, that icy land called Poland. And why was it I wanted to go? What had ever possessed me to make such an insane plan? Answers vanished in the frigid air as I slipped on some ice. I managed to grab onto the post of a No Parking sign, and merely grazed one knee on the sidewalk. Shaken, I wandered into the lobby of a large office building to assess the damage. Holding up the hem of my coat, I saw blood seeping through the stocking around my left knee. It began to hurt and I hobbled toward the security desk for some tissues or a Band-Aid, only to be told, "Madame, this is not a hospital."

"Thank you," I foolishly replied and limped away, tears brimming. Men in camel-hair coats and cashmere scarves strode past, briefcases in hand, unaware of my distress. I leaned against the marble lobby wall, watching the parade of the powerful as they pushed open the door and dashed out fearlessly onto the glacial street. I longed to reach out, attach myself to one of those sturdy arms, slip into a limousine beside one of those smooth-coated bodies and glide off to a cozy apartment where my Galahad would bandage my knee and brush away my tears and take care of me, forever . . . just as one of them once had offered, so gallantly, with such leonine strength, such prowess, such devotion. "I will love you, always," he had said to me. "I'll be there if you ever need me or want me. . . ."

Theo Bradshaw! He would pluck me from this turbulent sea of doubt and despair. He would save me from my self-imposed exile in Poland. We would have a life together, and a good one. . . .

I wheeled around and lurched toward a bank of telephones that lined the wall like life rafts.

"Darling," Theo groaned as he held me in his arms, spooned behind me on the bed of his still-bachelor apartment.

"Yes," I whispered back, wanting this as much as he. Worried that my knee would hurt, he was gentle and tender and carefully positioned me so he would inflict no pain. His thrusts intensified and he cried out with pleasure, but I felt neither rapture nor anguish. I lay very still as he caught his breath and murmured, "My darling, my poor, poor darling. Are you all right? Did I hurt you?"

"I'm fine." I assured him, wishing I were, wishing that our encounter could be the cure, the answer to everything. This solicitous man had rushed to my rescue on Park Avenue, scooped me up and into his waiting car, doctored my wound, listened to my sad story with all the tenderness and care of a chivalrous knight. He had pledged his love. He would take care of me. He would protect me. I would want for nothing. "Nora," he had said, his eyes glistening. "I can't bear that you've suffered and I didn't know. Why didn't you call me?"

"I did. You were out of town."

"I was gone when you most needed me?" He had showered my face with kisses. "I'm sorry. I'm so sorry. But I'm here now. We're together, as we're meant to be. We'll be happy. I promise you."

It would be like dancing with Apollo all over again, wouldn't it? Yet no cloud came to carry me away, no heavenly music resounded. And I lay beside Theo, earthbound.

"What is it?" Theo asked, when he felt my body stiffen after we made love.

"I don't know. I just didn't feel . . . I couldn't . . ."

He sat up and turned me gently toward him. "You've been through a terrible trauma, Nora. Be patient with yourself."

"I'm trying."

"Don't try. Let it happen. We have time, all the time in the world. There are no barriers between us now. We're free to be together forever."

Theo buried his head in my breasts, and I stroked his hair, wondering why, without child, without spouse, without responsibilities, I did not feel free, not at all, not the least bit. Nor did I feel the rekindling of love I had hoped this moment would inspire. But what could I expect? I had not often thought of Theo over the past months, I had not longed for him, I had not needed him. Where was the love I had felt for him, the love that had kept me so attached, during the steamy days of our liaison, the love that had once compelled me to recklessly risk my marriage, my family? And what was it about Theo I had adored? He was so refined, so godlike. Or was he? Had I been the one to put him on that pedestal? By making him divine, I had kept him distant, and by keeping him distant, I had remained safe. But Nicky's death had shattered all security, grief had shrouded all feeling, and now it was Theo Bradshaw, not the god of light, who lay beside me in the shadows of his bedroom.

I thought of his mother and imagined her sitting in a corner, wrapped in a blue blanket, watching me with her piercing eyes. "You're not a kid," she would say. "You should know what you want."

"What is it?" Theo asked, sensing something, some drawing back, some retreat. He looked up at me, with his kind, intelligent eyes. "Nora?"

I gazed at his fine, patrician face for a long moment. "I can't be with you, Theo," I said. "Maybe it's too soon after my son's death, maybe it's . . ."

"Don't." Theo touched my lips with one index finger. He smiled at me, a bittersweet, knowing smile. "I understand."

"Do you?"

"Yes. And someday, so will you." He looked at me for one last, lingering, affectionate moment. Then he pulled away, got out of bed and slowly reached for his robe. He tightened the sash and, attempting small talk, asked, "How's the knee?"

"It's okay," I said. "Thank you for coming to my rescue."

"You didn't need rescuing," he said sadly. "You never did."

"Will you ever forgive me?"

"Of course." Then he smiled at me, a smile that was a little off center, just slightly, just the perfect touch of imperfection. "Question is, Nora," he added, dead on, "will you ever forgive yourself?"

❧ 53 ❧

"I'M AT KENNEDY," I SHOUTED OVER THE DIN AT THE AIRPORT.

"You're on your way, then?" my father asked, as if surprised. He had not objected when I told him my plans. If he suspected my intentions to look for Mr. Ciesclaw, he said nothing. "Watch out for the Poles," was his only advice.

He might not have approved of my destination, but we both knew it was time for me to leave. His lady friends knew it, and made a going-away party for me, complete with gifts, including long underwear, a flannel bathrobe, and a pair of slippers with rabbit ears that I deftly managed to leave behind.

I had a job and I had a mission. I had severed old ties. I was, finally, free to experience, to explore. But now, as I stood at a phone booth at the international terminal, about to depart, my eyes were filled with tears, and, just to remind myself that it was actually happening, I yelled, "Yes! I'm on my way!"

"Call me when you get there."

"If I can. I'm told the phones are few and far between."

"Then write. And be careful. And . . . Nora?"

"Yes?"

I heard him take a sharp breath before he said, "I love you."

I could see him standing in the kitchen, rubbing the stubble on his chin. "I love you, too, Pops. And take care of the ladies, and . . ."

My farewells were punctuated by tears and a deafening announcement: "Lot Polish Airlines, flight two-five-two to Warsaw, is now boarding at gate B-6."

I said goodbye to my father and, heaving my canvas bag onto my shoulder, I left the world as I had known it and walked like a robot toward the machine that would transport me to another planet.

2

. . . The sun, lying by the roadside
with magic wands
commands the travellers to halt.

They stand still
in the glassy nightmare
while the cricket scratches softly
at the invisible

and the stone dancing
changes its dust to music.

NELLY SACHS

❧ 54 ❧

FLIGHT 252 WAS PACKED SO TIGHTLY I COULD FEEL THE KNEES
of the man behind me pressing into my lower back. The
seats were upholstered in a hideous floral pattern—murky
brown roses, navy carnations, mauve daisies. The passengers were silent. A woman in a beige uniform tossed me a
plastic tray with supposedly edible objects floating in a
muddy sauce. "Drink?" she barked, and when I hesitated
for a split second, trying to determine which tiny bottle of
alcohol would put me out fastest, she walked away. A male
flight attendant finally acknowledged my frantically waving
arms, and brought me two vodkas. Soon I stopped worrying
whether or not the head of the rotund sleeping woman
beside me would slip onto my shoulder, as I fell into a
welcome stupor of my own.

The voice of the captain, muttering in Polish, jarred me
awake. Window shades were opened. Gray clouds rolled
by like dust balls. A breakfast of rock-hard buns and bitter
coffee appeared magically before me. Landing cards were
passed out, and we were approaching Warsaw, the captain,
now speaking in English, told us, where the temperature
was minus 10 Celsius, and dropping. Fast.
    Snowflakes brushed my face, waking me up, as I followed
the flock of passengers down some stairs onto the whitened
tarmac. We traipsed toward the terminal. Inside, it smelled
of disinfectant, and I tried not to breathe as I shuffled in
line to passport control. Now that travel restrictions were

easing in the East, entries and exits would be a breeze, so I assumed. Life was perking again in Poland. I was suddenly excited about being there. I would see the first stirrings, the new awakening. A man in an olive-green uniform was pressing an iron stamp into a round ink box, then making circles on papers, nodding impassively as people handed him their pertinent documents. When it was my turn, he took my passport, looked at my photograph, then at me, then at all my papers. He smiled. He was handsome, with a thin mustache and warm brown eyes. A nice man, I thought, until he pointed at my work permit, and asked, in English, "You have brought a flute with?"

I nodded, and held up my canvas bag.

"You will show ownership paper at customs," he instructed, and waved me impatiently toward the baggage claim area and my impending doom. I had no ownership papers for my flute. No one told me I would need them. It was *my* flute. I would tell them that at customs, if they spoke English. I would show them my flute, a Haynes, American made. I would prove it was mine. But how? As I nervously pondered my strategy, a giant of a man in white overalls, pushing a luggage cart, sidled up beside me and smiled, a big friendly smile. "Help?"

A porter, I realized. I nodded. Yes, I could definitely use help. He stayed by my side, humming softly to himself, as the conveyor belt squeaked and began to move.

As soon as my bags arrived, my giant scooped them up and plopped them like toys onto his cart and wheeled me right past customs, despite the mumblings of a seemingly irate official who, with his leering eyes, seemed to want to make a thorough examination of me as well as my luggage.

I had to run to keep up with the white giant, who was wheeling his cart at Olympic speed. He stopped near a crowd of neck-craners who had obviously come to meet friends and loved ones.

"No customs?" I asked, winded.

"I fix for you."

"How?"

"I promise him half my tip."

Tip? Money. I needed to change money. "Can you tell me where the bank is?" I asked. "I need to get some zlotys." The jolly white giant smiled and leaned down to whisper, "Dollar. I am happy for dollar."

I gratefully pulled out a ten-dollar bill. But he looked at me, waved a finger at me and clucked, "No. *One* dollar. Only *one*. This is what I ask." He pushed my hand away. "Be careful, lady in red. You will have your advantage taken." And he left me standing in the crowded terminal, bewildered.

Stephanie's secretary had telexed my flight information to Marek's office, as requested, and Stephanie had assured me I would be met with great fanfare at the airport. If so, where were the trumpets? Where were the little children with flowers? Where the hell was Marek? And why was there not at least someone holding up a sign with my name on it? Panic set in as I looked around. Okay, I told myself, calm down, figure it out. Change money, take a taxi to the train, a train to Cracow. I had the address of the apartment at which I would be staying. I was digging around in my canvas bag for it, when a man chewing on a pipe, wearing a big sheepskin jacket tapped me on the shoulder, making me jump.

"Wasserman?" he asked.

"Watterman, Nora?" I asked back, ready to leap into his arms as he nodded and said, "*Tak. Dzień dobry.*"

That much I had learned from the tourist vocabulary in my recently purchased guidebook. *Tak* = Yes. *Dzień dobry* = Hello. I even tried it out myself while enthusiastically shaking his hand. "*Dzień dobry.*" I liked the sound of it, the way the words slipped hissingly through the teeth.

"*Proszę,*" he said, picking up my bags, indicating that I should follow him. And we marched out into the snow toward a parking lot where he opened the door to a small red mud-splattered car, and I tumbled into the back onto a sheepskin-covered seat.

I watched, bleary-eyed, as we drove through slush, down wide boulevards with stately buildings. Traffic was heavy, and the smell of diesel fuel filled the car. But we inched our way through intersections and seemed to be moving faster, heading out of the city of Warsaw, toward the countryside, toward Cracow.

We wound through small towns on our way, passing quaint old houses, and ugly new cement constructions, many only half completed. Horse-drawn carts piled high with everything from hay to herrings shared the road with cars that looked like sardine cans on wheels. Big yellow buses and smaller blue ones belched black smoke and blocked the roads as they labored up and down hills. The snow was melting, and as we drove into more rural areas, glades of pine trees dripped with ermine snow capes. Fields were glistening, and red-cheeked peasants riding on their carts returned the friendly waves I sent their way. The landscape changed constantly—now an ugly town of brick boxes, now a glistening stretch of orchard and forest, now a village with bundled figures hurrying in and out of busy shops.

"Music?" I asked the driver, pointing to the radio, hoping for Chopin, or at least a polka. Loud rock music jarred me, but the driver was happily nodding to the beat, and I did not know how to request a change of station, anyhow. So I watched houses and hills roll by to the sounds of Polish heavy metal.

By afternoon, we approached Cracow. The sun gleamed like copper, lighting the church spires that rose above the distant city. But just outside that glowing city, my driver slowed down, turned right, off the highway and into a road where big white houses with sloping roofs, garden plots and bird feeders stood. He pulled up in front of one particularly grand home, and a heavyset woman in a kerchief, wearing a skirt with almost the exact same floral print as on the airplane seats, plus brown ankle boots and a brown sweater with a sheepskin vest over it, came down the walkway to greet me and lead me inside.

Confused and unsteady, I followed her into the house, wiping my boots and removing the black felt hat with the wide brim I had proudly purchased myself. It made me look mysterious, I thought. Intriguing. Ready for adventure.

"Welcome!" a deep voice bellowed, and a small bouncy man in a suit and tie extended his hand and said, "Lukasz Slezick, deputy minister of culture." He clicked his heels together. "I have the keys to your apartment, and I was eager to meet you, of course!"

"Oh," was my scintillating reply.

"You must be fatigued."

"I am. And a little . . ."

"Bewildered? Frightened? Voracious? Anxious? A,B,C,D, or none of the above?" He laughed. "You can see I have studied in America." He clapped his hands, and ushered me into a living room, where a roaring fire warmed me, and a glass of tea was served by the lady of the floral skirt, along with sugar-coated cookies that looked like snowballs and tasted delicious.

"Call me Luke," he insisted, and proceeded to give me information about the ins and outs of life in Poland faster than a bumper car at a carnival.

"So, you'll remember, it is prohibitive to exchange money on the black market. The exchange is almost the same now at the bank. And really, you can always pay in dollars. We are becoming a hard-currency economy—dollars, marks, the more the merrier! So, use your hard currency at the hard-currency stores for items like toothpaste, candy, cigarettes, and mineral water. You don't want to drink the water. You don't want even to brush your teeth with it, unless you'd like to glow in the dark." He chuckled.

"It's that bad?"

"It's worse. And the air? In Cracow, you don't take a breath until afternoon, especially now in the winter. It's all the filth from the factories in Nowa Huta spewing into the air, and in the morning, with the smog? I'd stay inside if I were you. Well, don't look so worried!"

He offered me more snowballs and even less encouragement when he said, "If you have trouble finding meat or fruit and vegetables, or if you have a medical problem, give me a call and we'll arrange something. Now, let's get the keys to Professor Millbank's apartment. You must be eager to see it. It's a prize! Right in the old city. You are one lucky lady!"

Luke led me into a hallway where, hanging on great hooks were all sorts of medieval-looking keys. He handed me two unbelievably heavy ornate bronze keys. "Millbank's apartment dates back to the late Renaissance. You know, Cracow was the only city that was not destroyed by the Nazis, so everything is intact. Even the plumbing. It's perfectly sixteenth-century!" He laughed and explained that the larger of the two keys opened the outside door, the smaller opened the apartment itself. "Maestro says to tell you your first rehearsal will be tomorrow at ten at the Philharmonie."

My heart sank. I had hoped for a day, at least, to practice, to look around. "Tomorrow?"

"Not to worry. Maestro will visit you tonight. He will bring you the music, and he said to tell you how sorry he is that he could not come personally to meet you, but he had pressing matters. So, I suppose you will want to be on your way."

On my way back to America, that's what I wanted. But I smiled and said a polite, "Yes."

"You will adore Cracow. You see, Warsaw is the New York City of Poland. But Cracow is its Boston, its brain. You will be happy. And we are really so pleased you have agreed to help out, so creatively. It is so important right now, creativity."

"It is?"

"Of course, my dear. You create goodwill. Goodwill creates public relations. PR creates investments. Investments create prosperity. I was not in America for my health!" Luke laughed, then handed me his card. "Now feel free to call me if you need anything. . . ."

He offered me the use of his twentieth-century toilet, telling me I would be wise to take tissues with me everywhere, since Polish toilet tissue could double for sandpaper.

Then he sent me back out into the now sunny day, waving a jovial goodbye as my chariot putt-putted away into meatless, airless, cranial Cracow.

"Vistula!" the driver told me, pointing to the river we were now crossing to enter the city. Water undulated beneath us in the pearly light. Barges glided by, and on the opposite bank, high on top of a fortified hill, stood an impressive complex of Gothic buildings—"Wawel Castle!" I was told. The driver turned his wheel sharply to avoid a trolley car that whizzed toward us. Streets narrowed as we circled inward toward the center of the old city. Alleyways afforded glimpses of spacious courtyards. Rows of elegant buildings in muted pastels summoned visions of a grand era when commerce and culture must have flourished. Now omnipresent scaffolding hinted of decay, and people in drab overcoats hastened in and out of doorways in the dimming shadows. But as we pulled into a cobblestoned square, streetlamps lit up, as if on cue, announcing our arrival. I looked at Number 10 Floriańska, with its pale pink facade, and my spirits brightened.

One of my keys opened the heavy wooden front door, leading me and the driver, who was grumpily carrying my bags, into a large entrance hall with high arches and a floor made from squares of rough wood. Behind a stained-glass enclosure, a concierge wearing many layers of scarves and gloves looked up, disinterested.

"Millbank," I said, as assertively as I could. And without blinking, he waved us through, into an inner courtyard, where glass lanterns illuminated four floors, each with wraparound balconies bounded by wrought iron balustrades. Oak stairs twined around and up to each floor, and, seeing three doors per floor, I calculated twelve apartments. That would mean plenty of neighbors, some friendly, I hoped. But the courtyard was eerily silent, and there were no signs of life, no children laughing, no dogs barking. I followed the driver up one flight, where he nodded toward a door marked Millbank. My second key opened that door, and before I could say thanks, or offer even one dollar, the driver had plunked my bags down behind me and disappeared, his footsteps beating heavily on the stairs.

Alone and chilled, I cautiously entered the dimly lit hallway of the apartment that would be home for some time. Off to the left was a kitchen, with a two-burner stove, a small refrigerator, a sink, and an empty cupboard. A large square room opened out to the right, and once I found a lamp, and turned it on, I saw that the room was sparsely furnished, with a table and chairs, its walls lined with shelves stacked with leather-bound books, and its wooden floors polished to a chestnut luster. Heavy drapes opened to reveal large windows that looked out onto a darkened side street. An archway in that room led to a smaller rectangular chamber with a massive mahogany wardrobe and a sofa that, with some pushing and prodding, turned into a bed of sorts. A sudden creaking sound made me jump. I held my breath. But silence reigned, and as the cold, clammy air in the apartment began to seep through my coat, a sense of gloom and an urgent need to urinate converged, sending me scurrying to find the antediluvian toilet.

At least it flushed, and there was a sink, a medicine cabinet filled with empty brown bottles, and a bathtub balancing on four iron lion's paws. I concluded that a box on the wall was a water heater, but when I turned the knob, nothing but the smell of gas came out, and I knew I would have to find a match, or face an ice-cold bath.

Fumbling through the kitchen drawers, I found an assortment of grotty utensils, a pot or two, but no match. Do something, I told myself. Or you will die. American Flutist Found Frozen in Cracow. How would that be for publicity? Not funny. I did not laugh. And it was important to laugh in Poland.

With a sudden idea for salvation, and my last ounce of energy, I forced myself to my feet. I scuttled out of the apartment, back down the stairs and through the courtyard to the stained-glass cage.

"Cold!" I tried, and shook, to show the concierge what I meant. He looked at me, expressionless.

"Brrr!" I shivered more violently, but he was unmoved. Then I reached into my coat pocket to find the ten-dollar bill that had been rejected by the giant at the Warsaw airport. The concierge's face crinkled up into a smile. He nodded excitedly, pocketed the money, and, limping ahead of me, he climbed the stairs to Professor Millbank's apartment where, babbling away in Polish, he showed me how to regulate the heat in the apartment, how to use the stove, where the sheets and blankets were kept, and where matches for the water heater were hidden. Then he disappeared for a few minutes, and came back carrying a steaming bowl of broth and dumplings, a loaf of bread, and a bottle of wine.

"*Dziękuję*," I tried. "Thank you!"

"*Proszę*, proszę," he said, the all-purpose word that seemed to mean both "you're welcome," and "please." We smiled uneasily at each other.

"Nora," I said, pointing at myself as introduction.

"Waclav," he said and, bowing, backed out of the apartment, leaving me to a supper of soup and silence.

❦ 55 ❧

FRESHLY BATHED AND IN MY FLANNEL BATHROBE, PREPARING to flop into my fold-out bed, I heard a buzzing noise and walked into the living room to investigate. "Yes?" I asked through the closed door, tightening the belt on my robe.

"Nora? Here is Marek," he announced.

I opened the door, and in a big wool coat, with a long

scarf wrapped around his neck, his cheeks flushed, and his eyes twinkling, the maestro looked like trouble.

"But you are feeling so tired, I can see!" he boomed, kissing my hand in that formal detached European manner before presenting me with a big bouquet of flowers and a box of chocolates. His eyes danced all over me, making me nervous. But casual kisses on both cheeks reassured me, and when he came in to look around, his presence and avuncular pronouncements made me relax. "But, my dear child, this is wonderful, this Millbank mansion!"

"It's very nice."

"It is completely splendid, with space and quiet! Do you know now we have in this country a wait list of more than twenty years, for young couples wanting apartments?"

I did not know. And I felt piggish not to have realized what a palace I had been given and what a privilege it was.

"Yes. Young people marry and then must live with Mama and Papa and have their babies. Can you know what a cacophonia this is, all in one little apartment?"

"I can only imagine."

"But here you are having much room and private and the ability for playing your instrument, with no restrictment. And you have below, on the street, every shop for food and eating. I have here for you an advancement of zlotys for your purchasing." He took a large manila envelope from under his arm, and gave it to me. "And with it you have Haydn and Mozart. Music and money. A nice combination, yes?"

"Yes," I said, sliding the zlotys and the music out of the envelope, placing the money on the table, then looking at the flute parts for Haydn's "Le Poulet" and Mozart's "Prague" symphonies. Flipping through the pages, seeing all those delicious passages, I wanted to take my flute out on the spot and try them. Excitement and gratitude made me offer Marek a glass of the concierge's wine.

He declined. "We will drink together, my sweet. But not tonight. You are sleeping now. Tomorrow morning you will pass please to the Philharmonie, which is walking distance from your apartment, just across the market square."

He handed me a map from his pocket, and pointed to an X. "Come to our office, for the introductory to our administrative at nine, and then you will have your first rehearsal with the Cracow Chamber Players. Will you be ready?"

Nine A.M. here would be 3:00 A.M. for me. I had not played the flute in a day and a half. Would I remember how? "Of course I will be ready," I bravely promised.

Marek left me to sleep, but anxiety was battling fatigue and I padded nervously around the little apartment, unpacking, hanging my carefully chosen Eleanor Outfits in the wardrobe, finding a plug for the dual-voltage blow-drier Stephanie had insisted I take, arranging my things, popping chocolates into my mouth. I placed the picture of Nicky and me on the living room table. Then I picked the prettiest rose from Marek's bouquet—a bright pink one—for Nicky's blue vase. I had packed it carefully, in newspaper, and as I unwrapped it, I glanced at page thirty-three from *The New York Times* of February 11. "Sale of the Century!" was bannered across the full-page advertisement. A willowy model, draped in rags, gazed up from the page, bereft. "Life breezes by and you may miss it!" said the breathless copy below. I dropped the newspaper and, grabbing the heart-shaped photo of Nicky and me, I pressed it tightly to my aching chest. Then I crawled into the fold-out bed, curled up, and cried myself to sleep.

I woke to the alarm, bathed in sweat. Kicking off the down comforter that buried me, I stumbled like a zombie toward the bathroom, pausing to glance at the living-room table. Dingy green light flowed through a chink in the closed curtains, splashing onto Nicky's vase. The rose was opening, turning its radiant pink face toward the windows, blooming, even on this brackish morning.

Outside, the smog was so thick I could barely see where I was going, and the air smelled putrid, metallic. Luke was not kidding, I thought, as I groped my way across cobblestones, pulling my coat collar up and the brim of my hat down. My eyes burned, and a tickle in my throat made me cough. Have I come to Cracow to suffocate? I wondered, but then a shop window filled with breakfast cakes powdered with sugar made my stomach growl, and I entered. Bells above the door tinkled. A woman with wide cheeks and wet brown eyes looked at me expectantly. I pointed to a cake on her counter.

"I'm sorry, I don't speak Polish," I said and smiled, hoping to charm her, but she grumbled, held up some fingers, and when I did not understand, she tsk-tsked, then wrote down the sum on a scrap of paper, glowering as I wrestled to pull my Polish money from my canvas bag. She yanked some bills out of my hand, tossing me a bit of silver change and I backed out of her shop, vowing never to set foot in it again.

As I wandered down the street, eating my cake, heading in what I hoped was the right direction, the smog seemed to be lifting, leaving a green residue like algae in the air. Church bells rang. I munched the sweet, doughy confection and stopped in my tracks as the hoped-for square spread out before me, like a sunken treasure in the watery light. A vast cobbled expanse was bounded on all sides by pretty pastel buildings. Standing like a palace in the center of the square was a splendid Renaissance structure, surrounded by vendors selling flowers, pretzels, peacock feathers, paintings, and handicrafts. Pedestrians in moonboots clomped past, bundled in bulky coats and jackets, looking tired but purposeful. Pigeons strutted, pecking at crumbs and crusts, and a young man with scraggly hair was playing a guitar, singing plaintively. A church with two spires of unequal height stood off in one corner of the square. The map Marek had provided told me it was called St. Mary's. I finished my cake, dropped some coins into the guitarist's open case, and followed the faithful into the church. Falling to their knees just inside the front door, men, women, and children crossed themselves, closing their eyes in an ardent display of religious devotion. I heard a hissing sound, and realized it was the shush-shush of Polish words being whispered in avid prayer. Carved wooden saints hovered over the altar, their faces smiling, their wooden robes seeming to flow. I smelled incense, and listened to the murmuring of the devout. Was it an urge to fall to my knees that made them buckle? I took a seat in a pew. What did these people pray for? Forgiveness? And who would grant it? Expiation comes to those who believe. If I could believe, could I be forgiven? Would my son then be restored to me? I closed my eyes and tried to pray, but no words came to mind, no divine inspiration bolted into my brain. The sweet smell of incense began to sicken me, and the murmuring swelled to a hiss. I stood up and hurried out of the church, making a flock of pigeons take flight. Strollers stared at me, so I slowed down, checked the map, then getting my bearings and my breath, I marched in a diagonal across the square toward the Philharmonie and the offices of the Cracow Chamber Players.

✵ 56 ✵

IN THE LONG MARBLE HALLWAY OF THE PHILHARMONIE'S foyer, a woman wearing the omnipresent kerchief, flowered skirt, ankle socks with plastic sandals, and sweater with a vest over it, was on her knees, mopping the floor, dipping a filthy rag into gray water and squeezing it with her bare, reddened hands. She looked up as I walked past, heading for the grand marble staircase that would lead me, so the sign said, to the orchestra offices.

. . .

. . .

"Pani Pawlick, and Pani Michnik," Marek said enthusiastically, "meet Pani Watterman."

I shook hands with two women who got up from behind their paper-strewn desks to greet me.

"*Pani*—does that mean 'Mrs.'?" I asked the maestro, who clapped his hands and said, "Flute players. They are so clever!"

The small office was dimly lit, smoky, and hot, a combination that conspired to make me feel sleepy and nauseated.

"Now we have some official documentation to complete," Marek told me, and the pair of Panis passed me various papers—receipts, in triplicate, for money advanced, money to be advanced, receipts for music taken, music to be taken, receipts for the receipts, etc., etc.

"We have a computer, from America," Marek bragged, pointing to an IBM sitting on top of a file cabinet in a corner. "But we have not yet the capability of using it."

"Soon we will," Pani Michnik explained, then blushed. "My English is very much improper."

"It's excellent," I disagreed, smiling at these two women, who seemed so kind, so eager to make me at ease.

Pani Pawlick lit a cigarette, closing one eye, the other inspecting me. "You are from New York City?" she asked.

"I was born and raised there."

"With all the Jewish people?"

"Well, I am Jewish. But there are many other ethnic types in New York, and . . ." I stopped mid-sentence, realizing that her question had been hardly innocent, that instead, it signaled a sentiment I had never in my entire assimilated American life experienced. Her cold eyes gleamed at me. Her head tilted arrogantly. I wanted to lean across her polluted desk and push her face in.

"So, come!" Merek intervened, clapping his hands. "I will take you to our hall."

"But she's an anti-Semite!" I whispered to Marek, as he led the way.

"Pani Pawlick? Why do you say so?"

He looked at me, surprised. This is the man, I remembered, who had told my father he played with Jewish children before they "went away." Was he naive? Or was I?

Painted pale yellow, with white wedding-cake trim, the hall was a baroque beauty. Players were already onstage, warming up, and the sounds resonated as we stood at the back, listening.

"Good acoustic. I show you." Marek clapped his hands, making players stop and turn their heads. He yelled at them in Polish, and taking my arm, pulled me with him toward the stage.

"You are welcome," said the bassoonist, a stout man with bushy eyebrows. "I am Janusz." His eyebrows wiggled like caterpillars. Then he guided me to my chair, bowed to me as I sat down beside the oboes. The first oboist, a woman, glared at me, and without a smile, identified herself. "Zofia."

"Nora."

"La," she announced, and, cheeks puffing, eyes blinking, she played her "A" for me even before I had pieced my flute together. Janusz leaned forward in his chair to tell me, "I can help with language. If you have any need, only to ask, yes?"

"Thank you," I said, then tuned to Zofia's "A" and nervously tried to warm up. Players wandered onto the stage, looking very tired. They took their seats, and acknowledged my presence with a nod or a polite smile. No one came over to say hello. I assumed they were shy, or simply showing consideration, allowing a colleague to warm up uninterrupted.

"Danila," a sultry voice to my left said. The second flutist had arrived. Hand extended, she shook mine, hard. A young woman in her twenties, Danila had pasty skin and dull eyes, hair that was bleached to death and teased to perdition. Her polyester blouse ponged with many days' perspiration and her short leather skirt hiked up to her thighs as she sat beside me. I could tell from her forced smile that she was less than delighted by my presence.

"I'm really looking forward to working with you," I said, hoping that appearances were deceiving.

"No English," she said and, raising her fragrant arms, she blew into her flute, making a big but ugly sound.

Marek began the rehearsal by asking me to stand. He introduced me to the orchestra, and I waved and said, "*Dzień dobry!*" There was applause at my attempted Polish. A few players even smiled at me. My spirits lifted, and when Marek raised his baton, I was ready.

If my heart beat fast at the syncopations of the first movement allegro of Mozart's "Prague" Symphony, it beat even faster at my first entrance with Danila, who was flat and whose articulations did not match mine. I expected her to adjust her pitch, and when she did not, I thought that Marek would stop the rehearsal and say something. But he did not even seem to hear the discrepancy, not even when we played supposedly in unison later in the movement or entered together so out of tune in the andante that I cringed. We piped painfully through the final presto. But when Mozart's burning passions blended with the lighthearted gaiety of the music, I forgot all about Danila and concentrated on the lacerating rhythms that spoke to me of a deeper struggle, that mingled joy with sorrow, that took me, for a brief moment, far from all dissonance.

At the break, everyone scattered. Danila disappeared before I could attempt to talk with her. I wandered around the halls and found a stuffy little café upstairs. I seemed to be the only customer, but I bought myself a coffee and sat sipping it alone at a table, wondering where the others went for refreshments.

"There you are!" Marek entered the café and rushed toward me. "You are a great success! They love you!"

"Really?"

"Yes. Really!"

If his smile was a tad too affectionate, I attributed it to gratitude. After all, I was helping him out. And he, too, was helping me out at a difficult time. "I'm happy to be here," I gushed, "but a bit worried."

"About?" He snapped his fingers at the waiter, and as he sat beside me at the table, a coffee was placed before him.

"I'm having an intonation problem with the second flute."

"Adjustment," Marek said, dismissing my concern with a wave of his hand. "In a few rehearsals, you will be perfect together. You must not be worried. You must not be wrinkled, here." He touched my forehead a little too tenderly.

"Where is everyone?" I asked, pulling away. "Don't they have coffee at the break?"

"They can't afford it."

"They can't?"

"Inflation." He drained his cup. "The times are bad. Very bad. But we are better off than the Romanians!" He laughed and leaned his hand on my arm. "Do you know why there is no minuet in the 'Prague' Symphony of Mozart?"

Not a joke, I wanted to say. Please, no. But I smiled and asked, "Why?"

"Because the Czechs can't dance!" Marek slapped his knees, doubled over with laughter.

I wanted to cry. Had I come to Cracow for stupid ethnic jokes that I couldn't even understand? But I faked a giggle and said I really had to get back to the stage to look at the Haydn.

The ensuing run-through of "Le Poulet" was a mess. Marek waved away like a windmill, letting sloppy entrances and ragged passages fly by. Occasionally he would stop and scream in Polish at players who, to my ears, had sounded just fine. By the end of the rehearsal, the musicians were exhausted and disgruntled, and they packed up their instruments, fleeing the hall as fast as mice.

"Everyone has another job, to teach, or to play. We must work like the dog here, in order to eat," Janusz explained, when I asked him to help me speak to Danila. "Don't worry about her," he quickly counseled as he rushed off to his next commitment. "She is jealous. She wants to be number one. You know how it is. Forget about it. Go home. Relax. Have a nice day."

❧ 57 ❧

TO GO HOME AFTER REHEARSAL, I CROSSED THE MARKET square again and decided to have a peek inside the large Renaissance building at its center. Stalls with Polish handicrafts and trinkets were doing brisk business. Embroidered blouses, costumed dolls, strings of amber beads, carved wooden objects, felt slippers, sheepskin coats were all for sale at amazingly low prices—for those with hard currency. I was gazing up at a ceiling decorated with charming masks when I felt something tugging at my coat. I looked down to see an urchin of a boy, with a dirty face and large brown eyes. He held up a tattered piece of paper for me to read, but the primitive block letters were in Polish.

"I don't speak Polish," I told him, while shoppers turned to look, and he flipped the paper over and shoved it at me. More block letters in another language. "Or German."

He grunted and clung to me, and from the way we were being observed, I had the feeling this kid was a regular here at the stalls, a tiny con artist who preyed on the tourists. I was no sucker. But his grunts turned to pathetic cries, and he was so poorly dressed and so filthy, I felt sorry for him and reached into my canvas bag to give him some zlotys. I slipped him a ten-thousand-zloty note—equal then to some two dollars—and he gurgled, grabbed my hand and began kissing it. Revolted, I pulled my hand away, but he lurched at me, grabbing my coat sleeve, kissing it, falling to his knees, kissing the hem.

"Please!" I pleaded with the boy. "Get up! Go away! Go!" His supplications made me frantic. Silent eyes watched us, but no one intervened, until one stall owner, an old lady, tired of listening to this fuss, rushed at the boy, shouting at him, hitting him on the head.

"Don't!" I cried instinctively, as the woman roughed the boy up, and he raced off, bobbing and weaving through the crowd. "Amerikanka!" she shouted at me, then pointed in the direction the boy had run. "He gypsy child. Bad!" She waggled a finger in the air and angrily returned to her stall. People in the crowd glared at me, before going on with their business.

I could feel my cheeks burning. What was wrong with these people, all so gruff and unsympathetic? And what was wrong with me that I could be so repulsed by an unfortunate child? Confused and abashed, I rushed out of the building, into the square. It was well past noon, and I was hungry, but the idea of going to a café did not appeal to me. I decided to try my luck at purchasing some food at the shops near the apartment. I would cook for myself. I would eat by myself, away from the strangeness of strangers. I would have a nice day.

Plastic crates in one shop window were filled with an odd assortment of items—onions, lemons, dried lentils, small bruised apples, dried fruits, something that might be cereal, many jars of pickled foods, and plenty of cigarettes. Pushing aside a heavy curtain that was undoubtedly there to keep out the Cracow cold, I entered the shop. A long line of customers stood silently, waiting patiently to purchase what few things were left. Heads turned to stare at me as if I were intruding. Was it a store closed to foreigners? Or was it my stylish red coat and black hat that made them wary? I should never have borrowed it. Something in gray or sludge brown would have been more appropriate. But I defiantly took my place at the end of the line, and after fifteen minutes, it was my turn. I pointed at things that I wanted, and used my hands to show how much, and I uttered many all-purpose *"Prosz̨e,"* hoping to sound polite and confident. I could see the smirks on faces around me, but instead of evading eyes, I turned to stare back, smiling insistently. And when it came time to pay, I gestured for the amount to be written down for me, and once it was, I quickly counted out my money, accepted my change with many *"Prosz̨e,"* and sauntered out of the store, package in hand, feeling triumphant.

I would make a soup out of the lentils and onions, but now I needed mineral water and bread and milk, and where would I find all that? Don't be discouraged, I urged myself, and, seeing bread in the window where that morning I had found breakfast cakes, I entered the very shop to which I had earlier vowed never to return.

"Dzień dobry," I said to the sour-faced lady. *"Prosz̨e,"* and I pointed to the desired loaf of bread and paid with a flourish, smiling at my nemesis, whose stiff reserve I thought I saw bend just the slightest little bit.

I pointed at myself, then stuck out my hand. "Nora Watterman. I live near here. I will be a good customer." The shopkeeper looked at me blankly, then she broke into a big smile, squeezing my hand between her two so hard that I winced.

Outside again, confidence growing, I turned a corner, mineral water on my mind, when something pushed at me from behind, making me stumble. I grabbed onto a street-lamp with one hand, holding my packages with the other, when I saw the "gypsy boy" racing down the street, my canvas bag in his hand. I felt as if part of my body had been torn off. "My flute!" I screamed. I dropped my groceries and ran after him, shouting. But no one came to help, and after two blocks, I was out of breath, and he was out of sight. I was frantic and furious. In all my many years in New York City, I had never been mugged. Had I come to Cracow to get ripped off, and by a kid? He took my flute, the little bastard. My flute! "Come back here!" I screamed, and took off at top speed in the direction the boy had run.

❦ 58 ❦

CHASING THE TINY THIEF DOWN NARROW STREETS, I WAS about to give up, when I caught sight of his tailcoat turning a corner. I ran after him. Avenues were widening, the buildings seemed more dilapidated, and I was entering an even older part of the city, with Gothic archways and ancient churches. I skirted some scaffolding and demolition sites, and barreled into an open square, almost bumping into a young man with thick black hair, a brown sheepskin jacket, a leather tool bag slung over his shoulder.

"Excuse me," I panted. "Do you speak English?"

His eyes were two onyx ovals, and his mouth, with full lips, curved decidedly upward at the corners. He did not answer me.

"Forget it," I sighed and turned to walk away, winded.

"Hey!" the young man called. I turned back to meet his insouciant eyes. "Kiss me. I love you. Change money."

His outrageous banter took me so by surprise that I burst out laughing. He smiled back at me, arms crossed staunchly across his chest. "I make you laugh," he said. "This is good." His dark eyes drifted across my face, resting on my mouth, making me uneasy.

"It's important to laugh in Poland. Someone told me that."

"Someone told you right." His eyes flickered across my body and I felt myself blush as I asked, "How come you speak English?"

"You live in Pulaski Park for a year you pick it up."

"Chicago?"

"You got it."

"Why were you there?"

He smiled again. "Why are you here?"

"I asked you first." Crossing my arms in front of my chest, I stood my ground. I would not let this cheeky young man with a swarthy complexion intimidate me.

"My wife has relatives in Chicago."

"I see."

"Oh you do, do you?" His head was tilted, and his smile was broadening, his white teeth looking sharp, his stance feral. "Want to know what I see?"

"No," I said sternly. But he was not to be stopped.

"I'll tell you anyhow. I see a lady in a red coat who is looking for something."

"My bag!" I said, having momentarily forgotten. "I was mugged. Robbed. Near the marketplace, the big one, with the big palace thing in the middle?"

"Sukiennice."

"Whatever. Near there. By a little boy. He was begging for money in Suki . . . inside, and I gave him some. He must have followed me out into the street. He grabbed my bag and ran. . . ."

He hissed. "At the market, he holds up a piece of paper?"

"You've seen him there?"

He nodded knowingly, angrily. "Come." He took me by the elbow and led me to a beat-up old car parked at the curb. "We'll get it back."

"We will?"

"Just come."

"I don't want to impose. . . ." I objected, not out of politeness, but out of fear. Never go anywhere with strangers. Hadn't I been warned? But I was weak, my legs were wobbly. I was lost, and hungry, and weren't strangers supposed to be sometimes kind? Maybe this one will be, I

224

thought, as I slid with a resigned sigh onto the front seat and the car lumbered off down the cobbled streets.

✥ 59 ✥

I WAITED IN THE CAR, AS COMMANDED WHILE MY KNIGHT IN shining sheepskin ran into the jerry-built tenements that stretched with a stunning sameness as far as the eye could see. We were in Nowa Huta, the "new town" constructed at the command of the Russians in the heyday of their control. Besides ordering factories to be built right on the edge of Cracow that would belch smoke and filth into the beautiful old town, they raised these ricky-ticky cement boxes for the several hundred thousand factory workers who were squeezed into tiny apartments, with walls thin as cardboard. Ideologies might have changed recently, and freedoms been promised, but the long-faced, heavy-stepping Nowa Hutans I saw heading home did not exactly look liberated. Not at all.

"Here!" my knight announced, opening the car door, holding my bag in one hand, the little thief by the other. He spoke gruffly to the boy who tried to look at me, averted his eyes, and said, with some coaxing, "Sorry."

"That's okay," I told him, checking for my flute, my wallet, my passport, finding everything intact. "Thank you for giving it all back."

Sharp words were said to the boy, in a language that did not sound like Polish or any other I had ever heard, and when he was released, he raced, zigging and zagging like a jackrabbit into the tenements.

"How did you know where to find him?"

"A gypsy is a gypsy," was the cryptic reply.

"And what language were you speaking to him?"

"Romany."

"So you are . . .?"

"My grandfather, on my father's side was of Romany people. A real tzigane." He looked at me, defiant. "I am proud of it."

"Of course you're proud of it. Why shouldn't you be?"

"Because there are gypsies who steal and lie and make enemies everywhere." He reached in his pocket and pulled out the piece of paper with block letters that the little gypsy had pushed at me.

"What does it say?" I asked, as the paper was torn in half.

"It says, 'I am a deaf orphan and I cannot speak. Please help me.' "

"Is he really an orphan?"

"Of course not. And he hears just fine. And he speaks, too. Lies. Endless lies." He shook his head.

"He does need help, though, doesn't he?"

"We all need help. But even a child, especially a gypsy child, must know that without honor there is nothing."

My honorable champion's name was Mikolaj Branko. "Call me Miko. Everyone does," he told me as he guzzled a mug of beer and ordered another in the smoky café where we were sitting. I devoured a greasy treat called *zapiekanka*, a slice of bread baked with tomato sauce, cheese, and mushrooms—the Polish version of pizza. It slid into my stomach heavy as a torpedo, but still I gobbled.

"But you are starving," Miko noticed.

"And thirsty, and exhausted," I told him.

He watched me chew and swallow. "And very sexy."

I choked, and took a gulp of coffee. It tasted metallic.

"Excuse me for saying this," Miko apologized. "I am a man." He shrugged, his open hands gesturing. I could not help noting the grace of his fingers, or that dirt was embedded under his nails, or that his skin was rough, or that although he seemed older, he was probably less than thirty. Much less.

"I had no time to wash." he said, catching my glance. "I am a plumber. And an electrician. I fix things with my hands."

"That's great," I said, "to be able to fix things."

"What is great about it? Today, where I met you, I went to repair a sink. I need a simple quarter-round piece of copper for the job. But you cannot find this. Nowhere. There is not a piece of copper pipe left in all of Poland. There are leaks everywhere. Soon all our pipes will be broken but, to look on the bright side, there are no light bulbs either. So this is fine because without light no one will notice the leaks!" Miko guzzled his beer, lost in dank thoughts.

I wanted him to feel better. I wanted to cheer him up, comfort him, this young man with the graceful fingers. "Things will get better."

"Sure," he said, with no little sarcasm, "easy for an American tourist to say. Did you come to see the new Poland, with its freedom, equality, and fraternity?"

When I told him why I was in Cracow he was amazed. "A woman, by herself, comes here to work for zlotys. But you are crazy!"

I laughed. The return of my bag and a full stomach and a companion had cheered me considerably.

"It's good to laugh," he repeated, watching me eat. "Yes?"

"Yes." I wiped my mouth with a waxy napkin that merely rubbed the tomato sauce all over my chin.

"I help," he offered. His eyes looked deep into mine, as he took another waxy napkin and wiped my chin slowly, deliberately. "There," he announced. "You are good now."

"Thanks," I said, liking the turn of phrase, smiling at this young man with eyes that sparkled like coal, with hands that fixed things.

"I would like to see you play your flute," Miko said. "With that mouth. Those lips. I would like that."

I blushed. "You like music?"

"Very much. And art and poetry."

"Really?"

"You find this strange, a plumber who likes poetry?"

"It's not strange at all," I said, studying his suddenly vulnerable expression. "Do you write?"

"There are many things in life we would like to do, and cannot."

"You've tried?"

Miko deflected the question by signaling for the check.

"Let me pay," I said.

"No."

"Please?"

The waiter put the check on the table. I grabbed it, but Miko grabbed it back, catching my hand as well as the paper. His skin was warm, his hold firm.

"Okay. You win."

"Naturally," he grinned, and winking at me, he released his hand and slid it slowly down his hip into a pocket of his faded blue jeans.

On the way back to my apartment, Miko took me to a hard-currency store where I found some of the things I needed. There was no toothpaste or soap, but he suggested baking soda as a substitute for both.

"In Poland now you must use this for that, or that for this. And if you want meat, you must boil your shoe."

I laughed, but it was not amusing when, at the market, there was nothing left on the shelves but dried legumes and a slimy sprig of parsley.

"You must wake up at five on a Thursday," Miko told

me, and pointed out the square where the farmers came with fresh produce once a week. Then he dropped me off in front of my pink pastel building.

"How can I thank you?" I asked, as he looked up at me from the open window of the driver's seat.

A broad smile was his only reply.

"You've been so kind. Could I invite you and your wife out to dinner one night?"

"I don't think so."

"Oh," I said, disappointed. I had hoped for friends.

"She lives in Chicago." His eyes were sad.

"You're . . . separated?"

He shrugged. "We went to study. We finish, but she wanted to stay in America. I had no choice."

"You couldn't extend your visa?"

"I *wanted* to come back. I am crazy." He laughed, a short, harsh laugh. "And you?"

"I'm separated," I said, without hesitation.

"And children?"

I could not say, My son is dead. I simply could not say it. "I have one son," I said, easily. "One beautiful eighteen-year-old son. Nicky. Living in New York City, going to art school. . . ."

Miko studied my face. "You love him very much."

"He's everything to me."

"But you came to live in Poland, so far from him?"

"I'll only be here for a few months. Besides, he's an independent young man, living on his own."

Miko nodded. "I see."

Was my sudden discomfort due to the heaviness of my packages, or to the glassy darkness of Miko's eyes that stared at me, prodding, penetrating mine? "I'll go in now," I announced.

I expected Miko to offer to help me take my bundles upstairs. I expected to have to say, "I can manage, thanks anyhow." But instead, he shifted into reverse and said, "I hope you will enjoy your stay in my country. I wish you beautiful music."

As he backed away, I called after him, "Thank you! Thank you so much!" But his car had already turned the corner.

❧ 60 ❧

LATER, LEAVING A THICK LENTIL SOUP SIMMERING ON THE stove, I allowed myself a long hot bath, and it was only then that I felt the fatigue wash over me. I had been in Cracow only twenty-four hours—one very long day, a day of frustrations and disappointments, a day of robbery and rescue, a day of echoes—whispered prayers in St. Mary's Church, the fulsome sound of Mozart in the Philharmonie, the baritone of a stranger's voice yelling, "Kiss me. I love you. Change money!" I smiled at those remembered words, and soaping up, I thought about Miko Branko, who was part gypsy, part handyman, who spoke of honor, who wished me beautiful music. He liked poetry and art. Nicky was studying art. He would probably like Nicky. One day maybe I could introduce them, and . . . I submerged myself completely under water, head and all. You're losing it, I told myself. You're starting to believe your own fantasy. Get a grip on yourself! I came up for air, vowing never to pretend, to a stranger or to myself, ever again.

Looking into the ancient bathroom mirror, I examined my hair, now shoulder length and manageable, if I took the trouble to blow-dry it and tame my troublesome tresses. But I was too tired to fuss with it, and the curls that dried around my face were not too frizzy, I thought, and made me look young, even girlish. Would my father approve? I had promised to call him. I had not even looked for a phone in the apartment. Now, concerned that my father might be worried, I poked around, looking in bookshelves, in cupboards, along the walls for signs of a telephone. But there was no phone. And what if I got sick? How would I notify the orchestra? How would I get help? Then I realized that there was no television or radio in the apartment, either. If something happened or was about to happen—a calamity, a war, a killer storm—I would have no way of knowing. My neighbors would inform me, wouldn't they? But I did not hear any sounds coming from the other apartments. Were they unoccupied? Was I the only person in this entire building? The thought made me jumpy.

I ate my soup, and broke my bread, aware of creakings in the walls, cracklings in the flooring. As I was mopping up the last of the soup with a piece of bread, voices startled me—a man and a woman, the sounds of an argument. Were they above or below my apartment, or next door? I could not tell, and the yelling got louder. A plate smashed. Then there was silence. But at least there had been signs of life, I told myself, as I washed my dishes. I wondered who was angry at whom, and if the man and woman were now lying side by side in a fold-out bed, not speaking.

I wrote a quick note to my father before going to sleep:

"Hi, Pops!

I'm in Cracow. The trip was OK, and I'm just getting settled in a really nice apartment in the old town. There is no phone, but please don't worry about me. The city is glorious, and I know this will be a great experience. My first rehearsal with the orchestra went very well and everyone was very welcoming. Take care, and let me hear from you.

I love you,
Nora"

It was the sort of letter I used to send home from music camp, omitting all anxieties, not wanting to worry my dad. But wasn't this like music camp? I was roughing it in this Renaissance bunk, surrounded by strange noises. I smiled and, cuddling under my down blanket at Camp Cracow on the Vistula, far from home, I fell instantly asleep.

⚜ 61 ⚜

"COULD YOU TELL HER THAT I AM HAVING DIFFICULTY ADjusting to her pitch?" I asked Janusz during our rehearsal break the next day. I smiled at Danila, trying to be diplomatic, collegial. "And that our articulations do not seem to match."

Janusz turned red. "She say you play sharp and your staccato is too short."

"Perhaps we could compromise," I suggested. "Meet in the middle?"

Danila hissed through her teeth at Janusz's translation, looked at me, and walked off.

Janusz shrugged. "Forget about it. Have a nice day," he said and disappeared for the rest of the break.

After rehearsal, Marek passed by the woodwind section. "*Bravo, bravo, tutti!*" he told us and, turning to me, blew a kiss. "We will have a drink very soon. But these days I am so busy. Forgive me!" He rushed off the stage. Danila gave me a look before diving for the doors herself. Everyone packed up and took off, slipping by me in silence. No one stopped to ask me whether I needed anything or offered to show me around or invited me to their home. Surely they would warm up in time, I told myself. Surely they would become my friends. It was inevitable.

I walked briskly out of the Philharmonie to the market square, wary that the gypsy boy might attack again. But there was no sign of him. It was freezing, and vendors stood by their stalls, slapping their arms against their bodies to keep warm. People moved like robots in their moonboots across the square, leaning into the wind, jaws clamped.

I pulled my collar up and my hat down and braved the buffeting winds as I wended my way home.

❦ 62 ❦

FOR LUNCH, I HEATED UP THE LEFTOVER LENTIL SOUP. THEN I practiced. After practicing, I paced, trying to keep my perspective, trying to remember why I had left the sunny little home I shared with my father to come to ice-cold Cracow, where I had no friends, no family. There was, of course, Mr. Ciesclaw of Szeroka Street, whom I intended to visit sometime during my stay. What was I waiting for? Why didn't I go visit him today, right now? He would make tea, talk about my mother, make me feel at home. I pictured him, a man in his mid to late sixties, a bit older than my mother would be, with a ready smile despite his sufferings, a man who had seen everything and could tell me all about Elena Miklavska.

. . .

I handed the taxi driver a piece of paper with the address written on it. He turned to see his foreign customer, smiled, then reached into the glove compartment and pulled out a small yellow tin, offering it to me for five dollars. "The best Russian beluga." Just to please the driver, I bought the caviar and was treated in return to his life story, told in a mix of languages on the way to Szeroka Street: "My *frau* leave me for a Yugoslav and take the *bambini*. Life is war, *n'est-ce pas?*"

I made my peace with the driver when we arrived at Number 7 Szeroka Street and rang the bell, my pulse racing.

"Hello. Do you speak English?"

The old man in slippers and a tattered jacket who had answered the door shrugged.

"I'm looking for Stanislaw Ciesclaw."

"Ciesclaw?" repeated the old man.

The cold was penetrating, but I was determined to be understood. "I am looking for Stanislaw Ciesclaw. He lives here." The man shrugged again. A woman's voice called out from somewhere in the dark recesses behind him. He turned and yelled back, and I heard another door creak open and in a few moments, an old woman, wrapped in scarves and blankets peered out at me suspiciously. "Yes?" she asked, her voice hoarse.

"Do you speak English?" I asked, hopeful.

"Yes?"

"Stanislaw Ciesclaw? Do you know him?"

"Ciesclaw? Stanislaw?"

"Yes! Yes!" I nodded eagerly. "He lives here. Number Seven."

She raised one knobby hand and crossed herself. "Dead. Many years."

Frozen with cold and disbelief, I stared at her. "Did you know him?"

"Yes."

"Do you know if he has any family, or friends, or . . . ."

234

"He has nothing. Nothing here. You go. Go!" She made a clucking sound and shut the door, leaving me chattering with cold on the doorstep of a crumbling brick house in some godforsaken part of Cracow. I stumbled down the steps and back out onto the street, furious with myself for having let the taxi go. How stupid could I have been? And what did I expect to find here? Mr. Ciesclaw's letter was more than thirty years old. Things change in thirty years. People die. What a fool I was!

I kicked at a stone on the sidewalk and looked around. No human beings were on the street. The houses seemed abandoned. It would be dark soon, and I would have frostbite unless I moved, and moved fast. A cat skulked past me on the sidewalk, a skinny, pathetic creature. It stopped and looked over its shoulder at me, as if to say, Follow me. It was the first helpful gesture any living soul had made all day. I followed it.

At the end of the street, the cat stopped, and began mewing pathetically, rubbing itself against my legs. I remembered the tin of caviar and took it out of my pocket, lifted its handy metal tab, and left my feline friend with a fine gourmet meal. At least one of us would survive the night, I thought, as I turned the corner, looking for transportation. But it was a desolate area, and the only vehicle that passed was a bicycle, its rider oblivious to my shouts. I came to a square and, crossing to the other side, I found myself walking toward a wooden door with Hebrew letters above it. Was there a synagogue in Cracow, and had I found it? Sanctuary! I rushed to the door, but it was locked. I walked around to the side, where a flagstone path led me behind the building to a massive cemetery. The ground was muddy, but I walked among the tombstones checking names, wondering if Mr. Ciesclaw had been buried here. Intricate carvings and astonishingly ancient dates diverted my attention. There had been Jews in Cracow in the fifteenth century, perhaps my ancestors, perhaps my very own family! Hearing footsteps, I turned to see a woman in a floral skirt and kerchief coming toward me, a feisty expression on her face. I was trespassing. I was in trouble.

"Do you speak English?" I asked. "I'm just looking, only looking."

"I am welcoming visitors," she said, smiling, her cheeks lifted into two wrinkled pouches. "I know all the stones. Do you look for one in particular?"

She was friendly. Even helpful. I wanted to kiss her hands. "Mr. Ciesclaw, Mr. Stanislaw Ciesclaw?"

She looked at me oddly. "Why do you look for him here?"

I began to babble. "Because he knew my mother. In the camps. He knew her. And she died when I was little and I never got to know anything, so I came to Cracow to see him, and I went to his house and they said he is dead. Is he buried here?"

The woman seemed to be thinking. "No," she said. "I am afraid there is no Stanislaw Ciesclaw here."

"Thank you," I said, tears blurring my vision, "Thank you anyway," and I turned and ran out of the graveyard, out into the square, where a taxi was turning the corner, its light glowing like a small miracle.

❦ 63 ❦

MY DISAPPOINTMENT WAS DEEP AND PAINFUL. I WOULD NEVER know more about my mother. At least I tried, I told myself. And coming to Cracow had not been in vain. I had a job. I was helping a colleague. There was consolation in kindness. And there was consolation in the music.

We had two more rehearsals, both equally uninspiring and unnerving. The closer we came to concert time, the higher Marek's temper flared.

"Flutes!" he screamed in English. "Intonation, please!"

I tried to approach Danila again about our disparate pitches, but Janusz whispered to me, "When is the concert, Danila is getting nervous, excited, and the pitch will go up to meet with you."

"I hope you're right," I told him, and just to make certain her adrenaline would pump, I asked Janusz to tell her the deputy minister of culture of Cracow would be present at our concert, listening very attentively to the flute section.

Luke was present at that concert, and he brought with him some photographers who snapped pictures after the concert of me with Danila, me with the maestro, and me standing beside the deputy minister himself.

"This is for UPI. America. Poland. Everyone must see how happy you are here. Smile!"

And smile I did, since the concert had gone well. Everyone had risen to the occasion, including Danila and her pitch. Our "Poulet" was done to perfection. Our rendition of the "Prague" Symphony was lively and passionate, with dark clouds racing across the pastoral landscape at just the right moments. The audience demanded an encore, and we tossed off a Mendelssohn scherzo as if no one had a care in the world.

"Come and have dinner to celebrate!" Marek insisted. Madame Rudiakowski, a rhinoceros of a woman, trudged wearily along beside her husband. Luke took my arm and we marched across the market square to the oldest restaurant in town, where we had meat that might have been fresh five hundred years before. Brandy helped wash away the taste. If Marek leaned too close and touched my knee once or twice, I let it all pass. I was safe with the watchful Madame Rudiakowski across the table ready to charge. And

I had played my first concert in twenty years with an orchestra and played it well. I would let nothing spoil my celebration.

❧ 64 ❧

THE NEXT FEW WEEKS PASSED MORE EASILY. LASZLO WAS recovering slowly, I was told, and I knew my stay was temporary. I was patient with Danila, calm when accosted by the maestro, and confident at concert time. I lived like an ascetic and learned to like it. I discovered that it felt good to be cold and hungry and alone. In a strange way, it made me feel as if I were experiencing something my mother experienced, sharing it with her. I kept the heat turned low, and subsisted on bread and tea for breakfast. I skipped lunch. Then in my long and lonely afternoons *chez* Millbank I made myself read the only books I could find on his shelves in English—written by him, on medieval iconography. Not one sentence made sense to me, but I would plow through them, hour after hour, just for the discipline of it. Then there was practicing, and the daily ceremonial changing of the flower in Nicky's vase, which included a moment of silence, and a summoning of images— Nicky at school, Nicky on his bike, Nicky with Prince Hal, Nicky laughing. I could see him very clearly. I could almost feel his presence. Then I would kiss his photograph, and prepare a modest evening meal for myself. I would scrounge around the stores in my neighborhood for ingredients, and it was not until I noticed that my gums were bleeding and that I looked more pale than usual, that I realized I needed some fresh fruits and vegetables or I would get sick. And if I got sick, I would just be a burden again.

The smog was thick, green, and icy at five-thirty in the morning, as I attempted to find the square that Miko had pointed out to me. I held a scarf to my face in an attempt to keep warm as I wandered in the murky light, looking for signs of that mythical market where farmers supposedly brought fresh produce. A distant hiss seemed to grow louder, and I recognized the sibilants of Polish, now crescendoing, and through the mist I could make out the stalls and stands just up ahead, filled with fruits and eggs and plants and vegetables. It was not yet 6:00 A.M., but the market was crowded, people were bartering, money was clinking into tin cups, and I stood on line, first for oranges, then for bananas, placing them all in the string bag I had purchased for my shopping. The ruddy faces of peasant women, with flowered babushkas tied under their thick chins, were animated. Voices were lowered, but the occasional peal of laughter rang through the air. I added a dozen eggs, speckled and fresh, to my bag, then wended my way up and down the rows of stalls, looking for any fresh vegetables besides onions. Broccoli! I saw the green stalks on a table in the distance, and tried to elbow my way through the crowd in order to join the buyers' line.

"*Proszę!*" a man said, just behind me, jostling me.

Proszę yourself, I was about to say, and shove him back, when I turned to see the smiling face of Miko Branko.

"Hi," I said, feeling myself blush as he took my arm and pulled me out of the crowd.

"You are shopping like a proper Pani," Miko observed.

"I am a proper Pani." I could not stop smiling.

"Will the very proper Pani give me the pleasure of a cup of coffee?"

239

I hesitated. Pleasure? I had not planned on any. But I certainly owed this helpful young man the courtesy of a quick coffee.

❧ 65 ☙

MIKO HELPED ME TAKE MY COAT OFF, HIS BIG WARM HANDS touching my arms, his eyes surveying the long skirt and baggy sweater that I had thrown on for my early-morning marketing.

"With that hair, those eyes, that clothing—you look like you just stepped off the caravan."

I laughed. "Maybe I have some gypsy blood."

"Hot gypsy blood," he whispered, making my legs feel weak. We followed a waiter into the cavelike coffeehouse that had just opened for business.

"How is your work going?" I asked, just to keep the conversation on track.

Miko seemed amused. "Good. And your work?"

I warmed my hands on the mug of hot coffee that had been placed before me. "Difficult."

"Why?" He lit a cigarette, and took a deep puff.

"Orchestra politics."

"Politics, politics." He exhaled, head tilted back as he blew perfect rings of smoke into the stale air. "You must try to keep away from politics."

"Do you?"

"Me?" He took another long, thoughtful drag. "Men come and go. Their promises and their lies do not excite me."

"But what about all this freedom, all these extraordinary changes in your country?"

Miko shrugged. "If freedom means that I can pay my bills, then I am for freedom." He puffed on his cigarette. "Frankly, it all makes me nervous."

"Why's that?"

"No more excuses, that's why. We can no longer blame 'the system' for holding us back. The individual can express what is in his heart. A writer can write freely." He took another deep drag of smoke. "But he must have something to say."

"I take it you would like to write."

He exhaled, and smiled ruefully. "You have much—how do you call it—intuition."

"I'm a woman."

"You certainly are," he said softly, provocatively. I did not want to be provoked.

"And you're an angry young man, with lots to say. You would be a good writer."

Miko sucked on his cigarette again. "I'm not so angry, or so young."

His gaze made me uncomfortable. "You shouldn't smoke," I chided, to remind him I was older, much older, and unsuited to such scrutiny.

"Why not? We are dying anyhow, every day a little bit."

"Why do you want to speed up the process?"

"Who's speeding?" Miko asked, taking a long, slow drag to illustrate, then slowly exhaling, his lips pushed forward in a pout. Then he stubbed the cigarette out half finished and smiled at me. "But, since you wish. I quit." He brushed his palms together. "From now on, I do not smoke. I eat only oats, and I am healthy as a horse. How do you like me?" He whinnied, shaking his head, making me laugh, then laughing with me.

241

"So," he said finally. "Work is hard. Life is sorrow. But hope is an eternal spring."

I giggled, until I saw that he was not joking, that his mood had darkened. "What do you hope for?" I asked.

He shrugged. "For more freedom. For more justice. For an end to misery."

I nodded. "These are good things to hope for. I admire you for them."

"Hopes are not to admire. Only the way we live our lives is to admire."

I looked directly into his dark, fathomless eyes. "Is your life admirable?"

Miko picked up his pack of cigarettes, crinkling the cellophane. "I have tried my best. I can say this."

Could I? What had I done in my life that was admirable? Raised a son only to lose him. Devoted myself to a marriage only to destroy it. Life *is* sorrow. And as for hope, it died in me when my son died.

"And you," Miko was asking, as if reading my mind. "What do you hope for?"

I have no hope, I was about to say, but I did not want pity or platitudes, not from this brash young man. And, despite my resolve to stop pretending, I did not want to tell Miko the truth about Nicky. "That my son finds the happiness he deserves," I said.

"This is a beautiful hope also." Miko raised his mug to clink with mine. Our eyes met, and I looked away quickly, unnerved as I was by the sharp sensation I felt, somewhere in the very center of my body, as if something hibernating deep inside had suddenly rolled over and growled. "I must practice before rehearsal," I announced firmly, quieting the rumblings.

"Then you will. I'll drive you to where you stay."

"Do you have time? I mean, don't you have to get to work, too?"

"I work when I want."

"You're not with a company?"

Miko smiled mysteriously. "Haven't you heard? Times

242

have changed. Private enterprise has come to Poland. I am private."

I nodded, as if I understood, as if I could possibly understand this young man who had the hands of a plumber, but the eyes of a poet, whose manner was rough, but whose words were thoughtful. And what did he want with me? Or I with him, for that matter? And why did his hand touching my arm as he helped me on with my coat cause me to tremble?

"It's only seven now," he said. "You have until ten-thirty to practice."

I looked at him. "How do you know my rehearsal is at ten-thirty?"

He smiled, his teeth flashing white against his dark cheeks. "Because I have watched you walk there, every day, across the market square."

"You've been watching me?" I felt my cheeks burn. "Why?"

His eyes narrowed, and he leaned toward me, his black hair gleaming like the pelt of a panther. "To make certain that no one takes again from you something you do not wish to give."

Miko took me back to his car and drove me home, where he handed me my string bag and said, "When you squeeze the oranges, you must drink the juice before twenty minutes pass, or the vitamin will lose its power."

"I'll do that," I said.

"*Nazdrovia!*" he yelled as he drove off. "To your health!"

⚜ 66 ⚜

Waclav, the concierge, eyed my string bag as I walked past his post.

"*Dzień dobry.*" I smiled at him and gave him two oranges, at which he gurgled and rushed out from behind his glass cage to help me carry the rest of the groceries up to my apartment.

As I crossed the market square to rehearsal, I looked at every black-haired man in a sheepskin jacket, afraid that it might be Miko Branko. Or was I hoping it would be? But he was not in the square and I could not decide if I was relieved or disappointed. The sun was bright, the air was clearing, and the temperature felt warmer. Children jumped and played, chasing pigeons, their mothers watching with pleasure. I bought myself a pretzel from a vendor, and stopped to listen to the ten o'clock bugle call from the church, an hourly call that halted abruptly as a memorial to the sentry who, aeons before, was killed by an arrow in the throat as he trumpeted a warning to the countrymen of the imminent attack. Cracow, I was discovering, was full of legends, mysteries, and dreams.

That night, sleepless, I paced the living room. I heard voices. A woman laughed. A man moaned. I held my breath. Was that rhythmic creaking noise another sleepless pacer, or was it a bed being rocked by the writhings and intertwinings of two bodies? I crawled back into my lonely bed and thought of my trysts with Theo, the heedless embraces, the wanton excitement. Then I thought of our last encounter, just before my trip to Cracow, and my coldness, the discomfort of it all. Would I ever lie in someone's arms again and feel complete? Would I ever feel that wild abandon and the warmth after? I curled up, craving comfort, wanting to be loved.

The market square was empty and covered with freshly fallen snow. The sky was clear and bright sapphire blue. Sunlight danced across the snow, making it sparkle, and not one footprint marred its perfect surface. I stood at the edge of the square, wondering where all the people had gone, hesitating to take a step, not wanting to blemish the beauty of that vast white expanse. But in the distance, I heard a woman's voice singing so sweetly, so tenderly, that I could not help myself, and I began to walk across the snow, sending a wake of ice-diamonds into the air. As the voice grew louder, I walked more quickly, running now, slipping, but eager to find the source of the singing. I determined that the sound was coming from St. Mary's Church, but when I stood in front of the black iron doors, they would not open. I pushed and pushed, and finally, the doors parted, and the smell of incense filled my nostrils and there, sitting on a chair, on the distant altar of the church was the most ethereal woman, her golden hair flowing in the breeze. She reached her long arms out to me, and I walked toward her, down the long central aisle, between the wooden pews, and as I got closer, I recognized her. "Mommy?" I whispered.

"Nora!" She smiled, her lovely face lit by the glow of candles. Then she pointed at me. "The red coat! It is yours, finally! Show me!" And I began to twirl for her, making the skirt billow. Her laughter rang like little silver bells, echoing against the stone arches, echoing and echoing, and I twirled and twirled, until, dizzy and tired, I fell in a heap at her feet and my head was in her lap, and she was stroking my hair, and singing to me, "*Ai, lu lu, kolebka z marmuru. . . .*"

My alarm clock jarred me awake. I opened the drapes in the living room and was blinded by brilliant light. When my eyes could open to look out the window, I saw snow everywhere, blanketing the road, decorating the rooftops, draped across the streetlights, and garlanded along the scaffolding, the fluffiest, most glittering layer of milk-white new-fallen snow.

❦ 67 ❦

EVERYONE WAS IN A GOOD MOOD AT REHEARSAL THAT DAY. We played Schubert's Fourth Symphony, written when he was nineteen, with all the sweetness and soft complaint and urgency of its youthful creator. The streams of melody, flowing from winds to strings and back, were in tune and touching, and even Marek cracked a smile when the horns danced with grace and agility in the final movement. And, most surprising of all, Danila turned to me, as we sat side by side at the end of rehearsal, swabbing out our flutes, and said, "*Dobrze*, yes?"

"*Tak*," I told her, and, after many weeks of working together, we actually smiled at each other.

Children were throwing snowballs at each other in the market square. One hit my shoulder as I passed. I quickened my pace, but another caught me on the side of the head, harder. "Hey!" I yelled, and whirled around to shake a finger, only to find a young man in a sheepskin jacket grinning boyishly at me.

"Hay is for the horse, and here I am," Miko announced. "To take you to see the castle that is magic in the snow."

I smiled at him. "I don't know. . . ."

"What do you not know?" I had no answer except a shrug. He took my canvas bag from my shoulder, and I did not protest as he heaved it onto his own and offered me his arm.

We strolled through the arcaded courtyard of Wawel Castle, and gazed at the snow-covered city from the top of the cathedral tower and looked down at the Dragon's Den, as Miko told me the inevitable legend.

"There was fire coming from his mouth, and he ate virgins, and no one could stop him, until one shoemaker tricked him into eating a sheep that was poisoned with salt and sulfur," Miko said. "This made the dragon thirsty and so he went into the Vistula to drink, and he blew away into tiny thousands of pieces. Poof!" He threw his arms into the air, puffing his cheeks, making me laugh.

"So," I said, simmering down. "There's no dragon in Cracow anymore."

"And no virgins."

"Oh?"

"I don't like virgins anyhow. I like my women older, more experienced."

I looked away across the brick wall, out at the icy water, where a few hardy swans bobbed and floated. "My son is only a few years younger than you," I announced coolly.

"I will be thirty."

I looked at him, disbelieving.

"Someday," he said, smiling, undaunted.

"And someday you'll find the girl of your dreams."

Miko turned his back to the river, leaned his elbows on the wall, and said, "Maybe I already have."

I could not begin to consider the implications of that comment. I would not. I deflected it with, "My son thinks he's found the girl of his dreams." My son? To keep pretending he was alive was positively pathological. I knew it, but I could not let go of the imaginary thread that kept me connected to Nicky.

"And do you like her, your son's girlfriend?" Miko was asking.

Kelly. I had managed to keep her out of my thoughts. Now I wondered if she had forgotten Nicky already, if he had been replaced by another boy, easily, effortlessly. I hesitated. It was time to end the pretense. I knew it, yet I answered, "Not really. But *he* likes her. And that's what matters."

Miko leaned closer and I could feel his eyes tracing my profile. "You are a wonderful mother, I can tell."

"I have a special son. He makes it easy. He's so loving, and he's very considerate and caring and . . ." I turned to meet Miko's eyes.

"You are sad. Something about your son. I can tell."

I shrugged. "I miss him."

"Do you talk to your son?"

"Every night."

Miko looked surprised, and I must have blushed at my blunder because he touched my arm and said, "You are sensitive and easily upset. I can see that."

"Can you?" I asked, feeling my eyes fill with tears.

"I can tell many things about you," he said, as he touched my cheek with a bare hand that was gloveless yet strangely warm.

"How?" I asked, letting a tear spill, unashamed.

"I inherit this ability. My grandfather, they say, could see a person's past, present and future, just by looking into their eyes."

"He could tell fortunes?"

Miko nodded, brushing his lips gently against my cheek. I closed my eyes. I should have pulled away, but I liked the feel of his warm breath on my skin and when he whispered, in a hoarse and urgent voice, "You taste of salt, but I will devour you anyhow," dragon flames of fire ignited in my belly and it was I who flew into thousands of little pieces as his mouth covered mine and his strong young body pressed needily against me.

"Miko," I whispered, trying to collect myself, meaning to push him away, but drawing him closer, kissing him hungrily, clinging to him, until the cold stopped us both and he hugged me hard against his woolly lapel and said, "I think you must take me to your bed."

The thought both terrified and excited me. "I can't. We mustn't. . . ."

Miko stroked my hair. "The first night of a new snow, it will be very cold," he murmured soothingly. "I will keep you very warm, very, very warm."

✵ 68 ✵

ON THE WAY BACK TO MY APARTMENT, MIKO STOPPED AT shop after shop, looking for a bottle of wine, a bouquet of flowers, some bread and cheese. "We need supplies," he explained, kissing me. "You may not want to go out for a week."

"Aren't you awfully sure of yourself?" I teased, kissing him back.

"I have much energy," he whispered, nuzzling my neck like an eager colt, "and much need."

We went into stores together, standing on line after line, holding hands, touching, laughing like truants, searching for the "necessary supplies," as Miko called them. Customers stared at us. Was it shocking—an older woman with a younger man? Were we ridiculous together? Miko noted my concern. "Let them think what they want," he whispered. "Does it make a difference?"

"Of course not," I agreed, planting a large kiss on his

cheek to prove it to our observers as well as to myself.

"What's this for?" I asked as Miko stopped at one last store and picked up a large red scarf with flowers and black fringes and wrapped it around my neck.

"So you will remember the first time," he whispered, looking into the mirror with me, his head leaning on mine as he arranged the scarf.

"It matches," I told him, meaning scarf and coat, but he was studying our faces in the mirror. "Black hair, big eyes, hungry mouths . . ." He covered mine with a kiss, then paid for the scarf and, arm in arm, we walked out into the twilight, into the twinkling, snow-covered streets.

The dining-room table was laid out with bread, cheese, fruit, and wine. Miko and I stood looking at it, a sudden awkwardness between us. Nicky's vase stood at the center of the table, with a fresh rose in it.

"That was the first piece of pottery my son ever made," I said proudly.

"I see why you take it with you. It is wonderful."

"Isn't it?" I touched the vase, telling myself to stop there. "But of course, his work is much more advanced now." *Nora!* I warned myself.

"He works still with clay?"

"Yes," I decided, ignoring my own warnings, "And he sculpts."

Miko nodded and poured one glass of wine. He took a sip, then pressed his lips on mine and let the wine trickle slowly from his mouth into mine and it was hot and delicious and not one drop was spilled. There was another intoxicating kiss, and another and the awkwardness disappeared and we were kissing, and inching toward the bedroom. Miko deftly opened the sleep sofa and, eyeing the lamp, he disappeared and came back carrying my new scarf, the wine, and a chunk of bread. He covered the lampshade with the scarf, turning the light into a deep roseate glow and he sat me down on the edge of the bed, knelt down in front of me, ceremonially placing a piece of bread on one of my knees. I giggled nervously, but he looked at me with his dark, probing eyes and, putting his hands behind his back, picked the bread up from my knee with his mouth. I felt his lips nibbling against my skirt and the giggles ceased as he grasped the bread between his teeth, then raised his head and leaned toward me, for me to take a bite. As we gnawed toward each other our lips met and we chewed and kissed; then Miko reached for more wine, and we drank. Then he lowered his head onto my lap and slowly lifted my skirt, pressing his face into my thighs, his hands removing my panties, parting my legs, his tongue darting and flicking, and I fell back onto the bed, my legs thrown over his shoulders as tremors shook my body and I groaned and writhed at wave after shock wave of sensation. Then, wet-faced and uninhibited, Miko disrobed, standing before me, revealed, ready. His body was young and firm, his chest hairless, his skin the color of creamy caramel, his eyes vibrant. I worried that I would disappoint him, but as he removed the rest of my clothing slowly, piece by piece, he seemed pleased with his discoveries, whispering to me, now in Polish, now in Romany, now lying beside me, and I closed my eyes and held onto the mane of his black hair as he entered me, and carried me off and away, into a world where flesh and feeling merge, where time and place disappear, and life's sorrows are swept aside.

We took a hot bath together, toes touching, hands holding. Miko washed me, everywhere, soaping, kissing, splashing.

"Don't be such a baby," I told him, when it was my turn to scrub him and he flinched when I rubbed his right shoulder.

"It was broken," he explained. I apologized profusely, and he told me the story of how years before he had taken part in a pro-Solidarity demonstration and a policeman smashed him on the shoulder with the butt of a rifle and carted him off to prison where he was forced to remain, without medical treatment, for three months. "This is why I say you should stay away from politics."

"But don't you feel some satisfaction that your efforts caused all these changes?"

"My efforts? All I did was stand on a street corner."

"You took a risk by being there."

"I am no hero, Nora."

"You are to me." I kissed his sensitive shoulder gently, and he pulled me around for a kiss, his eyes glimmering. Then he began to massage my back and my neck, hard, making me groan.

"Who's the baby?" he taunted.

"Occupational hazard," I told him. "Flute players get stiff necks."

"I will unstiff you," he promised. I craned my neck to kiss him, saying, "You already have."

69

"YOU ARE LOOKING SO BEAUTIFUL, YOU ARE PLAYING SO BEAUTIFUL, that I must ask you to have some drink with me," Marek announced, at the intermission of our concert the next night.

"Thank you, maestro," I demurred, "but I am busy."

"Busy?" He was confounded.

"Yes," I told him, feeling radiant, confident, and eager for the concert to conclude so that I could rush out the stage door, into Miko's arms. "Perhaps another time."

Janusz had caught our exchange out of the corner of his eye. "Attention," he told me, his caterpillar eyebrows arching, "Madame Rudiakowski has gone to Prague for a cure. The cat needs another mouse!"

The second half of the concert went without incident, so I thought. We played a short piece by a contemporary Polish composer, a jagged, atonal, alienated piece, with plenty of forte high notes in the flutes, meant to sound dissonant. Danila and I outdid ourselves, and since there is only one flute in Mozart's Symphony Number 39 in E flat, intonation was no problem. I executed my ascending motif boldly against the descending notes of the violins in the introduction. I played lightly in the first allegro, tenderly in the andante, energetically in the minuet, and dashed through the final allegro with what seemed the proper wit and brilliance.

At the end of the concert, I packed my flute, threw on my coat, and was hurrying toward the door.

"You are in a race?" Marek asked, blocking my path. "Perhaps in the future you will save your rushing for *after* the concert only?"

Stunned by his comment, I asked, "Did I rush?"

"Only like a train, only like the Orient Express, only two hundred kilometers per hour!"

"I thought I was in time with the violins, I thought . . ."

"I thought! I thought! A simple apology will be correct and a pronouncement of intention of good tempo."

His bloodshot eyes did not intimidate me. "I will do my best in the future," I told him, and, excusing myself, I walked past him and out the door.

"But what is it?" Miko asked me as I rushed into his arms and he looked into my face.

"The conductor is an asshole!"

He buttoned my coat. "Tell me what he did."

"It's what he'd like to do."

He smiled. "You mean, he has a desire for his first flute?"

"He's just a snake!"

"There are many in the grass. You must be careful." Miko hissed, then buried his nose in my neck and playfully nibbled me.

"Don't," I protested, looking around nervously. We were standing on the curb, on a darkened side street near the Philharmonie. No one was around, yet I worried for some reason about being seen.

"But what are you afraid of?" Miko asked. "Or are you ashamed of me?" He backed away, waiting for an answer.

"Of course not! I . . . I don't know why I did that. You frightened me, with that talk about snakes."

"This is not the reason you jump from me, is it?"

His question was straightforward, without the judgment and reprimand to which I had become accustomed with Bernie's inquisitions. And then I knew, it was because of Bernie that I had backed away, because I remembered the running and the hiding and the pretending of my adulterous past and the punishment that followed.

"Tell why you jump from me," Miko insisted. "Please."

"I haven't been separated from my husband for very long. I guess I suddenly thought what we are doing was wrong. That I was being unfaithful."

Miko nodded and put his arms around me. "You were a good wife. I know this."

But he was wrong. I had lied to him about Nicky, and that falsification was already one too many. "I was not a good wife," I confessed, pulling back to look into his eyes. "That is why my marriage ended."

"No," Miko said, kissing my forehead. "That is not why."

"How do you know?"

"Because it is never about good and bad. It is always because the wife needs this. The husband needs that. They cannot meet in the middle anymore. They are like two people, standing on opposite sides of a lake, looking at each other. Both know to swim. But neither will step into the water."

I smiled at his metaphor. "Was it really so simple in your case?"

"Simple?" he asked, a sadness dimming his eyes. "What is simple about being stuck on your side of the lake, suffering, confused, unable to come closer?"

"I would like to come closer to you," I whispered, wanting him. "Right now."

Miko pressed my gloved fingers to his lips. "Then I think you must take me to your bed again," he said. As he opened the car door for me and I slid inside, I thought I saw, standing in the shadows at the corner of the street, Maestro Marek Rudiakowski, leaning against a brick wall, watching us, his beady eyes glowing in the dark.

❧ 70 ❧

I HAD NEVER BEEN SO WITHOUT RESERVE BEFORE, SO EAGER to please, so greedy for pleasure, so aware of the delectation of two bodies. Miko's delight was mine. His every move fascinated me, thrilled me. He was my jungle cat, wily, knowing just when to purr, when to pounce, when and where to touch, to taste, to tease. Professor Millbank's apartment was our wilderness, and we romped and played in it, now rolling around on the floor, now splashing in the bath, now chasing each other, playing games.

"You make me feel so free," I said, stretching my arms. "So young."

Miko rubbed against me. "You are free. And young."

"I'm much older than you think," I announced, expecting shock. "I'll be forty this year."

"December 19." He grinned at me. "I saw your passport. When I found your handbag the first day, remember?"

"You looked?"

"Is that bad of me?"

"No, just . . . surprising, that you knew all along, and it didn't bother you."

"Does it bother you, that I am twenty-four?"

I stared at him. I knew he was young. But *that* young? Seeing my worried face, he kissed me. "You thought I was older?"

"I didn't think about it."

He smiled. "You see?"

What did I see as this young man put his head in my lap, and I stroked his hair? I closed my eyes and saw a mother cradling a son. I saw Nicky. I saw myself. The image made me recoil.

"What is it?" Miko asked, looking up, feeling my body stiffen.

"I was just thinking of my son," I said. "And how I miss him."

"Then we will call him," Miko said, pushing back on his heels, standing up. "I will find you a phone. But now I go to fix the refrigerator of Pani Moskowitz, and you go play for The Snake."

"When will I see you?" I asked, suddenly worried that he, like Nicky, might walk out the door and never return. Miko took my hand, looked at my palm.

"This is the mirror of your destiny," he said saucily. "I see, in the mirror, a meeting at five o'clock in front of St. Mary's. Can you see it, too?"

I folded my arms, and tilted my head. "Maybe."

"Nora," he said softly, rolling the R.

"Yes?"

"Just saying your name." He winked, just as Nicky would, then disappeared out the door.

MAREK WAS PARTICULARLY MEAN TO ME AT REHEARSAL. IT
was a particularly cold day. And when Miko was particularly late, I found myself in front of St. Mary's
Church in a particularly poor mood. I could have gone
inside the church. But I was in no mood for genuflec-
tions and piety. I had decided to end my relationship with
this boy-man. He reminded me too much of my son. There
was something wrong with such a connection. It could go
no further. I would tell him it was over the minute he
arrived.

Finally, half an hour late, Miko rounded the corner at
top speed and swept me into his arms. "I'm sorry, it was
the traffic," he whispered, kissing me. "You will forgive
me? Please?"

A lock of jet black hair was dangling across his forehead.
His cheeks were red, his lips moist. He was a bright spot
on a grim landscape. To give up the light would mean to
live in a dank, gray world. "Of course I forgive you, silly!"
I said, taking his arm, and we went into a café for some
hot, metallic-tasting coffee and some *lody*, the one food the
Poles had plenty of—ice cream.

"Your rehearsal? It was okay?" Miko asked, licking his
spoon.

"It was okay."

Miko sighed and gazed at me. "Did I tell you when I
saw you on the stage the other night, I was very proud.
Me, Mikolaj Branko, I am with the premier flute of the
Cracow Chamber Players. And she plays like an angel. I
was very proud."

"You did not tell me. But thank you."

He took my hand and licked some ice cream from my
spoon, then kissed my wrist. "And are you not a little

ashamed to be with just an electrician, just a plumber? You, the artist with me, the—how do you call it—'blue-collar worker'?"

"Why would I be ashamed?"

Miko shrugged, a troubled expression crossing his face. "You should be with a poet, a man who can fix things with his head, not only with his hands."

"I admire and respect you, and I am in awe of what you can do with your hands." I took his hands in mine and kissed them. "I am with a poet."

❧ 72 ❧

"SURPRISE!" MIKO CALLED OUT, AS I ENTERED THE APARTment one day, and he handed me a telephone, just installed, by him.

"But I was told it was impossible. How did you . . .?"

"A friend. High up," he explained. "I have fixed his toilet many times for free. I flush for him. He flushes for me. So it is in my country!" Grinning, Miko pressed the receiver to my ear to let me listen to a crackling dial tone. "Call your son," he suggested.

I stood frozen. Tell the truth, I urged myself. Now is your chance.

"You are too excited. So I will ask the operator for you. What is Nicky's number?"

"He doesn't have a phone," I whispered, despite myself.

Miko looked at me oddly.

"He doesn't want one," I invented. "It interrupts his work, and he just finds it easier without one."

There was a strained silence. "But I would love to call my father. He's in Phoenix, Arizona, and . . ." I gave the number to Miko who placed the call for me, and, after a delay of several minutes, the operator called back. Miko diplomatically left the room just as my father said hello and I shouted, "Pops! Did I wake you up?" I chattered at my father excitedly, telling him about the orchestra, the apartment, the city, raving about it all, leaving out the part about the young man who was my lover and virtually living with me. I assured him I was being treated wonderfully, like a queen. Pops told me the news of the ladies and Doc, and said everyone was well. I promised to write.

"Well, I'm glad it's more pleasant for a Jew now in Cracow," my father commented. "You haven't had any problems have you?"

"Of course not. Don't worry. Please." And I gave him my phone number and he promised to call me very soon.

"You are sad," Miko noticed, when he came back into the room.

"No," I insisted, then revised the answer. "A little."

"It is hard to be away from family."

"It is."

He stood behind me, gently massaging my shoulders. "Are you happy with your telephone?"

"I was so surprised, I forgot to thank you!" I said, turning to give him a kiss. "I am very happy with it."

"And I am very happy with you," Miko said, folding me into his arms, into his always eager embrace.

IT WAS MARCH, AND THE SWANS HAD RETURNED IN GREAT
numbers. Gliding along the Vistula, they were a stately
escort to my afternoon stroll with Miko down the pathway
on the riverbank. There was a hint of spring in the air, and
Miko opened his coat, closed his eyes, basking in the sun.
Arm in arm, we lingered at the water's edge, comfortably
wordless. After a while, we headed up toward the market
square, wandering aimlessly, amiably.

"Here is a store that can send to the States," Miko said,
pulling me into a shop filled with painted wooden boxes,
embroidered cloths, and other handcrafts. "Perhaps you
would like to send something to your son. Some bowl to
keep his clay, like this." He pointed to a large, carved one,
ornamented with colorful designs.

"He keeps his clay on a table, covered with plastic," I
resisted, but seeing that suspicious look on Miko's face, I
added, "but I know he would like this bowl."

Miko talked to the saleswoman, who smiled and nodded,
and when they asked me for Nicky's address, my heart
seemed to flop around in my chest. I gave them my address,
or rather, Bernie's address, saying that it would be safer to
send it to a house in the suburbs than to an apartment in
New York. While they were busy organizing the shipping
papers, I browsed around the shop.

Small carved birds caught my eye, and then on the shelf
above them, in a corner, was an object that drew me like
a magnet. It was a little wooden figure, a man, fixed by
two small springs to a square, so that when you touched
him, he bobbed back and forth. His face was a caricature,
with a big, bulbous nose, his puffed lips turned up in a
hideous grin. His large black hat had two sidecurls that
jiggled when he bobbed on his springs, and under one of
his arms he carried a book, with some kind of writing on
it. Hebrew? I blinked. Surely I was not seeing this cor-

rectly. But I picked the object up and held it in my hand, and it was indeed what I thought it was—a grotesque little Jewish man holding a prayerbook, davening on his springs.

"Is this a joke?" I asked the saleslady. Miko looked at me, touching my arm, but I avoided his eyes and pulled away.

"It is folkloric," she said.

Disbelief made me splutter, "But it is a Jew. A Jew made to look like a clown!" The saleslady seemed surprised by my agitation.

"Nora," Miko said, putting an arm around me. "Leave it."

"I can't leave it. It's horrible." I stared at the little Jew doll that davened in the palm of my hand. "This is racist," I insisted, holding it up in front of the saleslady's nose. "Why do you sell it?"

"It is folklore," she repeated, smiling insidiously. "It is from the happy time in Poland, when the Jews sang and danced and wore funny hats."

I was shaking, in a rage I did not begin to understand. "How much are they?" I asked, and when she told me, I asked her to cancel the wooden bowl, and instead I bought all the Jew dolls in the store, every one that she had on the shelves and in the stockroom—five dozen—and I marched out into the streets, sixty tiny Jew dolls bobbing crazily in a box before my very eyes.

"Nora?" Miko asked, walking beside me, trying to make me stop, but I was storming toward the corner and a wastebasket where I deposited these insults.

"I think you do not understand," Miko was saying.

"I think *you* do not understand," I whispered, shaking. "Millions of Jews died, and here in Poland, where most of them were murdered, they still make little Jew dolls with hideous faces. And they have the nerve to call it folklore!"

"Nora, the Jews are coming back to Poland."

I stared at him. "Who says?"

"They are. The Philharmonic of Israel has played here. Jews come to visit. To live. They are filling the Ramu synagogue, here in Cracow."

"The little synagogue, with the big cemetery?"

"You have seen it?"

"I have. There's a reason that the synagogue is tiny and the cemetery is big. Poland is just a graveyard for Jews."

"You are wrong. It is changing. The doll is not meant to offend," Miko insisted. "The Poles are trying to understand the past. Many feel bad about the war and what happened. They make dolls. They also publish a Polish Jewish cookbook."

"I can't wait to try a recipe," I jeered. "Matzo balls made with ground glass?"

Miko shrugged hopelessly. "Nora, I tell you what is happening. In their way, the Poles are trying. They are sometimes clumsy. I know. I am half Polish."

"And that's the half you never talk about. How come?"

Miko was silenced for a moment before answering. "Because that is the half that looked the other way when the Germans came, the half that pretended they could not do a thing to stop them, the half that said, This is not our business."

"So my father is right. They would let it happen again, in a minute."

Miko was shaking his head. "You must not be—what is the word?—paranoid."

I looked at him for a long moment. "You're not a Jew."

"Gypsies and Jews. We are not so different."

"Of course we are. You just can't understand this."

"I can."

"No. No, you can't. And you know what? Neither can I. I can't even begin to understand what happened here. What happened to my mother, to her family. To my family!"

"They were in the camps?"

I nodded. "Everyone was killed. All of them. Except my mother. And she would never talk to me about it."

"Why not?"

"She just wouldn't. And neither would my father. But I had the address of a man here in Cracow who had been in the camps with her. I hoped he could tell me something. I went to find him. He died years ago. Now I'll never know what happened to her there. . . ."

Miko's dark eyes were fixed on mine. "I will take you there."

"Where?"

"To Oświęcim."

"To Oświęcim?" I whispered.

"My grandfather died in Oświęcim. Gypsies and Jews. We are not so different."

❦ 74 ❦

"Dear Mommy, I am well. I feel good here. . . ."

I read the postcard on the wall of one of the barracks at Oświęcim, or Auschwitz, as the Germans called it. Pressed behind a piece of glass, the handwriting was carefully controlled and the card, Miko explained, was dictated by the guards. Each child was required to send one. We were inside the barracks of Auschwitz, now a museum, filled with artifacts in glass display cases—piles of human hair, jumbles of eyeglasses, mounds of suitcases with names still scratched into the sides. Miklavska? Would I find the name Miklavska? But my eyes would not focus, and the letters blurred together, and I moved on to the exhibit of children's personal belongings—cotton dresses, tiny baby slippers, delicate hats, one sock, and a battered doll that must once have been held lovingly by some little girl. My mother? Was it hers, the doll she called Kasha?

"Come," Miko whispered, leading me out of that room into another, this one filled with documents and photographs of medical experimentation. Had my mother been here, in this room through which the sun now streamed in heedless profusion? Had her body been touched brutally? What butchery had she braved? What terror had she survived that was so inhuman she could not even tell it to her own child? Had her arm been injected with live viruses? Was this why she refused a polio vaccination?

"Dear Mommy, I am well. I feel good here. . . ."

"I feel sick," I said to Miko, and he put an arm around me and took me outside, where I leaned against a tree and tried to breathe while he asked, "There is more to see, or do you want to leave?" I had seen enough. More than enough. But I could not stop looking.

Auschwitz was a small operation in comparison to Birkenau, the larger, less comfortable camp, also part of Oświęcim, just down the road on an endless, flat, grass-covered area, where fifteen thousand people were killed daily, four million in all, mostly Jews, but many Poles, and several hundred thousand gypsies. A cold wind whipped around us as we walked down the train tracks, through the entrance gates, the Gates of Hell. Barbed wire was everywhere. Row after row of wooden barracks lined either side of the tracks with a stunning symmetry. The organization of it all was so appalling, so dazzling, such a monument to technology and to evil.

"It is here that my grandfather came. He was twenty-six. Strong like a bull. He went right to the flames." Miko pointed to a pile of stones in the distance—the crematoria, destroyed by the allies, and left in shambles as part of the grim memorial.

"How do you know he went right to the flames?"

"My uncle Angar saw him go. He was a little boy. Six years."

"And Angar? How did he survive?"

Miko pulled his collar up. "The kitchen workers kept him like a pet in the kitchen. They fed him potato peels. And when the Nazis came to get him, he hid in the bins. He was small."

How had my mother survived? She was small. Had she, too, been kept and hidden? Or did she hide herself, flattening herself into some secret niche when danger lurked, holding her breath until her chest was near breaking? How is it possible that she lived through this lunacy? Was it luck? Fate? Or was it cunning and spirit that kept her alive?

We were outside one of the barracks. "Don't!" I whispered, as Miko pushed the door open. It creaked like an old tree.

"Don't worry," he said. "There is nothing left inside." He beckoned me to go in with him. Late-afternoon sun sent shafts of yellow light into that huge building, with its tight rows of wooden shelves onto which human beings, barely alive, were stacked for sleeping, six to a slab.

"*Verhalte dich ruhig!*" a sign painted in German proclaimed on one wall. "Keep quiet!"

And it was very quiet, finally. Only the creaking of the wooden shelves, and the howling of the wind hinted that in that place, four million human voices had cried out in screams no one heard. And it was in that place, on that vast, windswept plain, that afternoon, that I began to understand my mother's silence, the silence of one who had lived to tell, but would not, the silence of one who had wished to spare her child the unspeakable.

That night, chilled into a silence of my own, I told Miko that I needed to be alone. He kissed my forehead, and left me to take a hot bath and crawl into bed to sleep, to dream:

An iron vise of cold clamped my body. I was hungry and in terrible pain. Splinters from the wooden shelf stuck into my sides. But I knew they would come in the middle of the night and take her from me unless I lay very still.

She moaned. "Shh!" I whispered to her, patting her golden hair, holding her tight. She clung to my red coat, pressing her face against my breast. She was all skin and bones, so frail that I feared breaking her.

Footsteps echoed right outside the barracks. She pushed her face harder against my chest. "They're coming," she told me.

"Shh!" I said, and rolled on top of her, to hide her. I held my breath, worried about crushing her. The footsteps came close. Closer. A light shone in my face.

"Out!" they shouted, and grabbed her from under me. "No!" I screamed. "Take me! Take me instead!"

But they pulled her from my grasp, and she did not cry. Her lips trembled, but she made no noise. I begged them to take me instead. But they hissed at me, *"Verhalte dich ruhig!"* and they took her—Elena Miklavska, my mother. They took my mother away.

❦ 75 ❦

I WOKE UP THE NEXT MORNING WITH A HIGH FEVER. MY throat felt as if broken glass were stuck in it. I made myself a cup of tea and tried to get dressed. Rehearsal was in an hour, but when the room began to spin around and I broke out in a sweat, I picked up my new telephone.

"Pani Pawlick?" I said. "This is Nora Watterman calling. I am sick and will not be coming to rehearsal this morning." She said she would tell the maestro for me. She even asked if I needed a doctor. I assured her that it was only a cold and that I intended to be present at rehearsal the next day.

"But let me give you my telephone number, in case the maestro wants to talk with me," I suggested.

"So you have a telephone?" Marek's voice asked, startling me out of a restless sleep.

"Maestro?" I croaked into the receiver.

"And your voice is damaged."

"It's just a little cold."

"Your candle is burning by too many ends, perhaps?" His tone grated. "No. In fact, I caught this cold at Auschwitz yesterday."

"Ah, Oświęcim. Yes, the tourists complain. There is always wind." He sighed. "What you will need is a special tonic, which I am bringing to you."

"That's very kind, but . . ."

"It is nothing, my dear Nora. A little bitter, but you will eat a bonbon after, and by this evening, your candle will be on fire. I am coming. *Do widzenia!*"

When the doorbell rang a few hours later, I could barely make it into the living room and down the hall to open the door.

"Pale like Camille!" Marek crooned, taking off his wool scarf, wrapping it around my shoulders, then propelling me back into bed, tucking the blankets in around me. He picked up my wrist, felt my pulse, clucking his tongue. Then, reaching into his coat pocket, he took out a brown vial and, opening it, he handed it to me. I sniffed it and wrinkled up my nose.

"How quickly I wish your health to be restored," Marek sighed.

How quickly I wished for Madame Rudiakowski to return from Prague as I downed the putrid stuff and shivered at its aftertaste.

Marek slapped his knees. "I promise candy, and I forget. How terrible I am!" He pouted, thinking, no doubt, that he looked adorable.

267

"It's okay," I assured him, still smarting from the taste. "This way I really know it's medicine."

Marek laughed and batted his beady eyes at me. "I am so delighted with your talents. You are being talked about in all our critics. Are you aware?"

"No," I wheezed.

"Big tone. Beautiful, they say." He kissed my hand. "Like you."

His grizzly face pushed closer and I could smell the sourness of his breath even with my cold. "I will have to tell Stephanie how friendly you are being," I bleated. "She so loves making music with you. I'm sure you would miss having her as soloist when you go on tour."

Marek sat straight up at my insinuation. "Yes. Our collaboration is very confident."

"So," I said, patting my blankets, pleased with my successful parry. "Thank you for the medicine. I feel better already."

Marek stood up, in retreat. "About your telephone," he mentioned, as if it were a sudden thought. "It is a shame for such an illegality to cause you difficulty."

"It's illegal?"

Marek smiled. "Well, of course. And I would be very careful about the kind of friend you are keeping."

"Oh?"

"A person who will install a stolen apparatus can make much annoyance for a visitor, you know." He blew me a kiss and walked toward the door. "I am letting myself out. Sleep, sleep, my dear. And tomorrow your flute will be once again silver!"

"Stolen! Of course it is not stolen! That pig!" Miko stormed, and continued cursing in Polish or Romany, I could not tell which. His anger seemed out of proportion.

"Why are you so upset?" I wanted to know.

"Why?" His eyes flashed at me. "Because I am no thief. How could you believe that man?"

"I didn't believe him!" I protested.

"Of course you did. Or why would you even ask me? How could you think this of me, Nora?"

Miko's chest was heaving. His mouth turned down at the corners.

"Please," I entreated him. "Let's not let such a small thing . . ."

"Small. Oh, to you this is small? To me it is very big. But of course, I am only a plumber. Only a small little electrician. And when some stupid idiot-snake-maestro-asshole-artist says I steal, and when the woman I love believes this, to me it is very, very big!"

I smiled at him. "I love you, too," I whispered, at which confession Miko stopped and stared at me.

"Good," he said, a sheepish smile printing out across his face. "This is very good."

"I think so," I said, putting my arms around him, kissing his neck. "Except you will catch my cold."

"Lady," he said, untying the belt of my bathrobe, pushing it off my shoulders. "I am not afraid."

❧ 76 ❧

IT WAS APRIL, AND AS THE DAYS LENGTHENED, THE LEAVES on the trees along the Planty began to appear, and the willows wept into the Vistula. The air seemed to clear and there was no more morning fog. Multicolored flowers blossomed in window boxes and courtyards, in every nook and cranny of Cracow. But the opulence of nature did not find its way from the great outdoors into the stores. Vegetables were few and hard to find, and cost more and more every day. The butcher shop was empty. My salary of zlotys barely bought one day's worth of food. My dollars were being depleted. Miko's work had dwindled alarmingly. He was worried and depressed. "I am useless," he complained. "I cannot let you pay for everything."

"It's my pleasure."

"But it is my shame." Miko's mood spiraled downward, until one day he came into the apartment cheerfully suggesting a trip to the mountains, to visit his grandmother, Mina. "I wish to present to her, the woman of my dreams."

I warmed to his wish. "I would be honored," I said. A trip to the country sounded like the very thing to lift our sagging spirits.

"Yes! Mina has vegetables! She has chickens!" Miko crowed. "We will eat like kings. And maybe we will see Bibijaka, who lives in forests and is a giantess and shines like gold and shows herself only to honest people." Miko puffed out his chest. "I, of course, have seen her many times."

A program of Handel concerti grossi and a Mendelssohn string symphony meant a week without flutes at the Cracow Chamber Players.

"Now you are free," Marek announced to me. "Perhaps you will find time to dine with me?"

"I'd love to," I pretended. "But I'm going away for a few days."

"Oh?" Marek sniffed. "To shop in Prague? To take the baths in Zakopanie?"

"To see Bibijaka," I told him, and left him sulking in his stuffy dressing room at the Philharmonie.

And so Miko and I piled supplies into his car, and drove out of Cracow, heading northwest. As the city receded behind us, so did all worries. We passed limestone caves and forests and medieval castles perched like eagles' nests high on the mountain peaks. We sang and laughed and ate pretzels, and the trip was over before we knew it.

Grandmother Mina lived in a small village in a valley. Her house was surrounded by a garden, chicken coops, and stands of tall pine trees. Hearing Miko's car approach, she hobbled out into her garden, a gnarled woman of eighty-five, dressed in long skirts, several shawls, and a bandana around her head.

Miko picked her up like a doll, and she squealed with girlish delight. Then, she looked me up and down, and mumbled something to Miko.

"She said you are pretty. For a *gadja*."

"What's a *gadja*?"

"It's Romany for outsider."

Mina shoved her grandson toward the house, and, taking me by the hand, she walked with me through her garden, pointing at blossoms, picking spices, letting me smell them, pointing at the sky, smiling, speaking to me with her eyes and with her hands. Chickens clucked in the background, and I jumped as a tawny cat rubbed itself against my leg. Bending down to stroke it, I saw a ladybug on a leaf.

" 'Ladybug, ladybug, fly away home. Your house is on fire and your children are all gone.' " I remembered my mother, chanting that gruesome rhyme to me, a frightened look on her face. Had she first seen ladybugs as a child in Poland? Was it here, in these mountains that she might have climbed, in springtime, when the world was full of promise and dangers were only in the words of nursery rhymes?

Miko and I spent the afternoon roaming through the hills surrounding the village. He was in high spirits, chasing me through the woods, showing me the stream where he swam as a boy, the cave he hid in, the hermit's cabin where the local kids went to tell ghost stories and plot their endless intrigues. He had lived in the village until he was ten. Then he moved with his parents to Warsaw, where they still lived, his father—Mina's son—working in a plastics factory, his mother in a dress shop as a seamstress.

"Are you close to them?"

"My parents?" He shrugged. "They did not approve of my marriage. I was too young, they said. They were right. So I came back from Chicago. I visit them. But there is always between us this tension. Do you have tension with your son?"

"I wish."

"Nora?"

Realizing my slip, I covered it with, "Sometimes we get along too well. We're too close."

I would never know the tension of differences with my grown child. Was I lucky? Had I been spared disappointment and distance? I stood in the peaceful woods, where nature was in harmony, and all was still. At that quiet moment I knew I would have given anything to trade the silence of Nicky's absence even for angry disagreement, even for the rowdiest argument.

❧ 77 ❧

MINA'S HOUSE WAS RUSTIC, MADE OF STUCCO AND ROUGH timber, with wooden floors and furnishings covered with decorative cloths. Her kitchen was cozy, with bunches of herbs hanging from the wooden beams. Braids of garlic and baskets of onions were perched on the sink, and Mina was busy chopping potatoes when Miko and I returned from our romp in the woods. I offered to help, and Mina put me to work with a fresh-killed chicken that was soaking in a bucket so its feathers would not fly around when it was plucked. I had no idea how to denude it, and Miko laughed at me when I tried removing feathers with a knife.

"Oh, you think it's funny, do you?" I asked.

He folded his arms and watched me struggle. "Yes. I do."

I picked the soggy bird up, and dive-bombed it toward my tormentor. Mina cackled, her face crinkling merrily, and she said something.

"Translation," I demanded.

"She said the dead can't fly."

"As her if the dead *can* do anything," I suggested, and Miko asked, coming back with an answer: "The dead can teach us how to live."

The temperature dropped quickly when the sun went down. Miko made a big fire in the hearth, and we sat in front of it, eating chicken stew. After the meal, I was told to drink my coffee slowly and not to shake the cup, and when I had finished it, Grandmother Mina asked to see the dregs. She looked at them for a long time, then told my fortune to Miko, who translated it for me:

"What you seek you will find. Happiness will be yours. You will live and be well."

I smiled politely.

"She tells the same fortune to all the tourists." Miko winked. "Only she charges them for it. You got yours for free."

A rooster crowed. I cuddled against Miko's warm body in a small wooden bed as darkness faded into day. He stirred, embraced me, then leapt out of bed, full of energy. "Today there will be excitement in my grandmother's house," he promised, pulled on some trousers and a shirt, and disappeared into the kitchen. I heard his voice, then his grandmother's. But a gentle conversation soon crescendoed into shouts and screams. I dressed quickly, and rushed into the kitchen. Mina was angrily jabbing at the air, ranting.

"What is it?" I asked Miko, when my entrance caused a sudden silence.

"I want to go into business with her, but she is not interested in money. She prefers to keep her food. She says it is worth more than zlotys. But she is wrong."

Mina squawked at her grandson, and I retreated to a corner to watch them battle it out. The sound of a car arriving stopped them both. A shiny black Mercedes sedan pulled up, and a driver in a dark uniform approached the house. Miko growled something at his grandmother, then took the man behind the house to the chicken coops, from which they soon returned, with a pair of freshly killed birds tied together by the feet. Money was exchanged, and the chickens were stashed in the trunk of the car. Miko waved goodbye as the Mercedes pulled away, a foxy smile on his face.

"What exactly are you doing?"

"There are no chickens in Cracow. People will go out of their way now to find their food."

I stared at him. "And to pay outrageous prices?"

"I am charging a modest amount."

I gave him a look. "Is this fair to your grandmother?"

"That is no concern of yours," was his truculent reply. "Now go into the kitchen and help Mina."

During the course of the morning, Mina and I watched through the kitchen window as more fancy cars arrived, and more chickens, necks broken, tied by the feet, were taken away. Miko strutted and preened, stuffing money into his pockets, his face cold, calculating. I could not reconcile the caring Miko I knew, and this self-appointed cock-of-the-walk. But, then again, Mikolaj Branko was very young.

His arrogance might have been the privilege of youth, yet it was troubling to me. I saw the haughtiness of a boy instead of the modesty of a man. I saw the makings of a tyrant. And I already knew that love is lost when tyranny triumphs.

I glared at him. "I knew you were young. I did not know that you were also a bully."

Miko scowled back at me, then stormed out of the house, slamming the door behind him, leaving me to smooth Mina's feathers and lick my own wounds.

Why did Miko's behavior pain me so much? I knew my discomfort was not just about the chickens, nor was it about his callow youth. Something deeper than disillusionment troubled me, gnawed toward the center of my feelings. Was it a growing realization of the impermanence of things with Miko? I knew ours was not destined to be a long and lasting union, like the one I once had. I pictured Bernie lying on the blue couch, sound asleep, and I remembered how that image, before Theo, used to make the world seem so very right. I remembered my husband. And, at that moment, despite everything, I missed him.

We drove back to Cracow a few days later, the car laden with chickens, bags of vegetables, and bunches of flowers. The trip was without incident, and without much conversation. I was disappointed in Miko. He was annoyed with me. A veil of discomfort had come down between us. We both wanted to spend the night apart. Neither of us needed to suggest it.

"Sleep well," Miko said.

"We didn't see Bibijaka," I noted.

"I think she has left Poland."

"Maybe she'll come back."

He smiled whimsically. "Who knows?"

"YOU WILL NOT LET A FEW CHICKENS COME BETWEEN US, WILL
you?" Miko had asked, the day after our return from the
mountains. His dark eyes and smooth skin convinced me,
and I willingly, wantingly, opened the door and let the fox
back in. If he had not been entirely honorable with his
grandmother, neither had I with him. I had allowed him
to believe that my son was alive and well. Our alliance was
uneasy but ongoing, and, since the Cracow Chamber Players had no summer performances, we spoke of spending a
few months together in the mountains with Mina.

"And after the summer?" Miko asked.

I shrugged.

"Then we must live for the moment," Miko said, embracing me, but I could see the concern in his eyes glimmering behind the bravado.

There were only a few more weeks of concerts left in
the season. One morning, Maestro Rudiakowski called me
into his dressing room.

"Laszlo recovers slowly," Marek said. "And it is my hope
that you will continue to honor us with your presence until
he is returned."

Could I really consider staying in Poland and putting up
with the maestro's harassment and with my colleagues' coldness? Could Miko keep me in Cracow? He was too young.
We had no future. Yet leaving him was unthinkable.

"I'm honored by your offer," I answered the maestro. "I
will see if I can find a way to continue."

Outside the Philharmonie, I stopped for a moment to
admire the blossoming trees, the blue sky, when someone

tapped me on the arm. A small, bald man with a gap between his front teeth stood before me, grinning.

"I hear you are looking for me," he said, in heavily accented English.

"Who are you?" I asked, startled.

He pulled a piece of paper out of his pocket and held it up. It was a photograph from a Polish newspaper of me with Marek at our first concert. He poked at the paper with one stubby finger. "You look just like her."

"That *is* me."

"What I mean is you look like *her*. Like Elena."

"My mother?" I whispered, leaning up against a kiosk. "Who are you?"

He laughed. "At the synagogue Rivka told me you looked for my grave!" He pinched my arm. "You remember Rivka, the woman who shows visitors the cemetery?"

I nodded.

"She remembers you. And she saw your picture in the paper. So she saved it for me. Smart, no?" He tapped his head, then began to walk away, fast.

"Wait!" I called, and chased after him. "Please wait!"

He crossed the market square, striding briskly. I reached his side. "Are you Stanislaw Ciesclaw?" I asked.

He stopped still. "He's dead, don't you know?"

"That's what they told me. At Number Seven Szeroka Street."

He looked around furtively. "Yes, Number Seven," he whispered. "Wasn't it clever of me?"

"What?"

"To arrange my own death?"

"What do you mean, arrange it? Why?"

He grinned. "Just like your mother, you look just like her." He tapped my arm. "Come to Warsaw. We'll talk there."

"Why can't we talk here, now?"

"Because here they are listening," he confided.

"Who?"

He put a finger to his lips to silence me.

277

"But I have so many questions."

"Shh! On Thursday at two o'clock at the Saxon Gardens in Warsaw, okay?"

"Where are the Saxon Gardens?"

"You will find them." He pinched my cheek. "And you will find me. Two o'clock." He saluted smartly, and walked away.

"You're not serious, are you?" Miko said later, when I told him I was going to Warsaw that Thursday.

"Of course I'm serious."

"But the man sounds like a crazy person."

"What if he is? He can still tell me things about my mother."

"How can you know if what he tells you will be the truth?"

I considered that thought, but it did not deter me. "I came a long way to talk to him. I can't give up now."

Miko nodded. "Then I will drive you to Warsaw."

"Thanks." I took his hand. "But this is something I have to do for myself, by myself. Can you understand?"

"I can," he said, and sent me off to the train station that Thursday with a kiss, an orange, and a big bar of chocolate.

It was a sunny day, and the countryside streaked by in long green ribbons. I stared out of the dirty window, thinking that my mother had traveled here by train, passing through this benign landscape, too, but she had not been allowed to see the rolling hills and blossoming fields and her destination had hardly been a garden.

The train arrived at Warsaw by noon. I elbowed my way through the jostling crowds in the vast gray central station, and, map in hand, I strolled slowly to the Saxon Gardens through the Old Town, reconstructed after the war, with its narrow houses, little winding streets, and horse-drawn cabs filled with camera-clicking tourists. I ate an ice-cream cone, and wandered through the open-air cafés. An art student sketched at his easel, drawing steep tiled roofs and wrought-iron grillwork. Nicky might have gone to Europe to study. I imagined him, with paper and charcoal, sketching in the open air, concentrating, the whole world his to capture with a sweep of the hand.

Tourists circled the Tomb of the Unknown Soldier at the Saxon Gardens, snapping photos of the eternal light. Stanislaw Ciesclaw was nowhere to be seen. Flower beds were laid out in the old French style, surrounded by geometric walks, and I began wandering along them, path after path, turn after turn, hoping to see a small bald head. It was past two, and I was beginning to worry.

"You must stop to smell the flowers." I whirled around toward the voice, and there was Stanislaw Ciesclaw, grinning like a leprechaun.

We sat on a cool marble bench beneath a budding tree. Lev, as he asked to be called, told me about his life in Pittsburgh, where he had lived and worked as a welder for the last twenty years. Two decades earlier, alone and unable to pay his debts in Poland, he had orchestrated a fake accident, documented his own death, and fled to Israel to reconcile with his wife. She and her new lover were less than delighted to see him, and so, with an Israeli passport and the new name of Lev Koblenz, he took a ship to America to join a cousin in Pennsylvania. Now an American citizen, he was visiting the land of his birth.

"The Jews are coming back," he whispered. "In Cracow, by the synagogue, they are building a hotel, with kosher food. Who would have thought?"

Slowly, inevitably, the talk turned to an earlier time, to the war, to what happened.

"I visited Oświęcim," I told him.

"So you have seen." He nodded solemnly. "But you have seen nothing. You have understood nothing."

"I would like to understand. I would like to know."

"I admire your interest," he said. "It is brave. But your mother was right, not because you should not know. Because you cannot know. Not unless you were there."

"But you were there. You can tell me."

Lev shook his head and stood up. "There is nothing worth telling you."

I reached for his arm. "Just tell me one thing. You wrote a letter to my mother, many years ago, and in it you said, 'But for you, I would not be here.' "

"Of course," he said. "Because of the rabbits."

"What rabbits?"

Lev sighed and sat down again. He tilted his head back and looked up at the new leaves. "Amazing, every year, how life comes back. Isn't it amazing?"

"Yes," I agreed, and sat in silence, allowing Lev time to gather his memories, and begin his story.

Toward the end of the war, Stanislaw Ciesclaw arrived in Auschwitz on a transport with other Jewish children who had been rounded up from hiding in the town of Zamosc. At the camp they were taken directly to Room One, to be *abgespritzt*—injected: "When they didn't have enough people to gas, they used this method, a little injection of phenol, directly in the heart. Very efficient. More economical. Zap! Right here." He pointed to his chest. "Ten, fifteen milliliters, and in fifteen seconds you are gone. So we children from Zamosc, we are there, Room One, waiting. They tell us we are going to be inoculated, against typhus. But we know. We know it is the end. We are huddled together, whimpering, waiting. The doctor comes into the room, in a white coat. He looks nice. I see, behind him, a girl poke her head into the room, then she runs away without the doctor seeing her. The doctor arranges the syringes, the assistants come and the first 'inoculations' begin." He stopped and shuddered. "Then suddenly this little girl runs back into the room, tugs at the coat of the doctor, and screams, in German, 'Doctor, the rabbits have gotten out!'

The doctor makes one more injection, and rushes away, leaving everything in chaos. The girl stands there, her eyes wide and staring at the body that just fell. Then she runs out after the doctor. The injections stop. A guard takes the rest of us to a cell block where we are imprisoned until the war is over." Lev glanced at me. "My life was spared, you see, because of the rabbits."

"I don't understand."

He smiled, a bitter smile. "They had pets, some of these Nazi doctors. They were so gentle and good to their animals, you know. This doctor raised rabbits, and your mother—he called her his Little Bunny—she took care of his rabbits. She got such a job, such a privilege, because she was blond with pretty eyes. She arrived at the camp with typhus. The doctor cured her and then let her watch his rabbits. From time to time, they spared one of us. To show how kind they were. She risked her life, your mother, letting the rabbits out of the cages like that, on purpose."

"Why did she do it?"

"She saw someone in the room. Someone she knew. She did not want him to be injected. But he was. He was that last body to fall, the body she saw."

"Do you know who it was?"

Stanislaw Ciesclaw nodded. He looked up at the leaves for a long moment, then touching my arm, gently, tenderly, he whispered, "It was her brother."

We parted at the Tomb of the Unknown Soldier. My mother's friend wished me luck and waved before darting down one of the garden paths, and disappearing among the flower beds. I stared at the eternal flame that flickered and glowed as tourists admired it, photographed it. I thought of my mother and the flames she had defied, the fate she had outwitted. Or had she? To see her own brother consumed was to burn for him for the rest of her life. Was the fate of the survivor yet more hideous than that of the victim?

I began to walk, trying to add Mr. Ciesclaw's piece of information to the puzzle that was my mother. I walked and walked along widening avenues, past statues and palaces toward another park where a pianist played Chopin waltzes for a rapt audience. I sat in the shade of a tree and listened, phrases tumbling like blossoms around my ears. But for all the loveliness surrounding me, I was blinded by an image that would not fade—Elena Miklavska, standing at a doorway, watching her brother die. She had risked her life, and still he perished. How did she absorb the anguish, the betrayal, the horror? How did she go on? How was it possible that in the midst of cruelty and carnage her will to live prevailed? And how had she managed to be a wife and a mother after all she had been through?

Mr. Ciesclaw's story had stunned me. Now it began to enlighten me. Now I could understand my mother's unwillingness to have a polio shot. Now I could understand her unwillingness to talk. Now I could also understand that through silence, her sorrow had become my sorrow. Taking it for my own, as children do, I had grown up, dragging an enormous invisible weight. I had added to that burden, too, with pounds of my own guilt, masses of my own misery. In a harness of my own making, I had been carrying a crushing load. Now that I had arrived at some understanding, could I allow myself to let go?

The healing sounds of Chopin vibrated through me. I looked up through the renewal of young leaves to the infinite blue above and I felt something wash over me, like a cooling breeze. And I knew then that if my mother's pain had been my heritage, her strength could be the more enduring legacy. I stood up, immeasurably lightened, and, feeling something close to power, something close to courage, I strode out of the park.

❦ 79 ❧

I TOOK AN EARLY EVENING TRAIN BACK TO CRACOW, WATCH-
ing the shadows fall across the land and a full moon rise.
Sometimes, on a hot summer night, my father and I had
taken folding chairs up onto the roof of our apartment building on West Twenty-third Street and had watched the moon
roll like a gilded plate over the jagged buildings. We had
sat there together silent, both thinking of my mother, missing her in the moonlight, until my father would turn to me
and say softly, "Enough, now. It's time, Nora." And we
would go home and get ready for bed.

Where was home for me now? Was it an apartment in
Cracow where a handsome half-gypsy waited for me? And
what were we to each other? He was my young lover who
had lifted me out of my misery and brought me light. If
he reminded me of my son, was it a sin? We had cared
greatly about each other. We had been kind and giving. But
as close as we were, I was still his *gadja*. I would always
be a stranger in his world, and was there really a permanent
place for him in mine?

Miko was waiting up for me. Sitting at the dining-room
table bare-chested, a towel wrapped around his waist, he
was sipping tea, smoking a cigarette.

"You're smoking?"

"I am nervous."

"But why?"

"I don't know." He blew a smoke ring into the air. It
floated like a halo over his head. "How was your trip?"

"Very long. Very tiring." I yawned. "Could we talk in
the morning?"

"I don't think so."

"Please." I began to unzip my dress. "I promise I'll tell
you everything in the morning."

"We will talk now."

I groaned. "Miko, what's so important that it can't wait?"

"You will be very upset with me."

"Why?"

He looked at me, troubled. "I broke something."

My eyes flew to the table, to Nicky's vase. It was gone.

"It was an accident," Miko was saying. "I was taking off my jacket, and a sleeve knocked it to the floor. I know it meant very much to you. I am very sorry." He looked at me. "I will glue it for you. Nora?"

I sank down onto a chair and stared straight ahead. "It's okay," I whispered.

"He will make you another, I am sure."

"He can't." I reached for one of Miko's hands and looked up into his face. "My son is dead."

His eyes searched mine. "Dead?"

"Yes. It happened less than a year ago."

Stunned, Miko stood very still. "But why didn't you tell me?" he whispered.

"I couldn't."

Miko's eyes filled with pity. He pulled my hand to his cheek and kissed it, his tears splashing on my wrist. "My poor Nora. I knew, I knew there was something about your son. My poor Nora."

"He was killed in a car accident," I said simply, sadly. "I'm sorry I lied to you."

"You wanted to keep your son alive. I can understand this."

I shook my head. "It was foolish. A foolish fantasy."

"No," Miko said, "it was a good fantasy."

"It's finished now," I whispered.

Miko sniffed and wiped his cheeks. He picked up a piece of broken pottery. "I will glue it for you."

"That's okay," I said. I did not need the blue vase to keep Nicky alive anymore. He was still with me, deep inside, smiling at me, winking, teaching me how to live.

❧ 80 ❧

"I'M AFRAID I CAN'T," I TOLD LUKE WHEN HE CALLED INVITING me to a cocktail party at Cracow's Intercontinental Hotel a few days later.

"But it is in honor of you," he said. "We have important business people here from America, potential investors. We wish to celebrate your successful stay in Cracow. We wish you to say a few words to them about the maestro, the orchestra, your happiness here. . . ."

Should I be the dog and pony show for visiting investors? Could I entertain my countrymen with praise for Poland? I would not be a hypocrite. I would not compromise myself.

"I would find it very difficult," I said. "Please excuse me."

"We all do difficult things," the deputy minister of culture replied. "When goodwill is at issue, we must extend ourselves. I will see you at the hotel at five P.M. sharp."

On the appointed afternoon, I extended myself into a simple black Eleanor Outfit, with pearls and high heels.

"Remember to say something nice about The Snake," Miko teased as he hailed a taxi for me. Then, kissing me, he added, "But don't tell them what you do in your spare time."

"Nora!" Luke called as I walked into the elegant marble lobby of the Intercontinental Hotel. Taking me by the elbow, he led me into a room crowded with people holding champagne glasses, drinking, laughing. "Americans," Luke whispered. "They are so congenial!" And he sent me to circulate among my visiting compatriots.

"You must just love it here," one woman said. "It's so exciting, all this new freedom. Is Lech Walesa as sexy as they say?" And she grabbed an hors d'oeuvre from a shiny tray.

"I understand you've been playing in a Polish orchestra," another person whispered. "Do you speak Polish? How do you communicate?"

"The language of music is international!" a voice interjected. I turned to see Maestro Marek Rudiakowski, who was working the room like a pro. He put a proprietary arm around me. "And Nora Watterman speaks the language of music with every eloquence."

I nodded and grinned my way across the floor, Marek by my side. "I am thinking," he whispered, "that you must play a Mozart Concerto with us next season. Perhaps this will intoxicate you to stay on, my dear, yes?"

Luke had failed to mention that dinner would follow drinks. Before I could protest, I was shepherded to a table, Maestro Rudiakowski seated to my left. Chicken was served, with salad and vegetables.

"I was told there was no food in Poland," the man to my right said, munching contentedly.

"You just have to know where to shop," I said.

"In Poland, there is always a way," Marek agreed, touching my knee under the table, pretending it was by mistake, infuriating me. But I chewed and swallowed, chewed and swallowed, and got through the meal, composed.

When the dessert was served, a door in the back of the room opened, and a phalanx of photographers entered.

"Oh no," I whispered. "No one told me this was going to be a press conference."

"Smile," Marek commanded, preening himself, as Luke summoned us to the center of the room: "Maestro Marek Rudiakowski, and your own extraordinary Nora Watterman!" Applause. Luke rubbed his hands together and began, with just a touch of hyperbole: "Nora's willingness to step in for an ailing colleague was a message for the entire world. Her successful tenure with the orchestra attests not only to her talents, but to the warming of relations between our two great nations. The seeds that Nora has sown cannot help but blossom into flowers of friendship and understanding, cooperation, and communication." More applause. Luke turned to me. "And now, I would like Nora Watterman to tell you, in her own words, about her musical adventures in Poland!"

I tried to seem assured. I smiled into the cameras, as flashbulbs popped, and videotape rolled. "To make music in Poland has been my great privilege," I began, trying to control the tremolo in my voice. Luke had said I would be asked to say a few words, not give a speech. I took a deep breath, and searched for something to say. "This is, after all, the home of so much great music, great art, great culture. It is here that Chopin lived. It is here that Wieniawski and Paderewski and so many musicians flourished. It is here that the Cracow Chamber Players, under the able baton of Maestro Marek Rudiakowski . . ."

Marek bowed as the diners applauded him.

"It is here, under his leadership, that the Chamber Players has grown to become one of Poland's cultural jewels. I'd like to tell you about Maestro Rudiakowski." I eyed him, noting perspiration beaded on his forehead. "Maestro is a man of enormous power and persuasion, a man who uses his authority to . . ."

Marek's eyes were wide, glimmering with apprehension. But goodwill was the order of the day, and I summoned the generosity to find the right words.

"Maestro Rudiakowski wields his enormous authority in the most benevolent ways. He brings out the best in his players, he is always generous and kind, and he challenges his musicians to give one hundred percent."

The room applauded, and relief as well as a handkerchief crossed Marek's brow.

"It has been quite an experience living in Cracow," I continued. "I find the people courtly and kind. I find their spirit in the face of continuing hardship to be a great inspiration. I have learned many things here. I have learned that there is life without vegetables." A gentle wave of laughter rose and fell. Then I spoke words that were not planned, that welled from a private source, and spilled over. "And I have learned that music provides solace where sorrow prevails."

Applause began slowly, then rose to a rousing acclaim.

"You could be our next ambassador!" a man called out. I smiled at the compliment, then stood attentively beside maestro as he made his speech. He went on and on, and, losing interest, my eyes wandered. I noticed, standing behind a camera, in the back row of the press contingent, a man staring at me, giving me the A-OK sign, smiling at me. Marek made his speech, but I could not hear a word. I stood frozen in place, until the talking was over, glasses were raised in the air, and the bright lights were turned down.

He led me outside onto a balcony. The night was balmy. The moon was full.

"Gus had been sending me to some pretty exotic spots—Pittsburgh. Omaha. Indianapolis. So I said, don't I deserve to go someplace exciting, someplace where it's all happening? Next thing I know, I'm on assignment in the Big Kielbasa. What do you think?"

What did I think? Bernard T. Watterman was standing in front of me. I was astonished. "I think it's nice to see you," I said.

"You, too. You look"—his eyes traveled up and down my Eleanor Outfit—"you look great. You cut your hair."

"It's growing back."

"So's mine," he joked, rubbing his bald monk's crown. He had lost weight. His cheeks were hollow, his features were eagle sharp. Except for the hair, he looked like the Bernie I had met so many years before, one summer in Vermont. He looked like the man I had married. He looked like the father of my son.

"How have you been?" I asked.

Bernie sighed. "It's been rough." His eyes met mine. "How about you?"

"It's been rough."

He nodded, then smiled. "Well, you were pretty smooth tonight. In fact, you were amazing in there."

"Good soundbites?"

"Wonderful." Bernie leaned up against the balcony. "You touched me."

"Did I?"

"Yes."

I held on to the railing beside him, gazing out at the moonlit garden below. "Is the linden tree blooming?" I asked.

"I'm hardly ever there. I haven't noticed."

I pictured the place neglected. The garden was probably overgrown with weeds. The driveway no doubt needed new surfacing after the winter, and the house would be due for repainting. And then the birches out back should be sprayed. . . .

"I've thought about you a lot. I've thought a lot about us," Bernie said. "I know I was no prize. Not as a husband. Not as a father. . . ."

"You don't have to do this. . . ."

"But I do," he insisted. "Let me." He looked up at the moon, then back at me. "I wanted to forgive you for Mr. Bradshaw. . . ."

Not again, I thought. Enough. Surely the statute of limitations had expired. "Bernie," I began, but his arm on mine quieted me.

"I tried," he went on. "But I couldn't. I blamed you and blamed you, even though I was hardly white as the driven snow, even though I had strayed, still I blamed you. Then I realized that what really got me about your affair, was that you *felt* something for that guy, you *loved* him. . . ."

"Please . . ."

"I was jealous, Nora. You could feel things so deeply. You could connect. And I couldn't. Not even to you. Not even to my son. You gave Nicky so much. You were a great mother." He wiped at his eyes with the back of one hand. I reached out to touch his shoulder, and he took my hand, held it in both of his. "I never got to say I was sorry," he said. "Not to you. Or—and this is the hardest—or to Nicky. Because I wasn't there for him. Not really. Not the way I should have been. Not the way you were."

I shook my head. "Nicky adored you. He worshiped you. His whole life revolved around you."

"No one's life should revolve around another's."

"But we're all satellites," I said. "We gravitate toward the strongest body. Nicky admired your strength. So did I."

"Strange," Bernie mused. "Because it was yours we both relied on."

"Mine?"

"Yes."

"Funny," I said. "And I always used to feel so helpless and weak."

"You never were."

I smiled. "I guess I know that. Now."

And on that balcony, at that moment, there were other things that I also knew. I knew that I had missed seeing Bernie asleep on the blue couch, and that what I had missed had not been merely the comforting vision of a familiar body. I had missed *him*. I had missed *us*. Granted, ours had been an imperfect union, but who was to blame for those imperfections no longer seemed important. Ours had been a bond founded on mutual respect and admiration. It had been founded on love, and it had been long. It had also been good. For that, we could both claim responsibility.

Bernie put his arms around me. "Nora. I'm sorry," he whispered. "I'm sorry for everything."

"So am I," I said, my arms circling him. "So am I."

In the moonlight, on a balcony in Poland, Bernard T. Watterman and I held each other, our bruised hearts beating fast, our tears spilling, and if sorry wasn't good enough, it was the best we could do.

"What are your plans?" Bernie asked, as we pulled away from each other and mopped our faces with wet, waxy napkins.

"I don't know," I told him. "Rudiakowski wants to renew my contract. I've got a life here."

He sniffed. "Is there someone in it?"

"Yes."

The muscles in his jaw tightened as he nodded. "I see." Visions of what's-her-name, Pamela, came to mind. "And you?" I asked, imagining her at Linden Hill, cooking on our stove, sleeping in our bed.

Bernie shook his head. "I'm alone," he told me. "Except for . . ." A look of great warmth came over him. There was someone in his life after all. Someone he really cared about. Deeply.

"If you come back," Bernie said. "There's a girl I think you'd like to meet. She's very beautiful."

He was probably dating an eighteen-year-old. How sad. Or was it? I was living with a man many years my junior. Who was I to pass judgment? We both were wounded. Did it matter how we healed ourselves?

"I'd be glad to meet her," I said, and I promised, if and when I came back to the States, my very first stop would be Corbin's Cove.

❧ 81 ❧

WE WERE REHEARSING MOZART'S "JUPITER" SYMPHONY, HIS last, the one that lingers longest after its final chord. There is only one flute in the "Jupiter" Symphony, and from the stage, I could see Danila lurking at the back of the auditorium, envying me those soaring solo phrases, those leaps and turns, burning with resentment. And why shouldn't she resent me? It was unfair that a foreigner had been hired, a foreigner who could come and go at will, who could audition for other jobs in her own country and probably get one, even though there were hot-shot young players out there, even though the competition was formidable. She could contend with the best. She could . . . We reached the final fanfare of the last movement, triumphant and jubilant sounds echoing through the hall.

"*Dobrze*," Marek told us, wiping his brow. "*Bardzo dziękuję.*"

Grateful myself, and with a decision finally made, I put my flute away.

I went immediately to Marek's dressing room, but he was gone. I looked upstairs in the office of the Cracow Chamber Players. Pani Michnik was shouting into the phone when I entered. She did not acknowledge my presence, although I am certain she saw me out of the corner of one reddened eye. I looked around the office, at the scrawny ivy plant that inched its dying vine toward the window, at the piles and piles of paper on the Panis' desks, at the IBM computer still stuck on top of a file cabinet.

"*Proszę*," Pani Michnik finally said.

"Have you seen Maestro Rudiakowski?"

"He is at the café, having his lunch," she said. "He will be back in one hour. You will wait?"

"I will go to the café," I said, and as I was leaving the office, I asked, pointing at the file cabinet, "Your computer—will it be functioning soon?"

Pani Michnik's mouth tightened in prunish wrinkles. "They have sent us cables for linkages in the American system of electricity. We are waiting for the adaptations."

"I see," I said, and smiled prunishly myself, noting the model number of the IBM as I left the office.

. . .

"But this surprise is wonderful that you will join me for lunch," Maestro Rudiakowski said, his mouth full of dumplings, as he stood to offer me a chair at the café. "Have you decided which concerto you will play?"

"I have made a decision," I said. "But it is not about the concerto. . . ."

The hourly trumpet sounded as I passed St. Mary's Church. I listened, and at the abrupt end of the bugle call, I quickened my steps and hurried toward the apartment on Floriańska Street.

Miko was in the kitchen, wearing a white shirt open at the collar. He was expertly peeling an apple, one long red spiral dangling from his knife.

He looked up as I entered. "What is it?" he wanted to know.

I could not tell him. "Nothing," I said.

Miko took a bite of the apple. "There are things about you I know. So you cannot say nothing when it is something. Tell me."

I took a deep breath. "I won't be playing the last concert."

Miko looked at me. "You won't?"

"Danila will play. I have had my turn. Now it's hers."

He nodded. "You are leaving, Nora?"

My heart was racing. "Yes," I said. "I love you. And I am leaving. Can you understand this?"

Miko smiled bravely. "Yes, I can understand."

"Will you forgive me?"

He pulled me into his arms in response. He seemed older and wiser than when we met. He was manly, mature. I felt his strong heart beating against mine. I heard his resolute sigh. Then he released his embrace to cut two slices of peeled apple. He handed a piece to me and we both crunched. Then he kissed me slowly, sadly, his lips wet with apple, our salty tears mixing into the sweet taste.

"Do you remember the first time we made love?" he whispered, wiping my cheeks with his warm hands.

"I will never forget it."

"And I put a piece of bread on your knee?"

I nodded.

"It is a Romany custom, to take the bread from the knee, when we marry. I knew you would never be my wife. But I wanted our time together to be a union, like a marriage. I wanted our time together to be blessed." He kissed my forehead. "For me it was."

I stood looking up at him, my Miko, the young man who had brought light and laughter back into my life, the young man who had tried his wings and now would soar. "For me it was, too."

❧ 82 ❧

MIKO TOOK ME TO THE AIRPORT. LINES WERE ENDLESS, FACES were long, and there were tears tumbling everywhere. People were holding each other, embracing as they prepared to depart their homeland, some for a few weeks, some forever. Miko stood beside me staring stoically ahead, his arm around me. As we inched close to the ticket counter, we attempted some small talk.

"How long is the flight?" he wanted to know.

"Ten hours, I think."

"And this Stephanie, she meets you in New York? You are all arranged?"

"Yes."

"Will you write to me?"

"Of course."

"Nora," he said, as I handed my ticket to the woman behind the desk. "I will never forget you."

"Passport!" the woman demanded.

"And I will keep you in my heart forever," I said.

"Luggage?"

"Two bags," I told her, and Miko lifted them for me onto the scales and I felt my stomach drop as the moment came for me to move on into the customs area.

We clung to each other for a last goodbye, and I kissed him. Then he took an envelope out of his pocket. "For you," he said, pressing it into my hand.

I watched him walk away, and disappear into the crowd. I put his envelope in my pocket, and waited my turn at customs, imagining Miko getting into his car, driving down the streets of Cracow toward the Philharmonie. I had told Maestro Rudiakowski that a certain Mikolaj Branko could obtain the proper adapters needed to hook up his IBM computer, and that he would be very pleased to do this for the Chamber Players for the proper fee.

"This is wonderful!" Marek had exclaimed. "But I was told such adapters are impossible to find, and you must wait, for many, many months."

"Maestro," I said, "you have taught me about things in Poland. There is always a way."

❧ 83 ❧

"Papers of ownership?" the English-speaking customs official asked when he opened my canvas bag and saw my flute.

"This is my flute," I told him. "I brought it here with me from America."

"When you enter Poland, you must show papers, you must obtain certificate of ownership."

"Well, I didn't. No one asked for any papers."

"This is incorrect. You must have a certificate. How do I know you have the right to this flute?"

What right did I have? Every right. "I have just played this flute for months as the first flutist of the Cracow Chamber Players. It's mine. Why do I need a certificate?"

"Certificate of ownership," he repeated and began to yell in Polish for another official to join us, no doubt to take my flute away.

I looked around for a pair of compassionate eyes. But no one gazed my way. No giant porter appeared. No influential maestro was anywhere to be seen. My flight was scheduled to depart in ten minutes and I feared that my flute was about to be confiscated. While the customs officials conferred, I quickly pieced the flute together. Putting it to my lips, I began on B flat, playing Debussy's "Syrinx." Astonished faces turned in my direction, but I kept playing, the haunting melody reverberating through the huge gray space of the Warsaw airport. The two customs officials looked at each other, stymied. I stopped mid-phrase to ask, "Now do you believe it is my flute?"

A debate in Polish began between them. I calmly put my flute away, and they finally stopped arguing. "Thank you," I was told, and they waved me through, as a scattering of applause resounded behind me.

. . .

The airplane lifted off and I took the envelope Miko had handed me out of my pocket and opened it. Dried rose petals fell into my lap, their sudden scent filling me with sweet memories. I opened the folded paper, and read what Miko had written:

TO NORA
a poem, which is better in Polish, but at least in bad English you will have some of my thought, and all of my love, which is for you, forever.

> Bibijaka would not come to me.
> She shows only to the honest and
> I was not one.
> But love is truth, and shines like a rose,
> And it was you which lighted my path.
> It was you which led me
> through shadows and doubts
> like a bursting of sun on a black winter sky.
> You are disappeared,
> But I keep the rose of you inside of me
> to clear the way.
> Now Bibijaka comes.
> She shows herself.
> She puts kisses on my eyes.
> She gives me her golden wine.

I held Miko's poem in my hands and wept as the land of my ancestry faded behind me, the land of old sorrows, the land of new dreams.

"WHERE ARE WE GOING?" I ASKED, WHEN STEPHANIE PICKED me up at JFK and told her driver to take the Major Deegan Expressway.

"Someplace," she answered coyly.

"Hey," I objected, "even in Poland, they tell you where they're taking you."

"To Linden Hill."

"No way!" I moaned, the lingo of the land coming back to me in a rush.

"I'm under strict orders," she insisted. "Bernie asked me to take you there."

"Well, excuse me. But I am no longer under the jurisdiction of Bernard T. Watterman."

Stephanie sighed. "He really wants you to go to the house."

I folded my arms in front of me. "I'm not staying there."

"Who asked you? He's leaving for a long trip tomorrow, so he wants us to pick up some of your stuff."

I gave her a look. "What's going on?"

Stephanie batted her long lashes at me, arranged her hair, and said, "He really wants to see you. That's all."

"Why?"

"You'll find out. We're almost there."

"The hell we are!" I exclaimed, looking out the window as we passed the George Washington Bridge.

"Nora, we're going. Don't ask questions. Don't be a pain in the ass, okay?"

I was too tired to argue anymore. I sighed, and gazed at Stephanie. "You look great," I grudgingly told her. "How's Jill?"

She seemed embarrassed. "You won't believe this."

"Try me."

"She's with her father for the weekend."

"You're kidding!"

Stephanie shrugged. "She kept asking how come other kids had daddies and where was hers. He's been lobbying for visitation rights, so . . ."

"Good for him," I said, kissing her on the cheek. "Good for all of you."

The highway curved away from the water, through the woods, heading toward Corbin's Cove. I knew the way blindfolded. I closed my eyes. Now a stoplight. Another. A right turn onto Main Street and in three blocks and one more left turn, we would be there.

It was dusk when we arrived at Linden Hill. The house needed painting, but I could not help thinking it looked lovely in the twilight. It looked like a home, a haven.

"Should I ring the bell?" I asked Stephanie, as we approached the door. It opened as I reached for the black buzzer.

"Hi, Nora," Bernie said.

"Hi."

"Come on in," he said, and he ushered us into the living room, eyeing Stephanie nervously.

"What's going on?" I asked. "You two are acting like it's my birthday and this is a surprise or something."

"Mrs. Watterman?" a young woman's voice asked. Startled, I turned to see a familiar person, standing in the doorway to the dining room, holding something in her arms.

"Kelly?" I asked, recognizing her, but barely. She had filled out. Her hair was curled and combed, and she looked at me with confidence, with ease. I heard a noise. Something gurgled.

"This is the girl in my life," Bernie said, taking the baby from Kelly. "I told you she was beautiful."

I peered into a small pink face, with a rosebud mouth, strong features, and bright, wide-awake eyes.

"Would you like to hold your granddaughter?" Bernie asked me.

I could not breathe. My chest was bursting. I tried to

say something, and reached for the baby instead. She was a beautiful little girl, my granddaughter, the blood of my blood, the bone of my bone. I looked up at Kelly. She smiled shyly at me.

"She was born in January," she said. "Seven pounds, eleven ounces. She's really good. She hardly ever cries."

The baby's eyes were on mine. She was looking up at me, studying me.

"She's beautiful," I murmured. "She is absolutely beautiful." I kissed her gently on the forehead. "What did you name her?"

"Her name," Kelly said, as her daughter's tiny fingers curled around one of mine, "is Elena Nicole."

❦ 85 ❦

THE BABY WAS ASLEEP IN NICKY'S ROOM, IN THE CRIB WE had bought for her visits to Linden Hill. Kelly had left her with us for the weekend. She was going skiing with a young man who worked in the real estate office where she was a secretary.

"I'll get up with her tonight," Bernie offered, as we sat together, reading, in the living room.

"I don't mind."

"You've got a concert tomorrow," he reminded me. "You need your sleep."

I looked up at him, teasing, "You just can't get enough of her, can you?"

"I have this weakness for little girls who spit up on my shirt."

"Put a diaper on your shoulder when you burp her."

"And lose the thrill of the spill?"

I smiled and put my magazine down. "Okay. You get the night duty. Only I get to go check on her now."

"She doesn't need checking."

"Maybe she doesn't," I conceded, "but I do."

I stopped at the door to the den on my way upstairs. A playpen was on the floor, filled with stuffed toys and rubber balls. I wondered what Hal would have made of all this paraphernalia. I could almost see him, in this room, sniffing around the baby's gear. Then he would curl up on the floor near Bernie's feet and join his master for a long, peaceful nap. I lingered over the image. Then I walked over to the blue couch, fluffed the cushions, and went upstairs.

I stood for what must have been many minutes, watching the baby, bending over her. I brushed my lips across her forehead and felt a wondrous coolness against my kiss, like a swim after too much sun. Bernie, concerned at my long absence, came into the room.

"Shh," I said. "You'll wake her."

He smiled indulgently at me, then joined me at the side of the crib.

On her belly, backside in the air, Elena Nicole, was oblivious to her grandparents. Her blanket was pulled up over her head. I gently folded it down, bending over to make sure, yet again, that she was breathing. Her chest rose and fell comfortingly. I closed my eyes while I inhaled her powdery, apple-sweet smell. Then I stood up, took my husband's hand, and tiptoed with him out of the room.